Cold-Blooded Carnival

Katherine Black

Katherine Black Books
TWISTED MYSTERIES

Best Book Editions

Best Book Editions

1 3 5 7 9 10 8 6 4 2

Copyright © Katherine Black, 2023

The right of Katherine Black to be identified as the author of this Work has been asserted by her in accordance with the Copyright, Designs and Patents Act 1988

All rights reserved

Paperback ISBN 9798862198508

This publication may not be used, reproduced, stored or transmitted in any way, in whole or in part, without the express written permission of the author. Nor may it be otherwise circulated in any form of binding or cover other than that in which it has been published and without a similar condition imposed on subsequent users or purchasers

All characters in this publication are fictitious, and any similarity to real persons, alive or dead, is coincidental

Cover by Best Book Editors

A CIP catalogue record of this book is available from the British Library

---

There is no animal abuse or animal triggers in this book.

Welcome, ladies and gentlemen. As you take the best seats in the house, leave the cares and stresses of the working day behind. Be amazed at the spectacularly low price of your circus ticket to see the fifty-nine acts that make up the new wonders of the modern world. Don't forget your hotdog and candyfloss—and prepare for the spectacular extravaganza that is... Quinn Brothers Flying Circus.

What happened to the human oddities and animals when they were banned from circus performing?

Put perfect reality aside as we bring the conventional circus tradition into a modern-day experience.

Do we still have freak shows? No.

Do we still have animal performances in the UK? No.

Should we? Absolutely not.

However, in this alternative history, I have taken the story elsewhere, to a place where the rules aren't as rigid. We explore the intricacies of circus life in a society that makes it work.

As of 2023, when this book was published, the use of animal acts was still in existence in the Czech Republic with certain restrictions. Active groups are lobbying for the disbandment of all animal acts, and I expect that will come into force within the next few years. And this author applauds that future decision. The book has been researched for accuracy as of today's working standards—but this book isn't about the horrors or ethics of the modern-day circus experience, it's about escapism and is—just a story.

Contents

1. Chapter 1 — 1
2. Chapter 2 — 10
3. Chapter 3 — 16
4. Chapter 4 — 24
5. Chapter 5 — 32
6. Chapter 6 — 43
7. Chapter 7 — 50
8. Chapter 8 — 56
9. Chapter 9 — 64
10. Chapter 10 — 73
11. Chapter 11 — 82
12. Chapter 12 — 92
13. Chapter 13 — 104
14. Chapter 14 — 114

15.	Chapter 15	124
16.	Chapter 16	137
17.	Chapter 17	150
18.	Chapter 18	164
19.	Chapter 19	174
20.	Chapter 20	181
21.	Chapter 21	190
22.	Chapter 22	197
23.	Chapter 23	204
24.	Chapter 24	212
25.	Chapter 25	221
26.	Chapter 26	233
27.	Chapter 27	249
28.	Chapter 28	259
29.	Chapter 29	270
30.	Chapter 30	277
31.	Chapter 31	285
32.	Chapter 32	293
33.	Chapter 33	299
34.	Chapter 34	308

35.	Chapter 35	320
36.	Chapter 36	333
37.	Chapter 37	345
	Dedication	357

Chapter One

Isiah Quinn looked across the field at his carneys.

He felt an ill wind at his back. There was unrest in the camp, and his seasoned eyes recognised the signs. Trouble was brewing. He saw it in his people's mannerisms. The tension rippled along their muscles and was evident in the way they moved and interacted. A simmering discord was ready to overspill into anarchy if he didn't do something to stop it. And it was his place to stomp their grumbles into the ground before there was any murmur of an uprising.

'Jimmy, bring her around,' he shouted to a man leading a lame horse five times his height. 'Get a poultice on that leg, and I want her rested up for this entire site. You can replace her with Enchantress for the eight-up.'

'Yes, boss.' Jimmy winked to show he'd do as he'd been asked.

'I don't want to see her out of the stalls until I've examined the fetlock myself, got it?'

'Boss.'

The soft rays of the early sun dappled the ancient city of Prague. It was seven o'clock, and the camp had been active like an ant farm since five. Everybody had a role, and each man, woman and child was expected to pitch in. The enormous rolling field in the old Vysehrad Castle grounds was transformed into a vibrant wonderland when the travelling circus arrived. It brought the promise of magic and excitement, lighting the faces of every kid in town. It was coming into tourist season, and Quinn loved hearing his tills singing.

The carney riggers, a group of weathered men used to hard labour, scattered across the field. Their faces glistened with perspiration as they pulled on ropes, hammered boards together to form the sidings, and put up the magnificent stalls and marquees.

And when they were ready for the big top to go up, the colourful canvas rose into the sky. The call of 'Tops-up' went around the camp, and people fell in from their trailers. Every able pair of hands gathered in a circle around the rumpled canvas. With one accord, while the boss shouted the count, they hauled on the ropes to erect the tent in a billowing mass of vibrancy. What had taken an hour to straighten out went up in two minutes. The display was a kaleidoscope of childish joy. Red and white striped tents jostled for space, next to vivid blue and yellow pavilions. The effect created a dazzling artwork against the backdrop of the brilliant Pragian sky.

'Bobo. Get the lever,' Quinn shouted. The ten-year-old untethered chimpanzee ran with his lolloping gait to the lever operating the breakers on the running boards. He pulled the handle to slide them into position. Even he had his job to do. Jumping on the spot, he clapped his hands and let go with a string of chatter, waiting for his praise.

'Good boy.'

The chimp screamed in delight, and ran to Quinn, climbing his leg and presenting his face for kisses. He reached into the circus owner's breast pocket and helped himself to a mint. They were always in there.

All over Europe, it was illegal to use animals under six months old for performance purposes. But, when Bobo was five weeks old, Quinn Bros Circus was asked to take on the orphaned infant who spent the next five years attached to Camilla, his foster mother's teat. The female chimp taught him manners, and Melissa, his human trainer, turned him into a circus performer. It was a good life, and Bobo was high on living.

'Morning boss,' A young girl shouted as she flung the door open to air her trailer.

'Morning, Belinda. Gorgeous day.'

Isiah Quinn was already giving thought to the chimpanzee's future. He only had three years left with them, at which point Bobo would be an adult male, with his breeding dander up. He'd be at his most dangerous—the age when males fight for supremacy in the troop. He'd be too unpredictable to have around camp—and after ten years of thinking he was human, Bobo could never be chained.

'Ignatius, you're late for rehearsals. You should have been there ten minutes ago,' Quinn said to a young man in black leggings and a tight shirt. He was in his rehearsal uniform with no spare material to interfere with the fire. His performance costumes, however, were magnificent fire-retardant leotards in a myriad of vibrant colours.

'I told you I'd be late this morning. I had to go into town to pick up some accelerant because the order wasn't delivered to the site when we arrived yesterday.'

'So you did. Good man.'

England, and some other countries, had already outlawed animal acts—Quinn said it had killed the circus, never mind all the sideshow attractions that no longer had jobs. Public safety had to come first and was paramount, but the welfare of his animals and special people was important, too.

They had other chimps, and Bobo was used to being with his own kind. And they had Billy the Orangutan, but sometimes an animal came into the family that was special. Bobo was that guy, and Quinn was dreading the day they had to let him go. He vowed to find him the best damn monkey land on the planet to live out his retirement reverting to life as an ape. Quinn said Bobo was nine-tenths human to one-tenth hustler—with no room left for any monkey business. And he'd laugh at his joke.

He laughed now as Winnie ran out of the animal enclosure with her trainer chasing her. 'Don't just stand there laughing, help me catch her,' Carly shouted.

'You've got this. Let her stretch her legs, the park isn't open yet. Just keep an eye on her.'

'She's an arse.'

'And you wouldn't have her any other way,' Quinn said.

'Like I've got time to be standing around watching her all day.'

Winnie, the ostrich, realised that she wasn't being chased anymore and the game lost its appeal. She trotted back to Carly and nudged her under the elbow.

'Go on, chase her,' Quinn said.

'You bloody chase her.'

Quinn was proud of the life he'd built for his people. The troupe were a motley band of performers, concession workers, and ground crew. There were no locked doors around here, it was a community built on trust. The most a closed door ever warranted was a knock. Bad apples were identified early, and either changed their rotten ways or were moved on.

The carnival's history held the shadows of a time when the freaks were a spectacle. They were commodities for gawking eyes. Years ago, Caspian and Gideon, Isiah Quinn's brothers, had wanted to shed the past. The winds of change whispered that it was unacceptable to exploit human differences for entertainment. And so, when they ceased to have any financial value, they championed the cause to dismantle the freak exhibits and throw the people onto the scrap heap. They were cruel times, and circuses the world over were struggling. Shows from the four corners sloughed their freakshows like calloused skin. The better ones took their human oddities, exhibits—objects with no current worth—and left them at orphanages or mental institutions. The ones with even less humanity dropped them from the circus caravan on the road between towns. Isiah Quinn wanted better, and the disagreements between the three owners of Quinn Brothers Flying Circus were bitter.

As he reflected on the old days, not so long ago, he wondered about the current state of his business. The circus was going through times of movement. The oddity acts were gone, the animals were going, and motorbikes doing the Wall of Death had replaced the elephants in many circuses. *Cirque du Soleil* had moved with the times, combining performance art with traditional acts. What the bloody hell was performance art? Quinn's elephants performed, and they painted, didn't that count?

During a performance in 1979, Gideon, the eldest Quinn brother, was murdered when the trapeze rig was tampered with, and Caspian was blamed and imprisoned. Their parents had died years before—and neither of them to the circus ring. It left the very young Isiah, a complex man of ego, empathy and devotion, at the helm. He was twenty-two, a circus owner, and the youngest ringmaster on the circuit.

He went inside his trailer and brewed another pot of coffee, and when he came out, Octavia was singing. He went down the steps this time and sat at the side of his trailer. The morning, the Vyseyrad gardens, and the song were beautiful. There wasn't a much better life to be found than this—if you took to it. The circus was all he'd ever known.

He wasn't the only one listening to Octavia. Her voice was rich and pure and she often sang in the Critter Cave if the horses were restless. Quinn said her lullaby could put an angry bear to sleep. Not that Huckleberry was ever angry, he was just a goon.

Mac Makenzie, his boss hostler didn't know Quinn could see him. He'd asked for Octavia's hand once, but she turned him down and he gave up trying. The fool yearned for her from afar, and Quinn wished she could yield and make them both happy.

As the owner, Isiah had sought to mend the wounds of the past. In the 1980s, public opinion was that, far from being entertaining, the freaks were uncomfortable to watch. Isiah looked at his extensive band of human oddities and offered them new positions. The word freak was obliterated from the circus vocabulary and he called them staff—or arsehole if they did something wrong. Freak was their dead name.

They were given jobs to match their abilities. Quinn refused to believe that there were any of them incapable of fulfilling some position of worth, right down to the conjoined twins, and Tobias, a man with no limbs or lower torso. Octavia, the bearded lady was trained as his special effects coordinator, a role she took to with enthusiasm. And everybody was given their new occupation. Tobias was more of a challenge. He was the self-proclaimed Worm Boy. Quinn offered him the role of audio technician, but Tobias said, 'I thought you were a man with his finger on the financial pulse, boss.'

'And your point is?'

'Think with your head, not your heart. I would be far better as the first point of contact. Don't hide me away. I won't have it. I'll walk.' Quinn laughed on cue. 'Put me right at the front gate in the ticket booth. I'll sell more tickets than anybody else could,' Tobias said.

'To be stared at again?'

'I'm a handsome guy. Why wouldn't they stare?'

Tobias was the only one in the direct public eye—and that was at his insistence. Nobody at Quinn Brothers Flying Circus ever wanted to hide away, they were proud people. Tobias loved his job and cracked jokes with the customers from the side of his mouth as he sold them tickets using a mouth-operated grabber.

Isiah's pride swelled every time he saw one of them thriving. They weren't exhibits. They were Quinn's staff. A family. The circus had bloomed into a new era where diversity was celebrated.

The carneys had seen it all before. The tent went up, the tent came down, and in between times, they travelled. There was no romantic illusion about living the carney life, it was backbreaking work. You either loved the circus, or you left. The youngsters came, and Quinn gave them their chance. There was no lack of work for a good carney, but once they realised it wasn't all taming tigers and chatting up the performers, most of them couldn't hack it.

As Quinn watched with a cheerful expression masking his concern, the men sang their hauling song to keep time as they pulled on the guy ropes. The sun rose in the sky, and the gentle warmth turned into the blistering heat of the summer morning. There was nothing glamorous about this life, not until showtime, when the overalls came off, and the sequins went on. Some of the team had dual roles as shit-shovelers by day, and circus stars when the lights went up.

The carneys worked with the odour of sawdust and manure wafting on the air when the morning muck-out was underway. Laughter took the strain out of petty rivalry, but there was still that feeling of a storm on the horizon, and Quinn wasn't thinking about the weather. A current of tension hid underneath the banter and tomfoolery.

As it always did, the set-up attracted onlookers from the neighbouring towns, and the handlers would exercise some of the animals in the field, just to heat the punters up for the ticket jockeys to go out and sell them a dream. An occasional fleeting glimpse of his conjoined beauties as they crab-stepped up the ramp to their trailer, and the lookers were putty in his hands. Never one to miss an opportunity, Quinn had left many holes in the security fence, big enough for people to see through.

The camp was safe. He had night patrollers, and the security fence had one purpose. When there was a barrier, people wanted to know what was on the other side. It was the gateway to unleashing curiosity. Peering through the fence gave them a delicious sense of getting away with something, and the ticketers made a killing.

'It's psychology, my friend,' Quinn would say to his accountant. 'The circus has its foundation in grease paint and psychology. Make them want what you've got, and it's like stealing sex from a hooker.'

Chapter Two

The Meeting Place pub was filled with laughter and clinking glasses as some of the homicide department met after work. DCI Silas Nash had called the impromptu night out after a day of dealing with the usual assortment of witnesses and ploughing through their secrets and lies. He mentioned meeting up at the end of the team debrief and didn't expect anybody other than Molly—who was always up for a drink—to say yes. He was warmed and humbled by the turnout at such short notice. And then spent the first half hour worrying that they'd only come because he was the boss and they felt they couldn't say no.

'Boss, can I speak out?' DI Molly Brown asked.

'You usually do.'

'I just wanted to tell you that you're a dick. Of course, we aren't here out of duty. We're here because we all think you're bloody awesome.'

Nash blushed. 'Behave yourself.'

Sergeant Phil Renshaw, who'd heard Molly, leaned in and added his take on it. 'And if you're putting your hand in your pocket to buy a round, I want to be there.'

Nash was working on being less socially awkward and more spontaneous, but it didn't come easy. He'd spent a lifetime as a reserved man, and it was only in the last twelve months that he'd realised he could be fun. And he liked it.

Nash, Brown, Sergeants Renshaw and Mo Patel, and PCs Bowes and Lawson occupied the big corner table by the window with the comfy sofas that tried to eat you. They were enjoying the camaraderie and relief that came with the sentencing of the infamous serial killer, Robin Hill.

It was a tough case—especially for Brown, and the trial had been protracted as evidence was compiled against the murderer to make sure he went down for a long time. Hill was found guilty, and they had to wait again for the sentencing.

During this time, Brown had been in deprogramming therapy to rid her of the after-effects of the case. It was done now. And with Hill's sentence beginning, Brown's had ended.

'Sent down and staying down,' Mo said, raising his glass of orange juice for the drinkers to clink.

They repeated the toast back at him, and Renshaw caught Brown's eye and winked at her. It didn't go unnoticed by Nash, and he read it for exactly what it was. A gesture of support from one colleague to another. Six months earlier, the looks between them would have set the building on fire.

Their affair was something else that was finished as Renshaw and his wife looked forward to the birth of their new baby in a few weeks. Until the next drama threw a tiger in the puppy pen, the team was more settled, and Nash had all of his obsessive tendencies stuffed into his case files.

'While I've got you here, I have an announcement,' Nash said. He waited until he had their attention. 'I was called into the boss' office today.'

'Have you been sacked?' Bowe's asked.

'No, I have not been sacked.'

'Shame, I was going to ask if I could have your swivel chair, so I could spend all day twirling in circles like a DCI, sir.'

'I do my best thinking in that chair, Bowes. It would be wasted on the likes of you. Anyway, getting back to the point. DCS Lewis has been in meetings with PACE.'

'Who?' Renshaw asked.

'Come on lad, remember your last inclusion course, it was covered in that.'

'Yeah, he slept through that bit,' Lawson said.

'No, he was awake through that bit. It was the other four and a half days that he slept through,' Renshaw said. He dodged a flying beer mat.

Nash held his hand up before it descended into throwing things across the room. 'PACE is the Police Action for Community Empowerment agency. They were set up in 2022 during the Kiev troubles to oversee policing for sensitive communities.'

'Not sure I'm following you,' Renshaw said.

'You really did sleep through the course, didn't you? They are a European police department that came about to help the refugees from Ukraine, and then grew to encompass any sensitive community such as gypsies, travellers, transients, and some ethnic minorities.'

'Sounds like more red tape hogwash to me,' Brown said. 'Why do they need a special department to police them? Surely we know when to employ tact and a bit of extra TLC.'

'Apparently not. And in light of that, it looks as though you might be getting rid of me for a few weeks later in the year.'

'Why?' Brown asked.

'Because PACE wants all its member countries operating from the same rule book, so they've been awarded funding for an international exchange programme. Each country will take a ranking officer from one of the others when they have a suitable case to barter police procedures.'

'Sounds reasonable,' Lawson said.

'As you know, every country has a very different method of policing, and PACE aims to unify protocol and procedures, especially when dealing with cases in sensitive or vulnerable communities. I've been chosen to represent Cumbria in the UK delegate.'

'Nice one, boss. Congratulations,' Lawson said raising his glass. They all clinked glasses and shared their good wishes.

'I just hope we're not balls deep in a case of our own when you have to go,' Renshaw said.

'I'm sure we'll be given notice, and you kids will just have to play nice in the sandpit when I'm away.'

'Yeah, bagsy being first to pee in it,' Bowes said.

Before Bowes could pull the conversation any lower, Nash's phone rang and he discreetly pulled it out of his pocket. 'Excuse me.' He looked at it before sending a quick reply and turned the screen off fast. The team saw his face light up. Old poker-faced Nasher was losing it.

'Nash, you should text Kelvin and invite him to join us,' Molly said. Nash was shy when it came to his personal life.

'Eh up,' Bowes said. 'And who's Kelvin, might one ask?'

'No, one might bloody well not. And stop talking in the third person, you dickhead,' Brown said. 'Kel's a right catch.' She was on her second glass of wine and Nash gave her a warning look, but it wasn't very serious. There was an iconic boundary glare to tell her when she was overstepping the mark. This was just a frown to say that his private life was just that.

'What? You've met him, Brown?' Lawson asked, and they all leaned in for the answer. Nash hated being the centre of attention. He picked up his glass and wished it was something he couldn't be seen though.

'Oh yes, I've met him all right. I've been to dinner.' Molly said. 'Go on, boss. Get him to come along. It's about time the team gave him the once over.'

Nash blushed, but he couldn't keep the smile off his face. 'I don't think so. I'm sure he'll be busy. Maybe next time.' He stammered, which was so unlike him that it, evoked more laughter and nudges from his colleagues.

Molly's eyes were gleaming with determination. Nash knew that look.

'All right. If you won't do it, I will.' She pulled her phone out, tapped out a text message, and sent it to Kelvin Jones.

Seconds later, before they'd even got onto a new conversation, Nash's phone buzzed with a text notification. He read it without pulling it all the way out of his pocket, and he set his face into his stern DCI expression.

'Is it him?' Molly asked. 'What did he say?'

Bowes was just as curious. 'Come on, boss. What's he saying? Is he coming?'

Nash blushed redder, and his eyes shone with happiness. 'He says he's on his way.'

As they waited, the team engaged in playful banter, teasing Nash about his love life. 'I can't believe you've been hiding this from us,' Bowes said. 'Do you have matching slippers and drink cocoa together?'

Nash wanted to shock him by saying, 'No we spend a lot of time having sex, and drinking way too much wine,' but he didn't. He laughed and realised that laughing came a lot easier than it used to—just like he did. His cheeks were still flushed and he willed them to cool. 'You can mock all you like, Bowes,' he winked at him. 'But Kelvin's amazing and he's made me a very happy man.'

'You're going soft on us, boss. You'll be reciting poetry in the team meetings next.' But the smile he gave Nash was full of approval.

It had been horrendous at the time, but when Nash had been outed by force at the hands of a spiteful ex, it was the best thing that could have happened. He'd hidden the fact that he was gay from his various colleagues for thirty years. And it took him thirty years to realise that, these days, nobody cares.

Chapter Three

The parade through the streets the day before had given them a sell-out for three of the five dates. Tumblers, acrobats, trapeze artists, jugglers and stilt walkers performed on the cobbles, while the grinders, or ticket guys, went among the crowds with their spiels, and card tricks. The clowns brought up the energy with comical antics, and after every skit they'd be in the crowd, cooing at babies and selling balloons and battery-powered light-up windmills.

But the animals were the stars of the show—and they knew it.

After travelling, they were always on form and ready to entertain. They loved the stimulation, and the big parade was led by the magnificent family of elephants.

Chandra was at the front, with his big ears flapping, and trunk waving in the hope of snagging some treats. Indira, the female, was only slightly smaller, and her calf, Sabu, delighted the crowds with his mischievous tricks.

'Make them smile, my beauty,' Quinn would say to the bull elephant as he rode him through the town.

The bally broads, or circus girls, came next, they were the dancers, aerialists, ribbon artists, magician's assistants, and other female performers. They danced in the streets, wearing skimpy costumes and fishnet tights, with pearly smiles applied as professionally as their scarlet lipstick.

'I'll see you tonight, under a million lights, my handsome,' they'd say to the gaping boys who were lovestruck with lust.

The big cats roared. The lions were freshly groomed, and the tigers were rubbed with oil to bring out the colours of their hides. Sheitan, the panther, was sleek and shone like polished coal. He feigned aggression to elicit gasps from the crowd and was rewarded with a panther-sized cat treat.

Ignatius Vulkane, the renowned fire-eater, manipulated flames with the practised skill of a trained professional.

Dressed in a striking red and gold bodysuit, he strutted along the parade route with confidence, and every step maintained his air of showmanship. A hush fell over the spectators as Flora, one of the bally broads, handed the lit torches to him.

Ignatius filled his mouth with accelerant and drew in oxygen ready to exhale a stream of fire into the air. He went through his routine and the plumes of dazzling fire roared above the crowd.

Flora handed him a new bottle of firewater and Ignatius filled his mouth. As he released the flames, he stumbled in shock and almost swallowed the accelerant that would have stripped his throat like acid. The size of the fire was tremendous and the crowd ducked. The plumage of flame was too big and couldn't be controlled. Instead of the expected Dhalsim flame, a violent ball of fire engulfed him, setting his body ablaze.

Panic heaved through the crowd as they gawped in horror. The controlled exhibition had transformed into a wild inferno, and its intensity was burning Ignatius. He dropped and rolled on the pavement to extinguish the flames. Screams filled the air as parents hid their children's faces from the horrific sight.

The crew acted fast, rushing to his aid. Amid the chaos, Cassandra, the contortionist sprang into action. Despite the danger, she manoeuvred through the panicked crowd and wrapped Ignatius with a fireproof cloak, suffocating the last of the flames and cutting off their oxygen supply. It was over in a matter of seconds. Ignatius had already extinguished most of the fire with his instant response and wasn't badly hurt. But as he was led into the back of one of the ambulances to be checked over, he was furious. The carneys started the round of applause for Cassandra, and the crowd joined in.

Ignatius shouted to Mac Makenzie, the boss hostler—circus manager. 'That was no accident. Someone tampered with my apparatus. I could have been killed.'

'Calm down, Nat, you're upset. I'm sure it was just an error.'

'I don't have accidents, Hoss—and I never make mistakes.' He was hustled into the ambulance before spitting his last statement at the boss. 'Someone tried to kill me.'

'I'll investigate. If there's anything to find, we'll find it.'

The performers were trained in what to do during a mishap. They leapt into an extravaganza, an addition to the usual parade. Although people wouldn't forget, they needed to diminish the accident in the eyes of the crowd. Above all else, the circus had to be seen as safe. Despite the agony, Ignatius stopped before going into the ambulance. He shrugged off the fire blanket and did a somersault that must have hurt against the burns on his legs. He raised his arms for applause. 'Ta-dah.' He waved to the crowd and limped into the ambulance where he could submit to his burns in privacy.

On command, Chandra lifted his giant foot for Quinn to climb down and the ringmaster landed on the floor and bowed. He spun his cane with the calyx top in a display of speed and precision. He sent it behind his back and under his leg as he twirled it like a baton.

'Is he all right?' A man from the crowd shouted.

'That? All part of the show, sir. A well-practised example to show how the circus performs in a crisis. Our amazing, world-famous fire-eater will be back to perform for you under the canvas tonight.'

In truth, Ignatius was on his way to the hospital to be thoroughly checked over, but the game was to adopt deception and sleight of hand. Never admit the truth when a crowd could be bamboozled.

The circus was a cauldron of tension and uncertainty, as the performers went into their routines by rote.

The primates showed off. Bobo the chimp ran into the crowd to steal somebody's hat before Melissa wagged her finger at him in a mock telling-off. His response was to blow a raspberry.

The proud, regal horses, in their full show regalia, were always popular, and every child wanted to stand on their backs, riding through the streets like the bally broads. The big cats, small dogs, and Winnie the Ostrich, all took their part and did what they were trained to do. And then there was the giant brown bear, Huckleberry, a happy-go-lucky guy, who was everybody's friend.

The clowns played the fool, and Madam Selena, the Romany fortune teller, rode in a gilded carriage. Bence Jaeger, the magician, performed tricks under strict instruction to keep his personal issues with Selena out of the parade.

'Philistine pig,' she hissed at him as he stalked past her carriage.

'Charlatan,' he countered. 'All-seeing eye, my arse. The only thing you can profess is an all-encompassing backside.'

Selena stuck her leg out of the carriage door and tried to kick him, but missed.

'Be careful, woman, or somebody might set fire to you. Isn't that what they do to witches?' He smiled at the crowd and shook a man's outstretched hand.

Madam Selena waved through the window, copying Queen Elizabeth II's iconic gesture. 'Make your mind up, little magician. Either I am a witch or a fraud, make your selection and have the conviction to stick by it?' She'd latched onto the fact that Bence hated being called a magician, and insisted on the term mentalist. She knew it would get his hackles up.

'I'll have you out by the end of the season. You're as fake as a Dickensian medium spraying ectoplasm from her bustle.'

Quinn waited until he could get alongside Jaeger. 'I've told you before Jaeger, you aren't indispensable. Get on with Selena or you can find yourself another circus to play games in.'

'Why me? I don't see you threatening to kick her out.'

'Grow up, man—and smile, damn you.' Quinn raised his cane aloft and twirled it, smiling his perfected plastic smile at the crowd.

They came to the glorious landmark of the famous Charles Bridge, and the walking performers branched off to cross the six-hundred-meter iron construct, dancing and back-flipping. The little people formed a walking pyramid, and the clowns tumbled. Jolene, Jimmy's wife, played her mini accordion, while Huckleberry stood on two legs and danced. He loved to dance almost as much as he loved scratches. The bridge was ablaze with colour and pomp.

The swish of canvas being attached to easels ran the length of the crossing as the Pragian street artists, lining both sides of the bridge, rushed to capture the scene in caricature. The clowns teased them, and the little people, knowing the artists would use the results for their own marketing purposes, jostled them with an outstretched hat for a fiver—'to buy the elephants some peanuts, sir.'

After the drama of Ignatius' accident, they were all glad when the parade was over.

The next day Quinn was perturbed. Ignatius hadn't been badly burned, but it was enough to scar him. The day before, The Big Parade was magnificent—a spectacle, though it could have had a very different outcome, but for the professionalism of the troop. Quinn was philosophical, there was no such thing as negative publicity. Their fire-eater going up in flames would hit the evening papers—with photos if luck was with them. It'd swell ticket sales and fill those last two days. Every cloud. He wanted Quinn Bros Flying Circus talked about by every family in Prague at dinner that night.

After checking on the fire-eater's progress, he had matters to attend to, and town bigwigs to schmooze, but he came back to the field later that afternoon. Time was getting on, and they were opening in four hours.

Mac knocked on Quinn's trailer door, his face was dark with worry, as the sounds of unrest echoed through the circus camp. Quinn poured them a generous shot of whiskey and slid one over to Mac. They clinked glasses before Mac spoke.

'Shit's getting real out there.'

'I know. I feel it, too. Superstition and paranoia are lighting fires that are going to spread out of control. We've seen our share of challenges, but this feels darker. What's going on? Where's the rot coming from?'

Mac swirled the amber fire in his glass. 'I don't know, nobody's talking, but something's brewing, and it isn't just the danger of the ring. I believe Ignatius. That accident wasn't in error. Someone wants him dead.'

'Don't be jumping at shadows. We don't know that yet, and there's enough superstition going around,' Quinn said. He kissed his fingers and anointed himself with the sign of the Cross. 'I'll thank you to keep your thoughts to yourself outside this box. However, he's right and if there's any truth to it, the question is, who could set one of us on fire? We've always been a family. But trust is slipping and the snakes are hissing.' He kissed the talisman around his neck.

'Something bad is going down, boss.'

'I agree, but fear can't destroy us. We need to stick together and keep our eyes open. I've known most of these folk for years, and I won't let any harm come to them.'

'You're right, Isiah. Our circus deserves better than this.'

They raised their glasses. 'Salute.'

Performers and animal keepers saw to their charges in the summer heat. The horses were groomed again and dressed, and the pool had been filled for the three sealions and Cornelius, the walrus, who was only eight but looked like a whiskery old man.

Each trailer was an enchanted microcosm, bursting with characters straight out of a fairytale, and the smell of baking bread and roasted meat danced on the air as the performers gathered in a vibrant circle. They ate early to be fully digested before their performance. Some of the routines required great stamina, and like the animals, the human acts needed fuel.

It was an hour before showtime, and he prayed for a great opening night. Somebody had watched his fire eater burn with malice. Bad omens were coming at him from every angle. The circus was under threat from the authorities, animal protesting do-gooders and the spirits themselves.

Chapter Four

The door swung open, and all eyes turned to look. Kelvin Jones strode into the pub, and his huge smile was already in place and radiated across the room. He walked straight, and with confidence to their table with his eyes fixed on Nash.

Nash stood up to greet him. Damn, Kel looked hot. In the same situation, Nash would have aimed for confidence but would've come in like a mouse and tripped over a stool on his way. Before Nash could say a word in introduction, Kelvin closed the distance between them, cupped his face, and planted a kiss on his lips.

The team's jaws dropped, and like cartoon figures, they looked at each other with their mouths open. Bowes' eyes bulged, and he elbowed Lawson, who tried to suppress a laugh and failed. Molly broke the silence.

'Nash, your boyfriend is a master of grand entrances.'

Nash's face was the colour of a scarlet letter, and he stuttered in embarrassment. 'I didn't see that coming.'

He knew they weren't shocked by anything about Kelvin. It was Nash who had floored them. And he was surprised to find that he liked them seeing him in a new light.

'Hey, Si. Hi, everyone,' Kelvin said.

They returned the greeting, and Bowes pounced. 'Ha, got you at last. Simon. Your first name's Simon, boss.'

Nash just grinned, and Kelvin, very aware of the reactions around him, let go of Nash, his eyes sparkling with affection. 'Sorry for stealing the limelight, folks. Pleased to meet you all.'

Mo clapped him on the back. 'We're just impressed you can make the boss turn into a human traffic light. That's some superpower.'

'Boss, you're a dark horse. And if you don't mind me saying, Kel, you didn't get a tan like that lying on Walney Beach,' Renshaw said.

Kelvin winked at Nash as he sat down and indicated everybody's drinks. He used the same line Nash had blurted out the night they met. 'I'm the dark horse, he's a palomino.' They fell about laughing, and Nash was delighted that Kel had them eating out of his hand within seconds. Kel told them the story about Nash saying it and then wanting to cut his tongue out, and how it had broken the ice between them. He mentioned being from Ghana and that he'd come to England to complete his education at Oxford. 'Si, come and help me get the round in, will you?'

They spent the rest of the evening sharing stories and toasting to Robin Hill's imprisonment. In a sombre moment, Nash raised a toast to Hill's victims and they all stood to honour them. 'Let's never forget them,' he said.

Bowes recovered from his initial shock and was intrigued by Kelvin. He and Nash were so different and he said he'd never have put them together.

'Why? Is it because I is black?'

Bowes didn't miss a beat. 'No, Ali G, it's because you're not what I expected. I thought you'd be older than the boss.'

'Si's not old. Ugh, I don't want to be snuggling up to an old man. It'd be one step away from snogging a corpse.'

Bowes had to get as much mileage out of this one as he could. 'It's official, sir. Kel is younger and good-looking. How the hell you pulled him, I'll never know. It's brilliant. You know when your boss got laid the night before because he comes in happy.'

They laughed often, filling the pub with a relaxed atmosphere.

The evening wore on, and stories flowed. Phil recounted an amusing incident from their current investigation without breaching confidentiality protocol, and Lawson shared an embarrassing moment from his early days as an officer. The banter created a bond between the homicide department and Nash's partner.

While the others were engrossed in one of Kelvin's stories, Molly leaned into Nash. 'He's besotted with you, you know?'

Nash smiled. 'But what if I'm not enough, and he gets bored of me? Look at him, he's outgoing and people love him.'

'Are you freaking kidding me? Have you seen how good you two look together? You could pass for forty, and you have the best banter going. He's as lucky as you are. You're perfect together.'

'Thanks, Molly.' Nash did look good. He worked out at the gym at least three times a week. And he went running sometimes but mostly took brisk walks along the ocean path outside his house. He was tall—but fell four inches short of Kelvin—slim and still had all of his hair and a goatee that suited him and gave him a chiselled look. He loved seeing Kel's body against his. Kel's skin wasn't just black, it was tonal, it looked almost liquid and had several shades of the darkest black merged together. It fascinated Nash. He loved when they entwined and his white skin was against Kel's. And though he said it himself, together they were beautiful.

Some of the guys were getting ready to leave and Nash was pulled away from his thoughts. He clapped the younger officers on the shoulder. He was learning that, by relaxing, he commanded more respect. Not less.

With the three of them left, they relaxed into their seats when the others were gone. 'How's it going with the new boyfriend? You're being very cagey, Miss Molly and you haven't updated us on that front,' Kelvin said.

Nash was in awe that Kel had such an easy way about him. He was interested in people, and it could be said that he liked a bit of gossip. And that was probably why he and Molly got on so well. Nash would have asked the same question, but he'd have asked it in a stuffy avuncular way.

Molly chuckled. Her cheeks were tinged with a rosy blush. 'Danny and I are doing great. He's a roofer and he's been helping me do up my house.'

'Sounds like you're a dynamic duo, solving crimes and building houses. That one's a keeper.'

Nash laughed at them. His arm was resting on the back of Kelvin's chair. 'I'm glad you're happy, Molly. Nobody deserves it more.'

'Don't get me wrong. It's still early days and nothing serious, but I like him and we get on okay. But enough about me. When are you going to take some time off? It's time we talked about you and Kelvin going on your first holiday together.'

Nash blustered. 'Molly. It's not something we've even discussed.'

'Do you know, I was thinking the same thing. I think it's an excellent idea,' Kelvin said and Nash felt an ambush coming on.

'I know. We've been so caught up with work that we haven't had a chance to plan anything. But we'll make it happen soon, I promise,' Nash said.

'Molly's right. You're due a break. Maybe it's time we escaped the city and enjoyed some relaxation.'

Molly's face lit up. 'That's the spirit. Let's talk destinations. How about a luxury villa in Spain?'

'Or a romantic getaway to the country? Rolling hills, charming cottages, and long walks hand-in-hand,' Kelvin suggested.

'I have a thought about that,' Nash said.

'Go on,' Kelvin was intrigued. They looked at him.

'I have a camper van.'

Kel spluttered and had to wipe Guinness from his chin. 'You have a what? The concept of you in a camper van is preposterous. It's like putting a king in a council house.'

'I made a stupid promise to a dying man, and I'm ashamed to say, up to now I haven't kept it.'

'Max Jones,' Brown and Kel said together.

'Yeah. Maxwell bloody Jones. I might as well tell you because you're going to wheedle it out of me. When he was dying, he bought an awful, dilapidated old camper van. The rest is history, and he never got to use it much. Anyway, on his deathbed, the bastard said he was leaving the damned thing to me and made me promise—promise no less—to use it. I had no choice but to say I would.'

'And now you're going to inflict a fate worse than death on me. I couldn't imagine anything worse than being trapped in a sardine tin for any length of time. Thanks, Si.'

'That's about the size of it,' Molly said.

'Max told me I'm uptight and don't know how to have fun. His punishment was inflicting his camper van—no doubt smelling of his sweaty feet—on me, and making me promise to use the blasted thing. He said I needed to loosen up as if that thing would be any kind of fun.'

'Loosen up? We'll probably both end up in traction. Does it even have a proper bed or air conditioning? Where the hell will we hang our clothes?'

Molly couldn't stop laughing at the horror on Kel's face. 'It'll be brilliant, you'll have a ball.'

'We'll break our balls, you mean.' Kel said.

'Only if you play your cards right.'

'Jones really was a bastard. I love that man,' Nash pulled a face and then stopped talking to rub his lower leg.

A breeze blew around their feet. They were in a sheltered space at the bottom of the room away from the door. There was nowhere for a draft to originate. They felt cold air around their ankles and looked at each other in shock as it travelled up their bodies and swirled around their heads. Molly had long hair and the breeze from nowhere blew it out of place. Nash felt a hand touch his shoulder for a second, and then it was gone. He felt where the hand had been.

'That was Max, wasn't it?' Molly said.

'Yes, I think it was.' Nash was smiling.

'That settles it, then,' Kelvin said. 'A promise is a promise, and I'm not going to be a party to you breaking it. We could go to a tropical paradise. Sandy beaches, crystal-clear waters, and maybe even some scuba diving—but no, a few days in a rotten old camper van it is. You owe me, Nash.' Kelvin laughed.

'She's called, The Good Lady Diana, if you don't mind. And it doesn't mean we can't have adventures. I'm sure there's somewhere in England where we can go scuba diving. I'm up for it.'

Molly laughed. 'Scuba diving? Nash, are you sure?'

'I'm up for anything with this guy. But, I might need some convincing at the time.'

Molly said, 'It's not about the destination. It's the memories you create on the road. Wherever you end up, what matters is that you enjoy each other and make memories. Max's death has taught us that.'

Nash took Kelvin's hand and squeezed it. 'You're right, Molly. We'll cherish it, no matter where we go.'

They discussed camping ideas and destinations until the bartender cleaned their table around them and they took the hint. Leaving the pub together, they said goodbye to Molly and tried to get a good look at Danny Wilson as he pulled up to take her home. She jumped in his car and gave them a wave as they drove away.

Nash and Kelvin strolled to the nearby taxi rank, holding hands. As they chatted, Nash remarked that Kel had been spending a lot of time at his place, and a smile tugged the corners of his lips. 'You've practically moved into my house. I think it's about time we cleared some drawers and a permanent space in the wardrobe for you.'

'I'd like that. If you're sure I'm not outstaying my welcome.'

Nash flagged a taxi, and he saw the soft glow of the town's lights reflected in the car's window—those and his own face. He was full of beer and love and didn't think he'd ever seen his reflection look so happy.

They reached Nash's oceanfront house and gave the driver a generous tip.

'As we've been talking about home, I have something for you,' Nash said.

He pulled two keys out of his pocket and held one up for Kelvin to see. Attached to it was a keyring that read, *You're Nicked*.

'Is that for me?'

'My home is your home.'

'I don't know what to say.'

Nash leaned closer as he whispered, 'You don't have to say anything. Just always feel loved in our home.'

'Drumroll, please.' Kelvin put his key in Nash's lock.

With the promise of a shared home—and camper van, Nash and Kelvin leaned into each other. When they had a nightcap in their hands Nash raised his glass.

'To the Good Lady Diana and beyond.'

'Bed Time?'

'But I'm not tired.'

'Exactly.'

Chapter Five

After the performers had eaten it was time to prepare for the evening show. Trailer doors closed as showers were taken, and the sound of hairdryers rang across the camp from the dressing tent. The animals were sorted first, people second—it was the first rule of Quinn's Law.

Always, and in every corner of the bustling scene, a group of diminutive figures caught the attention of passersby. The small people were part of the ground crew and scurried around with an energy that made them invaluable. With the exception of Moody Morton, who could be an angry, aggressive sod, especially after a few beers, the dwarves were a cheerful bunch, governed by Jimmy's wife, the camp cook, Joleen—who terrorised the whole camp. Quinn and Mac didn't give Joleen instructions—they made polite suggestions, otherwise, they didn't get fed.

Everybody was adjusting their outfits, and adding the pizzazz of sparkle and glamour.

Quinn's harsh words with Bence Jaeger were forgotten, and he clapped him on the back and wished him good luck as he passed. Jaeger had been through some problems in the past, especially following the tragic death of his mother, but the man was a genius and a great asset to the circus, and he always gave his time to mentor the younger members of the troupe. Quinn allowed him a certain amount of temperament and vanity.

A few steps away, Octavia brushed her full chestnut beard and ran fragrant oil through it until it shone like burnished gold. She carried herself with dignity and a regal countenance. Octavia had strength and an air of presence. The woman of keen intelligence was confident and ambitious. She was the circus mother and people bowed to her influence. Her face and body were covered in a full coat of hair that mixed with the flowing beard. It gave her an air of mystique and she said it kept her warm in winter.

Octavia worked backstage as the Special Effects Coordinator and, working with Bence Jaeger, she'd produced some amazing illusions. She was diligent in her work, but the haze of shining hair was her pride and joy. Once, when Jimmy's son, Little Rory, had teased her with a pair of scissors, she'd put him over her knee and spanked him on her trailer steps, causing all-out war.

Tonight, her eyes were dusted with a shimmering eyeshadow that sparkled like jewels, and the colour drew Quinn to her eyes—until she started yelling.

'Noor? For Goodness sake. Noor? Where is that girl?' Octavia stood on her trailer steps and hollered. 'There you are. Come on. You said you'd oil my back.'

'I'm sorry, Octavia. And it's not as though you're in the spotlight. The performers need help first. And anyway, I couldn't get away because Saar was playing kissy-face with Damien'

'Standards are essential no matter where one is. And what Saar wants, Saar gets? It'll end in tears. Mark my words.'

The other girl scowled.

'Careful Saar. If the wind changes you'll stay like that, and Isiah will put you in the ring as a gurning act.'

The Danish strongman, grinned, 'Aye, but at least she'll scare the protesters away.'

'Protestors.' Octavia spat on the grass, but nothing came out. 'If they aren't up in arms about the animals, they're trying to liberate us.'

Magnus was six foot eleven, and it caused consternation between him and Berdini, who claimed he was the world's tallest man. It was a lie.

Berdini missed the old days when he'd worked as a sideshow exhibit, but he'd adapted well to his role on the ground crew and enjoyed his job title as Head of Tall Maintenance.

Magnus had muscles bulging beneath his tight-fitting leotard. His arms glistened with a sheen of sweat which was evidence of the rigorous training that shaped his strength. He had the aura of Herculean invincibility, and dared anybody to challenge his might, if not his height.

Berdini was seven foot eleven inches, and exactly a foot taller than Magnus. And, as a prank, he'd had it written into his contract that Magnus would stoop in his presence. The men were good friends and hung out together, but they were still rivals.

Berdini fell three inches short of the world's claim. Pandering to his vanity, Quinn had ordered handmade size fifteen shoes fitted with elevated heels, and Berdini wore his trousers long enough to hide his secret. They took him to the world record height of eight foot three, and even though he wasn't in the public eye, he took his false record seriously. As long as nobody made him take his shoes off, he was fine.

Quinn was in his trailer brushing lint from his red tailcoat ready for his ringmaster's duties, when there was a knock on the door. What now? He always moaned that people only knocked when something had gone wrong, but it wasn't true. He was surprised to see Tomasso, the youngest acrobat.

'What's up? Come in.'

'I need to talk to you. It's about Fauna, one of the dancing girls.'

'I'm well aware of my staff, Tomasso, and the roles they play. Fauna? What's wrong with her? Is she okay to go on tonight?'

'Tonight, yes. But the problem is, boss—well, she's pregnant.'

'Pregnant? How?'

Tomasso didn't answer but blushed to the roots of his hair.

'I mean, is the baby yours?'

'Yes.'

'And what does Fauna want to do about it?'

'I don't know. She's confused. I'm only twenty-one. I came to ask if you can help me arrange a termination while we're in Prague. It would be best for both of us, and she'll listen to you. Fauna has her career, and having a child at nineteen would ruin it.'

'Tomasso, I understand your concerns, but have you considered how Fauna feels? You kids, you think it's all a game until it comes to bite you on the backside. But you're only thinking about what you want.'

'I know she has attachments to the idea of a baby. But it would be a huge setback for her, Mr Quinn. She's a vital part of the magic act with Flora, as well as her dancing and the horses. Having a child would mess up everything.'

'You're pretending your concern is about Fauna, but you're selfish. Her feelings should be your priority. It's her body and her choice. You can't make decisions like this for her. Have you even discussed it? Your mind should be on your performance, boy. If you aren't concentrating, you're asking for an accident. Does she know you're here an hour before the curtain lifts?'

'No. I wanted to see if you can help first. I understand what you're saying, but I'm trying to do what's best. She's being sick all the time and I don't want her to face being a young mother in this industry—and I don't want that for my child.'

'Being a parent is a life-changing responsibility, and it's not something to be taken lightly. Fauna will make her own decision. You should talk to her, Tomasso. Find out what she wants.'

Quinn saw him hesitate. Tomasso had seen his options as being shoehorned into one box and this was the first time he'd looked at it from the other side of the fence, but he was still frightened of it affecting his career. 'I am thinking about myself. I want to be the best in my field, and I can't be tied to a wife and child—not now. But I'll talk to her, and we'll make a decision together.'

'That's the right thing to do. However, I'll be talking to her as well, because I won't have her bullied into doing what you want. Remember, the circus is a family, and we support each other. No child would have more people to love it and see that it grows happy. I'll be here if you need my assistance, whatever you decide.'

'Thank you, Mr Quinn. I appreciate your advice.'

Tomasso left the trailer and Quinn watched him go, hoping the boy would approach the situation gently. Quinn saw something change in the acrobat's eyes when he realised having a child wasn't the end of the world and that his people would be there to support him. He'd come to Quinn in shock, and he needed time to process the news.

Quinn was a surrogate father to them all. The boy was a mass of bluster and fear. He'd acted on his first impulse with a knee-jerk reaction. He was calmer now and in a better place to see the whole picture and make an informed choice with his girlfriend. His mind might be more on the job that night and the risk of an accident reduced. Even if it would be another mouth to feed in difficult times, Quinn hoped he'd have to get out his special box of cigars. They only emerged at the birth of a new circus baby.

Backstage the girls were arguing. Noor and Saar were conjoined twins. They were Dutch, and locked in an embrace of attachment at the stomach. They time-shared, and both had demanding and very different careers to juggle that had taken a lot of compromise. They could walk, but it was difficult They preferred sitting, and had flatly refused a wheelchair wide enough to accommodate them both. Quinn had only dared offer once.

Saar was the dominant sister and the primary decision-maker. Their intricate dance with limbs in awkward places defied the boundaries of the physical world, as their bodies moved in unspoken unison. They were gifted and had a remarkable bond. The twins used telepathy for communication, had their own made-up language—and knowing their worth—they demanded exorbitant salaries. It caused bad feelings among the others, and the twenty-eight-year-olds weren't always popular around camp.

Their expressive eyes held a depth of emotion and intelligence, reflecting the complexity of their existence. They'd been at odds with each other and didn't speak for weeks when Saar started seeing Daft Damien. But things seemed to have settled lately.

An hour before showtime, the opening night jitters were evident. The performers went through their rituals and superstitions and they heard the crowd outside waiting for the gates to open forty-five minutes before curtain. That gave the punters plenty of time to browse the concessions and buy burgers and candyfloss.

The troupe made their preparations, readying themselves for the greatest show currently treading the sawdust in Prague, and prayers were heard being uttered by acts as they chalked their hands under the canvas. The keepers tended their animals, calming them, and ensuring they looked perfect. Majestic horses gleamed ebony, chestnut, and the purest white aided by talcum powder. They were brushed again and adorned with regal harnesses. Plumes of feathers rose from their heads, and the sound of their soft wickers added a feeling of well-being.

Chandra, the bull elephant, stood tall. He was a symbol of majesty, ready to open the show. Isiah Quinn, the ringmaster, sat across the elephant's immense shoulders, resplendent in his red suit and top hat. It was time for the grand entrance.

Quinn was ready. He caressed Chandra's rough skin and whispered words of encouragement to him, as the elephant trumpeted and sent his trunk over his head to caress his master with the sensitive tip. Chandra was content in his place within the family and loved the ring.

The curtain lifted and they walked out of the wings.

In a distant corner, cages housed a menagerie of exotic creatures. From sleek big cats, with their eyes gleaming an untamed fire, to playful dogs. The feline predators had sinewy bodies and hypnotic gazes. They prowled the enclosures, and their presence was captivating. This was the diversity of humans, and the animal kingdom working in harmony.

The scents of the Big Top created a sensory blast that was as rich as the visual extravaganza. The aroma of hay, mixed with the musk of animals, was a heady concoction. And the tantalizing fragrance of popcorn being buttered, and candyfloss spinning, drifted through the tent, tempting the crowd.

The symphony of activity reached its crescendo. The carneys were dressed in their costumes. The side stalls were lit up like fairyland, open, and adorned with colourful banners. They enticed the crowd with promises of entertainment, unforgettable tastes, games to chance their arm, and experiences they'd never had.

The performers were made up and primed. They gathered in the clown alley backstage, and despite having done it hundreds of times before, the first night was a magical night, and their excitement was infectious.

A trumpet sounded, and its call echoed across the field. It was a clarion summons bringing the audience and drawing them into the wonders waiting inside the big top. People streamed in, taking their seats.

As the curtain opened, Chandra led the entrance. Behind him, the vibrant performers surged forward, their voices rising and exuberant. The circus was a world within a world. It transported the audience to the realms of their imagination, where exotic dreams danced.

The acrobats soared through the air with breathtaking precision. Their bodies defied gravity in a display of strength and grace. The trapeze artists swung with agility, leaving the audience breathless with admiration.

Quinn was thankful that he had another fire-breather to mesmerize the crowd with their mystical prowess while Ignatius was resting up in his trailer after his release from the hospital—he was still screaming sabotage to anybody who would listen. Like every night, the flames danced in hypnagogic patterns, casting a glow to illuminate the faces in the ringside seats.

The contortionists twisted into unearthly configurations. Their flexibility pushed the boundaries of human possibility. Each movement was met with applause and astonishment, as the performers bent and stretched, defying the laws of physics. They were living sculptures, painted gold. Wondrous people of beauty who twisted into something less human-looking.

The horses, guided by their skilled riders, galloped in perfect synchronization, their hooves pounding the earth in a rhythmic symphony. The elephants, with their colossal forms swaying, and a gentle grace, showcased their intelligence and power. With a wave of their trunks and a command from their keepers, they stood on their drums. They ran around the ring holding each other's tails and the crowd 'Awed' on cue when little Sabu couldn't keep up and had to run to catch his mother's tail.

The finale of their act was painting canvasses with watercolour paint, using brushes held in their trunks. The paintings were auctioned with a forty-pound reserve. Quinn was shrewd. They could have created many paintings, stockpiled to sell to the crowd before the show started, but he kept the number to three per performance, and forced value into the canvases. They were coveted, and fights had broken out in the crowd more than once. In ten years, they'd never been left with a single elephant painting after the show. 'Psychology is a game of wits,' Quinn would say to his accountant. And Jack Devine would smile—at three hundred pounds an hour, he could afford to.

'Good choice, my dear lady,' Quinn would say to a punter. 'Our sweet baby Sabu paints magnificent pictures—perfect for your child's nursery.' The splodges sold like grandmasters, and the money—rarely less than a hundred pounds a painting—was secreted away in the ringmaster's pocket every night—and twice on Saturdays.

The big cats stalked the ring, their movements were lithe with natural grace and predatory instinct. They leapt onto their platforms with the potential for danger in every taut sinew.

When the clowns ran out in ridiculous costumes with the energy of a dervish, they brought laughter to the ring and delivered a respite from the breathtaking feats of other performers.

The smell of sizzling burgers teased and heightened the sensory experience. The fragrances were sent into the tent by electric fans ten minutes before the final curtain, and wrapped around the audience, making their stomachs growl.

And then it was over. High on a rush of adrenaline, the performers took their bows. Their faces were radiant with accomplishment—nobody died tonight, folks. That's a win. The audience filed out of the tent.

The circus had fulfilled its promise of transporting people to a world of make-believe. In the realm of the carnival, every sunrise brought new excitement, and every performance was an opportunity to live through another night of danger.

The darkness embraced the circus ground with tranquillity and cast an indigo cloak over the field. The muffled sounds of settling animals and the echoes of laughter floated into nothing as the performers wound down.

In their enclosures, a peace drifted over the animals. The horses nuzzled each other with affection, and their whinnies resonated with a soothing melody. The elephants swayed, and communicated in low rumbles, with a language of vibrations expressing their bond.

The night held its own brand of enchantment, and the colourful trailers shimmered in the moonlight. Prague, with its ancient charm and storied history, was the backdrop for the fantasy. The circus, born from the passion of the misfits who called it home, unwrapped its secrets for the crowd. They ignited a memory in the audience that left an indelible smile. And then—when it was done—when the animals were bedded down, and the performer's adrenalin quieted—they slept.

Chapter Six

Isiah Quinn's charismatic leadership commanded attention. His red tailored suit, cast with black velvet and embroidery made him stand out as the main man. With a top hat perched on his head, his hawk eyes surveyed his circus. He was tired but had a school group to enchant before he could get out of his costume to siesta in his trailer before the evening performance.

As the morning sun reached its zenith, a rumble filled the air, growing louder as he listened. He turned to the entrance to see who was coming and was surprised to see an enormous truck materialise from the warped perception of the heat haze. The metal behemoth pulled up near the colourful canvas of the big top and concession tents, and its engine roared, sending vibrations through the foundations of the earth.

The lorry shuddered to a halt, unleashing a grumble of creaks as its doors swung open. A group of burly men jumped out of the cab, like clowns from a Mini. They wore old leather jackets despite the heat, and their faces were etched with lines and oil smudges.

With practised ease, the men hoisted the tarpaulin off the flatbed. The sight of the cargo took Isiah's breath away. It was a carousel of unparalleled beauty—a French masterpiece of craftsmanship and artistry.

The merry-go-round was an artist's palette of vibrant colour and intricate detail. Its decorated wooden panels gleamed. The hand-carved horses were the best he'd ever seen. Their horsehair manes and tails flowed in flaxen beauty. Each steed had been painted with tones that shimmered in the sunlight, and their eyes were crafted with an uncanny lifelike quality that stared at you no matter where you were standing.

Gilded mirrors dressed the outer edge of the French carousel, reflecting flashes of light. Above the moving parts and central control booth, a lace-effect canopy of ironwork would stretch like delicate filigree, completing the carousel's craftsmanship.

Isiah reacted to his astonishment. He checked for the speakers. It would play traditional calliope music. This was an object of outstanding beauty and he was possessed by it. The carousel had a presence—a magnetism that sparked a need to have it. But it was a fairground ride, and they were a circus. Carneys and fairground types didn't mix. Circus folk were performers, and fairground types were gipsies with no discernible talent in his opinion. When the two crossed paths, there was trouble. Beautiful though it was, the ride had no right in his circus.

His voice carried authority as Isiah waited for the delivery men—they could come to him, he wasn't showing deference by moving. His gaze locked on the carousel. 'What is the meaning of this?'

A grizzled man with calloused hands and a weathered face sized him up. He met Isiah's stare, and his voice implied that he didn't give a damn about much. 'Are you the gaffer? We were told to deliver this.' His next words were tinged with mystery. 'We've been given no further instruction.'

'Who ordered it?'

'Are you Isiah Quinn?'

'At your service, my good man, but you haven't done me the courtesy of answering my question. So I'll set you another one, maybe something simple. Who sent it?'

'I don't know. I've got a sheet with an address, and that's all I need to know.'

'Do you have any paperwork for it?'

'I do indeed. I have my worksheet with an address on it, like I said.'

'Are you being purposefully dim-witted? Do you have anything else?'

'Nope.' The driver nodded to his men and they unloaded the carousel.

They hefted the disconnected parts off the truck, ready for assembly. Performers paused in their show preparations, drawn to the unexpected delivery.

Isiah's eyes traced the curves and details. He felt an inexplicable connection to the magnificent artwork—it was meant to be here. It had come home—but he reacted stubbornly.

'You can't leave it there.'

'Well, there it is, and there it stays, so that's your problem, sir.'

It was a rare occurrence for Quinn to be flummoxed. The upper hand of any situation belonged in his court. But without another word to him, or even each other, the men jumped back in the truck and drove away.

It took a while to back out of the entrance. He could have stopped them and forced their hand, but he wanted them to go. He coveted that ride. He hadn't been given a bill of sale, and didn't know where it had come from, or who it belonged to—but some force at play made him desire it in the same way that a man in the desert craves water.

With a click of his fingers, Isiah motioned for the workers to gather. They waited for Quinn's guidance. And his voice resonated across the field.

'My friends, we find ourselves on the tide of a mystery. This carousel, though unexpected, holds a promise to make our tills ring. We are the keepers of wonder, seekers of the extraordinary, and it's our duty to give this magnificent lady a home. Rig her up in the east corner, boys—and if the tallyman comes knocking, tell him possession is nine-tenths of the law. She found her way here, and this is where she's destined to be. It's mine now.'

'You heard the boss, lads. Relay it down the field, and let's get it up and tested ready for tonight.' Mac McKenzie had been with Quinn for over a decade. He'd worked his way up the ranks to become boss hostler, a term referring to the person in charge of overseeing circus operations. He managed the groundcrew and was responsible for the care and movement of livestock. His word was second only to Quinn.

Isiah's voice rose. 'We'll gather our resources, our talent, and our curiosity. We'll tell great stories about the hurdy-gurdy's past, and weave them into the loom of our circus canvas.'

'All right, Guv. You're not wowing the crowds now. It's a bloody roundabout, not the Holy Grail.' The strongman clapped him on the back and laughed.

'My dear Magnus,' Quinn said. 'Spoken like a true man of brawn over intellect. Don't you see before you our new golden goose?'

The men, including Magnus, applauded its arrival, and one of the trapeze brothers, fifteen-year-old Alessio, begged to be the first one to ride it. And Isiah's eyes were lively with greed. The circus took the arrival of the mysterious carousel—and the enigma that wrapped it.

Later, as the sun dipped below the horizon, casting hues of orange and pink across a caramel sky, the circus grounds buzzed with electric anticipation. The carousel was a beacon of fantasy and took on added beauty in the moon's glow.

The circus came to life. Daft Damien was entrusted with running the new carousel, and when it was turned on, the band of carneys cheered.

Alessio was given the first ride as promised.

And as daytime surrendered to the evening, lights came to life in competition with the stars. Every human sense was catered to, and the calliope sent its circus jingle across the grounds. The hulk of the castle walls behind them were in silhouette and illuminated by the carousel's light. It was a looming sentinel over the darkness. The bustling atmosphere settled into a hum of anticipation, and the performers were ready for another evening of Plasticine smiling as they trod the sawdust of the ring.

A figure emerged from the shadows, an old man with weathered features and a hint of something unholy in his eyes.

A stranger.

His steps were slow and the carneys looked on.

Jimmy ran up to Quinn's trailer and was shouting before he knocked. 'Boss, you'd better come and see this.'

Quinn walked tall behind the small man, his suit tails blowing in the evening wind, and his open-legged gait displayed his authority.

'Proper chased Damien off with a flea in his ear, he did,' Jimmy was talking about an intruder on the field. 'Said as how he was taking over.'

He got close to the new ride, and Quinn saw the man standing between two horses. He was talking to them and Quinn sensed trouble.

'You're in the wrong place, my friend. The backstage area is private,' he said.

'I've come for my first evening's work.'

Isiah sized the stranger up. 'And who might you be?'

'They call me Ambrose Ravenswood.'

'What's your business here, Ravenswood?'

'I've sent something ahead of me—this carousel.'

'The carousel? Why have you brought it here?'

'I'm bringing an honest day's work, for an honest day's pay.'

'We have all the labour we need. And if I might be so bold, a man with a staff and old age apparent, is as useful as a three-legged chair. Be on your way, sir.'

'A tri-legged stool would be a triumph of balance if the legs were set just so.'

'We can barter quips all night, Mr Ravenswood, but I have a circus to run. I bid you adieu, sir.'

Ambrose's stare penetrated Isiah's as he leaned forward. His voice was barely a whisper. 'But I can't leave, sir. You see, this is no ordinary carousel, Mr Quinn. It carries a curse—a rare malevolence that has plagued those who dare try to rob a man of his rights.'

'Then why have you thought to bring it to our circus? It arrived without an owner and under my name. I believe it belongs to me.'

'It seeks a new home—a place where the spirits dwelling within its confines can find peace. The carousel has chosen your circus, Mr Quinn. It senses what it needs here within these grounds.'

Like most circus people steeped in folklore and myth from birth, Isaiah was a superstitious man. A cursed circus ground was a deadly place. His imagination conjured images of ghosts and apparitions, and in his head, he heard the calliope turning on without a human hand in the night. It would play its sinister melody at half speed and out of tune. The haunting notes came to his imagination as though he'd called them up, and he knew them to be true.

'It has taken many lives. Are you willing to risk incurring its wrath?'

'Is my circus in danger?' Quinn asked. Concern for his performers and staff was evident.

'Of course not, Mr Quinn, my good man. Your circus is not in danger—only the people in it.'

Chapter Seven

Ravenswood's eyes twinkled. 'The curse plaguing the carousel has a peculiar safeguard. It spares the public visitors. They are safe from its malevolent grip and you will make your money out of it. However, your people, working within its enchanted reach must be cautious.'

The dread of having the cursed carousel near him made Quinn apprehensive. 'And what of you, Mr Ravenswood? How are you unscathed by this aberration?'

'I'm the guardian of the ride. I navigate its treacherous realm, and it's my destiny to protect people from its dark enchantment.'

'And if I ask you to take your contraption and go?'

'I cannot, sir. You took delivery. You have it assembled on your field. It has been ridden by your people. The curse sees this as a binding contract. You can't get rid of it, burn it or—should the thought cross your mind—murder me to aid your endeavours. We are inextricably linked, it and I. Keep your people out of the saddle, Mr Quinn, and it will serve you well, and bring much revenue to your pocket.'

A feeling of trepidation chilled Isiah as he thought about the curse, but greed broiled in his belly like undigested offal. It took him thirty seconds to come to his decision.

Isiah Quinn extended his hand to Ambrose, a gesture of reluctant partnership. 'I welcome you to Quinn Brothers Flying Circus, Ambrose Ravenswood. May our time together be joyful, profitable, and blessed. I will have a contract drawn up.'

Ambrose eyed the gambit like a player in a chess game. He spat on his palm and grabbed Quinn's hand in a firm grip. 'With the solidarity and serendipitous spirit of this circus, we shall meet the darkness inside the carousel. If the spirits within the grain are appeased, its music will warm the hearts of many. But take heed, Mr Quinn, no carney or grease monkey affiliated with this institution must ever ride the carousel. If they do, they will be dead by the moon's wane.'

Isiah looked at the roundabout. He knew his stuff when it came to carney equipment, and this was a valuable antique of over a hundred and fifty years old—the condition was remarkable. Its presence whispered ancient stories, and the wooden horses were frozen in a gavotte of days gone by.

Some of the circus workers had paused in their preparations, drawn by the mystery surrounding the ride. They all had an opinion which was as varied as the intellect in any classroom of children. Their eyes mirrored curiosity as they gossiped, sensing a pivotal moment had arrived in camp with the stranger.

With a sweep of his hand, Isiah beckoned his performers and staff to gather around his trailer steps. Their emotions ranged from intrigue to apprehension, but trust in Quinn's decisions anchored their acceptance. He stood next to the old man.

'I have an announcement,' Isaiah said. 'This carousel is a harbinger of light and shade. It comes to us bringing both luck and curses. It's a gateway to wondrous and treacherous realms. But don't be afraid of its dark past, we will be guided by the wisdom of our new brother, Ambrose.'

A murmur of disapproval rippled through the crowd, and they focused on Isiah and Ravenswood.

The new arrival cleared his throat and tried for a smile that was grizzled and failed. 'Welcome my brothers and sisters. Fear not, the carousel and its curse will not harm you,' he said.

They were suspicious of the old man dressed in a shabby black suit and a felt bowler hat. He looked as though he wanted to be smart, like a funeral director, with his white shirt and everything else in black, but fell short of the mark. His shoes were scuffed and his clothes bore the age and fashion of many decades past. He spoke in a soft West Country English accent. But he talked gibberish.

'What kind of curse?' Mauritzio Silvestri asked. His family had one of the most dangerous acts, handed down through generations, and it made them among the most superstitious of the crew. 'The last thing I need is a curse flying on my heels.'

'It's nothing for you to worry about, my friend. All will be well,' Quinn said. He didn't like the way this was going.

Ambrose took a step forward and raised his hand to draw everybody's attention. 'On the contrary, that is not true. Our esteemed employer makes light of the issue. Indeed all will not be well. If certain conditions are not adhered to, all will be far from well. The carousel is guarded by the spirits of children killed in macabre ways by carneys down the centuries. They are drawn to the carousel by its haunting music.'

A murmur of dissent ran through the field.

'Get rid of him,' Magnus shouted, and a ripple of agreement echoed him.

'He jokes. What a cad.' Quinn tried to lead Ravenswood away, but he wasn't for being taken anywhere and carried on talking.

'Fear not, friends. The demon children will do you no harm, as long as you do not ride the carousel. No circus employee must ever sit in the saddle of one of my beautiful stallions.'

Mauritzio clasped his hands as if in prayer. 'My son has already ridden your cursed ride. Are you saying harm will come to Alessio?'

'I rode it, too,' Madam Selena spoke up from the back of the crowd. 'Am I doomed?'

Ambrose Ravenswood waved his hand and forced a smile that was cunning and insincere. 'My dear lady, don't worry. I will conduct a cleansing ritual to ensure your safety. It is selective and won't take every carney. After all, you didn't know about the dire curse when you rode it. Take heed for the future.' He grinned at the people, and his pointy yellow teeth put Quinn in mind of a weasel.

The mood was one of fear and it came minutes before they were due to gather in the clown alley for the performance. Grumbles and complaints rang around the field but one of the crew came to Quinn's aid by speaking up.

'Look at you all jumping like rabbits. Superstition is so ingrained in your blood that you've lost all sense of logic. The old man's come with a story to thrill the punters. But, it's just a story.' He addressed Ambrose. 'Save your doom-mongering for the people with wallets, old man. These folk have a dangerous job to do. Dead children and curses—what a load of rubbish. I'll ride your carousel and prove there's no curse. Troupe, let's focus on what's important. There's a crowd waiting outside. We're going to give them a show they'll never forget.'

Quinn could have kissed Ross Finley. His level head and common sense were good for business. A cheer went through the performers and crew, and for now, at least, harmony was restored. Quinn saw the worried look on the carney's faces as they turned away. Concentration was imperative for the performance and the last thing they needed was another distraction.

Quinn acknowledged the dedication to their craft. And shouted glad tidings after them. It was the glue holding them together. But, he'd picked up on the unwelcoming vibe, and one bad apple could ferment the lot of them and pickle the circus in sour vinegar.

'Remember,' he said. 'We are a family—we protect and support each other no matter what. We'll break any curse attached to us, and brave the fated ride as a united force.'

Quinn gave Ambrose a nod of affirmation. 'Let's go. It's showtime.'

As the group closed ranks against Ravenswood, a black energy hovered over camp. They said the bad spirits of the ride were among them. Finley had taken his valour ride against mutterings and murmurings from Ravenswood. He dismounted in better humour and wandered off, but not one of the others was brave enough to defy Ambrose Ravenswood and mount the horses.

The moon cast a silver glow, illuminating the way with shimmering stars and a thousand LED fairy lights. The stage was set, and the artists, acrobats, contortionists, and dreamers lifted the curtain for the second night of their run in Prague.

The carney folk walked away from the carousel in the direction of the big top for their performance. They were still grumbling. Behind them, the haunting melodies of forgotten tunes echoed through the air. The story about the spirits of the ride scared them, and the presence of superstition may have been unseen but it was felt.

Ambrose traced the intricate carvings on the carousel's surface. 'My touch awakens dormant energies. Listen for the whispers that dance on the edge of time,' he said. And the stragglers ran away to the sound of his mocking laughter.

That night, the contortionists twisted their bodies into impossible shapes, defying the laws of physics, while acrobats soared through the air, evoking the beauty of aerial dances.

The artists did their job and put superstition behind them. The jugglers manipulated balls of shimmering light until they spun so fast in the air that they lost all form—like the carousel spirits.

Isiah Quinn stood at the front of the ring. He watched his people come alive through the nature of their art.

And the curtain fell for the intermission. The show was going well.

Chapter Eight

The anticipation was palpable as the Silvestri family prepared to astound the audience with a breathtaking trapeze act. Mauritzio, Aurora, and their three children stood in the ring. They felt a torrid and nervous excitement as they did before every performance.

However, Mauritzio was more agitated than usual. 'I want excellence tonight. This show could be a tragedy that will haunt us forever if anything goes wrong. *Porca miseria*, rotten curses. Take extra care with your holds tonight. Luca, your third dismount was sloppy in rehearsal. Ensure that it's strong tonight.'

'Yes, Dad.'

Aurora spoke in a stage whisper from the side of her mouth between smiling at the crowd. 'Shut up Mauritzio. You'll frighten the children with your loose talk.'

The spotlight illuminated the trapeze rig, casting a glow on the family as they took their positions. Mauritzio, Aurora, and fourteen-year-old Isabella took to the air first while the two boys held the ropes in the ring. The strong patriarch gripped the trapeze bar. His taut physique rippled with the sheen of applied oils and his stance was confident. Aurora soared through the air with elegance and precision and Isabella emanated youth and beauty with her long-limbed adolescence.

Twelve-year-old Luca, the mischievous youngster, swung the rope leading to the platform, ready to play his part. Quinn always told him off for complaining when he wasn't under the spotlight, and he hated spotting the ropes—but he knew that the kid's real ambition lay with another act that had nothing to do with the trapeze. He wanted to be a clown.

The music swelled, setting the rhythm for the performance. The Silvestri family twirled and flipped through the air, captivating the audience with their feats. The spectators marvelled at their skill, and the applause fuelled the family's adrenaline.

Isabella and her parents descended to massive applause, and it was the boys' turn. They had the most dangerous and gymnastic sequence of the family. They climbed the ropes in showman style, and as the song *Anything You Can Do, I Can Do Better* played, Alessio performed the routine, while Luca followed his every move like a shadow, and played to the crowd for the biggest applause.

The pivotal moment of the act came. Alessio, as the most athletic performer in the family, was performing the ultimate sequence. Luca stood at the back of the platform. The lights went down and a spotlight took the focus from the skies to the ring below. Isiah Quinn strode into the ring of light and a drum roll raised the tension. He gestured to Alessio.

'Ladies and gentlemen, boys and girls. We beg your absolute silence. The world-famous trapeze artist, Alessio Silvestri, is about to perform a manoeuvre never before seen by any audience, in any ring, in any circus the world over. He's just fifteen years old, and he's flying for you tonight. Remain silent as he completes five continuous somersaults in a stunt so dangerous it has its own name. Alessio will perform *Solto Mortale*, The Deadly Leap.'

The spotlight travelled from the ring to the rigging.

Alessio was elevated away from the first platform sitting on a trapeze swing and suspended at the second level plank high above the audience's heads. Luca climbed the rope with agility, reaching the platform and positioning himself to push Alessio on the swing. It was a move they'd performed in rehearsal, the thrilling highlight of their act. Quinn could tell the boys were nervous about the sequence. They'd been rehearsing in secret, and even Quinn wasn't allowed to see the most dangerous move until they were over an audience.

Something was wrong with the lighting and he was furious. This was the highlight of their act, and yet the lighting technician had the spotlight on a strobe effect. He went to find out why the spotlight on the swing wasn't as bright tonight. The boy was performing in partial shadow. It wasn't good enough.

The first push went smoothly. The audience watched the trapeze artist drop from the seat and cling to the swing with his hands. He dangled high above the ring. The crowd held their breath, their eyes locked on the trapeze. A haunting voiceover came from below and warned the audience not to blink, as they were about to see something that had never been done before.

Luca pushed harder on the swing the second time. Alessio's body jolted, his grip on the swing slipped for a fraction of a second, and he let go of one hand. The audience gasped in terror. But Quinn smiled, knowing it was part of the act.

As the swing came back for the final push, Luca, gave a powerful shove and it reached an alarming height, almost grazing the roof of the big top.

The swing recoiled with a force that made some of the audience hide their faces. Others hardly dared look. The boy on the trapeze desperately clung to the bar with one hand, and they saw his strength waning under the strain. His body looked almost opaque in the flickering lights and he seemed to dip in and out of focus with the velocity of the swing. The crowd watched the danger unfolding before their eyes.

Then, in a moment that would forever haunt the Silvestri family, Alessio let go of the swing and somersaulted into the air. The gasp from the crowd was deafening. But he didn't complete his five somersaults. As he went into the fifth and final turn…

…Alessio vanished.

Gone.

In front of two hundred spectators, the boy had disappeared into the sparkling dust nodes. Luca descended the rope as the audience and carneys alike held their breath. He had the centre ring, threw his hands in the air, and took his bow.

Straightening, he threw his arm wide. His open palm was directed at the curtain that Alessio would come through.

And he waited in a frozen tableau as time stopped.

Panic surged through the spectators with a mixture of disbelief and confusion, but the carneys held their nerve.

They waited for Alessio to reappear, assuming it was part of the act. But as seconds turned into minutes, it was evident that something had gone wrong.

Mac Mackenzie, the boss hostler, waved his arms and sent in the clowns. Aurora came in and guided her youngest son through the curtains with a wave to the audience. Quinn ran backstage and demanded to know what the hell was going on. And Mauritzio and Aurora demanded answers from their son.

'Where is he, Luca?' Aurora asked.

'I don't know. He was supposed to come on to take our bow.'

They were the last words Luca spoke.

Within minutes, every carney that wasn't performing went out to look for the missing boy. His disappearance was impossible. One second he was there, and in plain sight, he'd vanished.

'It's the curse,' Noor's voice rang across the field like the ringing of a doom bell.

Ambrose had stopped the ride and came over to see what was happening with some of the other side stall holders. 'Aye, it may be,' he said.

Alessio was nowhere to be found.

Luca was the only one who knew the truth. He looked into the darkness between two wagons, and the person lurking there put a finger to their lips. Luca was terrified. His family called Alessio's name. Their voices ranged from concern to disbelief. The vibrant circus atmosphere had transformed into a chilling one of worry.

As the final notes of the encore music faded into silence the ringmaster read the gravity of the situation. Quinn stepped into the ring, and his voice, boomed through the tent, commanding attention and maintaining his air of composure.

'Ladies and gentlemen, we apologize for any disruption to your printed program this evening and hope that you have enjoyed your experience at Quinn Brother's Flying Circus. We are addressing a technical difficulty, and our utmost priority is the safety and well-being of our performers, and you, our cherished audience. We ask that you leave the grounds quickly and in an orderly fashion as the gates will close in ten minutes.'

A ripple of uneasy applause spread through the crowd as they tried to understand the situation. Whispers filled the tent, and their questions hung in the same air that the boy had disappeared from. There was no smoke, no mirrors, he was flying through the tent and he vanished.

Mauritzio's face was etched with worry, and he pushed Mac aside to speak to the carneys directly. His voice was steady but ragged with terror.

'Where's my boy? I don't know what's going on.' The Silvestri family, still in their costumes, went to their trailer to ask Luca what had happened. They were in time to see a dark shadow running into the woods behind the field. Was it Alessio? Inside, their youngest son was as white as a sheet and terrified.

The atmosphere around the big top was charged with tension. The circus crew and performers cleared the tent in record time. People tried to hang back to find out what was going on, but they were herded through the entrance, and patrols were set up along the perimeter to keep the public away. Concerned onlookers gathered in groups, exchanging worried glances and hurried whispers. They were moved away. 'Nothing to see here, folks.'

Isabella clutched Aurora's hand with tears streaming down her face. 'Where is Alessio? He can't just disappear.'

Aurora was worried. She held her daughter close, but her focus was drawn to her youngest child. He was shaking and refused to speak. She asked him a dozen times, 'Where is Alessio? Where is your brother?' but the boy didn't answer. His eyelids were low, and he was in shock. His father threatened him with his belt if he didn't speak up, but Luca shivered on his bunk at the back of the trailer without responding.

'Lay off him, Mauritzio. Can't you see he's upset? If he knew anything he'd tell us. We must pray and have hope. We'll find him,' Aurora said.

After every inch of the castle grounds were searched, and came up empty, people split into groups. The search parties were better organised now, and Alessio's name was called and recalled in fading waves until the searchers were out of range.

Luca was alone. When his mother left him to speak to Mauritzio in private, Quinn saw that his eyes darted between the familiar and the empty expanse outside the trailer.

The moon cast long shadows over the city, as the search for Alessio intensified. Crew members scoured every street and alley, and their flashlight beams sliced through the darkness.

Only a few carneys stayed on the grounds, and they talked about their concern for the Silvestri family. Everybody knew Mauritzio pushed the boys hard and the general feeling was that Alessio had run away. Madam Selena took Luca by the hand and led him out of the trailer. 'I see great trouble,' she said to the other carneys.

Luca was incapable of making decisions for himself and had to be guided to the cook tent where the people left in camp had gathered. Jolene said that food helped any situation, no matter how bad. The homestead carneys spoke gentle words of encouragement, then offered silent prayers for Alessio's safe return. But the whispers behind the traumatised child's back were about the curse that had suffocated the field like a black depression. Daft Damien Belman was the first to threaten a visit to Ambrose Ravenswood's trailer with clubs. He was slow of mind and walked with a limp since an accident when he was Alessio's age. But he had the brawn to spare, and he was strong. 'We'll burn the bastard out,' he said.

The night wore on, and hope faded. Alessio was an Italian teenager alone in a strange place. He didn't speak the language and was in a city where the locals refused to speak English—though most of them could. Given the nature of his disappearance, even at this early stage, foul play was suspected but wasn't spoken aloud. Mauritzio and Aurora clung to each other, their faces etched with worry and exhaustion. They exchanged a few words, and their shared anguish was a bond strong enough to hold them together.

The morning sun peeked over the distant hills. As the hours ticked by, their hope waned. More talk of the supernatural abounded, and the fear in the camp escalated.

Despair engulfed the searchers and their steps were laboured as they came to a designated meeting place to swap notes. Every head lifted as a rustling in the trees disturbed the air. The carneys turned, and their hearts pounded in anticipation. But it was Luca who appeared from the shadows. His face was pale and his eyes were troubled. He'd wandered off to find his parents, and he'd heard the cry, too.

An hour later, a voice came from the woods. 'He's here,' the shout rang out again, and Little Rory ran out of a thicket with his dad behind him.

Chapter Nine

As the figure Jimmy pointed to emerged, everybody strained their eyes to see in the dim light of early dawn. The boy walked towards them, and Aurora gasped to see that he was dragging one of his legs—he'd been hurt.

Their hearts sank, and their elation turned to bewilderment. It wasn't Alessio striding across the field.

'It's just Daft Damien,' one of the crew said. They shouted insults and some of them threw sticks at him in frustration.

'What?' Damien said as he drew closer. 'What have I done? I've come to help you look.'

'What were you doing in the bushes with two midgets?' somebody asked.

Jimmy said, 'I could answer that, but now isn't the time for punchlines.'

'I came from the grounds and followed the sound of voices. There was no sign of Alessio' Damien said.

Confusion washed over the Silvestri family. Mauritzio's voice was frantic.

'Damien, have you seen anything? Why were you waving your arms?'

Damien's breath came in ragged pulls. He looked embarrassed for giving them false hope and his words tumbled out. 'I thought I saw Alessio, but it was a tree. I'm telling you that Anlose has got him.'

'Ambrose,' Jimmy said.

'No, that dirty old man with the carousel.'

Jimmy punched Damien on his arm, as silence settled over the crew, and disappointment weighed them down. Alessio's vanishing had left them sinking into their superstition, and their glimmer of hope was shattered. But somebody lurking in the shadows took their moment of opportunity.

Turning away from Daft Damien, Mauritzio clenched his fists. 'Alessio is still missing. We have to find him.'

People questioned how a young acrobat could vanish in front of two hundred pairs of eyes. Murmurs of something supernatural at play rumbled around the fields again.

Nobody had any news and nothing belonging to Alessio was found. Mac called a break and said they'd return to base and have breakfast together, then resume with full bellies, 'I don't want to hear any more talk about curses. The boy's out there somewhere and we're going to find him.' He clapped Mauritzio on the shoulder and led the march back to camp.

The search team numbered more than sixty. They'd been out looking all night, and they'd covered a lot of ground, but they came up with nothing.

The discussion over the communal breakfast was heated. It wasn't the carney way to call in the authorities. They'd never had good reason to trust the police. With constant opposition to the circus, and calls to extract the disabled crew, they had a deep mistrust of anybody in power. One of the strongest voices against calling in the police was Mauritzio.

'It is our business. We will deal with it in our own way.'

'Brother,' Mac said. 'We've been all over the city and he's nowhere to be found. We have to call the police.'

'He's my son. And I say no.'

'Have you got something to hide?' Magnus asked.

Mauritzio struggled to free his legs from the long bench that seated twelve people. He sent food and mugs of tea flying and almost overtipped the people on either side of him as he flew at the strongman. 'I'll kill you. You lowland bastard.'

'Enough.' Mac stood and held his hand up for quiet. 'Fighting among ourselves isn't going to solve anything.'

As the others had trudged back to camp to eat and prepare for the next search, Quinn refused to give up. It was his circus and the missing boy was his responsibility. He couldn't settle to eat while the child was out there. Without saying a word, he snuck away to continue searching hedgerows and riverbanks along the Vltava River. It was hopeless, and he gave up. Quinn went to the police station to report the missing boy. He was the owner and this had gone on long enough.

The Silvestri family were at their wit's end, and the circus was a melting pot of gossip. Everybody had a theory, and every occupation was swapped for the role of detective. They dissected every moment and scrutinised the details. The swing, the platform, and the trajectory were all examined and found to be in order—nothing made sense. Their circus was tainted with unease and melancholy. A black crow flying overhead brought with it a bad omen.

The crew were still arguing when several police vehicles drew onto the circus grounds. Quinn got out of one of the cars. He was still in his costume from the night before, and his steps across the field showed his exhaustion. His shoulders slumped and Alessio's disappearance hit him hard. He'd known the boy since the day he was born.

Aurora was taken to her trailer with the rest of her family to be interviewed. Luca still hadn't spoken a word and the child seemed unnaturally heavy and sleepy. A doctor was called to examine him. The police brought in reinforcements and soon the grounds were awash with people being interviewed in their respective trailers as timelines were built and challenged.

The townsfolk gathered, and as they watched, their initial curiosity transformed into empathy. They volunteered to join the search parties and were organised by the professionalism of PACE and the Pragian Police Search and Rescue Unit. The circus and local community united, and their collective strength charged everybody with a new energy to go out and search again.

The hours bled into five days, but when others gave up, the determination of the Silvestri family never wavered. Their love for Alessio fuelled their search, and faith in his resilience kept them strong when they wilted.

People who'd witnessed the vanishing asked a lot of questions that nobody could answer. Their voices were loud as they spoke to the police, and the loyalty of the locals shifted and swayed the other way. Accusations fractured the allegiance. The townspeople turned, blaming the carneys for the disappearance of the young man. The bleachers at evening performances were emptier with every show. The Silvestri's couldn't work, but even they said that the circus should stay open—it was the carney way.

The people of Prague boycotted the circus and only the new waves of tourists attended. Mothers stopped their children from playing near the castle grounds. The voices of blame were louder every day. The word murder was whispered on every new gust of wind.

The Sylvestris knew the truth would come out, and disperse the shadows hiding Alessio. Until then, they didn't rest. The hunt for their boy continued. Everybody wanted to know what happened, and the pressure mounted to provide answers. Leaflets with his photograph were distributed, urging anyone with information to come forward. The police pursued leads, following even faint traces of a clue. The circus routines were intertwined with the search, the animals still had to be fed, and the performance went ahead to a smaller audience every night. To close the show was to admit guilt. Quinn wouldn't allow that.

Whispers of conspiracy and stories about supernatural forces drifted from the grounds to the outside community. Most people believed the boy had run away, but some thought Alessio was victim to dark magic or otherworldly powers, while others speculated that foul play was involved.

Despite the rumours, the Sylvestris were focused. Alessio's disappearance had a rational explanation. Even Mauritzio put his ingrained beliefs to one side and refused to give in to unfounded superstition. He said he'd cling to rationale or go mad. But his rosary beads were never far from his hands, and when he wasn't searching for his son, he knelt in prayer.

The police had nothing. Due to the many nationalities represented in the case, they passed it up to PACE: Police Action for Community Empowerment. After five days, they were no closer to finding the boy and any leads were stone cold.

On the morning of the sixth day, some children from the outskirts of town claimed to have seen a figure resembling Alessio in the forest. Maurizio and his family didn't get their hopes up, but a ripple of prayer rang through the community as they mobilized.

The police ventured into the depths of the forest and broke through bramble and undergrowth in the area where the local boys had been playing. Initial optimism turned into the same old drudge when they found nothing new except the tracks of the local kids.

And then a miracle happened.

A shout went up from one of the police officers. Hidden in the dense foliage, a body lay half buried, battered and bloodied—but miraculously still alive. Shock passed through the ranks as they hurried to help him.

Alessio lay on the forest floor. His face was pale and his body trembled with pain. He was barely conscious and unaware of his surroundings. He'd endured a brutal attack. His clothes were torn and dirtied, and the immediate scene around him bore signs of a struggle. There was a broken branch, scattered leaves, and a feeling of lingering violence.

They couldn't get an ambulance to the scene because the forest thicket was too dense. As it was closer, they carried Alessio back to the circus camp. Rather than calling the family to the fallen boy, they took him to them until the ambulance got there from the city. The police didn't want the carneys running into the forest en masse. This was a crime scene.

At the circus grounds, there was always somebody milling around to see everything. By the time they'd carried Alessio through the entrance, a crowd of carneys had gathered. Mauritzio, Aurora, and Isabella rushed to Alessio's side, and cradled him, whispering words of reassurance.

As the Silvestri family returned to their caravan with their son, the camp's atmosphere shifted. Murmurs of the cursed carousel circulated among the carneys again as their superstitious beliefs resurfaced. Mac had forbidden Damien from accosting Ravenswood or inciting trouble, but it hadn't stopped his murmurs and stirrings of unrest.

Some whispered that the carousel's powers had lured danger into their camp. They said the curse had claimed Alessio as its first victim. News of Alessio's discovery spread, and they were delighted that he was home, but a sombre cloud settled over the vibrant community as they waited for answers.

Alessio couldn't speak and after being picked up, he'd lapsed into unconsciousness. His brother was like a shade and hadn't spoken a word since the night Alessio disappeared. Because of his condition and deep psychological detachment, Luca had already been taken into a psychiatric unit during the police involvement. This was against his parent's wishes, and after a committal order had been obtained to safeguard the traumatised child. It sparked a new wave of rumours that the police thought the family were involved.

The Silvestri's needed to heal. Alessio was safe, but he was lying in a hospital bed. With two of their children in different hospitals, the family were at a low ebb. In hushed tones, the carneys exchanged their thoughts, coming to terms with the unexplainable in the old ways that they could understand.

Alessio came home from the hospital before his brother, but he had no recollection of what had happened to him. He had a total mental block, and his only memories were of events before his last performance. The family focused on his recovery. They refused to succumb to whispers of curses and superstitions. Aurora said they should rely on more than folklore to find out what happened to their son.

In the following days, they rarely left their trailer. They tended to Alessio's dressings and did their best to provide comfort. As they nurtured him back to health, their determination to find justice was unyielding. The police operated outside their world, and Mauritzio resented the intrusion. But even he had to admit, they kept a lid on the tensions plaguing the circus community.

Their next engagement in Budapest was cancelled and they weren't allowed to move on. The castle authorities weren't happy, and the protestors and bigots came out in force.

Decisions weighed on Quinn because it meant exposing his beloved circus to the scrutiny of outsiders. He knew one thing—whatever happened to Alessio, it came from inside his circus grounds.

'Why haven't you got any answers for us yet? We're grateful to have our son back, but my family is in tatters. We're scared for our lives,' Mauritzio said to one of the initial police team.

'Rest assured, we're doing everything we can, Mr Silvestri. We won't close the case until we've found your son's attacker.'

The following day, nine days after his brother's disappearance, Luca was released from the mental health unit. It was at his family's insistence and against strong medical advice. Mauritzio said the doctors weren't helping him. He needed to be at home with his people and to have the healing reassurance of the animals around him.

It was a sombre homecoming. The family was intact, but barely. They ate goulash in their trailer. Neither of the brothers talked about what happened. Alessio's last memory was of being in the dressing tent before the performance, and Luca hadn't spoken at all. The conversation between the rest of them was forced.

That night, when the kids were in bed, Aurora and Mauritzio sat outside on a bench at the back of their home watching the stars. They discussed trying to resume some gentle training to regain a semblance of normality, though it was clear that neither boy was ready for intense practice.

Mauritzio's arm was around his wife and she snuggled into his warmth against the night chill. He kissed the top of her head and said it would be all right.

Later, she couldn't believe that she was humming as she went back into their trailer. Paranoia made her want to check on the kids. The first thing she saw was Luca sitting on top of his covers with his knees drawn to his chest.

'Hey, sweetheart, what are you doing out of bed?'

His eyes flickered. It wasn't even a proper blink, they barely moved but it was enough for her to follow them.

Alessio was in the other bunk with his throat cut.

Chapter Ten

The day after drinks at The Meeting Place with the team, Silas and Kelvin used Nash's laptop to find the perfect place. They were planning their camping trip with great reluctance and some trepidation. Silas and Kelvin debated for hours about where to go on their first dreaded mission.

Being a busy solicitor with a previously inactive social life, Kelvin hadn't taken any holidays for years, much to the chagrin of his three grown-up children. After some bullying from them and gentle persuasion from Nash, he'd been persuaded to delegate his workload and take two weeks off. He'd go camping with Nash and then spend some time with the kids. He joked that he'd need the rest of the holiday to recover after a couple of days in the cramped van.

They discussed the highlands of Scotland and the mountains of Mourne. Nash laughed at the expressions on Kel's face. He was flitting between horror and a rising excitement at the thought of something adventurous. It was a million miles from anything either of them would have chosen.

'Okay, so I'm not caught on a wave of watery enthusiasm regarding the idea of camping yet. But I'm bordering the point of jumping in a muddy puddle in my cashmere suit,' Kelvin said.

'Hang on. Neither of us has ever done this before. We're convinced that we're going to hate it. Do you think we're being a tad ambitious going so far?' Nash said.

'Somewhere closer to home?'

'I reckon. It'll give us a quick escape if we're caught in the middle of a tsunami.'

'And the last tsunami in the English Lake District was?' Kelvin was laughing. He was always laughing, and it was one of the things Nash loved most.

'Do not underestimate the power of the mighty tsunami, my friend. There's a first time for everything.'

'Are you sure you don't fancy a five-star resort in the Bahamas? My treat,' Kelvin said.

'No. We're doing this.'

They looked at various campsites within an hour of home.

'Looks a bit cramped.'

'Play parks everywhere. Too many kids.'

'Dog friendly? That's ridiculous. It's bad enough sleeping in that bloody thing without being kept awake by barking dogs.'

'This one's just a field in the middle of nowhere.'

'Isn't that the point of going back to nature?' Nash asked.

'I need a toilet block. I am not peeing in a 7-Up bottle. It's undignified at our age.'

'It's undignified at any bloody age,' Nash said.

The laptop screen in his office went black and Nash clicked the mouse two dozen times as if it would make a difference.

'What's wrong with it? Is it plugged in?' Kelvin asked.

'Of course, it's plugged in. Should I force a reboot?'

As his finger went to the power button, the screen came back on. The picture showed a stunning sunset with a campsite at Keswick in the foothills of Latrigg fell. There was a stream running the length of the site, and a gorgeous wooded trail for romantic walks. It had an electric hook up and the toilet and showering facilities looked clean and welcoming.

'Was that Max?' Kelvin asked.

'I reckon so.'

'Trust him to pick for us. We're hopeless.'

'Let's face it, we needed the intervention. We'd have spent all night looking for something. Let's book it,' Nash said.

'If Max hasn't already done that for us as well.'

They laughed, and ten minutes later they'd booked their stay in Keswick for two nights.

They set off after work on Friday. The drive was uneventful and when they got there, they got out of the van with stiff limbs. They grumbled about the cramped space and the less-than-ideal sleeping arrangements. But, Nash's promise to Max compelled them to see it through—no matter how bad it was.

They were met by a gust of Lakeland wind that almost blew them over. It arrived out of nowhere. And as abrupt as the gust was, it came and went, leaving a cloudless sky.

'Do you think he's come with us?' Nash asked.

'I hope not because I'm looking forward to some private time later.'

The sudden gust of wind was otherworldly. It came in strong and was gone in seconds. Nash was happy to blame it on Max's mischievous spirit playing with them. He was used to his antics, and often found objects had shifted from one place to another.

He'd even got used to his Alexa turning on to some God-awful rock music or the TV switching channels in the middle of a show. Sometimes he came downstairs to find a pyramid of random household things constructed on the kitchen table. And once, his gardening boots were filled with cornflakes. Max liked to play.

'Let's get the van unloaded, and when the awning is up, we can have our first cup of tea,' he said. Nash reached into the cab for the keys that should have been hanging from the ignition.'

'Kel, have you got the van keys?'

'No. I haven't touched them.'

Nash looked up, exasperated, and he found them. His keys were hanging from an air freshener attached to the rearview mirror. It took him a couple of minutes to release the tight keyring, and he chipped his thumbnail in the process.

'Jones, you're an arsehole.'

'What have I done?' Kel said.

'Not Kelvin Jones, Maxwell bloody Jones.'

'If he's going to stick around I'll have to revert to my African name.'

'Only if you teach me how to pronounce it.'

Their first challenge was setting up the six-berth awning that would extend from the side of the van. Silas joked that he was better at all things practical than Kelvin, and took the lead.

'Pass the instructions,' Silas barked after several failed attempts at the first step. His arms were loaded with metal poles.

Kelvin rummaged through their things, searching for the guide. 'I swear it was right here,' he muttered, tossing clothes and camping gear aside. 'Nope, sorry. I remember now. It was on the coffee table at home. I don't think we packed it.'

'So we've got to put this monstrosity up blind? It's like the pyramid stage at Glastonbury.'

'Is that made of canvas?' Kelvin asked.

'I don't know, do I? I've never been.'

As the tension simmered, another gust of wind whipped through the campsite, knocking over their pile of organized tent pegs.

'Max thinks he's funny,' Kel said.

'He's not. And neither are you. Do you intend to help at any point, or just stand there? I'm doing all the work on my own.'

Silas grappled with the awning, struggling to connect the metal poles and thread them through the fabric.

'Pass me that pole.' He held his hand out without looking back.

Kelvin handed him the wrong pole. 'My bad,' he laughed.

Silas' frustration escalated and he gritted his teeth. His voice was loud and strained. 'This isn't the time for childish games. For Christ's sake, hand me the right pole. And don't stand on that ground sheet. Bloody hell, I've just straightened that.'

The tension between them increased. Kelvin had tried to keep the mood light but Silas's face was red. He struggled with the tangled mess. 'We're supposed to be a team.'

Kelvin's playful teasing faltered. His voice was tinged with annoyance. 'That's the third time you've snapped at me, Si. What's got into you? Maybe if you stopped acting like a sergeant major, we'd get it done faster. You've got it all tangled up again and it's a mess. This is supposed to be fun, remember.' He touched Si's arm, but he shrugged him off.

Their voices rose, attracting glances from nearby campers.

Realizing their argument had reached an impasse, they took a break. The absurdity of their situation sank in, and they exchanged a sheepish look. Neither of them had a clue what they were doing.

Kelvin was the first to start laughing. 'Your face.'

'What?'

Nash picked a handful of grass and threw it at Kel. Soon they were rolling on the ground amid the chaos of poles and flat canvas. They wrestled and laughed. Kel was on top of Nash, had his arms pinned—and tickled. 'Scream for mercy, I dare you.'

Nash screamed like a lamb being slaughtered. When Kel stopped tickling him, Nash said, 'I'm sorry for being an arse. Let's put our stubbornness aside and work together.'

'Was that our first argument?'

'We can call it an argument if it ends in some make-up loving,' Nash said.

'Keep it in your pants, we've got poles to put up. We survived that. But man, you're a dickhead when you're bossy.'

'Duly noted,' Nash laughed. 'Maybe this camping gig was a terrible idea.'

Kelvin nodded with a smile. 'The worst one you've ever had. Okay, Detective Nash. Let's solve the hell out of this case. Teamwork, remember?'

They tackled the awning. This time they collaborated rather than competing. It was a nightmare that took another two hours in the mid-afternoon heat. The metal poles slotted into place, the fabric stretched tautly, and the six-berth awning stood alongside the van.

'I'm proud of that,' Kelvin said as though they'd just built the Great Wall of China.

'It's an achievement, and a thing of beauty. Brew?' Nash said.

'We've earned it. You get the chairs out and I'll put that ridiculous little kettle on.

Kel was filling the kettle from their water butt when a bag fell over in the awning. A bottle of red wine rolled out and stopped near Kel's feet.

'I don't mind if we do. Excellent idea, Max.'

When it came, the sunset across the campsite was an artist's palette of inter-combining hues. They shared a moment of victory, and laughed together, as they toasted Max's mischief.

'You know what? I get it. After all that stress, now that the hard bit's done, this is brilliant, and I haven't felt this relaxed in years,' Nash said.

They sat outside the awning and pulled their table onto the grass at the side of the pitch. Dinner was corned beef hash made with packet mashed potatoes, tinned corned beef, and tinned peas and carrots. The onion was a pre-prepared pack taking up almost all the space in their tiny freezer compartment.

They agreed that rarely had they ever tasted anything so good.

They opened a second bottle of red as the stars shone in the sky. Something blew across the pitch and caught on the table leg. Nash bent down to pick it up and burst into a fit of laughter.

'Night buddy,' he said raising his glass to the heavens.

Silas turned the piece of cardboard over to show it to Kel. It was a Do Not Disturb sign.

The sun rose over the campsite, and Nash and Kelvin woke early. They stumbled from their duvet to put some clothes on and went straight to the toilet block. They could have gone native and opted for sleeping bags, but agreed that duvets were life essential. Camping or not, some things were non-negotiable.

They exchanged groggy morning greetings. Kel said that it wasn't the worst night's sleep ever, but at six foot four, his feet had been hanging out of the end of the bed. They showered in a row of cubicles with wet floors from previous occupants.

And then began the arduous task of preparing breakfast. Together they produced an excellent spread of burned sausages, half-cooked beans, bacon and rubbery egg.

Kelvin eyed the charred sausages with amusement. 'These have seen better days. They've had a longer cook than Joan of Arc. But damn, they're good. Why does food taste better when you're camping?'

'It adds to the rustic charm.'

Silas's phone rang, jolting them from their peaceful breakfast. He looked at the screen and groaned. 'It's Bronwyn. This can't be good.'

'What does she want?'

Silas's expression was serious as he answered DCS Lewis. 'Hi, Bronwyn. What's up?'

Bronwyn's voice was authoritative. 'Nash, I need you back in Barrow. It's an emergency. You're not going to believe this but PACE has found a case for their programme. An exchange has been scheduled.'

'What the hell do PACE want with me?'

Bronwyn sounded excited underneath the professionalism. 'I can't discuss the details over the phone. All I can say is that it's big. Get your backside here today.'

'Kel, I'm so sorry. We need to get back to Barrow. Something's come up at work and PACE need to speak to me.'

'Pace?'

'It's that international special agency for empowering sensitive communities, remember, I told you about it?

'Oh yeah, the thing where you go away and learn about how other countries do things.'

'Something like that.'

Kelvin laughed. 'Don't worry, let's get packed up and go. This camping trip just gets crazier. We go from sausages on the verge of extinction to international intrigue. Who would've thought?'

They dismantled the camp a lot faster than it came together. Throwing everything into the Good Lady Diana, the sound of zippers, clinking pots, and folding chairs competed with birdsong over the field as they rushed to get away.

As they drove along the winding roads, Silas' mind buzzed with questions. He felt a tremor of anxiety.

Kelvin was driving and looked across with a mouth-splitting grin. 'Do you know, I loved every second of that.'

'Every second?'

'Well, not all of them, but we know what we're doing now. It'll be better next time.'

'Next time? Are you mental?' Nash laughed.

Chapter Eleven

The countryside flew past in a blur of green fields and quaint villages, but Nash's focus was on the task ahead. Kelvin was proud of him and said so.

'You're going to be part of something big. This is the stuff movies are made of. International Crime.'

'Slow down, it's not to crack an international crime ring. The PACE guys just want me involved in this exchange programme. I was chosen randomly. They probably spun a wheel or something.'

'What else could it be, but a golden opportunity? They chose you, Si. Mind, if you're really an international drug baron or something, now would be a good time to tell me.'

Nash kissed his hand.

Kelvin pulled into Barrow police station, 'Call me when you want to be picked up,' he said.

'It's okay. One of the lads will run me home.'

They kissed goodbye and Nash didn't even stop to watch Kelvin drive away.

He was as ready as he'd ever be, but setting up camp the day before had given him a mild sunburn. His face was tender, especially his nose. He hoped he didn't look too red. Bronwyn was waiting for him and followed him into his office.

'Nash. We don't have much time. They've given me some information and I'm waiting for further confirmation. The inter-collaboration exchange programme across Europe is being moved up—and specifically for you, it's happening in Prague. There's been a murder there and PACE wants your expertise.'

He shut the door. 'Good job my passport's still valid. Can I claim the air miles?'

Bronwyn handed him a file with detailed intel about a horrific murder. And Nash wondered if there was any other kind.

He skimmed the file and his mind absorbed every detail.

He was confused. 'I don't see where I come into it. How can we help?'

'Not we, Nash. You.'

Interview Room 3 was a stark, windowless space, illuminated by bright fluorescent lighting that cast an unforgiving glow on the faces of the agents. Nash, wondered why they weren't holding the meeting in Bronwyn's office. He sat at the table opposite them. DCS Bronwyn Lewis introduced detectives Reynolds and Colianni. The air was heavy as they asked for absolute discretion and prepared to delve into the details of the murder.

Reynolds stared at Nash and opened the conversation. 'DCI Nash, we're glad to have you on board. We heard about your success in solving the high-profile murders in Kos last year and have looked into your service record. Your reputation precedes you, and we're looking forward to solving this one with you.'

'Thank you, I can only do my best.'

'With the reformation of circuses coming into force across Europe, times are delicate and tensions can run high. That's why we need a tactful hand at the people-facing end of the case. We're grateful for your profiling experience.'

'Can we cut to the chase, gentlemen? What do you need from me?'

Agent Colianni interjected. 'A trapeze artist named Alessio Silvestri was brutally murdered on the circus grounds. His throat was slit, and the killer left no clues.'

Bronwyn leaned forward, her voice was intense. 'This is one of the great circuses and a lot of people owe their livelihood to it. The authorities want to shut them down in light of this. They believe it was an inside job and it's just the excuse they've been waiting for to impound the animals and arrest many of the performers and staff on immigration offences.'

'Okay. It sounds like something I can get my teeth into.'

'As you can imagine with a circus made up of many internationals a lot of them are illegal. While we don't condone anybody working without the correct documentation, we are there to do a job. The police further up the ladder than us are jumping all over this as a means to shut the operation down. These are simple people making a living, and how they came to be there is not our concern—that's for other agencies to deal with. We only want to catch the person behind this kid's death.'

'It's starting to make sense. When do you need me?'

'Now, Inspector Nash,' Reynolds said.

'Now as in this month? This week? How now is now?'

'How does in the next hour grab you?' Bronwyn asked. 'Your plane leaves at four.' She flashed him her disarming smile, the one she used to stem any protest with a slick of honey, it was interchangeable with the assassin smile that could take him down before her lips finished moving.

'Oh, come on. That's unreasonable. I can't drop everything. What about the Holman case?'

'I've delegated any future work. Holman's in the report filing stage, and there's nothing for you to do with it until it goes to trial. You were already on holiday, remember?'

'Am I going to be used as some kind of fall guy when the shit hits the fan? It sounds intense out there.'

'Not at all. Let me level with you,' Colianni said.

Nash interrupted him. 'I wish you would because it seems to me that any one of a thousand officers could consult on this case. With respect, it's one dead kid, when thousands are murdered every day.'

'We've been out to the circus grounds, Nash. We feel that you'll see through the facts of the case and take into account the people behind it. We need somebody with experience and the right level of compassion. How can I put this? Quinn Brothers Flying Circus is a traditional circus. It's run on old-fashioned tramlines where not much has changed for two hundred years if you get my drift.'

'I'm not following you.'

'It's one of the good circuses. The animals are well cared for—and the people.'

'So?'

'Among the staff, there are thirty-eight special people. The ones that they used to call freaks.'

'It's a freak show. That's grotesque. You want me to help solve the case and have it shut down to get those people out of there?'

'On the contrary,' Colianni said. 'We want to you catch the murderer and help to keep the circus open.'

'I can't believe you'd condone the barbaric treatment of these poor people.'

'I believe that when you see it for yourself, you'll very much condone it.'

'I can't see that happening.'

'Before we move onto the details, let me ask you one question, Nash.'

'Go on.'

'When you swoop in and have the place closed down, what would you have done with those poor people as you call them?'

'I don't know. Call in Social Services, I suppose. My job is to catch killers, gentlemen, not to nursemaid Siamese twins. But I'm damned sure I'd get them out of the exploitation.'

Reynolds smiled as he told them about Octavia, the bearded lady. He'd met her twice, and she tore a strip off him on both occasions. 'And therein lies the crux of the argument. They aren't poor people. They are able, intelligent members of society. Proud people, living independent lives and making a living in the only way they can. If that circus is shut down they'll be imprisoned as illegals or farmed out to care institutions across Europe, and, believe me, some of them are grim. They'll end their days away from the circus community. And that's the only family they've known. Have you ever seen a polar bear in a zoo, detective?'

Nash shook his head but he was ashamed and silent.

'You wouldn't want to. But that's what you're endorsing for these people. Your job is to get in, help us solve the Silvestri murder fast, and save the circus from closure.'

'I apologise,' he muttered. 'I hope I can do your faith in me justice.' He was still embarrassed. Nash remembered what he'd read in the initial case file, and his mind was already compiling the order of interviews he wanted to conduct.

Bronwyn said, 'Given the upcoming exchange, now would be a good time to get you on the investigation, Nash. Your ability to read people and your track record of solving complex murder cases make you the ideal candidate.'

Nash grappled with the responsibility. The prospect of another international murder case and the convoluted ways of the circus intrigued him.

'How do we proceed?' he asked.

Bronwyn handed him another folder containing his travel documents, and more information on the case. 'We've arranged for you to go to Prague tonight. You'll be working with the local police and liaising with a small team of PACE agents stationed nearby. We need you to ingratiate yourself into the circus community, uncover their secrets, and catch the bastard that did this. And, you can get yourself a decent tan while you're out there.'

'I want access to all relevant files, surveillance footage, and witness statements. It was a nightmare getting full access in Greece. DCI Lewis, I need you to make sure that when I push a door, it opens for me.'

'You've got it,' Reynolds said.

'And our backing in anything else you need,' Colianni added. 'The other thing you're going to have to overcome is a lot of superstition. Apparently, they have a haunted merry-go-round or some such nonsense. Some of them say a ghost killed the boy.'

Nash had to hold back a smile as he remembered car keys fastened to a mirror and his own haunting. Twelve months earlier, he'd have shot that idea down in a second.

'We'll need to piece together the events leading up to the murder and identify potential suspects. I want the police reports from the first response.' Nash was fired up.

Reynolds' voice was composed. 'We suspect the killer is an insider, he had knowledge of the circus and its members. They knew Alessio's routine, his movements, and how to strike without being detected. But, be warned, the community are suspicious of authority by default. We need you to get them on our side. The local police have alienated themselves, and you'll be liaising with them and reporting back. Be prepared to face a wall of lies and deception. They have no reason to trust you. We chose you because you can win them over.'

'I'm ready for the challenge.'

The interview ended, and Nash shook hands with the PACE agents.

'Prague won't know what's hit it,' Bronwyn said.

The thought of the dark underbelly of the circus world intrigued Nash.

Silas burst through the door with urgency tugging at his anxiety. A car was picking him up to take him to the airport in thirty minutes, and he still had to talk to Kelvin, never mind pack. The PACE exchange programme demanded his immediate attention but they were supposed to be on holiday. He hoped Kel would understand.

Kelvin met him in the hall with a concerned look. 'How did you get on? What's happening?'

'The exchange has been moved forward. I'm sorry Kel, but they need me to fly out to Prague. A car's on its way.'

Kel puffed out his cheeks and whistled. 'Wow. They don't mess around, do they? What do you need, babe? Let's get you packed.'

Silas took Kelvin's hand. 'I'm sorry for letting you down. I have a chance to make a difference. I hope you understand.'

'It's okay. I get it. I'm so proud of you. I wouldn't have you any other way. But it doesn't mean I have to like it. Now, stop wasting time and move.'

'Wait.'

He was halfway up the stairs when he stopped, ran back down and grabbed both of Kelvin's hands. 'This isn't going to take long, a matter of days, a week max. Come out and join me.'

'What? Have you gone mad? I can't drop everything and come to Prague with you.'

'No, but you can drive out and join me. I'm sure Hayley will have Lola for us. We can still have our adventure. Come and meet me at a circus in Prague. It'll be romantic.' Silas leaned in, and his voice was laced with secrecy. 'I'd love you to be there with me, it's such a romantic city. But I'm going to be honest with you. It's more than that. Obviously, I'll have to put you in a hotel. You can't stay on-site with me, but I want you to drive the van to Prague. I need the advantage of being there and embedding myself in the community. People won't talk to me from inside a hotel room.'

'You have. You've gone stark raving mad.' But Nash heard the edge of excitement in his voice. Kelvin pushed past him and ran up the stairs, taking them three at a time with his long legs. He took both of their suitcases down from the wardrobe and put them next to each other on the bed. 'Yours first.' He started picking piles of clothing out of Silas' drawers. Si stood against the doorjamb and smiled. He'd never seen his boyfriend like this and two things struck him. Kelvin had impeccable taste and common sense. He knew exactly what Nash needed to take. Kelvin was like a daft kid going to Disney World. 'I love you. I love you. I love you.' He didn't speak the words, he sang them to Nash. Then he sobered. 'You want me to drive the van all the way to Prague? What if I get attacked by a hitchhiker?'

'Don't pick one up.'

'You have no idea, do you? They are the best kind of people.' He was giddy again. 'I'm so excited. This is nuts.'

'Once the case is over, we can stay on and I'll make sure there's time for us to do plenty of sightseeing. But I can't guarantee the circus owner will give me a caravan. He's pretty resistant to the police, apparently. And staying in the van will help me with the investigation. I'll be able to gather information, observe the circus members closely, and have a secure base of operations. Plus, it'll be good to have you close.'

While Silas finished packing, Kelvin worked out that it would take him two days to get to Prague. He gave the address of the circus grounds to Alexa to plan his route and told Nash he'd prepare the van for the long drive. He'd drive to Newcastle and take a ferry to the Netherlands. From there, he'd go through Germany. Then after driving across the border, he'd reach the Czech Republic. From there, the roads would be well-signposted to Prague. Kelvin rattled all this off to Nash who was looking out of the window for the car.

'Stay safe, Si. I'll see you at the circus. And don't solve the case without me. I want a piece of the action,' he joked.

'It's confidential.'

Kelvin pulled a face and kissed him goodbye. Silas got in the car and was dismayed to find that Bowes was driving him to the airport. He'd talk all the way to Manchester. Nash's mind was racing with details of the case and he wanted quiet to think it through.

Chapter Twelve

When he got on the plane, Nash familiarised himself with the intricate dynamics and key players in the circus community. He read the files and documents, studying the histories and backgrounds of the circus members. Most of them had been there a long time, but their glamorous allure of circus life had been tainted by suspicion and hidden motives.

As he studied the case, it was clear that this wasn't a random act of violence. It was a calculated message. Nash deduced that when the killer had left the boy for dead he didn't expect him to survive. It was a huge risk for the murderer to go back to finish him off. The boy's parents were sitting five yards away outside. The younger child was in the same room and was witness to it—and then there were the claims of the fire-eater having his materials tampered with. It was a warning. Nash profiled the personality of the murderer and by the end of the flight, he would have laid money on there being another death very soon. This could potentially turn into a serial murder case. He felt as though he had a handle on him, and the killer was inching towards more violence. There was no time to lose.

After going to the local police station for his initial briefing about the exchange programme, Nash settled in his assigned hotel and got straight to work. PACE had assembled a team of their best-skilled investigators. They'd be based at the station and were responsible for studying surveillance footage, witness statements, and every available clue. They'd be invaluable, and Nash hoped that each thread they unravelled would throw new light on the case as it progressed. He needed more intel to lead them deeper into the personalities and egos of the circus.

He was excited when he drove through the circus compound in an unmarked car PACE had provided for his use. He was looking forward to meeting the characters in the case and immersing himself in the community. He'd attend performances and mingle with the performers during their off-hours. His job was to take notes, ask questions and uncover hidden secrets and lies. He'd read the initial witness statements and there were so many discrepancies that he'd already highlighted. He had to work out which just had their own agendas and separate them from the person or persons of interest.

He'd watch the interplay of relationships, rivalries, and alliances that defined the circus dynamics. His first visit was going to be to Quinn—it would be rude not to start at the top with the owner. But first, he wanted to check out the scene of the crime for himself. He couldn't shake the autopsy images of the trapeze artist's lifeless body. And he was told that Mauritzio could be heard wailing in his trailer at night. The echoes of the family's grief were still too fresh for their mourning to be dignified.

Nash met his partner, Lyara Horvat. She was an attractive Swedish PACE officer in her twenties, and despite the blonde ponytail, she reminded him of Molly Brown. The last thing he needed was another gobby woman nattering at him all day. But he smiled and they shook hands. As they trudged over the field, she filled him in about what she'd been doing before his arrival, and where the team were up to. Nash was wearing his good suit and the wet grass soaked his trousers halfway to the knee. The staff trailers were quiet. It made sense that they'd use the afternoon to nap before the show. A young girl sat on the steps of one of the colourful caravans. It was hand-painted in the gypsy style with red roses expertly brushed around the sconces.

She was singing as she chalked the soles of her performance shoes, and Nash noticed that she had a prosthetic leg. Apart from her, the field was quiet and he looked at the map he'd been given plotting the pitches to find the right trailer. The girl looked up and he nodded. Her returning stare was hostile, so they walked on without stopping. She'd keep.

He found the Silvestri's van and knocked on the door. When there was no answer, he risked cupping his hands and looking through the open curtains. He didn't expect to see anybody but had his first glimpse of the boy he assumed to be Luca. He sat alone on the sofa that followed the shape of the caravan under the bay windows. The first thing that struck Nash was that a game controller was missing from the kid's hands. Weren't all boys attached to either a phone or games console these days?—Luca was just sitting.

He hadn't planned to speak to him yet, but he could see that the doors leading to bedrooms were open and the child was alone. If the family weren't napping, then presumably they were rehearsing. Nash tapped on the window.

The boy flinched but didn't raise his head.

'Can I come in?' Nash shouted, but there was no response. He tried the door and it was open so he went inside.

'We can't go in,' Lyara hissed from the pitch. No warrant and his parents aren't here to chaperone.' Nash gave her a withering look.

'Hi, Luca is it?'

With a keen eye for detail, Nash connected the dots. It didn't take a psychologist to see that the boy was troubled. He sat on the sofa with his legs dangling over the edge and not making it to the floor. His chin rested on his chest and he looked every inch the poster boy for misery.

'Hi, I'm Silas, what's your name?'

'Are you Luca? Heck, I don't even know if I've got the right trailer.' Nash said.

'Luca, do you know why we're here?' Lyara's voice was soft and she might prove to be an asset after all. The boy was unresponsive and didn't look at them or make any attempt to answer.

'I'm going to try and find out who hurt your brother. I'm on your side buddy, and I'm going to help you,' Nash said.

There was nothing. As he watched, he was convinced Luca was forcing himself to be still. Nash sat for a minute counting in his head to give the lad time to process. Luca was only taking thirteen breaths a minute. He was using meditation to control his breathing and slow his heart rate—either that or his mind was so damaged that it had taken him to another place where Nash didn't exist.

'Okay, Luca. We'll leave you in peace. But I'm glad I met you. I'd like to speak some more soon. Would that be okay?'

Nothing.

Breaking through the child's silence wasn't going to be easy. He was either too scared or too traumatised to speak. He still hadn't uttered a word since the night his brother disappeared under the lights of the big top. There were no clues, other than those that pointed towards superstition and betrayal.

Jealousy, and vengeance within circus communities were rife, and everybody had alliances and enemies. Secrets spilled out of these places like confetti, exposing the dark undercurrents festering behind the scenes. His spotlight was shining on several possible culprits lurking in plain sight among the performers. Truths, stained with blood and tears, hadn't shed any light on the secrets plaguing the circus. And he had to find a killer among the greasepaint, sequins and clown faces.

He resumed his investigation by visiting the circus owner with Lyara. Isiah Quinn treated them cordially enough but eyed them with a degree of suspicion and distrust. The owner was full of pomp and couldn't turn the ringmaster act off once the curtains came down on the show. Nash was torn between thinking of him as an egocentric airbag, and admiring him for the way he held his circus together and cared about his people.

Nash was too seasoned a detective not to see through most of his ego. He used his instinct for reading people and cut through lies to get to the truth. He was a showman too and strapped his stern demeanour in place as he stepped into the cluttered office trailer of the owner.

They went through the usual pleasantries and spent the first five minutes weighing each other up. Lyara had introduced Nash and tried opening the questioning, but Quinn brushed her away with monosyllabic replies. Nash saw a keen wit—Quinn was people-intuitive, too, and he couldn't afford to underestimate his intelligence.

The atmosphere was heavy with the pride of a community. They had the essence of sawdust in their blood. It was a lingering ghost built over centuries of old memories. Isiah was a weathered but still handsome man in his forties. He had a cunning gaze, that Nash knew from his notes, had seen triumph and tragedy. Charisma seeped from the ringmaster's sweat glands.

'You don't mind me recording this interview do you, Mr Quinn?'

'Actually, I do, sir.'

'I must warn you, that your reticence would indicate that you have something to hide,' Lyara said.

He shrugged and Nash pressed record. Quinn had an ashtray on his desk half full of dead cigarettes. He had a packet of smokes on his desk but he ignored those and made a show of opening the top drawer and taking out an ornate cigar box. It was clear that his custom was to smoke cigarettes and the cigars were only for show. He didn't offer Nash one of the expensive fat cigars.

'You don't mind me smoking a cigar, do you, Inspector Nash?' Quinn asked.

'Actually, I do.'

'Then I suggest we step outside. I have a rather pleasant veranda.' He used a cigar cutter to snip the end and made a performance out of lighting the Cuban. Nash picked up his recording device and they went outside to sit in chairs overlooking the grounds.

DCI Nash showed Quinn a photograph of Alessio Silvestri with his throat slit. Isiah's expression registered shock, but he composed himself fast.

'Let's talk about young Silvestri. He was found dead in your circus, Mr Quinn. Care to shed any light on that?'

Quinn rubbed his temples. 'I've got nothing to do with that boy's death. This circus is my life, and I won't stand for accusations tarnishing my name.'

'You misunderstand me. I wasn't accusing you. I was merely asking for your take on it. Nobody knows these people as well as you. I believe you call them your family, but like any doting father, you must have your favourites,' Nash soothed Quinn's ruffled feathers.

'Anything you can tell us could be of importance,' Lyara said.

'My staff excel in their roles, I have no need to play games with them.'

'If not favourites, what about the ones you secretly loathe? It's just you and us, Mr Quinn, you can speak candidly.'

'You, me, and a recording device taking down my every word to use against me.'

Lyara pressed the button to stop recording. 'Just us. Please, give us your thoughts,' she said.

'You're wasting your time, detectives. I'm as much in the dark as you. I have no idea who killed him. All I know is the effect it's had on my tills. And the crew are as jittery as hell.'

'How so?' Nash asked.

'They're like sitting ducks waiting for the next one.'

'Why would you assume there'll be more murders? I've seen nothing in the way of hard evidence to imply that it wasn't an isolated incident.' Lyara pushed him, and Nash saw Quinn bristling. He didn't like her.

Nash had read in Lyara's reports that she'd threatened to halt the performances until the case was solved if the troupe didn't cooperate. He sensed that Quinn was going to clam up, and was impressed when Horvat saw it too. She looked at her phone and tutted.

'I'm sorry gentlemen. I'm afraid time has run away with me and I have a prior meeting to attend. Inspector Nash, would you mind continuing without me?'

Horvat had just shown herself to be worthy of her stripes. She knew when it was in the interest of the case to relinquish control, and she rose in Nash's estimation by having the sense to remove herself from the interview. There was no way Nash was going to let her be diminished in front of the circus owner. They were equal in rank, but Nash said, 'I'll submit my report for your approval, later, Inspector Horvat.'

They watched her leave and Nash waited for Quinn to be the first to speak—he didn't.

'Instinct tells me that you may be right, Mr Quinn. And I've been going down the same track regarding further trouble. Why is that?'

'The curse. Ambrose Ravenswood is stirring them up like a nest of hornets. But I can't get rid of him because he comes with the carousel.'

'I've heard about that. You can't get rid of them both, and remove the superstition that surrounds the ride? Surely it's not worth the hassle it's causing.'

'I wish. I'd have Ravenswood and that thing out in a second. But that's just it. Once it's embedded in the circus, you can't get rid of it. It knows where it wants to be and I'm stuck with the damned thing.'

'You strike me as an intelligent man, Mr Quinn. Surely you aren't taken in by this hogwash.'

'And, with respect, you'd be a bigger fool than me not to at least consider the possibility of a curse. The boy took a ride, and two hours later he was gone. A week after that he was dead. You tell me if you think that kind of voodoo is worth messing with.'

'I'll be talking to Mr Ravenswood. Who else? I can't imagine the kid had many enemies, but what about his father? Anybody with a big enough axe to grind?'

'On the level? That kid was born in this circus. He came into the world in the very trailer he bled to death in. Even if somebody did have a spat with Mauritzio, nobody would take it out on Alessio. I swear if I knew who it was I wouldn't be telling you lot. But they'd be dealt with—our way.'

'That's a hostile approach to take Mr Quinn, and I promise you any attempt to pervert the course of justice will be dealt with—our way.'

'You misunderstand me, Nash. I'll offer every help I can. We want this person caught. Sometimes I let my mouth run away with me.'

'Let's talk about something else then, nice and informal. I've been reading your file.'

'I don't like the sound of that. But I've got nothing to hide.'

Nash flicked through the file he'd brought with him and found the relevant entries.

'Your younger brother accused you of murder before he passed away. He said you killed Gideon and framed him for it. Have you anything to say about that?'

Isiah gritted his teeth and Nash saw a flash of temper, that he quashed as soon as it rose. He was a man of quick rage but could suppress it. In Nash's experience, anger like that didn't stay sat on for long.

'It was all lies. Caspian was a bitter man and blamed me. I've dedicated my life to this circus, and I won't let his accusations destroy it. It's long dead. I see no need for it to be raked up and rekindled.'

Unfazed, Nash read through the papers in the file, a ploy to psyche the ringmaster out.

'Your wife's death occurred in the same trapeze accident? Tragedy was out to get you that night, my friend.'

'My wife's death was the worst thing that ever happened to me. Does it state in your sheaf of incriminating papers that she was carrying my child at the time? Accidents happen in a circus, but this was no accident. My youngest brother tampered with the trapeze rig. And he can rot in hell for it.'

'He was pretty adamant it was you. He held fast to his story until the day he died.'

'But for a groin strain that stopped me from flying, I'd have been up there with my wife. I'd have been killed too, leaving him the sole heir to the family pot. Do you think I'm cursed? Maybe I am, but I'm no killer.'

Nash wanted to rattle Quinn and show him they'd been digging into the past. So he pulled out a faded newspaper clipping and showed him an article about the fatal trapeze accident.

'Witnesses claim they saw you tampering with the trapeze rig before the show that night.'

'They were mistaken or lying. And there is a vital flaw in your argument. It's no secret that there was bad blood between us three brothers. Gideon was the eldest and swanned around like King Canute. It's true, I didn't do a lot of grieving for him, and Caspian was a weasel, out for what he could get. But I would never harm my beautiful wife. Miranda was my life.'

Nash grunted and flipped a couple of pages.

'And yet it says here that she was making plans to leave you and abandon the circus.'

'Lies spread by Caspian. He said she was warming Gideon's bed while I managed the business for my idle older brother. But I can assure you, she loved me with all her heart. We were devoted.'

The silence in the trailer was punctuated by the distant sounds of the circus outside. Nash was playing a game called Silence Top Trumps with Quinn and wasn't going to be the first to speak this time.

'Is there anything else, inspector? I'm a very busy man.'

'As are we all, Mr Quinn. Your eldest brother's death and your wife's tragic accident both occurred on the same night?'

'You've already established it was the same incident. We're going round in circles. I loved my wife. Her death devastated me but I didn't get on with my brothers. However, I would never spill their blood. The circus suffered, but not because of me.'

Nash glanced inside at the chaotic haphazardness of the trailer. He pieced together fragments of the past and present, looking for any connection beneath the surface.

'You say you're cursed, but to me, the opposite seems to be true. No evidence was found against you linking you to the murders. But you must find it fortunate that with your brothers gone, there was nobody left to contest your stake.'

Quinn steepled his fingers and made a point of not answering.

'It cleared your path to control the circus. And now, here we are with another murderer in the same ring. You get that eyebrows are raised?'

'They can say what they like, but the past repeats in concentric circles. More bloodshed is coming. Madam Selena has foreseen it.'

'I'm not pinning this murder on ancient curses. A hex sure as hell didn't slit that boy's throat. We'll park it there for now, Mr Quinn. But you can rest assured, we will speak again.'

Quinn crossed himself and kissed his pendant and Nash tried very hard not to roll his eyes. He said goodbye. Quinn stood and the chair creaked, 'If the curse is so insignificant inspector, I'll have Ravenswood crank up the carousel for you.'

Chapter Thirteen

Nash didn't tell Quinn about his plan to stay in camp when the van arrived. That would be fed to him on a need-to-know basis. While he was staying in town, the police wanted to set up an office for the officers to use on the grounds. Quinn had thrown a paddy and said it would be bad for the business to have an invasive police base on their fields. In an effort to reach a compromise, Mac, the boss hostler, had found them a tiny towing caravan to use as a discreet office. It used to be a costume storage and had seen better days. But after it was cleared out, it gave Nash somewhere to sit and a table to work from. It was all they needed, but he kept banging his head on the overhead rails and used some colourful language getting into the cramped space.

Lyara was away interviewing the dancers when Quinn came to speak to Nash about the case. Nash sat at the small table, surrounded by paperwork and notes. Even if there was room—impossible—it was too public to have any kind of incident board. And it played havoc with his OCD relying on hand-written notes. The lingering smell of stale mothballs and old cigarette smoke hung in the caravan and gave him a headache but it was too noisy to work with the door open until he had to.

The van was stifling, and noise or not, the sun would be overhead soon, and he'd have no choice but to fling his door wide. As he was contemplating a second cup of coffee and stretching his legs out of the contortion they were in, there was a knock on the door. He didn't want to go through the undignified rigmarole of extracting himself from behind the table to open it. 'Come in,' Quinn said before Nash had spoken. It irritated him.

An unusual person walked in—though given the surroundings, she wasn't the strangest. There were far more spectacular people here, but she was interesting in her appearance. It was the Romany fortune teller. He pulled her name from memory without having to search his many pages of notes.

Madam Selena was in her thirties and had black cascading hair, dressed at the top of her head with a comb covered in red roses. She wore a vintage maxi dress and had a sparkling silver shawl, around her shoulders. It put him in mind of a spider's web. Her eyes were heavy with makeup and filled with distress. She was trembling and steadied herself against the table. Nash was dealing with an actress intent on the melodramatic.

He rose as best he could, curling his head and shoulders into the ceiling as he motioned her into a seat. 'Madam Selena, isn't it? I was going to find you today so that we could talk.'

Her voice was uneven as she spoke and made a point of ignoring Nash. 'I was told you were here, Isiah. I had to come because I couldn't hold it in any longer. I've seen something dreadful.'

'Seen something? Where?'

'I've had a vision—it's what I do,' she explained for Nash's benefit and then clammed up.

'It's all right, Selena. Whether we like having them here or not, we have to get to the bottom of this mess, and you can speak freely in front of Inspector Nash. Everything is said in confidence.'

'Oh. I see.'

Nash's immediate reaction was to disregard anything that came next as fancy on the fortune teller's part. But reprimanded himself and he was forced to reevaluate his prejudice when his stack of neatly arranged and collated files overturned without interference and were scattered on the floor. Max was telling him to listen.

Nash bent to pick up the brown folders, and one of the autopsy photos of Alessio slipped out. Selena recoiled from it with a cry of anguish.

'Forgive me,' Nash picked up the last of the papers and stuffed them onto the traditional U-shaped wrap-around sofa that you find in almost every caravan the world over. 'Please, continue.'

'I rode the cursed carousel. And I thought I was so clever. I'm gifted in the black arts and have my methods of protection. No feeble curse was going to touch me. What I saw on that ride was horrific. I haven't been able to speak of it since and tried to forget it. Just because I saw them, didn't mean I was doomed, did it?'

'I doubt it. No,' Nash said.

'A curse is a curse,' Quinn said. 'It can't be disregarded or brushed away with fancy modern science. You've been foolish, Selena. You'll do anything for an audience.'

'That's rich coming from you, Isiah Quinn. You son of a whelping pig.' Her temper had fired up in a second and Nash noticed how fast her rage was prone to rising.

'I got on the painted horse, and as the ride turned, the world around me shifted. The merry-go-round came alive, spinning faster but not in this realm. I was taken into the shades of darkness where tortured spirits scream. It wasn't laughter that filled the air. It was the anguished cries of the spirit children riding next to me.'

'Did you see the spirit children?' Quinn's face lit up and his body thrust forward in anticipation. Nash wrote in his notes that the circus owner wanted to keep the ghost story alive. It was as though he needed first-hand proof of the ghostly children.

Madam Selena's eyes were distant as she relived the horrors she'd seen. 'They were the souls of children who suffered terrible deaths. There was a child, a girl, with half of her hair burned away. The skin on her bald pate and face was puckered and burned. She'd lost an eye and the socket was closed over with a sheet of damaged skin. No nose. Just a hole where it used to be and her lips were gone.'

'It must have been distressing for you,' Nash said.

'There was a woman, with a child on the saddle in front of her. The little girl was wet, she'd been in the water for a long time, and her face was bloated. It was blackened. The mother held the upright pole that was twisted into a pattern like a barley sugar cane. It was so pretty. It had coloured ribbons flying in the breeze, but the lady's bones were all broken. Her skull was smashed, and her arm was twisted the wrong way on the pole. Her joints were dislocated and grotesque. And she reached out to touch me. It was horrible.'

Nash had heard his share of paranormal folklore, but the horror in Madam Selena's tone held more than words of superstition passed down through the people. Her demeanour made her seem credible. The fortune teller was only in her thirties but seemed older with the burden of terror. The realism of her vision made him shudder.

'What did the spectres want from you, my dear? Did they give you anything I can use in the ring?' Quinn asked.

'They wanted me to come to you, detective, to solve the mystery of their deaths.'

'Oh.' Nash said.

'Oh?' Selena said.

'Oh.' Quinn said. 'Delicious.'

'Did they tell you that? Did they know I was coming?'

'No, of course not. But it's obvious, isn't it?'

'While I'm not convinced by all this curse talk, I will look into your claims.'

'That's not all. The worst part happened last night.' She broke down and buried her head in her hands as she cried.

'It's okay, you're safe here. You can tell me,' Nash said.

'The children came to me in my trailer last night. They were beckoning me to them, calling me to death. And this morning I found this lying on the floor.' She handed him a card. 'It's the death card. The messenger of death.' The tarot card showed a skeleton in a black coat, riding a white horse. 'I've been having blackouts. They happen in the afternoons several times a week.'

She reached into the folds of her shawl again and pulled out a worn photograph. It showed the same carousel, its vibrant colours just as resplendent fifty years ago.

'I found this,' she said. 'It's a picture of the carousel, taken decades ago when my parents were with another circus. Legends whispered that it carried a dark curse even back then, but nobody knew the full extent of its power. Word has it that a millionaire bought the ride to include in a private collection of the macabre. My parents were frightened and only stayed a matter of weeks until they could find a new placement.'

Nash took the photograph and felt stupid when a new emotion stirred in him. He was getting caught up in the mumbo jumbo and needed to take a step back and assess his professionalism. There was an eerie aura surrounding the photograph, nothing he could see but he felt it. He didn't find it difficult to believe that an unsettling presence emanated from the fibres of the old picture.

As he calmed the frightened lady, the atmosphere in the caravan was tense. She was convinced that she was going to be murdered. The walls closed in, suffocating them with the feeling of danger.

'My dear, Selena, don't you worry about death. It's just a gentle breeze that carries our souls to a grand and everlasting circus party in the skies. Cupcakes and clowns await those who embrace their final curtsy,' Quinn said.

Nash connected invisible dots between the curse, the spirit children, and the murder, where no lines may have existed. But if Max and police psychic Conrad Snow had taught him anything it was to keep an open mind.

'I'd like to uncover the carousel's history and find out how this Ravenswood character came to own it. I'll get the investigators on it today. I'm also going to put somebody outside your trailer tonight, Madam Selena. Just so that you get a good night's sleep.'

He held his hand up to stem her outburst of hysteria. 'Calm down. I don't believe anything bad is going to happen to you based on riding the merry-go-round, but it won't hurt to have somebody watching your trailer for a couple of nights.'

He wanted them to leave. All the talk of curses and ghosts was getting to him. The line between the supernatural and reality was blurred and Nash needed some outside involvement. He didn't know if the psychic could help, but he was going to give Snow a ring to see if he could shed any light on things.

Nash was glad when the last of Selena's tears were mopped and he could swing the caravan door open. A ray of sunlight pierced the dank atmosphere. The cursed carousel was right in front of his eyes. If he drew a straight line from it to him there was nothing in between. It freaked him out. The spirits of the children beckoned—or the rumours of them did. Nash wasn't buying it, but he was more inclined to listen than he would have been a year ago.

'Max, keep an eye on that bloody carousel and keep it away from me,' he muttered.

He got on the phone and arranged a guard for the fortune teller to cover the next two nights. Before she left, he'd advised her to stay around other people and not to isolate herself. He rang the investigators and asked them to trace the history of the carousel to get a timeline of where it was and when. He wanted to know if there had ever been any deeds of sale. And he asked for past ownership dating back to manufacture. He gave a little laugh and felt stupid giving his next order. 'And Marta?' he asked the PACE researcher.

'Yes, Inspector Nash?'

'Trace all circus accidents or fatalities on grounds where the roundabout was present. And find out about any ghost stories doing the rounds at the time.'

He waited while she translated what he'd said in her head, and he felt like an idiot.

'Excuse me, please. Ghost stories? You want stories of dead people coming back?'

'Just get everything you can on the history surrounding that carousel. Focus on facts, but if you come across any hearsay or written accounts of anything out of the ordinary, grab those too, please.'

'Okay. I've got it.' He heard her laughing and already talking in rapid Czechoslovakian to a colleague. They must think he was nuts.

He was putting two things off. He didn't want to speak to Snow until he had more to go on. And for the same reason he decided to talk to more of the circus people before getting to Ambrose Ravenswood. Everything he'd heard about the creepy man showing up with his ride, was weird. Nash didn't trust him and wanted a better idea of which approach to take before interviewing him. He delved into the circus' history and spoke with the performers. Some of it gave him new insight, and he unearthed fragments of long-forgotten tales. Solving the puzzle that was fracturing in too many directions wasn't going to be easy.

When asked if anybody had a grudge against Alessio Silvestri or Selena, they unanimously came up with a blank for Alessio. They said Aurora and the kids were lovely, though a few of them didn't like Mauritzio, who could be bad-tempered and had a sharp tongue. However, none of them thought that was enough to inflict a heinous act of revenge. When it came to Madam Selena, they were less vague. He heard several reports of a feud between her and the mentalist, Bence Jaeger.

Nash spoke to performers who had witnessed strange occurrences near the carousel. They talked about seeing shadowy figures and unexplained phenomena. Octavia, the bearded lady, said the air crackled with intense energy as she walked close to it and her hair stood on end.

Nash covered his smile with a cough. With the amount she had, that would be quite a sight.

Octavia laughed and it swelled the tiny caravan with its warmth, 'Nice try, inspector, but you need to work on that poker face. Go on, let it out, I laughed too when I saw it all sticking up.' She motioned with her hands at a foot's distance to her head to demonstrate and they laughed about it together.

'It was damned creepy, though. We all avoid going near it,' Octavia said.

'What do you make of Mr Ravenswood?'

'He's a slimy article. I wouldn't be fool enough to underestimate him, though. He's shrewd but in a sly and cunning way. If you know what I mean?'

'Unfortunately, I do.'

'There's no doubt that he's intelligent. He has tales to tell and can be entertaining in the cookhouse at meal times. If you're asking me if I think he's capable of murder,' she paused, considering it.

'Please, go on.'

'I don't know. Maybe. But if pressed I'd say he was more scoundrel than threat. I'd be concerned for my Royal Doulton over my life, I think.'

Nash liked Octavia. She'd have made a good police officer. He maintained his dogged determination and engaged the troupe with his dry wit to disarm them at mealtimes, and intermingled unrelated conversation with relevant questions. Getting some of them to open up to him was like pulling crocodile teeth, and healthy crocs have over a hundred. His sharp observations moved the investigation forward. However, some of the banter in the otherwise harrowing investigation was a welcome relief. As each day passed since Alessio's death, the mood in camp lifted. It was a far cry from the mundane cases he usually tackled.

As the sun went down and he returned to his office, he made a point of turning away from the brightly lit carousel with its nightmare-inducing music and slammed the door.

Chapter Fourteen

Nash woke up sticky from the hot July night. He should have rushed to the circus ground but felt that he was entitled to the hotel breakfast, seeing as it was included. And while he wouldn't wolf it down and give himself indigestion, he wouldn't linger either.

When he got there, the circus was alive with early morning activity and animal handlers tending their charges. They ensured the livestock were fed, groomed, and ready for training for their performances. That morning, though, the curtain was still closed around the big cat enclosures. It was unlike their keepers to be late. And Daft Damien was sent to find them.

The news of a new detective on the case had spread, igniting the curiosity of the townsfolk who had boycotted the circus. Word reached them that the investigation was sparking up, and they flocked to the ticket booths in increased numbers. What had been a famine was now a feast and everybody was riding high on good spirits. It was the boost they needed. Nash wanted to get a handle on how things were run and had been included in the general meetings—but with huge reluctance from Quinn and Mac.

The day before, they'd consulted the accountant to see where cuts could be made and the animal keepers were up in arms at the first suggestion that they had to reduce their animal feed by a scoop a day. Nash saw firsthand how tempers could rise in a second and a temperamental character seemed to be a prerequisite to any circus role. Gloria Mendez, the dog trainer, said she'd resign if that happened and everybody stood behind her in protest against the proposal.

'Would you rather run out of food altogether?' Jack Devine, the accountant said, pounding the keys of the old-fashioned calculator in Quinn's office.

'Cut my animal's food and I'll feed you to my cats,' Althea, the lion handler had said.

That was yesterday, and despite the carneys being furious after the meeting descended into rebellion, the tills sang that night. The circus saw a steady rise in sales, fuelled by the town's desire for the latest gossip and scandal. The animals would get their full quota after all, and the handlers were appeased. The townspeople realised that boycotting the circus was only keeping them away from the news.

Nash walked the grounds with Quinn as he did his morning reconnaissance around the carneys to see that everything was in order. It was still early when Althea and her husband, Dante, were roused from their trailer by Damien. They apologised and said that in eight years with the circus they'd never once slept in. They had woken with headaches and were uncoordinated. Rory the midget laughed when Dante fell over a bale of hay on his way to the cat's cages. The lion tamer pulled back the curtains and his kittens were pacing, wanting their breakfast.

Althea's piercing cry cut through the vibrant atmosphere of the camp, and Dante's shout of horror was followed by a wave of voices spreading like wildfire. The news travelled fast. Madam Selena, the fortune teller, had been found dead in the tiger enclosure. Nash told everybody to return to their trailers and declared the area an active crime scene.

Panic and disbelief spread across the circus grounds. The assumption was immediate—that she'd been forced into the enclosure by her killer to meet a gruesome fate with the tigers. Yet, silence had accompanied her demise. Nobody heard any commotion or struggle during the night.

DCI Nash and Mac McKenzie cleared the area and marked out a clearance perimeter around the enclosure. Nash wouldn't let them touch anything until SOCO arrived at the scene. And his first response was to forbid the trainers' admittance to the cage to calm the confused tigers. They hovered at the edge of the enclosure, demanding admittance to their cats. Quinn and Mac were the only other people on the scene and Mac pulled Nash to one side.

'I don't know if this is relevant but I think Althea and Dante have been drinking.'

'What makes you think that?'

'They were late getting to their animals for the first time ever, and they didn't seem themselves. They sobered up fast when we found Selena's body but they still appear sluggish and not as sharp as they should be for dealing with dangerous animals.'

Quinn said 'We had to tell you before we let them in with the tigers.'

'Do you have an emergency protocol in place for getting the tigers out of that cage without anybody getting hurt?'

Althea had come over as they were talking and heard the last part of their conversation. She had three strong leads in her hands.

'I need my cats out of there, but Quinn won't let me get them.'

'At my suggestion, Althea,' Mac said. 'I would never presume to tell you how to look after your animals, but I'm responsible for health and safety. We don't know how wound up they are, or how they'll react if somebody goes in that cage while Selena's in there with them.'

'React to me? Is that what you're saying? Do you think they'll attack me? Mac, I hand-reared those tigers from three weeks old. They are as harmless as kittens.'

'And yet there's a dead woman in their enclosure,' Nash said.

Althea turned on him in a rage. She stumbled, righted herself, and let go with a string of profanities in her native French. Nash understood some of them and blushed. He was reminded of a conversation from the day before when Althea had threatened to feed the accountant to her cats—unwise words indeed in the light of that morning's grim discovery. The lady had a wild temper.

'And who the hell are you, Mr Big Shot Detective? What do you know about my tigers? I'm going to get my cats out of there,' Althea screamed in his face.

'Madam, I ask that you stand well back while the tigers are removed. Any interference and I will have no choice but to have you removed, too. We have one body and don't want any more mishaps,' Nash said.

Althea made her displeasure known but backed down still yelling and threatening violence against everybody.

'What's the plan, Mac?' Nash asked.

'We have a holding enclosure that we'll put against the tiger cage door. Then it's just a case of persuading them from one to the other. They're hungry so they should move. On the other hand, they're confused by the change in routine and that can make them unpredictable.'

'I can't believe my cats would kill anybody. There isn't an aggressive bone in them. Where's the blood, eh?' Althea screamed. 'Where is the blood? They'll be put to sleep, won't they?' she sobbed.

Mac oversaw the transfer of the tigers with Ross Finley who covered for the keepers in times of sickness. They had a guard of carneys around the enclosure like fielders in a game of cricket. Nash complained about his marked-out area being contaminated, but Mac overruled him and said that safety was paramount. They compromised and put the fielders as far back as was considered safe for removal.

The transfer of the tigers went without a hitch and Mac told Ross to feed them. He said Dante and Althea weren't allowed near them until they were sober.

The trainers were furious. 'How dare you accuse us of being drunk,' Dante said. 'We would never abuse our position like that. Don't you think we know how dangerous these cats can be?'

'When you came out of your trailer, you were stumbling. Everybody noticed it,' Nash said.

'I swear we have not been drinking. I haven't had a drink since we celebrated Candy's new foal.'

Quinn had come over when the shouting started. 'Are you sure you didn't have a tipple last night and the effects have hung around until this morning? I'm sure you'll be fine to resume your duties in a couple of hours, guys.' He smiled trying to ease the tension between them and Mac.

'I am telling you we have not been drinking, not last night. Not this morning. Not at all. And I won't have my wife and I accused like this,' Dante said.

They lapsed into rapid French and Quinn led the angry couple away. Nash watched them go. They were sober enough now, but a corpse in your cage can do that to you. He squatted beside the empty enclosure and looked at the lifeless body of Selena Romano. Her pale remains lay against the metal bars. He used a pencil to push her trademark shawl back, and a closer examination revealed no marks or any sign of mauling on her delicate frame.

Nash was sure of one thing. The tigers hadn't touched this woman.

Althea and Dante were experienced animal keepers. They wanted to soothe their cats but they were kept away from them and stood around getting in the way. Althea was still crying and said she worried about the protestors hearing that one of the tigers had killed somebody. She said that every few months the animal rights crowd brought an unfounded allegation of animal cruelty against the circus.

Nash felt sorry for them and wanted to put them out of their misery. When he told them that he didn't know what had happened to the fortune teller, but it didn't look as though their tigers had anything to do with it, Althea burst into tears again and hugged him. They expressed their condolences for Madam Selena's tragic death but were relieved to find that the blame didn't lie with them.

'I shouldn't say anything, because we don't know for sure, yet. But I can't see a mark on her. We won't know the cause of death until she's taken for autopsy. But I'd say your cats are in the clear. I have a question, though.'

'What, Monsieur?' Dante asked.

'I don't know how to put it delicately so I'm just going to say it. I suspect that Ms Romana was already dead when she was thrown in with the tigers. So what I don't understand is, wouldn't they have eaten the body anyway?'

'My animals are well fed, inspector. We don't keep them hungry to make them perform, as the protestors accuse us. But, yes, under normal circumstances they would feed off, I'm sorry, anything they considered to be meat. However, I think I know why they didn't touch Selena.'

'Go on.'

'It's because of the scent of fragrant oils clinging to her body. She uses them in her spiritual practices. It's all hokum, but she stinks of herbs. Poor Selena, she was my friend and I'll miss her. But you could smell her for hours after she'd been in my trailer.' Fresh tears sprang from her eyes and she crossed herself.

'What you're saying is, the aromatic oils kept the tigers away, and preserved her body from further harm?'

'Yes.'

'On closer examination, I've seen some bruising around her neck. It suggests she may have been strangled. It indicates a violent struggle, but the lack of defensive wounds suggests she was taken by surprise.'

Nash waited for the doctor to arrive and pronounce her dead, and until the SOCO team had finished with the body. He went to find the security officer who was supposed to be guarding

Selena through the night. He'd come on duty at ten and it was still only eight o'clock. His shift was due to finish. But Nash found him lying in the long grass at the back of Selena's trailer.

His first assumption was that the guard was dead until he heard the first gruff snore. Nash shook him but he was slow to wake. When he did, he sat up and Nash was put in mind of the Rip Van Winkle story. 'What the hell is going on? Get up, you fool. I'll have your job for this.'

'I'm so sorry, Inspector. I don't know what came over me.'

'You'll have enough time in a jail cell to work it out. A woman's dead because of your incompetence.'

The man didn't seem to follow what he was saying.

'Wake up, man. This is gross negligence.'

The guard was groggy. His speech was slurred, and he lurched onto his side and vomited in the grass. 'I'm so sorry, forgive me.' He wiped his mouth on his uniform sleeve. 'I can't believe I fell asleep on duty. I swear, it's never happened before. Who's dead? How?'

First, the trainers and now the guard. Either there was one hell of a party on the circus ground last night, or it didn't take a genius to work out that they'd been drugged. Nash apologised to the guard for jumping to conclusions and took his statement, sealing his timeline of movements.

The guard kept apologising and was deeply shaken that somebody had died on his watch. He said he didn't feel well and that his mouth was dry. Nash gave him a rueful grin and asked that he didn't have anything to eat or drink until they could get a blood sample. He rang the medical investigator to come out immediately to test the three people he suspected had been sedated. Then he watched Selena Romana's body being taken away for autopsy.

When the deceased was gone, and the carneys had been let out of their trailers, Nash made a list of the order that he wanted to see people. He stood amid the bewildered staff and watched their body language. Some of them were angry, others sad and most of them looked heartbroken. One of them was a killer. He thought back to the ride. Including Finley Ross, three of the circus people had ridden the bloody thing, and two of them were dead.

'Our tigers are family. They'd never harm anyone unless provoked. We've spent years nurturing a bond of trust and understanding with them,' Dante said.

Nash listened. He admired the dedication and passion the trainers had for their animals. The absence of any signs of aggression from the tigers deepened the mystery surrounding Madam Selena's demise, but Nash wasn't as simpering as them. They were still wild animals and until the cause of death was conclusive, he ordered minimal contact with them. The three tigers were taken out of the act until further notice.

Nash instructed his team to secure the area and the SOCO team finished clearing the scene. They searched for any piece of evidence that could lead them to the killer. Fear gripped the performers and staff. Whispers filled the air, speculating about the identity of the murderer and the motives behind it. Nash had tried to speak to Ravenswood and Jaeger the day before but both were off-site. Quinn explained that while most people stayed in camp during their downtime, it wasn't a prison. They could come and go as they pleased. When the old man didn't get back by show time, Damien had been asked to run the ride but flatly refused. He said he'd rather die. And in the end, Ross Finley agreed to operate it.

Ravenswood appeared in camp as Nash was leaving after dark at ten o'clock. He almost fell out of a taxi and Nash watched him stagger across the field to his trailer. It could have been an act, and it was something to follow up on.

Jaeger had also come back by taxi a couple of hours earlier and ran across the field with fifteen minutes until curtain up, so Nash had yet to speak to him. Jaeger's name kept coming up. Maybe it was no coincidence that it was reported that Selena had also been off the grounds the day before. Too many people had spoken about their feud for it not to raise the hairs on the back of Nash's neck. Had Jaeger followed her?

As the day progressed, DCI Nash liased with the forensic team, ensuring that Madam Selena's body was processed for a thorough autopsy.

The mortuary's cold slabs played house to two corpses. They'd groan under the weight of the relentless brutality if Nash and his team didn't catch the killer soon.

Chapter Fifteen

Isiah was tired. And he was sad.

But he gave the world the ultimate showman. He flung his trailer door wide and it slammed back against the wood, alerting the field to the fact that the boss was in attendance. He didn't come out of his van—he made an appearance.

He'd contemplated starting the day in a suit, to show his people that he had no concerns, that life went on, and that a little murder or two wasn't going to flag his spirits—but that was a step too far even for him. He was brash, but he had intuitive intelligence and behaved as he always did. To stand out, you have to fit in. And even neck deep in a murder enquiry, the worst thing Quinn could imagine was fading into the background. He wore pale jodhpurs inside his riding boots and a tweed sports jacket with a paisley cravat. Bobo was on his hip wearing a matching coat and neckerchief.

'Beautiful morning,' he shouted to the carneys milling around. 'Today we will be spectacular, I can feel it. Flora, lengthen your neck. Your arabesque is lacking, dear. Better. Beautiful my darling, extend from the sweet earth, through your spine, and to the heavens. And Jimmy, why isn't Huckleberry on the field?

A bear should be out enjoying this splendid sunshine. How is Enchantress working out in Candy's position on the eight?'

'We put her through rehearsal with the other horses this morning and she's fine. But do you want to put Candy back for tonight's performance?'

'No, let's give her a couple more days. Enchantress needs the experience. Make sure you hold her back in training. She's trying to get her nose in front of Stardust all the time. Nip it in the bud. Where's Hos?'

'He's overseeing the feed delivery. Do you want me to get him?'

'No. Leave him. But that detective's going to be here again any minute and I want Hoss on the ball while I'm tied up.'

'I'll let him know.'

When Nash arrived with PACE agent Lyara Horvat, he came in throwing his weight around. He told Quinn he was annoyed at not being able to conduct his interviews the day before. He'd asked that the owner ensure people were around when he needed to speak to them. Quinn had made it clear that his staff were free to do as they pleased outside the performance and he had no intention of putting any restrictions on them.

'You don't seem to be taking the brevity of this enquiry seriously, Mr Quinn,' the jumped-up policeman had said.

'And you, sir, don't seem to understand that running a circus is a balancing act that requires the precision of a tightrope walker. These are highly-strung performers. Upset them at your peril.'

'Your point is duly noted. However, I do intend to speak to Mr Ravenswood and Mr Jaeger today. They aren't getting away from me. And I'd appreciate it if you could facilitate making that happen.'

'Indeed. On the other hand, we could just go and knock on their doors. As you would with any employee living in a house.'

'In that case, Mr Quinn, you won't need to shadow me and I can conduct my interviews with Ms Horvat.'

'*Au contraire*, detective. Without my paternal hand at their shoulder, you'll get no more out of my people than what they had for breakfast, and that porridge may be taken with a pinch of salt.'

'May I suggest we get on with it before the seasons change, Mr Quinn?'

'But of course, Inspector Nash.'

As they passed, Quinn looked at the animal enclosure, with a heavy heart. The tiger's powerful presence was a stark reminder of the dangers. The investigation had reached a critical juncture, and he prepared himself for what came next. He muttered some soothing words to Huckleberry in passing, as he led the way across the field.

'Jaeger or Ravenswood?' Quinn asked.

'Let's begin with Mr Ravenswood. From what I've read, I think we can process him quickly.'

Quinn rapped on the old man's door and stepped back for it to open. When Ravenswood first turned up, Quinn gave him a small tourer not unlike the one allocated to Nash as an office. Ravenswood's was the same size, but dingier, dirtier and more cluttered.

Quinn knocked again.

'All right. I'm coming.'

The door was flung open and Ravenswood appeared straight from his bed. He had a plastic jug filled to the half level with a yellow liquid that was closer to brown. Ambrose Ravenswood made no allowance for the two men and the woman standing in front of his door. He swept his arm wide to discharge the liquid over the grass at the side of his caravan. As the jug passed under his nose, Quinn was assaulted by a smell so foul that he deduced that Ravenswood couldn't be a well man. He'd been with Quinn's circus for shy of two weeks, but his urine had already killed a sizeable patch of grass on the castle grounds.

He wore a set of combination long johns that had once been white but now resembled pavement grey with darker sweat stains under the arms. Quinn looked away as the man turned his back on them and went into his van, leaving the door open for them to follow. His long johns had the traditional square trapdoor at the rear and Quinn wrinkled his nose at the dubious marks on show.

They crowded into the tiny caravan. Ravenswood spread himself wide on the bench couch under the window and none of them squeezed in far enough to share it.

'Perhaps it would be better if I waited outside,' Lyara said, addressing Nash. He nodded and she forced her way through the men as they shuffled around to let her out.

'Good day to you, Ravenswood. This is Inspector Nash from England, and that brief ray of sunshine that lit up your caravan was Ms Horvat. As I'm sure you're aware, they're talking to everybody regarding recent events. I made an announcement to that effect yesterday, but you were offsite at the time.'

'What's your concern with me? I can throw no light on your recent events, as you call them.'

Quinn moved an almost empty bottle of whisky so that it didn't touch the back of his jacket. 'Perhaps, you might want to put a pair of trousers on to speak to the detective.'

'Why? I don't see any need.'

Quinn turned his nose up.

'Don't cast your aspersions in this direction, Quinn, I wash these johns once a year as regular as clockwork. They go on in October and come off when May goes out. If my attire is offensive to the good gentleman, then perhaps you might both like to return at a later hour.' Ravenswood winked at Nash and Quinn turned his head sharply in time to see the detective's grin.

'Is something amusing you, detective?'

'No, Mr Quinn, not at all. I'm just getting a feel for the dynamics of circus relationships,' Nash said.

It was a warm morning, and the musty smell mixed with the odour of urine rising from the brown carpet where Ambrose had missed his jug was making him queasy. He tried to imagine where the old man stood to pee through the night. The smell was getting to him and he moved to the door and stood just outside the caravan. However, he wouldn't trust Ravenswood as far as he could fire him out of a cannon and didn't want to miss anything.

'Good morning Mr Ravenswood. It must be difficult coming into such a tight-knit community as this and trying to fit in,' Nash said.

'I can assure you, we've all made him very welcome,' Quinn said.

'Why would you assume that I want to fit in, inspector? I furrow my own field. All I need for my comfort is a place to lay my head and a few coppers in my pocket for a drop of the golden dew. And speaking of which, would you care to join me?' He didn't offer Quinn a drink, and for that, the circus owner was very grateful. Nash shook his head and raised his hand to decline. Ravenswood stood up and reached for the bottle. Nash handed it to him and he poured half of what was there into a blue tin mug.

'Your health, sir.' Ravenswood drank.

'You've caused quite a stir turning up here with your ride and your stories. May I call you Ambrose?'

'Aye, I usually do. And you can call me what you like.'

Nash didn't return fire with another question and Quinn watched with amusement as he let the silence hang in the air, waiting for the other man to speak.

Ambrose was happy to play and let the silence linger like the smell of his sweat.

'I'd like to talk to you about the curse that you've put on the circus, Mr Ravenswood, but first, since you brought the subject up, I'm going to address the problem at your last placement first.'

'You are mistaken, detective. I have not put a curse on the circus nor on anybody in it.' He took another drink from the dirty mug. 'Quinn accepted the carousel, and therefore he took on the children residing in our story.'

'You tricked us into it, Ravenswood,' Quinn said.

'A man and his greed are easily duped, Mr Quinn,' Ravenswood's smile allayed the undercurrent of malice.

'We'll come to that in due course. Tell me about Nebular Circus, please, Ambrose.' Nash said.

'Nothing to tell.'

'I think there's quite a story. Let's start with Miles Kravitz.'

'I had nothing to do with that.'

Quinn pricked his ears up. Nebular was currently travelling Russia and news on the grapevine was that they were struggling to stay afloat. When he'd questioned him, Ravenswood had told Quinn that he'd come from a show in England, and yet he'd just admitted his last placement was with Nebular in Russia. If this man was spreading doom around the circus grounds, he wanted to know more.

'But you don't refute that Mr Kravitz expired in mysterious circumstances after an altercation with your good self.' Nash realised he was copying the verbosity of the two men. His good self, Jesus.

'We had words when he accused me of theft. For the record, detective, I have never stolen anything in my life. I'm an honest man making an honest living.'

'Tell me about that night.'

Ambrose tipped his head in Quinn's direction. 'Maybe Kravitz shouldn't have ridden the carousel that night.'

'Your fight was grounded in reality though, and according to the report it had nothing to do with curses and ghosts.'

'The people of that circus would disagree with you. Feel free to ask them.'

'The police have. And apparently, Kravitz took the ride with one of the young circus girls.'

'Aye, that's correct.'

Despite the smell, Quinn went back inside the caravan and stood just the wrong side of the door to listen while trying to breathe fresh air.

'I have the reports, but why don't you tell me in your own words what happened next,' Nash said.

'I won't tolerate any magpies in my circus, let alone murderers,' Quinn said.

'I am neither.'

'We've had our spates of light fingers and they've been stamped on. Literally, before being removed from the grounds. There's nothing like a camp thief to unsettle the troupe.'

Ravenswood ignored him. 'As I said, they all agreed he was a victim of the curse.'

'Let's talk about the facts, Ambrose,' Nash said.

Ravenswood looked at a smeared stain on the caravan ceiling as though it could transport him to Russia and the Nebular grounds. 'It was cold that night. There was a lot of snow and a strong wind.' He chuckled. 'I think they rattled through the show pretty quickly. We only kept the amusements and side shows open for half an hour afterwards and closed early. Kravitz and his old lady had one of their fights. It was a regular thing most nights.'

'And she was?'

'Lucinda Kravitz, a pretty mean knife thrower. I wouldn't have wanted to marry her with that temper. My, she had a mouth on her. She wasn't blood, she was newshow.'

'Newshow? What does that mean?' Nash was writing notes and Ambrose opened his mouth to speak but Quinn jumped in first.

'Newshow is a gorja. Somebody who hasn't been born into the travelling community. They have academies all over Europe to teach flat-footed Neanderthals skills that we've honed over hundreds of years.' Quinn flicked his thumb under his chin to show his contempt, '*Cirque de Soleil*. Low grade, circus academies. You can't teach circus blood how to flow through an artist's veins, it just does.'

'Thank you, Mr Quinn. Please continue, Ambrose.' Quinn glared at Nash. He didn't like being snubbed.

'Lucinda stormed off that night and said she was going home to her mother in London. She did it often but never got as far as the airport. That cleared the pitch for Kravitz to make a catcall.'

'A catcall?'

'Yes, inspector,' Quinn said.

'It's okay, Mr Quinn. I think I can work it out.'

Nash thought he was funny, and Quinn didn't appreciate the way Ravenswood was cosying up to him.

'Kravitz was playing away from home with the magician's assistant.'

'What was her name?'

'Suki Wong.'

'And the magician?'

Nash was writing, but Quinn was watching the horrible little man. His expression was closed and his eyes were shrewd. It was a second before he saw Quinn watching him and he made a show of thinking.

'No. Sorry, it's gone. I've worked in a lot of places and met a lot of carneys. That night Kravitz left his door unlocked and went to visit Suki. He'd only been gone minutes when he went back to get some beers. We crossed paths on his way back to his trailer. Soon after, he came out shouting and screaming that his wallet had been emptied. And he blamed me. He was a lion tamer—big brute, and it took four carneys to pull the bastard off me.'

'Why wasn't his door locked?'

'Carneys don't lock their doors. We have no need to. Certainly not in my circus. It's an unwritten rule,' Quinn said.

'But surely in this day and age, and with a transient community constantly shifting, that's unwise.'

'You clearly don't know circus ways, inspector. And frankly, I'm offended by your inference that carneys are untrustworthy by nature.'

'I assure you, that wasn't my intention.'

'You might want to watch your prejudice, all the same. Remarks like that will have my people clamming up faster than shellfish on a clambake,' Quinn took his cigarettes out and lit one.

'Can I have one of those, boss?'

'It's boss now, is it? You wouldn't look at me before.' Quinn threw him a cigarette and offered one to Nash who he knew didn't smoke.

'What happened next?' Quinn asked.

Ambrose took a drag, laughed and choked on the smoke. 'Kravitz was a dirty old fecker. In his late fifties, and with an eye for the fillies, if you get my drift. Suki was legal—he wouldn't do them under—but only just. The ink was still wet on her birthday card. Rode him into the ground, she did.'

'Are you saying she killed him?'

'Good as. She sexed him to death. Apparently, they were going at it like rabbits on Good Friday, when he clutched his chest and started hollering for help. Said the ghosts of the children had come for him, and he ran out of her trailer with his knob shrivelling in the breeze. He was screaming his head off. Some of the carneys tried to calm him down but he was lashing out all over the place. I'd almost felt the weight of his fist earlier and he said he hadn't finished with me. I wasn't getting involved.'

He stopped and drained the last of his whiskey. 'They couldn't hold him. His fists flew all over the place but not aimed at anybody, just punching out. He had the strength of ten, they said.

Anyway, he managed to fling them off and stumbled away into the wasteland at the back of the grounds. The boss hostler said to let him calm down and went to look for him half an hour later. He found him as dead as a glue factory horse.'

'None of that accounts for the drugs found in his system,' Nash said.

'I don't know anything about that.'

'But you do. You were questioned about it extensively at the time.'

'I know about them, that they were found in his system at autopsy. What I'm saying, inspector, is that I don't know how they got there.'

'But you left the circus that week.'

'I did. I made arrangements for the carousel to be packed up and shipped.'

'Shipped to here?' Quinn asked.

'You have a remarkable reputation, Quinn. One of the best. Why wouldn't I want to be here?'

'We've established that you used, may I say, underhanded methods to secure your position, but why did you leave Nebular?' Nash asked.

'I am not a thief, sir. And will not stand accused.'

'And yet it was a murder that you were accused of.'

'Indeed. But there was no evidence to convict me on either count. An honest man slighted may be justified in killing his enemy. There is an honour to be had in the act of moral killing. But thieves are lowland scum. I will not be called a thief.'

'I assure you, Mr Ravenswood, there is no honour in taking another human being's life, and no justification can ever be taken from it,' Nash said.

'An eye for an eye, it's the carney way,' Quinn said.

'And I'm getting sick of hearing about the carney way. During this investigation, there is only one way. And that's the way of the law, gentlemen.'

Quinn had been watching Ravenswood. There was no doubt about it. If he had everybody running scared at his last circus, it would do his credibility no harm after somebody claimed to see the ghosts and then died. Like a fire needs oxygen, a story needs veracity to keep it alive. Ravenswood was an old man and Quinn reasoned that he used his curse story to keep him in work. But that didn't mean it wasn't true. Ravenswood rode into town, and two of Quinn's people were already dead.

'I have a question for you, Ambrose, my good friend.'

'Yes, Mr Quinn?'

'You won't be called a liar and subsequently left Nebular?'

'That is correct.'

'Therefore you can leave my circus at will.'

'Alas no, that is not possible.'

'You're talking in riddles, man. Can you or can you not leave my circus?'

'I cannot.'

'Why?'

'Because of the carousel.'

'What about it?'

'It's the curse, you see. The carousel tells me where I go and when I leave.'

'Can we stick to my questions?' Nash tried to regain order, but Quinn was having none of it.

He was dressed up like a country squire and saw himself as very dapper indeed. And the scrawny old man in filthy underwear had stood and was squaring up to him. They postured in the tiny space like a pair of fighting cockerels.

'What if I just put you out.'

'Try it, Mr Quinn.'

The dirty old bastard gave Quinn the creeps and he didn't know what to believe.

Chapter Sixteen

The mood was heavy inside Bence Jaeger's trailer. He felt the mind-bending power of the man. Nash was trained to be observant and noticed the tissues in the waste bin beside his table, and that Bence's eyes had a hint of red around the rims, as though he'd been crying not long before. He was sitting in the middle of the sofa in the same position that Ravenswood had during his interview, but in a very different caravan. This was a modern, spacious motorhome with beds that dropped from the ceiling at the touch of a button and state-of-the-art electronics. Bence was smart and clean, his cologne was citric and he burned candles in his trailer. He told Nash the Peony & Blush Suede scent helped to clear his mind and guide this thought process. He was dressed in casual loungewear but had his black costume suit on a hanger in his kitchen space.

When they'd knocked, he had grains of rice on a tray and was estimating their number. Nash had the feeling that Bence had been waiting for him. He showed off to Nash by performing this part of his act, and after guessing how many grains of rice were on the tray, he asked Nash to transfer them to a counting machine to get their accurate number.

'3,626,' Bence said.

'Correct.' Nash wanted to move the interview along but if this was what it took to get on the man's good side, he'd play along.

They played again. '2,982.'

'Correct.'

'3, 514.'

'You're two out, I'm afraid. 3,516, Nash said.'

'Please check them again, Inspector Nash.'

Nash put the rice onto the weighing scale again to get the calculation. 'Same.'

'That is incorrect. The scales are wrong. They need recalibrating.'

Nash didn't see how the first two times he'd performed his feat, it was correct and only failed on the third pass, but he wasn't going to argue with him.

The autopsy had been returned showing significant amounts of opiates in Selena's bloodstream, and her murder had cast a long shadow over the circus. Nash and Quinn sat at opposing right angles to the mentalist and gave him a moment to relax and come back into the room with them after focusing so hard on the rice trick. Lyara sat further back by the kitchen island.

Nash informed Bence that the interview would be recorded and looked at Quinn as he announced the people present. 'Mr Quinn, for the sake of the interview, please change places with PACE officer Lyara Horvat.'

The smile dropped from Quinn's face like wallpaper peeling from a damp wall. 'What? I'm comfortable here, thank you.'

'Your comfort isn't my concern. I must insist.'

'And make us all a brew, while you're at it. There's a good man,' Jaeger said.

Nash wanted to smirk but it would be unprofessional and he smothered it. He didn't think he'd ever seen somebody turn purple before. He'd heard about it, but there was definitely a faint purple hue to the blood rush on Quinn's face from his fury. Nash was irritated that he'd had to ask Quinn to move and Lyara hadn't had the drive to do it herself. She was a good officer, but he'd like to see more balls from her.

The murder of the teenage boy and the death of Madam Selena had shaken the circus. The troupe was on edge, and their sense of camaraderie gave way to whispered accusations. Everybody had a story about the feud between Bence and Selena. Jaeger was pompous and told Nash he was the greatest mentalist in the world. Quinn didn't dispute his claims and verified the hours he put into rehearsing his act and the dedication it took to do the things he did.

'What I do, inspector takes years of concentration and dedication. Selena never performed in the ring. She hasn't appeared on countless TV shows or created world records. She was merely a fake two-bit fortune teller. I appeared on the Graham Norton show, not to mention, *On N'est Pas Couché* and Letterman.'

'And yet you feel the need to mention it,' Lyara said in her deadpan Swedish accent.

Jaeger winced when he'd mentioned Selena's name.

'With every fakery that came out of her mouth, she discredited my talent and my obvious superiority. Of course, people wanted to see the great Bence Jaeger, but she was always there, outside, with her crystal ball and her stupid cards. Trust me, inspector, had I wanted to dress up like an old gypsy queen, I could have performed that act far better than her. Right up to the end, she claimed she had the gift of second sight. She was a charlatan.'

'I've been told things were heated between you.'

'There is nothing supernatural about what I do. I never claim to be a medium or a magician. I do an act of mediumship as part of my performance but I tell the audience upfront that it is merely a trick.'

'Very commendable,' Nash said.

'What I do is a mixture of cold reading, sleight of hand, suggestion and illusion. She puts my hard work into disrepute with her claims of psychic power.'

DCI Nash leaned forward as he brought Jaeger back to the interview. 'Bence, we need to ask you some questions regarding the recent incidents in the circus.'

'I've already spoken to the police and told them everything I know.'

Quinn's expression mirrored Nash's. His arms were crossed as he interjected, 'This is a serious matter, Jaeger. A boy has been murdered, and we can't ignore the connection between that and Selena's demise.'

Jaeger's eyes flashed at Quinn, the animosity between them was an open secret in the circus. Nash heard the rivalry always simmered beneath the surface, but lately, it had erupted into something more sinister.

Nash was only with them for a couple of minutes before he realised that Quinn was jealous of Jaeger. He was intimidated by the strength of the mentalist's mind and postured harder and bigger in front of him than the other performers. Quinn portrayed himself as a man of superior intelligence and a master of the spoken word. But here was somebody with a greater grasp of all things related to the mind and even showmanship. Jaeger looked down on Quinn in the way he had with Selena.

'It may sting, Inspector Nash. It could even bring you to tears but I'm confident that you will peel away the skins, layer by layer to penetrate the truth in front of your sore eyes,' Jaeger said.

DCI Nash's gaze was steady, and for some seconds he refused to back down when Bence stared him out, but when his eyes felt as though they'd been affected by onions, he scrunched them up and looked away. Seconds later, tears streamed out of his eyes.

'Onions have that effect, inspector. You are as susceptible to hypnotic suggestion as most people in my audience.'

'Cut the crap, Jaeger, and stop messing about,' Quinn said. 'Save your parlour games for the ring.'

'We need to know where you were yesterday when we tried to find you for an interview,' Nash said.

Bence hesitated. 'I had some personal matters to attend. Nothing related to the circus or the ongoing investigation.'

'Personal matters? I'm going to need more than that,' Nash said.

Bence's eyes narrowed. 'Look, Detective, I don't have to explain myself. I'm entitled to a private life, and my business is my own.'

Nash turned to Lyara. 'Do we have room in the cells?'

'It was quiet last night. There's room for one more.'

'Excellent.' He shook his head as though it hurt him to have to make the call. 'Bence Jaeger, I am arresting you on suspicion of murder.'

Quinn jumped in before Nash could complete the arrest. 'Please wait a moment, inspector, I'm sure that won't be necessary.'

'That's a shame. I missed the chance to dive into the delightful world of perverting the course of justice,' Nash said with a dash of wry amusement.

'Bence, we know about the tension between you and Madam Selena. You feel there was only room for one of you in the circus. Could this rivalry have escalated out of your control?' Lyara said.

'Where were you, Mr Jaeger?' Nash lowered his voice, always a dangerous sign, but his air of authority snaked around the room and was forceful enough to make their teeth rattle. He'd heard Renshaw joke that when Nash shouts you should take cover, but when he goes quiet, that's the time to run for your lives. The thought of his team back home gave him a sudden pang of homesickness.

'I know you would never do anything to harm her on purpose, but you have got a temper, and if you don't tell the police where you were yesterday, they are going to arrest you and there's nothing I can do to help,' Quinn was trying but the Mentalist was stubborn.

Jaeger's jaw clenched, and his eyes darted to the door as if he was contemplating a quick exit. 'This is absurd. I have no reason to harm anyone. Yes, we had our differences, but that doesn't make me a murderer. I was in a bar in town.'

'Which bar?'

'I don't remember.'

'Now we have a problem, Mr Jaeger,' Nash said.

'It was a bar, a couple of streets behind the bus station. It served beer.'

'You're lying. How does it go? "Bence Jaeger the world-famous memory man." You can count three thousand grains of rice on a tray in five seconds. And you remember every word written in a thousand books—but you can't recall where you were from two o'clock yesterday afternoon.'

Jaeger shrugged.

'I suggest you try harder.'

'It was called Crazy Daisy, inspector.'

'We need your cooperation. If you have any information that could help us find the killer, it's in your best interest to share it,' Lyara used a softer voice.

'Why did you lie?' Nash said.

'It escaped my mind for a moment.'

'Is this a joke to you, Mr Jaeger?'

'No. Not at all.'

Jaeger's shoulders sagged with the weight of the situation. 'I don't know anything, I swear. But I'll do whatever I can to help you find the person responsible.'

'And how do you propose to do that?'

'I have certain talents as you've just pointed out. I can cold read people, and probably a damn sight better than you can, inspector.'

'Is that so? Did anybody see you in this bar? One of the most famous and popular in the city? Would the bar staff remember you?'

'As you say, it was a popular place, I assume many people saw me, but where you'd find them again, I have no idea. Apparently, Madam Selena was the one with the supernatural gift. As to the bar staff, they may well remember me. You would have to ask them.'

'Did you perform any of your tricks in there?'

'Why on earth would I? I was off duty. Do you wave your truncheon around when you're having a quiet drink in a pub?'

As the interview continued, the animosity was thick. Quinn and Jaeger took shots at each other whenever they could slide one in, while Quinn displayed an irritating air of just wanting to help, which made Nash want to punch him. He might arrest Quinn just for being an arrogant bastard.

DCI Nash probed further, looking for any thread that could unravel a lead. And new lines of enquiry added a deeper layer of complexity to the case.

Outside the trailer, the sounds of the circus continued. Rehearsals were in full swing and Jaeger kept casting a look of annoyance out of the window. The laughter of children, the melodic tunes of the carousel, and the clatter of performers preparing for their acts seemed to set him on edge.

As well as the gossip about his feud with Selena, the rivalry between Bence Jaeger and Quinn had always raised eyebrows. Bence had been with them for eight years and Quinn had come up with an attractive contract to entice him away from his former placement. Three times over the years, rival shows had tried to bribe Jaeger to go with them, and each time Quinn had to up the ante and increase his salary. Nash had seen his performance and been left dumbfounded by the things he did. His act, and particularly his cold reading and self-professed fake display of mediumship, was astounding. It seemed like incredible magic. Bence Jaeger was one of the star attractions and his salary was second only to Quinn's. He drew a crowd and the dark atmosphere and mysticism in his act were legendary. Quinn would have been a fool to let him go, but it must have rankled every time Jaeger stole the show.

It crossed Nash's mind that if the circus owner was the killer, something had switched in his brain and he was escalating.

Quinn was high on Nash's suspect list and Jaeger had everything to fear from him. He made a mental note to make sure Jaeger was protected.

But Jaeger was by no means in the clear either and Nash would send officers to Crazy Daisy's bar to interview the staff and customers that afternoon.

His mind raced, trying to piece together the puzzle of the boy's murder, Madam Selena's death, and the animosity between many rival performers. But like the tricks of the illusionist, the answers were elusive.

The motorhome was spacious, but it was still a trailer with limited space, and the walls closed in, suffocating Nash with claustrophobia. Beads of sweat formed on his forehead despite the coolness of the room. And Nash knew Jaeger had insinuated the feeling of suffocation into his head. Quinn knew it too and smirked.

'Problem, inspector?' he said. No matter how much these two butted heads, Nash was the outsider.

'Not at all. May I have a glass of water, please, Mr Jaeger? Lyara would you mind getting it for me? And Jaeger, I know what you're doing so if you wouldn't mind releasing me from this effect, it isn't funny, and the fact remains that while you're playing games, two people are still dead.'

'I have no idea what you're talking about.' However, with his game up, Jaeger lifted the paranoia from Nash and the pressure in the trailer balanced to a normal level.

'Stop messing with the inspector's mind, Mr Jaeger, I don't want him clucking like a chicken in my car,' Lyara said.

Nash had no choice but to wipe his forehead with his sleeve. 'You say you had personal matters to attend to. For the record,

I need to know what those matters were. We have to account for everybody's whereabouts during the time of the deaths and details that you feel are irrelevant could tie into somebody else's statements further down the line.'

'The matters were internal. I was working out a new feature for my act. I walked around the Old Town and paid particular attention to the six-hundred-year-old astronomical clock. The new feature will require a complex level of hypnotism and using a replica of the famous clock. I'm working on an illusion of turning back time. It will be a composite routine with a lot of elements and work.'

'And the bar?'

'All that thinking worked up a thirst and I needed to clear my head. I work better with a pint in my hand. Don't you, inspector? Or is something fruity more your thing? Ah yes, a gin and tonic, but you only drink it during the summer months. You prefer a good old pint of bitter in winter. Am I correct?'

Nash was unnerved by his accuracy and it cast a renewed feeling of doubt over Conrad Snow's abilities. Had Nash been right all along and Snow was just a man who did parlour tricks? He couldn't have predicted Nash's choice of tipple any better than Bence Jaeger had. The thought brought with it an immense pang of loss. If Snow wasn't real, then neither was Max, and he couldn't handle that thought. He was due a video call with Snow that evening and he pushed all thoughts and doubts out of his mind. He had no intention of answering Jaeger's question. He was leading this interview.

'Boyfriend?'

'Pardon?'

'Your business of course, but how close to the mark am I? I'm never wrong.' Jaeger was waiting for adulation and Nash wasn't giving it to him. 'You were off clearing your head when you knew we were conducting interviews with everybody? It seems convenient.'

'The greatest misconception of the public is the impression that when the curtain comes down the work is over until the next night. Some of my illusions and feats of muscle memory have taken years to perfect.'

'What has that go to do with my case? You're talking a lot but not giving me much substance,' Nash said.

'One feature for my act can take four years to put into operation. So yes. Sometimes I walk to work out my new routines. The responsibility of stage show hypnotism is immense, a momentary lapse of concentration and somebody could be hurt. I walk. I clear my head. And occasionally I go to the pub to forget the pressure of my work. Does that satisfy your inquiry?'

'The timing of your disappearance gives cause for concern. Was there something specific that triggered your sudden need to leave? Something more than just your act playing on your mind? Surely that's a daily part of your work to deal with. The thing is, witnesses claim that you often leave the grounds unannounced and nobody knows where you go.'

'As is my right to do so. Selena and I had our differences, she'd been riling me and belittling me again, and I needed some time away to calm down.'

'Is there anyone who can vouch for your whereabouts around town? Did you go into any other shops or establishments to help us build a timeline?'

'I did not.'

'You can see my predicament.'

'After leaving the pub, I ended up by the river. I was alone, so no one can vouch for me.'

Nash went to speak, but Jaeger stopped him with a pleading look. 'I was contemplating suicide, inspector.'

Quinn gasped. 'I had no idea.'

'No.'

'The river? It's convenient that you chose a place where you could be out of sight and unaccounted for.' Nash recognised a smoke screen when he saw one.

'Would you have me jump off the castle ramparts and drum up more revenue for the circus? I didn't do anything. I'm telling you the truth. I didn't go near the boy, and I certainly didn't harm Selena. I give you my word.'

'You can understand why your disappearance on the day of the murder raises suspicions? And given the animosity between you and the fortune teller, it's not hard to imagine a scenario where things got out of hand.'

Bence shook his head. 'You're wrong. We had our issues, but I would never resort to violence.'

Quinn's voice was soft. 'We need your cooperation, Bence. You can't afford to harbour secrets. If there's something you're not telling us you need to come clean.'

Silence filled the trailer for thirty seconds. It was a long time with so much to say. Nash watched the gameplay. He'd seen a lot of suicides and even more attempted suicides and he knew that generally speaking, the ones that shout the loudest are the poor souls looking for help with no intention of taking their lives. The ones that keep their depression to themselves are the people in real danger of self-elimination. On the surface, Jaeger seemed too arrogant to harbour such thoughts. He seemed to be wrestling with his conscience, torn between revealing the truth and protecting himself, but in his own words, this man was the greatest illusionist of his time. His world revolved around deception. And Nash had to keep his wits about him and treat every statement he made with a degree of scepticism. More than any other suspect, with Jaeger, the only truths that counted were the ones that could be proven with solid evidence. Reasonable doubt was nowhere near good enough.

Jaeger's voice was hoarse with emotion when he spoke. 'I admit, I had a confrontation with Selena. She threatened me, and said she'd make sure I was driven out of the circus for good.'

Nash gripped his resolve. Jaeger could take facts proven beyond any doubt and make them dematerialise in front of your eyes. He could take fiction and turn it into proof. 'Threatened you how?'

'She said she had dirt on me that could ruin my reputation. It was rubbish, but I lost my temper, and we had a heated argument. But I didn't hurt her. I left the camp. I swear.'

The circus was a breeding ground for vendettas. The gritty reality of life damaged people. The performers lived in a goldfish bowl of having nothing sacred, and Jaeger could blur the lines between illusion and truth. Nash walked a tightrope of conflicting egos and had to navigate deceit. While talking to the carneys he experienced the fragility of human emotions and the lengths they would go to protect their secrets. The key to solving the murders was hidden in forensic evidence and psychological analysis. Nash had to cut through the mumbo-jumbo of smoke and mirrors to get to the science in this case.

Chapter Seventeen

As they left Bence Jaeger's trailer, questions from the interrogation gave Nash indigestion. His mind churned with the revelations and the need to know what hadn't been divulged. Bence might be the killer—Nash didn't have enough evidence to go on, but the magician was holding out on him.

As they walked, the sound of rehearsals and animals being trained blended with the rustling leaves of the nearby woods. Nash turned his head. Somebody was hiding in the trees. Or maybe it was just the wind.

'Who's there?' He walked into the woods. He didn't see anything and went back to Quinn who didn't follow him in.

Quinn said, 'I can't shake the feeling that there's more to this than he's letting on.'

Nash didn't tell him he thought the same thing. As they reached the edge of the circus grounds, Quinn said, 'Let me level with you. You're here to find the truth, Detective, but I'm warning you—this circus has secrets, and some of them are darker than you can imagine.'

'You're warning me?'

'No. I didn't mean it like that. I'm making you aware that my people are guarded around outsiders.'

'Tell me something I don't know. The darkness doesn't bother me, only the lies.'

Quinn left Nash to his thoughts, giving him space to reflect on the interviews. He said he'd given as much of his time as he could spare and had to prepare for the night's show.

Lyara went back to the station to write up the current interviews, and with a couple of hours to himself, Nash missed Kelvin and wandered the winding streets of Prague. He walked over the Charles Bridge and had coffee on the terrace outside Brick's restaurant. Sometimes the best way of getting into the heart of a murder was by evicting it from his conscious thoughts. He spent half an hour in the Kafka museum and bought a first-edition copy of *The Metamorphosis* as a gift for Kelvin. The streets were narrow and quaint, and the age of this part of the city was apparent in the architecture of the buildings. He found the creepy Marionette Museum and came close to buying one of the handmade puppets—but it reminded him of the sinister hand-painted carousel. The shopkeeper put the hard sell on him and he almost had to buy the damned thing just to get out of the museum. He was certain that before they left Prague, Jaeger would have one to incorporate into his act.

He rounded the corner in a picturesque street one row back from the tourist shops and restaurants and saw a building with a beautiful cottage for sale. It was so typically Czechoslovakian that Nash had the ludicrous idea that he'd like to buy it. It would be good to have a holiday home to retreat to for a couple of weeks and it would be a sound investment for his retirement. But the Good Lady Diana wouldn't be happy at being second-bested.

He smiled at the fantasy and put his dreamy ideas behind him. It wouldn't hurt to show Kel the house when he arrived, though.

It was getting late and the sun cast an orange glow over the ancient walls of the castle as he crossed the grounds. Nash wanted to catch the performance from the wings again before going back to his hotel. It was amazing how many snippets of conversation he heard when they were waiting to go on. He could hear that bloody ride in the background and the nauseatingly happy music repulsed him. He had a load of paperwork to do but didn't want to go back to his stuffy caravan office. It would keep until he could turn the air-con on in his spacious hotel room later. With time to kill before the show, he sought solace in the cool ambience of the castle walls. It was peaceful, and he'd found a favourite spot where he could look over the circus, or turn ninety degrees and see the looming majesty of the main castle in front of him. He perched on a moss-covered stone, and his mind found a place of quiet contemplation.

His tranquillity was short-lived, as footsteps came up behind him. Nash turned to see Jaeger in the glow of the early evening sun. He hadn't realised until that moment how great the drop from the wall was—a push and he'd be gone. He felt vulnerable but covered his unnerve by straightening his back. He put his hand up, palm facing outwards to stop Jaeger from coming any closer as he got up. He was grateful for strong thigh muscles from running and that he displayed no signs of age. He didn't want to show any weakness to Jaeger. He put several feet between him and the edge and leaned against the stone of the castle wall. The sun's heat was seeping out of it and it was cool against his back. Nash was determined not to look around to see if anybody else was in sight. Don't look down. Show no weakness. The man was younger and looked stronger than him.

'Can we talk?' Jaeger asked.

'Of course. What's on your mind?'

Jaeger fixed his gaze on the distant horizon. Eight miles, the thought came to Nash unbidden. The horizon was always eight miles away. 'I need to tell you the truth about yesterday, and where I was.'

'Go on.'

Jaeger picked moss from the wall. 'I wasn't at the circus because I was with Selena.'

Nash's surprise was evident. Whatever he'd been expecting he didn't see that admission coming. Jaeger may have been the last person to see her alive. 'With Madam Selena? What did you do to her?'

'Not what you're thinking. Use your imagination, detective.'

'I don't follow.'

Jaeger's eyes glistened with tears. His voice softened as he spoke. 'We were in a motel in town—together. I loved her with all my heart.'

This man was full of surprises and Nash had the wind taken out of his sails. He remembered that Jaeger had looked as though he'd been crying when Nash got to his trailer that morning.

'Our animosity hid our affair.'

The revelation hit Nash like an ocean wave, the complexity of the situation opened another wing of investigation. 'You and Madam Selena were in a relationship?'

Jaeger's sorrow was palpable. 'We've been together for years—had been. It was nobody's business. Don't get me wrong, my feelings about her act were genuine. I wanted her to give it up and take another role on the side stalls, but she wouldn't hear of it.'

'But why keep it a secret? I don't understand.'

'Dynamics. If anyone found out, it would have caused trouble.'

'What kind of trouble?'

'Gossip, spite, jealousy. Take your pick. And Quinn can be a mercenary bastard. He'd have pushed us to marry so he could pay us a married couple's salary and buy one of our trailers. That's what he did with the Balladonias a couple of years ago and they hated each other within a year. Killed the act. And almost killed each other. They got a divorce and went their separate ways to other circuses.'

'I see.'

'Do you? Our love was forbidden, and we were willing to do anything to protect it from them.'

'No. I don't see. Not really. What business was it of anybody else? Surely it's up to you if you choose to marry.'

Nash was stunned, absorbing the gravity of Jaeger's confession. The misery secrets caused was life-defining here, and the entwined lives of the performers contributed to the murkiness of every lead.

'We'd planned to leave and be free. But she's gone, and I'm left with this unbearable guilt.'

Nash put a hand on Jaeger's shoulder, his tough exterior softening in the face of the mentalist's vulnerability. 'You were in a hotel together. What happened next? Unless you're telling me more than you're saying, you couldn't have known what would happen.'

Jaeger wiped a tear with the back of his hand, his voice choked with emotion. 'I should have been here, protecting her. If I was, I could have saved her. I would have married her, you know.'

'Why didn't you?'

He laughed and the bitter sound of his sorrow felt final. 'She wouldn't have me.'

'Why not?'

'I wanted her to give up work so we could start a family. But she wouldn't hear of it. I said she could work on a concessions stall—there's always other work here—but she said I was controlling her.'

'Were you?'

'No, of course not.' He thumped the wall. 'Maybe.'

'She was feisty. I wouldn't have fancied your chances.'

'She was. She was like a comet blazing a trail of fire behind her. And now she's been extinguished. And you'd better find whoever did this because if I find them first, you'll have another murder on your hands.'

Jaeger's grief and guilt bore down on Nash. He knew the answer to the murders was in the circus, but he understood the fragility of the dynamics. The consequences of their love caused ripples that affected everybody.

This didn't let Jaeger off the hook. Passion was one of the greatest motives for murder.

Nash and Jaeger stayed there until he had to leave to get ready for his act. Nash dropped his guard enough to sit with the mentalist in silence. They didn't need to talk.

At that moment, as the last rays of sunlight faded into the twilight, Nash realised the truth wasn't a matter of facts and evidence, it was an intrusion into the lives of people. Lines were blurred, leaving him confused. They hadn't spoken for ten minutes and Nash was surprised when Jaeger started talking again. 'Our relationship started soon after I arrived eight years ago.'

'That's a long time to keep a secret. It must have been a burden.'

'Sometimes. But it was exciting sneaking away for stolen afternoons together.' His voice was tight with memories and pain. 'We were drawn to each other from the moment we met. The passion and emotion between us was incredible. But because of our feud, we didn't act on our feelings for a long time.'

'What changed?'

'Sex. We fought, and she drove me crazy. She crept into my head at night, and it reached the point where I'd do anything in an argument to caress her, a hand on her shoulder, a brush of her finger. But we would never be accepted.'

'It sounds like a passionate affair.'

'As I said, the feud between us was real. In eight years, there wasn't a day without fireworks. Now she's dead, and I don't know what to do. I could seek revenge, but it would only ease the pain for so many hours a day. What about the rest?'

'I don't think you've told me everything.'

'There's nothing else of relevance. Though, I suppose you ought to know, she was seeing somebody else at first. She was living with Magnus Volkov.'

'The strongman?'

He grinned. 'Would you want to get on the wrong side of him? Things were difficult for a long time after she ended it.'

'I see. Residual anger?'

'God no. Not now. He's been with somebody else for years. He's married to Creya Brieanna, the primate handler. She's used to dealing with hairy apes.'

'Hardly fair. I've seen that brute rehearsing in his trunks. Every inch of his body is shaved.'

'She must have a hell of a laundry bill. Imagine all that baby lotion on your sheets. But perhaps you already have, Inspector.'

Nash looked up, it wasn't the first jibe about his sexuality. He was learning to roll with strangers knowing, but Jaeger had been in the private parts of his mind again. 'Not my type, too primordial.' He winked.

The moment of humour between them released some of the tension and Jaeger had his emotions contained. 'It was a long time ago, but it was bad back then and because Selena insisted on keeping our secret, I couldn't do a damned thing to protect her.'

'Did she need protecting from Volkov?'

'Yes, she did. There were a couple of incidents. He was pretty wild.'

'Physical?'

'Now and again, but that came from both sides. In fact, I think his assault on her was defensive. I wanted us to come out as a couple, but she wouldn't.'

'Hurt pride can take a long time to get over after a relationship. The residue can linger.'

'Do you think he killed her?'

'I can't say that,' Nash said.

'But he's a suspect?'

'No more than anybody else, including you, Mr Jaeger.'

'I loved her more than I love me—and I'm a narcissist. I would never do anything to hurt her.'

Nash felt the depth in his words.

'By the time she was killed, I loved her so much. I'd have done anything to make her happy.'

The tears that he'd had under control came again. He recounted the stolen moments they shared—a tender touch backstage, a lingering gaze across the circus grounds, their clandestine meetings in the quiet corners of the city. They had risked everything for their love, knowing that discovery could mean the end of their careers.

'We dreamed of leaving.'

'You were going to another circus?'

'God, no. We were giving it all up. I'd talked her into moving home to Hungary with me and getting a nice house. She wouldn't give up her career but agreed to work privately.'

'You said you wanted to live without fear. What were you frightened of?' Nash asked.

'The curse. But it got her, didn't it?'

'I don't believe that. It wasn't a children's ride that killed her, Mr Jaeger. It was a human being.'

'Alessio had his throat cut, and his brother hasn't spoken a word in two weeks. Don't you think that's something to be scared of?'

'I'm sorry, I misunderstood you. Your decision to leave the circus only came about after Alessio Silvestri was killed.'

'Yes. She finally agreed. But our plans were just dreams. The fear of discovery, and everything else, overshadowed our happiness.'

Nash felt sorry for the pain and guilt he carried because of not being there to protect the woman he loved when she needed him. He understood the sacrifices they'd made to be together. Jaeger's intensity broke down the walls preventing disclosure, leaving a man who needed redemption and closure. But he was still a suspect. He'd spilled the truth about their love, but the mystery of her murder would be a shrouded question until Nash got the autopsy report back from the lab.

Why wouldn't a man as strong as Jaeger say to hell with them and do what he wanted? Unless somebody had a hold over him. Was Jaeger being blackmailed?

They walked back to their trailers, and the truth eluded him like the illusionist's tricks. Love and hatred, joy and sorrow, they all walked a tightrope.

They reached Bence Jaeger's trailer and something still puzzled Nash.

'It must have put a strain on your relationship keeping up that level of animosity. Why put on an act of rivalry in front of the others? And I still don't get the hiding away. Like any relationship, it would have been rough for a few weeks, but things always settle.'

'You still don't get it. We can't lock up our office and go home at the end of the day, like you. We all live, sleep and wash our underwear together.'

'Didn't either of you confide in anybody else? What about the fact that you were leaving? Could Selena have told anybody?'

'I don't think so. The circus is built on tradition, and new relationships are frowned upon. We had to pretend to hate each other to protect ourselves. And even though Magnus was over her, he could still be an arsehole.'

Nash tried to understand the position Bence and Selena had been in. Codes of conduct dictated the rules. Jaeger still seemed to be holding back, there was more. Nash was away from the danger of the castle walls. That made him looser with a man who could hypnotise him in a second and lay him unconscious to do anything to him. He was more comfortable with poking Jaeger to see how he'd react.

'I see how challenging that must have been for you. But you're holding out on me and that makes me suspicious. I want to know why. There's more that you're not telling me.'

'There is something else. I received a death threat this morning.'

'Who from?'

'I have no idea. A note was put under my door saying that I'm next.'

'I need it. I'll go and get an evidence bag.'

'I don't have it. I burned it this morning.'

He was lying. His eyes shot to the top left of their sockets and Nash watched him thinking. 'In the middle of a murder investigation. You get a death threat, but you burn it, destroying what could be vital evidence? Why would you do that?'

'Why would I do that?' He was playing for time. Repeating a question back was a classic delaying tactic. Nash watched him and saw him suppressing his reactions. He doubted there was ever a note. It added another layer to the onion.

The feeling of trust they'd built evaporated and Jaeger's attitude changed. It was harder. 'I have my own plans for finding the killer. I don't need you. I have skills that can make people reveal the truth, even against their wishes.'

'I've told Quinn, and I'm telling you, any interference in this case will be met with the full force of the law.'

'And what can you do to me now? I've lost everything.' In direct contradiction to his words, his mood changed again, his demeanour was sly but playful. 'I know something else.'

'If you have further information, you should stop playing mind games and tell me.'

'I have to get ready, but what I know isn't about the murder or my relationship with Selena. It's about you, Detective.' He was goading him.

Nash's eyebrows shot up in surprise. 'Me?'

Jaeger leaned forward. His hands came up to touch Nash's temples. His eyes were intense and Nash wanted to pull away. Jaeger began his mentalist act and Nash couldn't move. He was frozen in hypnotism the second Jaeger touched him and muttered words of mind-control. Nash couldn't do a damn thing to stop him. 'I can sense things about people. I look through them without them saying a word and I've been reading you, Nash.'

DCI Nash bristled at the lack of his title. He had full competence over his thoughts but couldn't speak. He wanted to tell Jaeger he hadn't given his permission to be hypnotised and he wanted to arrest him for assault. But it felt as though his tongue filled his mouth and no words would pass his throat.

Jaeger's eyes pierced Nash's soul as he continued, 'Relax. You're safe detective. No harm will come to you. Just clear your mind and let the thoughts come to you as they will. You're a man who has faced hardships in life. You've experienced loss and pain, but you've found strength when you've needed it. You're driven by justice, a desire to protect the innocent and seek the truth. But you feel like an outsider. And as if you don't belong.'

Nash tried to break the hold, but couldn't. Jaeger had touched on some key aspects of his life, and he wondered how much was a lucky guess and how much was genuine intuition.

'Being a gay man in your line of work brings its own set of challenges.'

Nash felt a surge of vulnerability he hadn't expected. Until recently, he'd kept his personal life private, even from his colleagues, and it was hard for him to open up. He controlled that part of him. He realised that the police force wasn't so different from the circus, they were a close-knit bunch and other than Kelvin, they were the only people he had in his life. They were his family. Kelvin's children were warming to him, but it was a slow process. Especially with his eldest daughter, the only one who hadn't accepted her father's sexuality after their mother's death.

'You're in a relationship with a civilian.'

Nash tried to keep his emotions in check. He knew he had to stay focused, but Jaeger's cold reading had struck a nerve.

'It's Kevin, isn't it?' Jaeger's voice was gentle. 'You care about him deeply, but this investigation will put a strain on your relationship.'

Nash's defences went up. His relationship with Kel was private. 'Kevin understands how important your work is but the high-stakes nature of your job throws up problems that you have to overcome.'

Nash tried to speak and was surprised to find that his words had come back to him. 'How do you know this?'

'I read people, just like you do, detective. But I do it better. It's nothing more than that. It's a gift, or a curse, depending on how you look at it. I'm not here to hurt you. I just want you to understand that we all have secrets. And sometimes, those things can drive us to do things we never thought possible. I've done things I regret.'

Nash collected himself as he felt his motor skills and competency returning to normal. Jaeger's abilities weren't supernatural, but his insights were uncanny. He didn't have to hypnotise him. Nash knew it was about control. Jaeger was saying, 'You're playing the big honcho around town, but I can make you pee in your trousers if I choose to.' Message received. He forced his brain to process what Jaeger had said.

'Is that a confession?'

'I haven't killed anybody, but don't we all have regrets? We put on a show for the world, but behind the scenes, we're all human, with flaws and demons. The truth is never black and white. And sometimes, it's the things we keep hidden that lead us down the most dangerous paths.'

'That's twice tonight that your words have sounded like a threat.'

'No threat, my friend.'

'I'm not your friend. I'm an investigating officer. And I warn you, Jaeger if you ever pull a stunt like that again, I'll have your back against a prison wall before you can say abracadabra.'

Jaeger smiled. 'Do what you must. You be a policeman and I'll use my set of skills, and let's see who can catch a killer first.'

Chapter Eighteen

A conversation had already occurred between Quinn and Nash about Selena's papers. It was a far-reaching minefield that Nash said was circus business and he had no intention of getting into it. 'But you must at least have a passport for her,' he said.

'Paper, paper, paper. We drown in a sea of paper. Some of my performers don't know their own names, never mind anybody else's. Tobias the Worm was born without limbs. He was left on the steps of a church in Berlin. Mercedes only has one leg and was also abandoned at birth. We took her from a Hungarian orphanage when she was seven—we stole her. One of the guys picked her up covered in filth and carried her out of there under his coat. She couldn't speak, couldn't walk and had no name. At the orphanage they called her, Stump. So you see where your need for paperwork presents a problem.'

Once Quinn was assured there would be no repercussions in that regard, he delighted in telling the policeman that they had many ingenious hiding places for ferry and border crossings.

'We are dealing with a murder and nobody knows the victim's surname,' Nash said.

'If she had no name, inspector, she had a reason for that. She may have been on the run from a criminal misdemeanour, or even escaping a terrible end-of-the-world suicide cult—we've had those, too. We take people on merit here. Their business is just that and we don't ask questions.'

'Don't you know if she had any living relatives?'

'That I do know. She did.'

'Great.' Nash was poised with his pen and Quinn smirked.

'With ground crew and transient workers, we are a band of over a hundred. We are all her relatives.'

Quinn took his scored points and Nash put his pen down. He confided in Quinn that the lab had run Selena's DNA through the criminal database but it had come up blank. They'd try to trace her background through the ancestry sites. But although they were given priority, it was still a long-winded process that could take days.

After his meeting with Nash, they stood in the centre of the circus grounds, surrounded by unrest. The discovery of things that would normally never see the light, had created subversive energy and darkness among the performers. The atmosphere was thick with suspicion, and Quinn had to act fast to quell the mutterings of a walkout.

He called a meeting with the troupe, and everybody had something to say. If they could run the circus so well, he was tempted to stand back and let them. He'd give it an hour before they came running back to him for leadership and guidance.

He spoke with authority and reassurance. 'We can't let our troubles divide us. We have to stand together as a family the way we always have.'

'Until somebody comes in the night and pops us off one by one,' Konrad Wolf said.

'There are enough people gunning for us outside camp without us turning on each other. We'll get through this, but it's going to take trust and cooperation,' Quinn said.

'It's like a cabin-in-the-woods horror novel around here. I'm not hanging around to get butchered in my sleep,' Damien said, and he high-fived with Konrad.

'I'm astounded,' Nifty said. 'Damien can read. Who knew?'

'I'm daft in the head, not stupid.' Damien squared up to the clown, and Quinn brought the crowd to order. Bobo screamed, pulling back his rubbery lips into an excited chimp grimace. He showed his teeth and jabbered at the carneys. The animal chose whether he wanted to wear clothes. If he did he picked what he liked and he'd gone for bright primary colours. He wore red trousers and a yellow T-shirt, with pink sunglasses. Bobo jumped on the trailer steps anxious at the prospect of a fight between the humans. Quinn motioned for him to climb on his hip and he calmed him as Bobo came in for reassuring kisses. 'It's all right, my boy, they're just posturing. It's okay.'

Quinn was losing them. The troupe sounded like a flock of sheep coming out in favour of Damien's proposal to leave. They made the same noises as the back-benchers in the British House of Commons, and that was never a good thing.

Whispers spread through the crowd, and accusations flew like the knife-thrower's daggers.

'All this started when he came,' Damien said, pointing at Ambrose Ravenswood.

'Enough, Dafty Belman. Still your tongue. I've told you before, that nobody stands accused in my circus. Not without hard proof to back up your running mouth. This is your final warning.'

Saar put a hand on Damien's arm to stop him from storming off and defended her boyfriend. 'He's only saying what the rest of us are thinking, Mr Quinn. And he's right. This only started when the old man turned up with his carousel.'

The performers suspected their fellow troupe members of murder, and accusations were rife. A murmur of consent rippled over them when Ignatius said he doubted the integrity of the circus or its ability to keep them safe.

Quinn scowled as the English detective took a step forward to speak. 'Most of you know me by now, and if I haven't spoken to you, rest assured you're on my list. I want to reiterate again that we are doing everything we can to get to the bottom of this. More importantly, I've arranged for patrols on the field at night.'

'Fat lot of good that did for Selena. Your guard slept through the whole thing,' Ignatius said.

'He was drugged.'

Quinn tried to regain control. 'It's hardly the same thing.'

'Thank you, Mr Quinn,' Nash interrupted him. 'All the results have come back from the labs. And unfortunately, I can confirm that, as suspected, Madam Selena was also a victim of foul play.'

'Tell us something we don't know. It was only a case of having it officially confirmed. We knew she'd been murdered. Have the strength of your conviction and come out and call it what it is,' Octavia said.

Quinn saw Nash's head turn to two of the clowns as Patches handed Jinx a twenty Czech Koruna banknote. The tiny mute clown pocketed it and made the loser sign on his forehead. The clowns ran books on everything, including whether Selena had been murdered, and Quinn smirked at the thought that Nash would find it distasteful.

Nash spoke up. 'I'm sorry to be the bearer of bad news, but as Madam Octavia said, most of you already suspected that both victims were murdered. As there's a press conference scheduled for today, I wanted to personally tell you where we are with the investigation before it's made public. I've been instructed to inform you that Selena was drugged and strangled. And while we can't prove it, it's natural to assume that both deaths were committed by the same person.'

A murmur of fear ran through the crowd. 'I want you to know that my door is always open and you can come and talk to me anytime. Information will only be used if it proves to be relevant, and you can speak in confidence. If you know anything, or have any suspicions, no matter how unfounded, come to me. We are particularly looking for any information regarding Madam Selena's background.'

Nash shot a look at Quinn who was offended by the accusation in the glance. He opened his mouth but the detective shot him down by getting in first. 'Her background is proving elusive to track down. If anybody has even a last name for her, it would be helpful.'

'She's dead. What are you doing about keeping the rest of us alive? Have you forgotten that we've already been drugged by this maniac? We could have been killed and I still haven't had an apology from Mackenzie for suggesting that my wife and I were drunk,' Dante said.

'Nor are you getting one. It was a natural assumption under the circumstances,' Mac said.

'All this turning on each other has to stop.' Quinn spread his arms to include everybody. 'Let's look out for each other.'

Nash waited for silence. 'That brings me to my next point. That's excellent advice from Mr Quinn and the best way of helping us catch this person is to be vigilant. Wherever possible make sure you spend your leisure time in groups. Tell each other where you're going. Be aware of what you're eating and drinking. And don't leave your food and glasses unattended. Most important of all, watch your troupe's back.'

'Does that mean we can all caravan hop?' Patches said, winking at Flora and Fauna.

'Funny, Mr Patches,' Nash said. 'But as stupid as that sounds it's good advice for the people living alone. Wherever possible make sure that there are three people in your caravans at night. Far be it from me to increase the paranoia in camp, but until we know for sure that this wasn't perpetrated by somebody around you, your best friend could be your worst enemy.'

Quinn watched Nash scrutinising the crowd to see who their eyes went to. 'Talk like that is hardly necessary, inspector. Can't you see, we're all on tenterhooks as it is?'

'Better to have you on your guard, than being complacent, Mr Quinn.'

Saar had her hand up.

'Yes, Miss Van-Dijk?' Nash said.

'What about me and Noor? I'm pretty sure I'd know about it if she was sneaking out at night to bump people off. And do we need two extra people each or just one between us?'

Quinn was grateful for the light-hearted moment and loved seeing Nash trying his best not to laugh. The gorja was still at the

PC stage of discomfort around the oddities and overcompensated by trying to be ever-so-casual.

'Please can I have the dishy older detective on my side of the bed,' Noor said. 'Who better to protect me?'

'Miss Van Dijk, it would be an honour. Alas, I have to return to my lonely hotel room at night. Seriously, though, guys, keep your eyes open and your wits about you.'

As Nash wrapped up the meeting Quinn was annoyed. He'd wanted to address each concern individually, mainly to hear his own voice and assert his dominance over Nash. But he was distracted from inviting more questions by a commotion at the gate.

A new wave of panic engulfed the grounds and Quinn ordered all the trainers to go the enclosures to protect their animals. Animal rights protesters had breached security and were running across the grounds to the cordoned-off area with the big tent that the troupe called the Critter Cave. The fools were intent on their goal of liberating the animals. There were always the new ones, local ones and the thoroughly misguided. But a rotten core of the most extreme had been following the circus across Europe for years. It was a game to them, following them around the world and holing up in local hostels planning their attacks. The purpose was to save the animals, but their objective was to open cages and let them out. Quinn called them stupid, but it was a well-thought-out plan to draw media attention. No matter that they professed to be animal lovers. If the dangerous wild animals got loose they may have to be shot for public safety. A few beasts put out of their supposed misery was worth it for the greater good of the cause. If any human was hurt—all the better, especially if it was a child—the press loved that. And a death or two for media coverage would be the icing on their brainwashed cake.

The troupe were waiting for news about the fortune teller being found in the tiger cage to break, and if it came while the protesters were there, it would be pandemonium.

The trainers went to their animals via the tack room to tool up with sticks and shovels. The rest of the carneys knew the drill and formed a human wall to stem the charge. Quinn was already on the phone calling the police and noticed that Nash had no idea what was going on. He moved his mobile away from his mouth to speak.

'Stand back, inspector. We wouldn't want you getting hurt. You'll be best off in your caravan until we've got this under control.'

He watched as Nash made a brief phone call and then joined the human barricade with Lyara. He was impressed that the police put themselves in danger to protect the circus. It was going to get nasty.

Quinn rushed to defend his company. 'Protect the animals. Keep them safe.' he shouted, directing his staff to secure the enclosures. The circus animals were the lifeblood of the circus, but they weren't just performers, every one of them was loved and had hours of attention spent on them in training.

If the protestors saw how much more stimulation the livestock got than the average domestic pet, maybe they wouldn't be so keen to judge. What got him most was the ignorance. In the beginning, he'd had a war council with several key members of the core group present. He'd invited them as his guests to see how things worked. He was shrewd and said he'd welcome any suggestions they had for improvement. The invitation was declined. They had no interest in being educated and wanted to keep their bandwagon-jumping blinkers on.

After the debacle of Mary Chippendale's animal abuse blew up, every circus was tarred with the same brush of neglect and cruelty. Every year laws were passed in another country to outlaw the use of live animal acts, and their circuit was ever shrinking.

The protestors split in a practised pincer formation. Some of them went for the animals, while others ran to the tents and trailers to throw cans of red paint over them.

Quinn's face was determined as he looked around the enclosures. The animals loved performing. There were no sad animals in Quinn Brothers Flying Circus, and Alexander Bavic a staff member and resident who travelled with them was one of the best big animal vets in Europe. Over the years, they'd had a few creatures, usually the ones that had already been subjected to abuse, that didn't take to circus life. Good homes in wildlife sanctuaries were sought for them. With the life offered, Quinn could count on one hand the animals that didn't settle.

The protestors, fuelled by anger and misinformed beliefs pushed forward, shouting slogans and demanding the animals' freedom.

'Kill the circus–not the animals.'

'Lock up the clowns and see how they like it.'

The horses, sensing the tension, were restless and jittery. Flora turned the radio on with some classical music to help soothe them.

Quinn had tried to reason with the protestors in the past, explaining that the animals were treated with the best care and love, but his words had fallen on stony ground.

As the protestors clashed with the circus staff, some of them cast disdainful looks at the curios. They didn't understand that every one of them had their independence and had always been embraced and celebrated within the close-knit circus community. However, the protestors' ignorance was evident in their scornful gazes and derogatory comments.

'Freaks,' a woman shouted. 'You should have been put in a sack and drowned at birth. Animal abusers, the lot of you.'

'The poor things. They don't have the capacity to understand the exploitation and degradation they are subjected to. They don't belong here,' a man said. 'We'll be calling Adult Protective Services on their behalf.'

One protestor pointed at Octavia, a graceful woman who spoke eleven languages. 'Look at her. It's unnatural. She should be free, not locked up in this circus. She needs to be somewhere with people who can shave her every day.'

Cassandra put her hand on Octavia's arm to hold her back. 'Don't rise to it. It's not worth it.' Octavia opened her mouth to speak, but there was no point. She didn't say anything and gave Cassandra's hand a squeeze.

'We'll see this freak show shut down,' somebody shouted.

'Time for battle,' Quinn said to Mac. 'Here we go again.'

The protestors' ignorance fuelled Quinn's determination to protect his people. He'd heard some of the comments from inside the animal enclosure tent and was incensed. After checking the livestock were safe, he took a second to compose himself and went out to stand at the head of the line. The carneys broke the chain to let him through and then linked arms again.

Chapter Nineteen

Quinn stepped forward and his voice rose above the clamour. 'Our animals are not your concern. They are well looked after and we have a top vet living on-site to oversee their wellbeing.'

'Bullshit.'

'You're a liar, Isiah Quinn.'

'No animal could want for more. As to my people, these members are not prisoners. They choose to live and work here because the circus is their home. We are family.'

'Man, you're going to make me cry,' One of the protestors laughed.

'We respect and honour their abilities. Our people with disabilities have careers just like some of you and, with the exception of Mercedes who is one of our exceptional dancers, they don't perform. Just as we care for our animals with dedication we care about each other.' He wasted his breath and the protestors chanted for the circus' closure.

'Please, you're frightening the animals.'

The human oddities were proud people and refused to hide away when trouble came. Those who could, stood or sat beside their brothers to protect what was rightfully theirs. Berdini was two feet taller than most people and stood out for victimisation. Their attention turned to the gentle giant with a heart of gold. He was a man who was proud of his immense size due to gigantism. He delighted everybody with his kind nature and impressive mastery of an array of musical instruments.

Somebody pointed at him, his voice filled with disdain. 'Look at that man. You're exploiting his size for profit. It's inhumane.'

'I am the tallest man in the world,' Berdini boasted. 'What sets you apart, little one?'

'This is a freak show. You should be with regular human beings, not treated like a slave attraction.'

Berdini bent forward with his hands on his knees like a benevolent parent explaining something to a child. 'You are misinformed, my friend. I am not a sideshow exhibit. I have a job in the maintenance department.' He pulled a ticket out of the breast pocket of his brown tweed suit. 'Perhaps you'd like to come to a performance and see the real acts.'

As a reflex reaction, the man took the ticket and was dumbfounded enough to look shamefaced.

Quinn said, 'These are talented individuals who have found a home here. Some of them have trained for years in their chosen professions to be more than a spectacle. They aren't here to be gawped at or ridiculed, but to earn a living and be proud of who they are.'

The spokesperson of the group stepped forward to separate himself from the crowd. 'So, what you're saying is you specifically hire freaks to not be freaks? Isn't that the epitome of condescension?'

'My we have learned some big words. I could barter a thesaurus with you all day, young man, but my people are happy here.'

Despite Quinn's attempts to educate the protestors, they were steadfast in their belief that the circus was exploiting its performers and animals. The tension escalated, and reasoning with them was a waste of time.

'If this is how they treat their human beings, I dread to think what state of filth the animals are in. We're going in.'

Quinn shouted above the noise. 'We know how this is going to end. The police will be here momentarily—and in the meantime, we are greater in number than you. I'm confident that we can prevent you from breaking through our defence. Please turn around and go back before people on both sides get hurt.'

'Let us through.'

'Please. I've seen this escalate into violence before. We are peace-loving people, I implore you to turn around.'

'On my count,' the ringleader said.

'Stop,' Nash shouted.

The man who was leading the protestors hadn't got past number one. The detective broke ranks and stood beside Quinn. His air of authority and the command in his voice caused the ringleader to falter. Nash stood out from the carneys as being different. He wore jeans and a T-shirt with trainers on his feet. There was nothing remarkable about his clothing. He could have been one of them, but his demeanour set him apart. 'Who here speaks English?'

Several hands went up. Quinn was only irritated by Nash's interference for a fraction of a second. The pack were about to charge the line and he was grateful for anything that could stall them until the police arrived.

'I am DCI Nash of the British police force, here on secondment. You people are trespassing. Anybody taking so much as one step further will be arrested and the full weight of the law will come down on you. Are you willing to risk that?'

The phrase *Are you feeling lucky, punk?* ran through Quinn's mind and he prayed that Nash could hold them back for a few more minutes. Where were the police? As well as Quinn ringing the emergency number 112, Nash told him he'd made a direct call for backup—lots of it.

'Please. Let's diffuse this before more police get here. We're all reasonable adults, aren't we?' Quinn said. He was following both conversations. The ringleader of the protestors was speaking to him in Spanish and he responded in that language. Nash was talking in English and somebody else was shouting at him in Italian and he responded to him as well.

The next voice was a Czech speaker and only Quinn, Octavia and a couple of the performers could understand what was being said. One of the protestors held his phone out and spoke in rapid excitement.

'Look. The tigers have killed somebody. It's all over the internet.'

'Who?' One of the local protestors asked.

'Report says it was a fifteen-year-old boy. And this fiasco is still up and running? It's crazy.'

'Negligence,' somebody shouted.

'The tigers were probably staving.'

'Or crazed with frustration.'

The protestors were made up of nearly as many nationalities as the carneys and the next few minutes were filled with chaos as everybody was brought up to date with the breaking news.

This was all Quinn needed. He grabbed the training whistle from around his neck and gave three sharp blasts.

When the story was related in English, Nash tried to calm the situation again. 'Listen to me. You have been misinformed. One of the performers did pass away last week, that's why I'm here in my official capacity. But I can assure you, the tigers had nothing to do with it. The animal care here is exemplary.'

The ringleader resumed his count. 'We're getting in there. After three. One. Two. Go.'

He couldn't even get that right, and Quinn saw some of them run and others hesitate, waiting for him to shout three.

The protestors had the initial advantage as the stronger carneys and ground crew pushed the vulnerable members of the troop out of the way.

When the news broke and Mackenzie and Finley saw the direction things were heading, Mac sent Ross back for more sticks and anything else they could use to defend themselves.

Quinn and Nash were at the front of the line, several yards ahead of everybody else and the protestors came in with fists flying. Quinn was knocked to the floor in seconds and a man with a knife stood over him about to plunge his weapon into Quinn's chest when Magnus jumped forward and grabbed the man's wrist. He disarmed him and threw the knife behind him. The ground was a mass of arms and legs as the protestors charged what was left of the line.

Nash was punched in the face and felt blood pour from his nose. He took the protestor to the ground with his arm behind his back, but Quinn could see that Nash was no fighter and the man had youth and strength on his side. He twisted away and rolled on top of the detective. Magnus came to the rescue again and pulled the thug off Nash. The detective rolled when the weight was lifted off his body and covered his damaged face with his hands. They heard the sirens.

'Get out of the way,' Magnus shouted to Nash. 'Take cover, sir.'

Nash muttered that he didn't need telling twice but he couldn't stand up.

Quinn shuffled over to him as he lay on the floor stunned. He put his arm around him and helped him up. Nash couldn't get his balance and stumbled against the ringmaster. Quinn had been punched in the stomach and ribs. He had trouble walking as well but didn't think his ribs were broken.

Soon, police in riot gear waded into the madness, and half an hour later the worst of the protestors had been arrested and taken away in vans or ambulances.

Only two of them had made it into the animal tent and were taken down by the crew as they tried to remove Huckleberry's collar. It was lucky for them that the confused bear was well-trained and didn't attack the strangers. Thousands of hours had been put into his husbandry and training since he came to the circus as a cub. Mercedes rushed over to the bear to calm him.

Ross Finley wasn't so well trained and brought a club down on a man's back. Once he was down, the wood was prised out of Ross' hands by one of the crew before he hit him again. Ross straddled the protestor, raining punches down on him. The man was put in the back of an ambulance and an official enquiry on this and several other injured parties, from both sides, would be opened.

The sound of a confused animal rang out from one of the enclosures—and a lion's roar sent shivers down Quinn's spine.

He rushed to the terrified animal fearing the worst. He found the protestors had backed off, but the scene broke his heart.

One of the lions, a majestic creature called Sultan, paced his enclosure, restless with fear and confusion. The protestors' presence had disturbed him, and Quinn felt the animal's distress.

'It's all right, my boy. It's over, you're safe now,' he whispered, stroking the magnificent beast through the bars of his cage. He gestured to his staff to give Sultan some space and left him with Althea to calm down.

Quinn needed to address the turmoil before that night's performance. 'I understand we're facing difficult times, but I'm proud of you. We must remember why we're here—to entertain, to share joy, and to protect the animals and each other.'

The day had an effect on the troupe, and the atmosphere shifted. Murmurs of doubt were replaced with hope. They were together and they were whole. Jolene made urns of strong coffee and laid out plates of homemade cake, then the performers disbanded to their trailers to prepare for the night's show.

While it was quiet, Quinn knocked on Nash's caravan door.

'Come in if you're handsome.' The voice was female and sultry.

Octavia was standing over the protesting detective holding an icepack to his face. 'Stop being a baby and put up with it. It'll reduce the swelling.'

'I came by to ask if I could tempt you to a drop of whisky, old boy.'

'I thought you'd never ask,' Nash said. No other words were necessary.

Chapter Twenty

Nash felt his broken nose and looked at the two black eyes caused by the break. If he was any kind of hero it wasn't borne of fists and brawn. He wore suits to work and could only manage four pints of lager. He read *The Guardian* instead of the more sensational tabloids. He'd used physical force to apprehend criminals in his time but he'd never been in a fistfight in his life. When it came to roughing up the suspects he always stepped back and let the guys in the riot gear take the heat.

He winced and put his coffee beside him on a circus flyer that he was using as a coaster. He missed Kelvin and it hurt like toothache. And he had a hangover after getting drunk with Quinn after the show the night before. This felt like the longest few days of his life. It was made worse by the fact that he couldn't reach Kel the night before and had no idea where he was or when he'd arrive. He was still incommunicado this morning.

Nash adjusted the laptop to get the best camera angle, and straightened his hair, making sure he looked presentable for the virtual meeting. Noticing that his tie was crooked, he adjusted it and clicked on the link to join the media call with the renowned police psychic consultant Conrad Snow. Nash had always been sceptical about the supernatural, but desperate times called for unconventional measures, and he hoped Conrad could shed light on the murders and the curse of the carousel.

As Conrad's face appeared, he looked at Nash's blackened eyes through the digital barrier. 'Silas, good to see you. Oh, Jesus.' He greeted Nash with a grimace. 'What the hell happened to you?'

'What? This hot mess? It's nothing. You should see the other guy.'

'No, thanks. I'm not sure I'm liking the Tyson Fury version of you.'

'Good to see you, too, Conrad. I trust you've caught up on the case files I sent through.'

'Sure have. It sounds as though you've landed in deep water. I don't remember murder being a headlining circus act in my day.'

'It's a bugger of a case here, and I was hoping you could provide some insight.'

'That's what I'm here for.' Conrad exuded confidence. Nash had sent him encrypted information so that he had the gist of the case, but he wanted to tell him in his own way from the beginning. He'd only said a few words when Conrad interrupted him.

'I'm being shown a red metal box with a key and a child. The kid has his lips sewn shut. I don't think it's literal—a metaphor.'

'I understand. That's Luca, the dead boy's younger brother. He's traumatised and won't speak.'

'Nash, you have to get through to him. He's in danger. The killer has ties and doesn't want to kill him. He's doing everything he can not to and the kid's under pretty tight guard from his family—but make no mistake, he will if he has to. They're saying he was safer where he was before.'

'In the mental health unit?'

'I'm seeing doctors, so yes, I think so. Can you get him back there?'

'I don't know. He's been released as fit enough to be at home, but there's no improvement since he's come back. Unless I can get a committal order to have him taken by force, there's no way the family will let him go.'

'But you can do it?'

'Technically, yes, though I'd need the testimony of three doctors to say it's in his best interest from a medical point of view. However, if I go down that route, it will undo any progress I've made in getting these people on side. On one hand, I might help the kid short term, but it's going to hamper the case overall. What do I do for the best? It's taking a lot of treading softly to gain these people's trust.'

Nash needed to blow his nose, reached for a clean tissue and then decided against it. Too painful.

'They're saying it might not do any good anyway. Sorry if this is too cryptic for you, but my guides are telling me the killer can get to him. The child is the key. He knows everything. You have to break through his defence.'

'How?'

'By gaining his trust.'

'Any suggestions on how I do that?'

'They're telling me he has no choice.'

'What do you mean?'

Nash had a drink of his coffee and regretted it when a pain shot through his nose and played pinball with his eyes. He waited while Conrad went into his trance state and connected with his spirit guides.

'They can't give me anything else. The mind is a complex thing and many doors have been locked in this child's psyche.'

'For Christ's sake, Snow. Tell them to give me something clear that I can work with.'

'Si, we've been through this so many times. You have to learn the art of patience.'

Nash wanted to throttle the psychic. They'd forged a friendly working relationship but he was still a pompous arse at times. 'I know you can only tell me what they give you, but I hate it when you do that.'

'I can't stress this strongly enough. Luca is in danger, and you have to get through to him. That's all I've got. Sorry.'

'Okay, let's try something else. Tell me what this curse of the carousel is all about.'

Nash told him more about the bizarre occurrences, the deaths of the boy and the fortune teller, and the suspicion surrounding the carousel's history. He mentioned the spirits of the dead children, hoping Conrad could focus on any relevance.

The psychic listened. 'The spirits of dead children? Interesting. But curses are usually more fiction than fact. This carousel voodoo is probably just a hoax.'

Nash's scepticism was reinforced. 'My thoughts exactly. But that was my opinion about you when we met. Now you've got me buying into this stuff, against my better judgement.'

'Ha. You can't fight the force, Inspector.'

'Can you get me anything on the carousel's keeper? He's a shifty little weasel called Ambrose Ravenswood.'

'My guide hasn't got much.'

'Hermes.'

'Yes, Hermes.'

'Not the delivery company,' they said together and laughed. Nash regretted it, put a hand up to his swollen face, and cursed.

'And he's not Hermes the Greek God, either. My guide was a 17th-century philosopher, who worked with metaphysics and ethics.'

'No offence to him but never mind all that bollocks, what has he got on Ravenswood?'

'He says much offence taken, and to watch yourself or he'll turn you into a toad.'

'Can he do that?'

'I don't think so. I paraphrased for dramatic effect. But he's telling me that Ravenswood's an interesting character. He has a connection with the supernatural world, but not in the way you think. He says, far from being the vagabond that he portrays, he's actually a wealthy man, and not of traveller origin. He's giving me a large office complex and I'm seeing a broken man walking away from his life. He's a traveller through choice, not heritage, and it's all an act he puts on because he enjoys the simple lifestyle. Hermes says that most of his persona is acting. I'm getting the distinct phrase, "Not as daft as he looks." He's showing me a storage facility.'

'What about it?'

'This is interesting. Our Ambrose is a collector of oddities and relics with peculiar histories. There may be something linked to the carousel. It's not a curse, but something darker and more obscure.'

'What do you mean? What could be darker than a curse?'

'That's for you to uncover. I can't do all the work for you. Follow the trail of the unusual and the forgotten. You may find more than you bargained for. His collection is said to be priceless and is made up of objects that are supposed to be haunted or possessed.'

'Creepy guy. The collection fits with what I've seen of him. Though not the riches-to-rags story. He just looks like a drifter.'

'Exactly what he wants you to see. Let's not invite him to dinner, eh?' Conrad said.

'I'm getting something else. Another person has no supernatural abilities, but he has exceptional skills in reading people. I don't think he's the killer, I'm getting charming but fake. Does the word fence mean anything?'

Nash raised an eyebrow. 'I think you're talking about Bence Jaeger. He's even more fascinating. His abilities are uncanny. Any insight on him?'

Conrad chuckled. 'He's a talented magician, but his skills lie in psychology, not the supernatural. He can wield the magical with delicate finesse. However, I'm not getting anything. There's a block on his energy. Hermes can't get through. It could be deliberate.'

'I bet Max could spy on him.'

'He does have an uncanny knack of being able to drop in on people. Being dead has some advantages. It's as if the mentalist knows something is trying to infiltrate his subconscious and has put a padlock on the door to his mind,' Conrad said.

'He's got something to hide, then?'

'Not necessarily. He plants ideas in people's thoughts for a living. It stands to reason that he'd have enough mental wherewithal to prevent it from happening to him. As a psychic, I can do something similar. It's like locking the front door so that spirits can only get in when I invite them.'

'That makes sense.'

Conrad laughed. 'Or I could, before the great lockpicker Max Jones burst through my portcullis.'

'I can't believe I'm going to ask this. It's inviting disaster, but is there any chance of asking him to poke around a bit?'

'I can try and make contact.'

'Thank you. I just want to go back to the carousel for a minute.'

Before the meeting, the Police Action for Community Empowerment research team had prepared a dossier on the carousel's history. It detailed the victims, and the various individuals associated with the circus. He shared the file with Conrad, hoping it would provide additional context to help in his readings.

As Conrad scanned the documents, he was quiet with concentration. 'Impressive research, Nash. You've covered all the bases.'

'We wanted to be thorough. As you can see, there have been at least thirty unexplained deaths soon after circus employees went on the ride.'

Conrad grinned. 'At the risk of being told off for being enigmatic, the most crucial information lies beyond the surface. Keep an open mind, and don't be afraid to follow your instincts.'

'Am I going to meet a tall, dark stranger and take a journey across the sea, as well?'

'Both points are already covered, I believe.'

Nash took note of the information Conrad had given him. Other than the possible story for Ravenswood—and nothing had shown on his background checks to corroborate it—there wasn't a single concrete lead to follow. The only other thing he'd said that might be useful was that the kid was in danger.

'You're a rational man,' Conrad said. 'But in cases like this, you must embrace the unexplainable. The human mind is a vast and mysterious entity, capable of extraordinary things.'

Nash nodded. The supernatural had always been outside his realm of understanding, but he'd grown to trust Snow, and if he said the key was breaking through Luca's trauma, at least that was something he could act on.

Conrad had a glimmer of mischief in his eyes. 'Remember the truth can manifest in unexpected ways. Ask the child about his dream of being a clown.'

'I think you're playing with crossed wires on that one. He's a trapeze artist, a good one.'

'I've got Hermes in my head saying that the boy hates flying and wants to make people laugh.' Conrad offered a final piece of advice. 'You know there's going to be another murder. You can't stop it. Just make sure it isn't the boy. Trust your instincts and keep pushing forward. The answers are there. You just have to unravel them.'

Nash thanked Conrad for reading, and went on to chat about life at home.

He thought about the enigmatic carousel and the dark secrets it held. He'd follow Conrad's advice, and investigate the supernatural connections, but he'd stay grounded in the reality of hard evidence.

Nash would interview Luca again. Then a word with Ambrose Ravenswood was on the cards. He wanted to glean better insight into the ride's history and learn more about the collection of oddities that captivated the old man. The carousel's ominous form loomed over him and it was fuelled by rumours, storytelling and superstition, but he refused to be intimidated.

As the meeting ended, Conrad closed his eyes and rubbed his temples. Nash knew better than to ask if he had a headache.

'Thank you, Hermes,' Snow said.

He opened his eyes and returned to Nash in the present. 'My guides have been working on your behalf in the spirit realm. This might not be helpful, but they have some leads for you to follow or, at least, Hermes says he's been working on the motives. Grab the pen from your breast pocket, Si, and take notes.'

Nash scribbled, adding the odd comment to the list. He was thankful for the help despite his scepticism.

'Thanks, Conrad. But, I have to ask, do you have a name for the murderer?'

Conrad shook his head. 'I'm afraid not. Reality is stranger than fiction, and the answers will be found in unexpected places. Don't take things at face value. I can't be more specific.'

'You've given me a lot to think about. Thanks again. Take care.'

'You too, Nash. Look after that face.'

The case had taken a supernatural turn, but solving it lay with human intent and Nash wouldn't be swayed on that. The consultant came good in the end.

Chapter Twenty-One

Nash hadn't been able to speak to Luca with his parents present yet, so he'd spent his time conducting more interviews. It would have to wait until the next day to speak to the boy, but he could get things ready. He didn't want to alarm them, but there was no time to waste. The air was tense as the performers grappled with their suspicions. They were unsettled after the intrusion of the animal rights protestors. Nash noticed that the animals were agitated as well, the unrest surrounding them made the livestock jittery. He'd already checked Quinn's documentation when he arrived, and his animal welfare paperwork was up to date for the Czech Republic. Nash didn't like it, but couldn't deny that the care the animals got was second to none and the law was different here.

As he walked past the carousel, it repulsed him. He forced his thoughts onto Luca and how he could reach him. He had a plan, but whether it was a good one remained to be seen. Again it was experimenting with things that he knew nothing about and it went against his police ethics code of conduct. Lyara was with him and spoke Luca's first language which helped with the child's trust issues, but she was also trained in child psychology.

He was going to ask Mauritzio and Aurora's permission to enlist Jaeger's help.

He'd ask Bence to try and hypnotise the boy to break through his mental block. If that worked, they could look at taking him back to that day through further regressive hypnotism. He wasn't all in with the supernatural or even the mind-altering stuff but he was at the point where he couldn't be closed-minded to anything. It was a long shot. He had no idea if it was ethical—or even legal—but it might work.

He saw one of the young women sitting alone, one of the troupe he'd interviewed called Belinda. She reminded him of somebody and he thought back to remember who. She looked troubled.

Nash remembered another case and another murder victim. In his job, he saw a lot of people after they'd died, too, but there was nothing supernatural in that. He saw what was left behind when the soul was gone, and they scorched their images onto the back of his eyelids. They were still people to him and he never forgot a name.

Zoe.

Belinda reminded him of Zoe, a vibrant girl full of life, though he'd only seen her after it was taken. She'd had youth and vibrancy—and a lot of tattoos. However, she also had patches of clear skin, unlike Belinda who didn't have so much as a millimetre of her body that wasn't inked, or so he'd been told.

'Are you all right?' Nash asked.

'I don't know anymore. Everything feels strange.'

Nash nodded, understanding the emotional toll the case was taking on everyone. 'I promise you, we'll get to the bottom of this. But I need your help. Anything you can tell me about the carousel, or anything unusual you've noticed, could be crucial.'

She hesitated before speaking. 'I've seen things.'

'It's okay. You can tell me.'

'There have been times when I've felt a presence like someone is watching me. And the carousel—it's like it has a life of its own, even when it's not in use. I've seen the shadows. They sit on the horses at night. I hear them.'

'You've actually seen them? And you couldn't be mistaken? A trick of the light, perhaps?'

'I knew you'd laugh at me.'

'Belinda, I'm not laughing. Far from it.'

She wouldn't say anymore.

He urged her to reach out if she'd agree to talk to him again. He could see she was trying to get away from him and didn't want to push any harder and frighten her. Belinda's trailer was one of the closest to the carousel and she had an excellent view of anything amiss. Had she seen something?

When he got to his office he made some hurried notes. After speaking to Conrad, he knew time was running out and he had to get to the boy before it was too late. Every time the sense of urgency hit him, he contemplated running to the Silvestri's trailer in a panic, like a man possessed. And then he'd have to explain to Mauritzio that he wanted to check on the boy's well-being. He was being ridiculous. Conrad didn't say he was going to be murdered in the next five minutes. His head was reeling with thoughts and he had to get them in order before charging off to Luca. He told himself to get a grip and behave like a detective. The jitters of the place were getting to him. As he sat at his desk, he heard that bloody ride start-up and the music tortured him.

When he'd finished his notes after the reading with Snow, he had ten items listed.

Isiah Quinn: The owner and ringmaster - motive: financial gain.

Quinn may have murdered his brother to gain control of the circus profits. He was against the human oddities being sacked and thrown onto the scrap heap. Perhaps the victim overheard something he shouldn't have. Quinn was a man who sailed close to the wind. Alessio could have discovered financial irregularities or intended to expose Quinn for something. But why Selena? She might have known about Quinn killing the boy. Or maybe the ringmaster knew about her affair with Jaeger and was jealous. It was tenuous.

One of the clowns: motive - jealousy and revenge.

A clown could have murdered the trapeze performer. He was just a man who played a buffoon, where was the skill in that? Selena might have been in the wrong place at the wrong time and seen something. But if that was the case, and she knew about Alessio, why didn't she come forward sooner?

The trapeze artist: motive – blackmail.

Mauritzio the trapeze artist - might have killed Selena to prevent the exposure of a dark secret that could ruin their reputation. But he'd never kill his son. Life had taught Nash to think outside the box. It might not be the father, maybe it was Aurora, or even Isabella insane with jealousy over her brother's success. Hard to believe that a child so angelic could be capable of brutal murders. It was hardly likely—but he'd seen murderers disguised as family innocents before—one as young as ten. Snow had named these as being the most likely, there were many more he hadn't suggested. Why these? Some of them wouldn't have been anywhere near Nash's top ten list, but if it came from Snow, they couldn't be discounted.

One of the animal trainers: motive – protection.

Snow had no idea how many animal trainers there were. At least there were only five clowns. The animal trainer may have murdered someone who was mistreating their animals. Did Alessio have a cruel streak? It made more sense than Selena who he knew was devoted to them, especially the dogs. But if Selena had been cruel it would explain why her body was staged in the tiger cage. Alessio was the more likely candidate for tormenting livestock. This was a strong motive, and he made a note to dig into Alessio's character.

The fortune teller: motive — predicted threat.

Selena Debois was the biggest surprise of all. When Snow was talking, he mentioned a last name. But he was speaking fast as his guide fed information to him. Nash couldn't interrupt with questions. She was one of the victims, and she didn't strangle herself. There was no evidence that the crimes were committed by one person, but it was the most likely scenario. This threw it wide open again. The fortune teller could have committed murder after foreseeing a dire event involving the victim—a mercy killing to save them from a prediction. If Selena killed Allesio, Mauritzio could have known about it and, not trusting the judicial system, he took matters into his own hands. Snow had given Selena a last name. A thrill ran down his spine. If this was correct, it would help to find out about the woman with no identity. But why would somebody from Romania—a true Romany—have a French name? Marriage?

The illusionist: motive – sabotage.

The illusionist might have murdered his rival performer. Their jealousy was well documented. But they were engaged in an affair and that complicated things. Jealousy over Magnus. That would put the strongman in danger, too. And where did Alessio come into the picture?

Magnus the strongman: motive: love and obsession.

The strongman had been involved with Selena in the past. He might have killed her for rejecting his advances after their affair ended. He could know about Jaeger—but it made more sense that the mentalist would be the victim. And again the same question: Why Alessio?

The fire eater: motive - self-defence.

This had come from Snow, but it made no sense at all. Alessio was nowhere near Ignatius when he disappeared. However, Ignatius could have found out that Alessio tampered with his apparatus. That was twice Alessio's character had come into question. Nash had been looking for a murderer, maybe this was the guide's way of saying he should be looking at what kind of person the victim was. And more often than not it came back to Selena having seen something that she shouldn't—it had nothing to do with peering into crystal balls.

The contortionist: motive - identity concealment.

This was an interesting one, that Snow had thrown in from left field. Cassandra might have murdered the victims to hide her identity using the chaos of the circus as a cover for something in her past. As always it came back to the transient lifestyle and difficulty in legalising the troupe. It was the perfect place for people that needed to disappear.

The sword swallower: motive - revenge for past injury.

Henri Roux was somebody that Nash hadn't interviewed yet. He was low on his list of suspects. Nobody had anything negative to say about Roux. He was a normal twenty-seven-year-old. He was good-looking and innocuous. He'd dated a couple of the bally girls but wasn't in a serious relationship, and there was nothing acrimonious to note. That made Nash suspicious. Maybe this one was hiding in shadows to be overlooked. The sword swallower may have killed Alessio for something he did in the past. A man seeking vengeance. He couldn't see any motive for killing Selena. He came back to her having seen something—and Alessio, far from being the golden boy around camp, was a fifteen-year-old shit.

Why these ten? Other than Quinn, none of them had ranked high on his radar. The circus was fractured, and Nash didn't know if he could put it back together again.

Chapter Twenty-Two

He needed to strike a balance between embracing the supernatural possibilities given by Conrad and grounding himself in solid evidence. Somewhere in the middle, the truth lay like a hidden monkey puzzle.

With new resolve, he had some persuading to do. His first call was to Mauritzio and Aurora. They had finally gone back to work with Isabella after the death of their son. He knew they'd be getting dressed and stretching for that evening's performance, but he felt the urgency to speak to Luca pressing down on him. There was no time to waste.

His phone vibrated in his pocket and he pulled it out. It was a message from Max's old number. The thought he'd just had was printed on his screen *No time to waste*. Snow had got through to Max, then. It comforted him to think of his friend being close. The show would be starting soon, he couldn't rally Jaeger to hypnotise the boy tonight. As the thought went through his head, his phone vibrated again.

Now.

Nash put his phone back in his pocket. He wasn't arguing with Max Bloody Jones, but he couldn't ignore him either. There was no way Quinn would allow him to pull Jaeger from the show tonight and it would frighten Luca going to him when things closed down after eleven. By then Lyara would be long gone, and Nash didn't want the Silvestris there when it happened—and that was something else he was going to have a fight on his hands about. It had been a long day and he wanted to get back to the hotel for some sleep, but he hit on a compromise. I'll stay here and guard the trailer tonight. Will that do? he thought. Having a mental battle of wills with a ghost was ridiculous. He waited and his phone didn't vibrate. Answer me, goddammit, he thought. In his frustration, he nearly said it out loud, but he drew the line at talking to the very dead Maxwell Jones where he could be heard.

When he saw them, it took all of his powers of persuasion to get Aurora to agree to his suggestion of hypnosis. Surprisingly, he won Mauritzio around quickly.

'If it helps to find my son's murderer, and it's safe for Luca, I'll do anything.' That went better than he'd thought. But, Aurora dug her heels in.

'Let me understand you, Inspector. You want a performance illusionist to hypnotise my son? Have you lost your senses?'

Believe me, Mrs Silvestri, I wouldn't suggest this if I didn't think it was necessary. Luca is traumatised, and I believe he's the key to finding out who killed his brother. He knows, but he can't, or is too frightened, to say.'

'Bence isn't a doctor.'

'I know, and I've considered calling in a professional therapist to conduct the hypnotism, but think about it, who better than somebody Luca already knows and trusts? Bence is his friend.'

'Isn't he also a suspect?'

'No more than anybody else on the grounds, and I'll be there to keep an eye on Luca.'

'I don't know.'

'Neither do I, Mrs Silvestri, but as your husband said, at this point I'm willing to try anything.'

They went around in circles before Aurora reluctantly agreed if Jaeger could convince her it was safe. As well as losing his job, Nash could lose his reputation over this. It was highly unethical to bring in a layman, but he was clutching at straws.

Jaeger was another matter. Nash thought he'd be the easy one. He opened by throwing the same argument at Nash that Aurora had. 'I am a performance hypnotist. I use my skills for entertainment purposes. What you're suggesting is suspect at best and I could lose my position in the Magic Circle if word of this ever got out. I'm not licenced to conduct medical hypnosis.'

'But of course, you're legally entitled to be in Prague. You passed the proper border controls, and your passport and work visa are in order?' Nash said.

Jaeger shut up.

'This boy needs help.'

'Are you threatening me, Inspector? I've heard the British police stoop to blackmail when it suits them.'

'No, absolutely not. If you refuse, I'll walk out of this trailer without another word and we'll say no more about it. I'll get straight on to the authorities in the morning to get him professional help. But I've been told that Luca trusts you. His dad said you taught him magic tricks and spent time with him. I'm not threatening you, I'm appealing to you.'

When the deal was done Nash left the trailer. He was scared for the boy's safety that night. He was tired and hadn't planned on being up all night sitting in a cold field. He had to stay awake, and wouldn't be able to leave his post even to replenish his coffee. His mind was reeling about whether he was doing the right thing. Hypnosis wasn't something to be messed with, but Jaeger had given him some balanced viewpoints about the safety and validity of trying it with Luca.

'The official line is that hypnosis can't kill you and you can't be put under against your will. But it's been the subject of controversy. Accounts of fatalities or harm from hypnosis have appeared since the beginning of time. In the seventies, a leisure hypnotist asked a mother to regress to childhood—he implanted that she was hiding from monsters. Later, she sued him and reported that the memories, which weren't hers in the first place, had resurfaced often and damaged her for years. Other reports say that trance subjects were left in comas or suicidal. But I can assure you it's all urban legend, and the stuff of good stories.'

'Are you sure?'

'When I convince a subject that there's a fairy under his chair, do you think he's haunted by that subsequently? When I give them vinegar to drink and tell them it's an ice-cold beer, do you think this damages them at a later date?'

'I can't imagine his gut feeling kindly towards you after downing a pint of vinegar.'

By the time Jaegar agreed to do it, Nash was even less sure that he wanted him to go ahead. But he had nothing else.

When he left Jaeger, the grass was wet with dew and he dreaded the next eight hours. The moon was high over the circus grounds as Nash heard the sound of an engine in the distance. He saw a familiar van driving through the gate, and relief washed over him. Forgetting the wet grass, the case and the traumatised boy, he ran.

Kelvin parked the van and Nash burst up to him in delight. 'Where the hell have you been?' Nash said. They hugged, finding comfort in each other's presence. Kelvin looked amazing.

'Van broke down, don't worry, it's fixed. I missed you,' Kelvin whispered. 'And boy have I had an eventful trip.'

'I missed you, too, but I'm glad you're here now. What kept you? You look worn out. Are you okay?'

'All the better for seeing you.' He kissed him.

'Three days on the road must have been tough. How are you holding up? I've got an idea for us so that you can tell me all about it.'

'I'm okay. A bit stiff from driving, but otherwise all right. Why do you sound Machiavellian when you say that? What have you got in store?'

'How does you, me, a bottle of wine, and a midnight picnic in this spectacular location sound?'

'It sounds perfect. But why have I got the feeling that there's more to it than that?'

Nash kissed him long and intense. 'Ye of little faith. You're right though. I've got work to do tonight but we can combine it with some catching up. I offer you romance and you distrust me?'

'Spill, Nash.' Kelvin kissed him again.

'Okay, so there might be a tiny little all-night stakeout required—but we can talk.'

'And cuddle?'

'And cuddle, all night.'

Kelvin couldn't have come at a better time. The last thing he would ever do was put Kelvin in danger, but he felt comforted with the firearm issued under his police license holstered under his arm. Kelvin said he was well rested after anticipating they'd be doing some catching up and had pulled over for a roadside nap. Nash could have cried he was so happy. He'd have been delighted to see Kelvin at any time, but now he'd have no trouble staying awake. And he had the gorgeous Kelvin on hand to replenish his coffee flask.

He'd planned a clandestine stakeout to try and catch the killer in the act of sneaking around. Plans change. He could have put himself in grave danger and an out-in-the-open picnic close enough to keep an eye on the Silvestri's trailer would act as a deterrent to the killer. They didn't need to be quiet, other than not waking the carneys, if he came, Nash wanted the killer to see them and back off. He'd already picked a place where he could see the door and both sets of windows.

Kelvin held Nash close. 'I wouldn't have missed this for anything. I want to be here for you, no matter how hard it gets.'

'Thanks for being here. Your support means everything.'

They shared a connection that dimmed the chaos around them. In Kelvin's arms, Nash felt peace for the first time since he'd left England.

They held hands as they walked through the circus grounds as though they didn't have anything to worry about. Kelvin listened as Nash shared some of the supernatural aspects of the case. Despite not blindly believing the complexities, Kelvin offered his support and belief in Nash's abilities as a detective.

'I may not grasp all the details, but I believe in you. When there's a bad guy on the loose, you're the man I want in my corner. You're a great investigator, and you'll figure this out.'

Nash stopped to show Kelvin the carousel and told him about its eerie presence. Kelvin squeezed his hand. 'You're right. In this light, it's a scary thing. Want to take a ride?'

'Are you out of your mind? Not bloody likely,' Nash spluttered and they laughed.

'Spoilsport.' Kelvin said.

Chapter Twenty-Three

The circus slept in the ink of night. The castle and big top loomed like spectral figures against the sky. Nash and Kelvin huddled together on coats spread across the damp grass, their faces lit by the dim glow of a wrought iron lantern pulled from underneath the caravan that Quinn had given him to use as an office. Nash was amazed that it worked. The scent of damp earth mingled with their thrown-together sandwiches. Nash made their picnic in a hurry which showed Kelvin more than words how urgent it was to get out there.

'This is the fanciest stakeout I've ever been on,' Kelvin said as he bit into his sandwich.

'Been on many?'

'Thousands. Regular Saturday night entertainment at my gaff when the kids were little. We couldn't afford a telly.'

'Idiot,' Nash laughed. His breath formed a misty cloud in the cold air. 'We've got gourmet sandwiches, wet grass, and front-row seats to the Luca Silvestri Show. What more could you ask for?'

'And all for the low, low price of sleep deprivation.'

'It could be the highest price imaginable if I fall asleep. You couldn't have come at a better time, Kel. I'm grateful to you for doing this with me.'

'I love you. There's nowhere else I'd rather be.'

As they settled into their picnic, their eyes were trained on the Silvestri trailer nestled on the edge of the woods. The task was simple—ensure that Luca Silvestri made it through the night. But in the darkness, the ordinary took on an eerie quality.

At four in the morning, a rustling came from the nearby trees. Nash and Kelvin exchanged a glance, their senses on high alert. The Silvestri trailer was a stone's throw away from the edge of the woods, offering a clear view and a sense of vulnerability.

'Did you hear that?' Kelvin whispered, his fingers tightening around his flashlight.

Nash nodded. 'Probably a fox.' His heart pounded in his chest. He pulled his weapon but left the safety on. Together, they aimed their flashlights towards the source of the noise, their beams cutting through the darkness like blades.

And there it was—a figure emerging from the shadows, its form fleeting and indistinct. It moved with a swift grace, weaving through the trees with the dexterity of a shadow dancer. Nash squinted, trying to discern its features, but the figure was elusive, like a wisp of fog.

'He's going to the trailer,' Nash murmured, his voice carrying urgency and caution.

They watched as the figure drew closer, its silhouette growing more defined. It was tall, certainly younger than Nash and Kelvin. It navigated the terrain with an uncanny familiarity and fluid movements.

'Who's there?' Nash wanted the stalking figure to know he'd been seen.

The figure halted. For a split second, Nash caught a glimpse of its profile—a hideous inhuman face illuminated by the moonlight. It had a gleaming luminosity and enigmatic intensity. He grabbed Kelvin's arm in terror—and then relaxed when he realised the person was wearing a mask.

'He's seen us,' Kelvin muttered, his grip on his flashlight tightening.

Without warning, the figure changed direction, veering away from the trailer. And then it charged through the trees like a thundering behemoth, crashing through the undergrowth with a deafening cacophony. It was as if King Kong himself was rampaging through the woods.

'Wait here. Watch the kid,' Nash shouted.

He set off in pursuit, and as he ran through the dense carpet of mulch, his footsteps were muffled by the undergrowth. The moon's light struggled to penetrate the canopy and cast long shadows that danced around him. The figure emerged a hundred yards ahead. He was dressed in a dark hoodie and a mask that concealed his features. Nash tried to identify him through other means, his gait, and the way he moved, but it was useless. He was a shade in the night.

'Stop. Police.' Nash's voice boomed in the stillness of the wood, but his command was swallowed by the trees. He held the handgun tight, aware of a film of sweat making the handle slick. 'Stop,' he repeated, but the suspect ignored him and carried on running. Nash raised the gun, firing a shot into the air. The deafening echo reverberated through the forest, but the figure didn't falter. He ran in a frenzied sprint. His silhouette was only a shadow with no discernible characteristics.

Twigs snapped and leaves rustled, his respirations were laboured. The suspect zig-zagged through the trees. His movements were unnatural in their fluidity. Each dodge was calculated, every twist designed to elude capture. Nash had chased enough criminals to know this one knew what he was doing.

They reached a stream where moonlight glinted off the rippling water. The suspect didn't hesitate and ploughed in, splashing through the icy flow. His footfalls echoed like drumbeats. Nash followed, and the surge of adrenaline clouded his vision. The rocks beneath the water's surface were smooth and that made them slippery. He wasn't as surefooted as the man he was chasing. Not expecting a crazy chase through unforgiving forestry, he'd left his work boots in the office caravan and opted for soft shoes instead. He felt every pebble beneath his feet and cursed his vanity. When he slipped, his knee slammed into a boulder with a sharp pang of agony. Damn, that would be painful later.

He gritted his teeth against the hurt and pushed on. The chase led them into the wilderness, and the suspect's form melted in the night as he disappeared behind tree trunks to reappear further ahead. Nash's lungs burned, and his muscles ached, but he didn't stop running. His focus was locked on the figure ahead.

The gap between them widened. The suspect's agility gave him the upper hand. Nash's shouts were a futile attempt to halt the escape. The trees conspired against him. Branches clawed at his clothing and slapped him in the face as he pushed through the underbrush.

The suspect vanished into the darkness, leaving Nash alone in the wild woods at night. He doubled over, hands on his knees, gasping. His blood flow was a pounding drumbeat in his ears.

The forest was still, except for the displacement of nature resettling. He swept the area in frustration. He'd been close, so close, but the masked man got away. At times he was feet from grabbing him and being able to tear the mask away from his face to reveal the killer. The thought went through his head that he should have shot him in the lower leg anyway. And to hell with reprisals.

He turned back to retrace his steps, and the wood closed around him. He wandered in the dark for a long time disorientated and the relief on Kelvin's face when he blundered into the castle field warmed him.

'I heard a shot?'

'It's okay, just warning fire.'

'I take it he got away?'

'He burst through the tree line and disappeared into the streets of Prague. I stood no chance.'

'You were amazing, a regular action man. I may demand a replay later.'

'You'll be lucky, I'm knackered.'

'Did you see him, though?'

'I only caught glimpses before he got away.'

Nash was processing the encounter. 'It wasn't a complete disaster. Whatever that was, we saved a child's life tonight.'

'You did, you mean.' Kelvin said.

'No, both of us.'

By the time he'd fired, Nash was far enough away from camp for it not to rouse the troupe. As the circus field returned to an eerie calm, Nash and Kelvin talked about the person who'd emerged from the woods. The only thing they agreed on was that it was human. Nash had fulfilled his duty, keeping Luca Silvestri safe through the night and, in doing so, perhaps saving his family's lives as well.

The next morning, Nash filed his reports, including the ream of extra forms to justify why his weapon had been discharged. He brought Lyara up to date on the mystery figure running around in the night and arranged a search. A group of operatives were scouring the woods looking for any hints of the killer. There was no definitive proof that this person was the murderer but why else would he be skulking around in the dark?

The family had been asleep in the trailer and Nash guessed his plan was to take them all out. He could imagine Luca's face if he'd seen the terrifying figure waking him from sleep and looming over him.

Nash was trained in profiling but in the dark, he hadn't been able to make out much even with the beam of the torch. The person was probably male, of average height and wearing a mask. It could be one of many people in the camp. In the brutal light of morning, he couldn't even be sure now that it was a man—hell he couldn't be sure it was even human.

Quinn and Jaeger stood outside Silvestri's trailer. It was a dull day and the cloudy sky cast a sombre mood over the camp. It was one of the better trailers on site. Luca Silvestri, the fragile twelve-year-old, was waiting for them to start his hypnosis. Nash imagined he'd be terrified.

He knocked on the door and they went in. Luca's eyes widened in terror when he saw the three men. His breath hitched and he seemed close to a panic attack. Nash was doubting his wisdom in not allowing the boy's mother to be there.

'It's okay, son.' Nash said. He remembered his battered face. 'Don't mind this. It was those silly protestors yesterday. But I did my Kung Fu Panda on them. They won't mess with me again.' He did a karate chop with his hand but the boy didn't smile. His eyes were on the floor, and he was apoplectic with fear.

'Luca.' Nash tried to reassure him. 'We're going to help you. You know why we're here, we talked about it with you and your parents yesterday. And Bence is going to be with you. He can help you remember what happened that night if you're willing to give it a go.'

Luca's lips trembled, but no words escaped. He looked confused as if deciphering something he didn't understand.

'Luca,' Jaeger spoke to him softly, 'I'm here to help you. I can end your pain. I promise this won't hurt. I understand you might be scared, but we're here to sort this out. Hypnosis is a powerful tool that can make you better.'

The boy was unresponsive. It was creepy.

'You'd like that, wouldn't you? To get well?'

There was a vulnerability in the child, the sense of a trapped animal looking for a way to escape danger.

'I can stop your pain, Luca,' Jaeger said.

'Hey, Luca,' Quinn interrupted. 'You're a brave kid, and you've got nothing to be afraid of. We're all here to support you and make sure you're safe.'

Luca's silence persisted, and Nash felt a new terror in him that went beyond what had happened before. As he watched the child, he saw the tremor in his hands and the way he clutched his T-shirt to seek comfort.

'I think it might be best if it's just the three of us. Too many people in the cramped space are overwhelming him,' Nash said to Quinn. 'You can wait outside if you don't mind. We'll call you in if we need you.'

Quinn smiled at Luca and glared at Nash on the way out as though he wanted to kill him. The door closed, leaving Nash and Jaeger alone with him.

'All right, Luca,' Nash said. His tone was a shade more authoritative. Many times he'd persuaded people—especially children—to talk by adopting a calm air of authority. 'We need to know the truth, son. We can't proceed unless you're comfortable. If you want to stop at any point, just let us know, but we do need to find out what happened to Alessio.'

Jaeger gave him a warm smile that Luca didn't see, to convey a sense of trust. Luca's anxiety deepened with every second.

'Luca,' Jaeger said, 'I can see how afraid you are, but I promise I won't let anyone hurt you. We're going to help you remember what happened to your brother. You want to tell us the truth, don't you?'

Luca didn't answer.

'Sure you do. Are you ready?'

Chapter Twenty-Four

Nash was aware of the weight of Luca's terror. He thought they might have to call it off. The boy was traumatised and Nash sensed it was more than a fear of the hypnotic process. He was shocked because the kid wasn't recognisable from the stories about him. The troupe talked about an outgoing lad with unnatural strength for his age, and a maturity about him. A daredevil flying through the air every night.

This child was a waif and seemed so much younger than his twelve years. Nash was used to interviewing kids. Some of them were younger than Luca, who smoked, and thought nothing of having a joint for their breakfast.

'We can take as much time as you need, Luca,' he assured him. 'There's no rush. Just tell us when you're ready, son.'

There was a darkness in the boy that he couldn't comprehend. He knew things they didn't. Was he more than just a witness? Something filled Luca with dread and kept him locked in silence. Nash remembered Carter Finch—the country's youngest-ever serial killer—and he shuddered.

He pushed his concerns aside to focus on getting results. Their investigation hinged on the boy's ability to break free from his trauma and find the strength to speak.

The tension in the room grew. He heard the distant noise of the troupe, and the murmur of the trainers in rehearsal, but it did nothing to calm him. If Nash's pulse was racing, he dreaded to think what the strange boy was feeling.

He looked as if he was gathering his courage, and Nash thought he was going to speak. But he didn't. He raised his eyes, his lips trembling in a silent agreement to begin the session.

Nash exchanged a look with Jaeger to take it easy, and the hypnotist opened the process in a soothing voice, guiding Luca into a state of relaxation. Luca resisted and Nash watched a formidable battle of wills as Jaeger worked to put him under and Luca fought against it. As the room settled into a hushed stillness, and only Jaeger's voice rounded the angles with sound, he saw the tension leave the child. He was powerless to resist the lure of Jaeger's voice. Nash wondered what terrible secrets were buried in the locked-in parts of Luca's mind, and what horrors they could uncover. Never mind Luca, Nash was apprehensive enough to crave a calming tot of whisky. If this went wrong, and the child was harmed in any way because of it, his career was over.

Nash saw the first trace of progress as the boy surrendered to the hypnotic state. They pressed on. The dimly lit room was filled with uncertainty, but the boy had relaxed into a form of sleep. Luca sat on a floral sofa. When Jaeger told him to open his eyes, he straightened. His gaze darted around the room as if expecting something dreadful to happen and he looked as though he didn't recognise where he was. Jaeger was a commanding but gentle man with a piercing stare. Although he was sitting, his presence loomed over the boy. His confidence met Luca's barriers head-on, but Nash could see that breaking through them wouldn't be easy.

There was an eerie pressure that amplified the tension and threw it back at them. Luca's fingers traced the ragged tassels of one of the rose-pattered cushions. He reminded Nash of cornered prey that had given up the fight. The shadows played cruel tricks. They cast haunting shapes on the walls that mirrored the darkness holding Luca's mind captive.

'Can we turn on a light?' Nash said. 'It might help him.'

Jaeger glared at him for speaking after the session had started, and Nash shut up.

The mentalist spoke in a hypnotic voice as he delved into the depths of Luca's psyche, and his eyes seemed capable of peering into the middle of his soul. Jaeger's demeanour was a paradox—a blend of soft compassion and powerful strength. The trauma locking Luca's voice needed resolve and unshakable belief in the power of the human mind to break through it.

Luca's distress was everything. It hung over the trailer and suffocated any space so that Nash found breathing difficult. The boy's silence was the steel fortress that gave him somewhere to hide from the horrors he'd seen that night.

'Luca, listen to the sound of my voice. You are safe here in this sanctuary of healing. Let go of the burden weighing you down. I can end this,' Jaeger said.

With each carefully chosen word, Nash saw Luca's shoulders relax more. His breaths were less frantic, syncing with the rhythm of Jaeger's cadence. Hope flickered in Nash as he saw a glimmer of progress. At least the boy didn't look as though he was about to start convulsing.

'Imagine yourself in a place where the warmth of the sun holds you, where gentle waves whisper secrets to the shore. Feel the weight of your burden lifting from your shoulders, like a feather caught on the softest breeze, and drifting away.' Jaeger's voice was out there as a lifeline for Luca to grasp onto.

Luca's eyelids drooped as Jaeger took him deeper. His body eased into the sofa surrendering to the pull of tranquillity. Nash saw the walls of the fort crumble one brick at a time, and a sliver of light penetrated the darkness holding Luca prisoner.

With the twelve-year-old in a relaxed state, Jaeger moved to the second part of the session. Nash expected it to test the limits of trust and vulnerability. Jaeger's voice was a gentle whisper, 'Luca, you are safe. You are in control. You can stop this at any time. But know now that I can end your pain. Listen to what I've told you. I want you to go back to the night your brother disappeared. Can you see anything? It's okay if you can't. I'm here with you to guide you.' Jaeger's voice maintained its calm tone as he said, 'Luca, I want you to recall the night your brother disappeared. You're holding out. Well done, you're a good lad, but secrets are dangerous. Do only what I have told you, and trust that what I say is keeping you safe.'

Silence filled the room, stretching into a dead space. Nash saw the struggle in Luca's eyes as he battled with the memories he'd locked away. The boy's lips quivered, but no words escaped. Nash's heart sank as he watched. The trauma ran deep, and the barriers were too hard to breach.

Jaeger persisted, 'It's okay, Luca. Our minds are in tune. Listen to my words and remember the secrets we used to share. You understand me don't you?—We understand each other. It's good to talk, but you don't have to say anything if it's too difficult. Just trust in me, and let your thoughts flow. If you feel comfortable, share what you can with me.'

The seconds ticked by, weightier than such a small passage of time should be. Luca's face contorted with emotions, and tears welled in his eyes. He opened his mouth to speak, but the pain held him captive. Nash fought his own frustration. Patience was hard, and giving Luca the time he needed was even worse when his life was at stake.

'Luca, I'm your friend. We're here to help you find closure, but you need to trust me.' Jaeger said. 'Sometimes our mind plays tricks on us, making things seem different than they are. Focus on the feelings, not the details. It's your feelings that are holding you in check. The way you feel is what's important. I'm more powerful than whatever's troubling you. Your brother deserves justice, and you deserve peace. Together, we can make that happen. I can take you to a place of peace. Listen to my voice and remember.'

Luca's breathing was out of control again as he grappled with his emotions. His hands clenched into fists, a reflection of the inner turmoil he faced. He looked terrified but there were no words.

'Relax. And be calm. Succumb to my will. I'm taking you back down to that calm, safe place. Come to me. Remember, I am more powerful than your fear. Submit it to me. I can end this.'

As the session continued, Jaeger tried different approaches to connect with Luca, but the boy's walls were impenetrable. It was as if the night of his brother's disappearance had swallowed him whole, leaving nothing but a shattered spirit.

Luca's gaze was distant, caught somewhere he couldn't escape. His fingers fidgeted, a physical manifestation of his turmoil.

The pressure weighed on his fragile shoulders, and his words were trapped. The hypnotist's eyes bored into Luca's, urging him to find the strength to unlock the prison of silence.

'You're safe, Luca,' Jaeger whispered. 'I am keeping you safe. Nobody will judge you, and no harm will come to you. This is a space of healing and trust. Do you trust me, Luca?'

Luca's eyes were wild. A spark of determination seemed to awaken in him. Nash tensed, waiting for him to speak. Luca swallowed as if steeling himself for his first words in weeks. But they remained unspoken, held back by an invisible force that was insurmountable.

The room was a pressure cooker of emotions simmering below the surface. Nash's mind raced, searching for a way to chip away at the castle Luca had erected around his memories. If this didn't work he needed a Plan B.

'Luca,' Jaeger said. 'I know it's painful, but sometimes the only way to find healing is to confront the past. The truth can be a powerful salve for wounds that run deep.'

Tears ran down Luca's cheeks, but he couldn't find his lost voice. And Jaeger couldn't force the boy to speak. It had to come from Luca's readiness to face the truth.

'I understand it's difficult, Luca. Listen only to me. I'll be here every step of the way, guiding you.'

Luca started thrashing on the sofa and Nash put his hand out to Jaeger to stop. The boy looked as though he was going into convulsions. But Jaeger's voice raised and hardened. 'Your brother's memory deserves to be honoured. You hold the key to what happened that night. Remember, I am powerful. Listen only to me. Do what I tell you. We can seek justice together.'

Luca had no control of his body as it contorted and twisted on the sofa. Nash was as terrified as the boy and wanted to stop. But Jaeger was still talking. 'Answer me. You saw what happened. You've been threatened and told not to talk about it. They've told you you'll die if you do. Secrets are dangerous Luca. Succumb only to me. I can end this.'

Luca went into a grand-mal seizure. Froth bubbled from his mouth. His eyes rolled into his head and he jerked like one of the marionettes in the Prague Museum manipulated under skilful hands.

'Stop, Jaeger. He can't hear you. You're killing him.'

Jaeger paid no attention. He put his palm on the boy's head and carried on talking. It put Nash in mind of a scene from *The Exorcist* and he wanted to end the session.

'Healing takes time. Be still, child. You don't have to speak. You don't have to speak. Rest. You don't have to speak. But hear my voice and know my words. Come back to us, now.'

Nothing happened. 'Stop this, or I'll have no choice but to arrest you,' Nash said.

Jaeger didn't miss a beat in talking softly to the child like a father. He took the palm of his other hand and pressed it into Nash's damaged face, making him shout out in pain. He pressed Nash back using all the force he could muster through his body and into the hand to keep pushing Nash out of the way so that he couldn't make a grab for Luca.

'Come back to me, Luca. It's time to come back now. Hear my voice and listen only to me. Let my words guide you back to a calm and pleasant state. You can relax and open your eyes now, Luca.'

Luca's gaze softened, and the convulsion stopped. Jaeger kept talking to him and with time he opened his eyes. It seemed as if he might say something. But the moment passed, and he retreated into his subconscious, his face a mask of anguish.

Luca, still in a trance-like state, looked more drained than before. Jaeger put a hand on the boy's shoulder in a gesture of fatherly support. His voice dropped until he was almost whispering, the words like gentle waves lapping the shore. Quieter. Quieter with every word.

The room was heavy and the ticking clock broke the silence. Luca's eyes glistened with unshed tears, and his trembling hands clutched the armrest. Nash couldn't stand seeing the boy in so much torment. What was Luca seeing that he couldn't express? He felt the tempest of emotions raging under the surface and saw the pulse at the side of his neck throbbing.

'It's okay, Luca,' Jaeger whispered. 'You don't have to say anything if it's too difficult. We're going to stop now. I need you to come back.'

The silence stretched on. Luca's gaze was locked on an invisible point, his mind lost to inner thoughts. The night of his brother's disappearance had taken him, leaving only fragments of him behind.

There was no passing time, only the hypnotic state. Bence tried different approaches to reach the depths of Luca's pain and make him talk. But the boy's walls were laid with strong mortar.

When Jaeger gave up and brought him back from his trance, Luca's eyes fluttered open with an emptiness that tugged at Nash's heart. He was more drained than ever. Trying to confront his demons had left him vulnerable.

'You did well, Luca,' Jaeger said. His voice was like a gentle balm. 'Well done. Whenever you're ready, we'll be here to help you try again. Remember, secrets have a tendency to choke you. I can set you free from your pain.'

Nash waited as Luca realigned with the present like a flower opening its petals to the sun. He blinked, his eyes heavy with the weight of the memories he'd tried to suppress. Jaeger's hand was still on the boy's shoulder, an unspoken assurance that he wasn't alone.

'You did well, Luca. Never doubt that or worry that you let me down. I'm not angry with you. You did well,' Jaeger said.

Nash had hoped for more progress in their session and that the hypnotic state would unlock Luca's memories. But he understood that healing was a process with no shortcuts. It was a maze of complexity that needed patience and support but he didn't know if he could put the child through it again.

Nash reassured Luca that it was okay if he wasn't ready to talk when in reality, he wanted to shake the boy until he broke through to him. He smiled and told him how brave he was. And he hoped to God he could keep him safe.

The hypnosis had failed.

Chapter Twenty-Five

Quinn was sulking. He was the ringmaster and star of the show. Nash had shut him out of Luca Silvestri's hypnosis. For the boy's safety, they'd said. He, Isiah Quinn, was like an uncle to that child. He spent the rest of the day in a sullen mood.

As evening fell, his heart raced as he watched the carousel come to life under the moonlit sky. The lights danced, casting a glow over the old circus. He was scared of the rumours that had taken hold of the carnival. There was the curse and the ghosts of dead children haunting the ride, and while he was superstitious, he wanted to believe it was all nonsense.

And that was easier in the afternoons and evenings when the grounds were open and the rides and stalls were in full swing. Something that spread joy to so many people couldn't be evil. The only screams he ever heard from the ride were ones of excitement.

Ross Finley was off duty. Quinn saw him swaying on his feet with a can of lager in his hand.

'Hey, kids. Are you going to ride the horses of death? Guess what these circus fools believe—they say that if one of us rides the carousel we'll die. But apparently, it's safe for you guys.' He flung his hands in the air. 'Roll up, roll up to the greatest show on earth. For one night only, I am going to thrill you by taking my life in my hands. I'm going to ride the cursed beasts into submission.' He stumbled and almost fell over one of the little girls. 'Ravenswood, tell them about the ghosts of the children with gouged-out eye sockets.'

Ross was a hard man who scoffed at superstition and he'd been trying to get a rise out of Ambrose. When Quinn intervened, an argument with the drunken ground crew member had drawn a crowd. The tension in the air was thick.

'Go to your trailer and sleep it off, Ross,' Quinn said.

'There's nothing wrong with me, I've only had a couple of beers.'

'And the rest. I can smell the whisky on you from here.'

'Why can't I have a drink to unwind after slaving for you all day?'

'You can drink yourself into unconsciousness for all I care. What I'm saying is, not in front of the customers, you're scaring the children.'

Ambrose said, 'Get this bloody fool away from the ride. The bairns are frightened to go on it with all his talk of ghosts.'

Mothers pulled their children away, and the crowd was thinning. Only the curious stayed to watch the argument.

'Come on, Quinn,' Ross slurred. 'Let's prove to these in-bred idiots that there's no curse. It's all in their stupid minds.'

Ambrose's lips curled into a sly grin. 'You're that confident, are you hard man? On your head be it. Don't say you haven't been warned.' He called out to Quinn. 'To hell with him, Quinn. If he's not prepared to listen, it's his hairy arse on the saddle.'

'Don't be stupid, Finley. Listen to Ravenswood,' Quinn said.

Some of the carneys had gathered around, taking the place of the nervous public, and Ross couldn't lose face in front of them. Brave with alcohol and swagger he stepped up to the ride and bowed to the crowd.

Ambrose Ravenswood, looked more like a weasel now than Quinn had ever thought. He was mean-spirited and unkind. He nodded as Ross mounted, and then pressed the button for the ride to start. He took pleasure in doing it with a grand gesture and a flourish. The crowd was restless, and hushed whispers of dread filled the air as the carousel turned. Ross rode the horse, pretending to be a cowboy at a rodeo and raised his can of lager in celebration.

'See? Nothing to be afraid of. It's just a bloody ride.'

The carousel music rang out with its joyful tinny melody, and the rhythmic sound effects of hooves hitting the platform echoed through the night. Quinn watched in worried silence.

But nothing happened. The horses galloped in syncopation. Their painted eyes stared into the distance with the usual vacancy. There were no ghostly apparitions or haunted whispers. Just the sounds of the circus, of Ross' laughter, and the rush of the wind.

Quinn let his tension release and laughed as Ross clung to the carousel horse. 'Okay, smart-arse. It looks like you were right. Maybe it only takes the ones God wants in heaven,' Quinn joked with a playful glint in his eyes. 'No curse, no ghosts. Just a bunch of superstitious claptrap.' He wished he believed that, but neither Alessio or Selena were killed as the ride turned. His false optimism was a show for the crowd.

He'd said it to restore the public's faith in the circus. If word got out that one of his rides was unsafe it would ruin him. The crowd laughed at Ross but cheered as he dismounted and bowed with a renewed swagger of bravado. Quinn and Ross exchanged a nod in agreement that he had debunked the rumours plaguing the carnival, and Quinn tried to believe it.

'Now go and sleep it off, you rebel,' Quinn gave him a playful shove toward his trailer. If he survived the night, Finley might have done some good after all.

The carousel spun and one ride followed the next as the tickets sold to eager children and couples in love. Its lights twinkled and danced with stars in the darkness. The laughter of the children drowned out the lingering doubts.

But as he scanned the grounds, he knew something evil was lurking out there. There was a black energy about the place, a tinge of unease clinging to the shadows. He brushed it off as his imagination playing with him, and the remnants of the spooky stories they'd all had a gutful of.

The carousel ride continued without incident until closing time, as it did every night, making the tills ring. The rumours of the curse faded into the background for another night—but every carney wondered if they'd see Finley again. Several of them took turns checking on him and reported back that he was sleeping in his trailer.

At the end of the working evening, Ambrose Ravenswood called Quinn, his expression grave. 'You will see the truth, Quinn. The curse is real, and the ghosts of the past are restless. They demand justice, and won't stop until they have it.'

'Shut up, Ravenswood, or I'll have you sent to an old people's home.'

'The spirits of the lost children are trapped between worlds, seeking revenge and release from their torment.'

'I'll release you from your torment in a minute.'

Quinn was drawn to mysteries, but a haunted carousel was a new one for him. The night had taken a strange turn. Ross wasn't normally a drinker and Quinn had never seen him drunk before. It was another sign of the times. He'd downed more than his share of alcohol, and it was clear the booze had taken its toll. Quinn couldn't rest until he'd checked on his worker. He found him out of bed and slumped on the floor of his room.

'Easy there, Ross. Let's get you back on your bed, mate. You've had enough excitement for one night.'

Ross mumbled something incoherent around a mixture of laughter and slurred speech. His eyes were unfocused, and his feet had no purchase.

Ross' trailer was a small rundown metal box tucked in a corner of the field. It was still covered in red paint from the protestors' attack but was smudged and faded after a first attempt at scrubbing it off.

Quinn helped him up. 'I'll get you some water.' Something was wrong and he tried to keep the concern from his voice. He went to the kitchenette and filled a glass from the tap. Ross followed him but couldn't stand and slumped on a worn-out couch. His eyes were dilated and vacant. He'd stopped laughing and terror replaced his mirth.

'Quinn. I'm dying. Make them go away.'

'Don't be daft, Ross. You've had a skinful, that's all. You'll be fine in the morning.'

'They're here. Can't you see them? They've come for me.'

'You're talking rubbish, old friend. Let's get you back to bed.'

'I can see them, the children from the carousel. They're here, in the trailer, surrounding me.'

Ross was terrified, his eyes couldn't have been any bigger and his face looked clammy with sweat breaking out on his forehead. He was uncoordinated and had no muscle control.

'You've had too much to drink, Ross. It's just your mind playing tricks on you. You'll be fine.'

Quinn watched Ross trying to swallow a build-up of saliva in his mouth. His tongue came out, thick and grey and as his head fell backwards the spit emptied from the corner of his lips. He couldn't swallow. He was trying to talk and it was difficult to make out anything he said.

'I'm not imagining it. They want me to go back to the carousel. They're telling me to ride it again.'

Ross was in a bad way and it was more than just alcohol. This was either a terrible psychotic episode—Quinn had seen similar in a young carney with schizophrenia—or Ross had been drugged with some kind of hallucinogenic. He was in his forties and one of the most stable and hardworking men Quinn knew. He was down to earth and rarely drank, not to this extent. He'd never take drugs. But this looked like a drug-induced state making him see things that weren't there. Quinn needed to stay with him so he didn't do anything reckless or hurt himself.

Ross swatted his visions. 'Tell them to go away. You see them, don't you? There. Look at their ghostly faces, their eyes are black. I have to go back to the carousel.' Ross was incoherent and deciphering what he said was difficult. Quinn tried to calm him. He assured him that it was in his mind, but Finley Ross' panic grew.

In the middle of the night, when the ground was shut down, a haunting tune filled the air. It came in through the open window and swirled around them in the semi-darkness. The eerie music of the merry-go-round made Quinn's blood turn to ice. Damned Ravenswood was terrorising the castle grounds to stir up trouble. Everyone was supposed to be asleep.

He rushed to the window and peered out. It was an impossible sight—the carousel was spinning on its own, the lights flickering in a psychedelic dance as lights went on in all the trailers. The horses looked more alive than the scenery around them—bright and colourful. Quinn fancied their painted eyes were glowing with an otherworldly light and berated himself for getting caught up in the craziness. He was cold and frightened, and Ross was interspersing gurgling with screaming and fending off invisible hands. Quinn grabbed him. 'Calm down, you daft bastard.'

Nobody had turned off that damned music.

When Ross was quieter, the fight left him and he wasn't moving or trying to get away. He slumped unconscious onto the sofa after mumbling a few words that Quinn couldn't make out. When he lifted Ross' hand it flopped back to his side.

He was out of it.

'I'm going to shut the ride down, Ross, and I'll be straight back. You just relax, I won't be long.' He felt ridiculous talking to an unconscious man.

There was no response. Finley's eyes were closed.

As he left the trailer, something barged into him in the darkness and pushed him off the steps. He sprawled in the grass but couldn't get up. He'd twisted his ankle. The man was on top of him. It was black and he wore a mask, and some kind of cloak. The attacker was stronger than him. Quinn was powerless to fight, and trying was a waste of energy when his arms were pinned. He felt a blow to his head and the world went black.

Quinn opened his eyes and the first thing he heard was the calliope music. That bloody music again. It was still playing. He didn't know how long he'd been knocked out but didn't think it was long. Surely only minutes. He put his hand to the side of his head and when he felt around the tender area, his fingers came away sticky with blood.

He used the steps of Finley's trailer to haul himself up and tried to walk. Somebody was calling his name in the distance.

As he gathered his wits and came to full clarity, he limped across the field to the ride. What chilled him was the crowd that had gathered around the carousel. Every performer and crew member had come out of their trailers, drawn by the music like the pied piper's rats. They all looked stupefied. They surrounded the eerie spectacle. He identified specific figures in the gloom and the detective was trying to push people back and maintain order. He had a phone to his ear.

'Where's Ravenswood?' Quinn shouted.

Jimmy was terrified. 'Do you see it now, boss? The carousel is alive. The children are calling us.'

Quinn's mind raced, trying to make sense of it. Everybody was confused and looking to him for answers. They couldn't look away from the horror. Their eyes were fixed on the spinning ride. The vibrant colours had taken on an otherworldly hue, and the lights pulsated like a psychedelic dream.

They were staring at one thing as the ride rotated and the horses rose and fell. Ross was slumped over one of the mounts. This was impossible. Quinn had just left him unconscious in his caravan. Hadn't he? How long had he been out?

This wasn't the same Ross who had bravely ridden the carousel earlier. This apparition was pale and lifeless. His eyes had been removed and the sockets were empty. His spirit had been sucked out of him.

Mac was at Quinn's side. 'The mechanism must be jammed, boss. We can't turn it off.'

'Have you been on it while it's in motion?'

'Yes, but only to try and stop it. We haven't been near the horses.'

'Where's Ravenswood?'

'Damien went to fetch him, but that was a few minutes ago.'

'He's coming now,' Jimmy shouted.

Damien was marching Ambrose across the field with his arm twisted up his back. The old man's face was bleeding and he was having trouble standing.

Two of the carneys ran over and Nash shouted at Damien to release him.

Ravenswood was bent over but looked up and saw Ross' body. He seemed surprised. 'I warned him. I have witnesses. You heard me warn him not to do it.'

'Just shut it off, man,' Nash shouted. How had Nash and his boyfriend got here so fast? He must have been knocked out for at least half an hour, maybe longer.

Ambrose jumped on the ride and pressed the red emergency button to bring it to an immediate stop. Ross' body was pushed higher onto the wooden horse's neck, forcing a stream of accumulated breath out of his diaphragm. Belinda screamed when she heard it.

Three seconds later, the ride was motionless. The music wound down like bagpipes expelling the last of the air.

There was total silence. And Mac was the first to speak.

'We tried that,' he said. 'We pressed that sodding button for all we were worth.'

'Maybe it was jammed,' Nash said. An oil can they'd used on the mechanism was on the floor by the side of the ride.

Quinn waited until it was still before he jumped on and rushed to Finley's side. 'Jesus Christ, Ross.'

Nash was shouting at him to get away. It was a crime scene now. The backup was on its way. Words. Just a lot of empty words that didn't mean anything.

Quinn was dazed. Nash and Mac pulled him away from the carousel.

'It's all right, Isiah,' Nash said. 'We'll look after him.'

'Nothing can hurt him now,' Kelvin said coming closer to support Nash and help in any way he could. Quinn saw him averting his eyes from the body.

Quinn was aware of Nash and the boss hostler selecting some of the carneys to move the rest of the crowd back and encourage them into their trailers.

With the hypnotic music and movement of the carousel, the troupe had been motionless, their eyes glazed, under the powerful spell. They had to be physically moved away, and their senses only kicked in when they'd turned from the ride. The lights had dimmed, and the silence broke their trance.

'What have you done?' Ambrose Ravenswood's voice boomed. His anger settled over the field. He stood at a distance, his eyes ablaze with fury. 'You were warned. This is not my fault. You were all warned.' His voice rang out like a prophet on a soapbox at Speaker's Corner in Hyde Park.

Quinn's legs went from under him and Nash laid him on the ground, keeping a watchful eye on him as the world came back into focus. Somebody produced a brown paper bag for him to breathe into and, despite fainting, he took a second to wonder where it had come from so fast. He felt the colour return to his cheeks, and his breathing steadied, but his eyes held a lingering fear.

'Are you all right?' Nash asked.

'Do I look all right?' Quinn was bewildered. 'He saw them. The children. They were calling to him.'

Nash helped him to sit up, supporting him as he regained his balance.

'I thought he was hallucinating. Off his head on drugs,' Quinn said, trying to understand what he'd seen. 'They play tricks on you—drugs. But now he's dead. Just like Ravenswood said.'

'There will be a scientific explanation, other than curses. We'll take him away, and find out what happened to your friend. Just try to relax.'

'It was real, Nash. Ross felt their presence and their pain. He knew they'd come for him. He said so. He begged me to help him, but I just left him on his sofa to be taken.'

The police arrived and put a white windbreaker around the side of the ride where Ross lay over the neck of one of the horses. Quinn was still on the ground, propped against Belinda's trailer. They tried to get him inside, but he wouldn't move until Finley had been taken away. He listened to the SOCO camera shutters and sipped the strong cup of tea that Belinda pressed into his hands. He hated tea.

Ambrose Ravenswood came over, his weasely expression softened by a hint of concern. 'I'm sorry you had to experience that,' he said. 'My carousel holds a history of darkness, and its past sometimes resurfaces in unsettling ways. Tonight, you saw that I'm the only one who can control it.'

Quinn was a man of reason but he lived his life following mantras and superstition. The events of the night shattered his belief in good karma and pitched him into a spiral of negative folklore. He alleged that Finley had seen the dead children and they'd called him to his death. He couldn't shake the thought of them haunting Ross.

'How are you, Quinn?' Nash's voice pulled him from his reverie.

'I don't know. Everything feels surreal. I don't know what to believe anymore.'

'Sometimes, the things we don't understand are the ones that hold the most truth, but I think what happened to Finley Ross can be explained in earthbound terms.'

Quinn shuddered. He thought about the ghostly visions that had haunted Finley and the eerie sight of the carousel turning on its own.

'I want to know the truth and understand what's going on.'

The circus was a battleground of illusion, and Quinn was relying on the detective to restore order. Otherwise, he wouldn't have a circus left to save.

Chapter Twenty-Six

Leaning against the faded wall of his trailer, Quinn took his usual position and looked over the bustling carnival grounds. After a restless night and no sleep, he still couldn't come to terms with the loss of Ross. Despite many disagreements, the two had been good friends. Sometimes the loneliness got to him and last night was no exception. He'd cried for the loss of his friend.

The setting sun did little to warm the scene because, in a trailer further down the field, he heard a storm brewing—a tempest of emotions that had been on the boil since Alessio was murdered. Quinn should have been more supportive of the younger members of his troupe, but with everything going on, he'd taken his eye off the ball. A question ran through his mind on a loop. How the hell did the killer get Ross on the carousel with all those people coming out of their trailers to see what was happening? The darkness might have been enough to cover him from sight, and Ross must have been put on the horse at the back of the ride in the shadows. But damn, it was brazen.

The voices of Fauna and Flora, the identical twins who were part of the dancing troupe, were battering his ears with venomous intensity. The pitch was getting more ear-damaging with every screech. He couldn't help but listen, his curiosity piqued by the unrelenting fervour of their argument.

'I can't believe you said that. What do you expect me to do?' Fauna's voice trembled with anguish. 'This is my life. I can't abort my child like it's nothing. This baby is your niece or nephew. How could you?'

Quinn winced at the emotion in Fauna's words. He'd known her since she was a young girl. She was the quieter of the twins, and her eyes were full of dreams. The sudden need for adulthood had landed on her shoulders as her career was taking off. She was having a baby that she hadn't planned for, and that was a lot for anybody to cope with.

The sisters had been shaping into excellent bare-back riders. But when Fauna was forced to announce her pregnancy after bouts of crippling nausea had kept her from the circus ring, Quinn had no choice but to drop them from the act. He was disappointed that she'd got pregnant and had been hard on them that night.

'I can still ride, Mr Quinn. Please don't ground us. I've got some sickness tablets now, and I promise I won't be sick during a performance again.'

'It's not about your sickness, girl. It's about the baby. You're part of a dangerous act. One second of distraction, the smallest wave of nausea while you're standing on a horse's back, and the consequences could be dire.'

'What about me? I'm not pregnant,' Flora said.

'No, Flora. I'm sorry about that, but one identical twin without the other is like a comedy without punchlines. It's a magic show without a lady sawn in two. Worse, it's a dance routine without music—and speaking of dance routines, you'll join your sister with the dancers for tonight's performance. Learn what you can and stay at the back.'

They weren't happy, but dancing was something Fauna could still do without harming her baby. She was almost three months pregnant and her sister's retort was sharp, her voice laced with bitterness. 'You selfish cow. You talk about your life, but if you keep the kid, it's as good as over. What about our career? What about the troupe? You're only thinking about yourself, Fauna. And you're risking everything we've worked so hard for.'

'Give it a rest. You call me selfish. But you just want me back on the horses.'

'Damn right. And because of you, I'm still grounded, too.'

'You'll be fine, you can work without me until the baby's born.'

'Quinn's made it clear that without my darling identical twin, I'm just another pair of high-kicking legs.'

Quinn clenched his fists, torn between intervening and giving them privacy. But sometimes revealing insights were whispered behind closed doors.

'Selfish?' Fauna's voice quivered with indignation. 'You have no idea what I'm going through. This isn't about me. It's about life—I can't discard my baby like the unwanted script for a tragic play.'

Flora's laughter was cold, a contrast to the warmth of the fading day outside. 'What about Tomasso? You know what he wants. He's even spoken to Quinn about it. Did you know that? He's barely older than you, Fauna. A baby will ruin him.'

The acrobat was a talented young man with ambitions that soared as high as the circus tent. And he was aware of the competitive nature of circus life, and the fleeting seasons of success before he was too old to be a sensation.

'He needs to know you're keeping it after everything he's said. And he deserves his opinion,' Flora said.

Quinn admired Fauna. He was still devastated over Ross' murder and the fallout still to come from that. He didn't have time for petty squabbles, but this went deeper than a sibling row. It took courage to stand against the people she loved. With time, Quinn knew she'd be all right. The troupe would look after her whatever she decided.

Flora's voice dropped, carrying an undercurrent of jealousy. 'You were always the centre of attention. Fauna the golden child, the one everyone adored. Even when we chose our stage names, you had to have the prettiest one. And now you're pregnant, and stealing the spotlight again.'

Quinn tried to make sense of the bitterness in Flora's words. They shared a special bond. But envy and resentment had cracked their connection, casting doubt over the relationship that only they understood. Quinn remembered what Flora had said to him once. 'When I look in the mirror I see Fauna looking back. And when she looks, she sees me.' At the time, he thought it was beautiful. He didn't want that image shattered.

'Are you crazy? This isn't about attention. It's about love. And I won't let fear—or you—dictate my choices.'

'It's not just your career on the line.'

'I know. And I'm sorry, but it won't be forever. I love you.'

Flora was quiet for a few seconds. 'Just think about it some more. I hate it when we fight.'

'I've thought about nothing else for weeks. I love this baby, and you will too. I promise. You'll be the best auntie ever,' Fauna said.

Flora grinned and took her sister's hand. 'I'll try and get my head around it. I'm sorry I yelled at you.'

'Me too.'

'Can I be at the birth?'

'Are you kidding? Of course, you can. I can't do this without you.'

Things heated up and cooled down on the turn of a sixpence—but with volatile temperaments and bruised feelings, anger was never far from simmering over. The girls shared their identity and the only other people that could understand were Saar and Noor—and they couldn't escape each other if they wanted to. Quinn noticed Flora and Fauna spending less time together. Fauna was often with the other twins, and jealousy always flared during rehearsals. Before Tomasso came between them, they were close.

Two minutes later they were arguing again and Quinn swore he felt the ground shake when Flora stormed out slamming the door behind her.

He wanted to bang their heads together. Alessio, Selena and Ross Finley were dead. The circus was stuck in the horror of an intense murder investigation. And they were tearing each other to pieces over what should be a time of happiness. A horrible thought came to him. What if one of the girls was next? How could they ever grieve? It would be so much harder for them than anybody else. He imagined the pain of being confronted by the lost one's face every time the survivor looked in a mirror.

Quinn feared the show would be cancelled after Ross's death but was glad when it was decreed that nothing would be gained by closing. The animal feed bills still needed to be paid. PACE had shouted long and hard about closing the circus, but Nash appealed to them and said the loss of revenue would cripple them at a difficult time. The carousel was closed, and at his request, they replaced the police windbreaker with less obtrusive fencing to protect the integrity of the crime scene. It was one less worry, but Quinn was only going through the motions. His grief and turmoil about who would be next made functioning secondary to getting out of bed. He missed Finley, and with three members down, things were too different.

That night, as they dressed for the show, the air inside the makeup tent was thick with tension, each stifled sigh was a lead-in for the next war of words. Quinn and the rest of the girls were unwilling witnesses to the twin's emotions.

Fauna and Flora were the same in almost every way but had hearts as disparate as fire and water. They faced each other, their voices sharp enough to slice through the canvas walls. Fauna's, fiery hair cascaded down her back, and she clutched her belly, her eyes brimming with defiance. Flora, the mirror image of her sister, radiated a toxic blend of envy and anger. It was unlike her and Quinn was worried. Was the jealousy directed at her sister strong enough to spill out into other areas of the circus? He wondered if Tomasso might be in danger from Flora. That was ridiculous—but he remembered a bitter argument between Flora and Alessio not long before his disappearance.

Flora applied a thick layer of scarlet lipstick and her voice trembled with a rage that was barely contained. 'You can't be serious, Fauna. You're going to throw everything away for a kid?'

They were at it again. Same song, different verse.

Fauna's gaze held steady, her chin high and defiant. 'This is my baby, my choice.'

Flora sneered. 'It's going to trap you into selling hotdogs for the rest of your life. You'll be fat and ugly after it's born. You won't look like me—we won't be the same, and you can't be bothered fighting to save what makes us special. Do you want to be tied down while the rest of us perform?'

'Knock it on the head, you two,' Malory said looking at them through her mirror as she straightened her hair. 'Having to do this eight times a week is a ball ache enough without listening to you two knocking lumps out of each other.'

Quinn felt sorry for the sisters and remembered the arguments with his brothers. The girls had been inseparable but were torn apart by conflicting needs. On the horses, they had mirror imagery. They were a showstopper. Their balance and the way they moved with an ethereal beauty that defied gravity was spectacular. And for them to do that perfectly balanced in a balletic pose and standing on a cantering horse's back was amazing. Now their graceful movements were replaced with harsh gesticulations. And their sweetness had been turned ugly with cruel words.

Flora wasn't finished and ignored Malory. 'Remind me again about Tomasso. What does he think about this? Oh, that's right, I forgot. He's the one who wants you to get rid of it,' Flora said.

'He's coming around to the idea. He just needs time to get used to it.'

'That's not what he's telling the lads.'

Fauna's eyes flashed, and Quinn saw the pain in the angles of her face. 'That's enough, girls,' he said. 'You're going on stage, save your energy and prepare for that.'

'Tomasso's scared, Flora. We both are. But that doesn't mean I should kill my child because it's inconvenient.'

'You're naive. This isn't a fairytale. You're not going to have a happy ending with him. He's not ready.'

'Maybe it's time we redefined what our happy ever after looks like. Yours and mine. If you can't support me, nobody can.'

Flora's laughter was a sharp contrast to their light-hearted giggles. 'You're a fool, Fauna. And fools get hurt. I'm warning you, you need to watch yourself.'

'Enough,' Quinn yelled.

Flora stormed out of the tent, leaving Fauna crying. He hesitated, torn between the urge to comfort her and letting her work through it on her own.

Fauna sank onto a stool, her shoulders shaking as she let the weight of her sorrow engulf her. Quinn went to her with a cough to let her know he was still there. His presence was a reminder that she wasn't alone, despite the chatter of the other girls.

'Mr Quinn.'

He knelt beside her, and his hand brushed a tear from her cheek. 'Fauna, I don't know what you're going through, but whatever you decide, I'll support you.'

'I feel so alone.'

'With all this family around you? People may fall out, my dear, but you are never alone in the circus. We look after our own. A new baby in camp is something of joy, a celebration—and the next generation. This little one is your branch of the circus tree to keep our tradition alive. So pick your face up and smile. Be happy.'

They sat in the dressing tent under fluorescent lights and bulbs around the mirrors. The other girls were flying between the dressing room and makeup tent preparing for their performance. As they finished primping, they left to stretch. Their faces were painted like China dolls to be seen at the back of the audience. Soon, Fauna and Quinn were alone.

Fauna's unenviable choice was a third entity between them. The circus, with its magic and wonder, couldn't shield her from reality and the things people were forced to do. The echoes of the argument lingered and made the tent sour.

Somebody had bought Fauna a congratulations card, and a pair of tiny yellow booties hung from her side of the dressing station. Somebody was happy for her. Flora's side had a Rage Against the Machine sticker.

Quinn went to get Fauna a tissue from one of the other stations so that she could start her ruined makeup again. She was just getting her breath back and her sobs had stopped hitching when Tomasso stormed in, his usual charismatic smile replaced with a stormy scowl. With curtain in twenty minutes, this was all Quinn needed. He hadn't got himself show-ready yet.

Tomasso cast a furious glance at Fauna, seething with frustration. 'You're being unreasonable. This isn't the life I planned.'

'It isn't about you, Tomasso. It's about me having a baby.'

Quinn put a hand on the boy's shoulder but he brushed him off. 'That's enough, Tomasso. Can't you see she's upset?'

Tomasso clenched his fists and Fauna glared at him.

'Of course, I can, but she's being naïve.' Tomasso's voice was laced with desperation. 'We're artists. What do we know about being parents? She's only nineteen.'

'You weren't worrying about that when you were between my legs, were you? Sorry, Mr Quinn.'

Tomasso looked furious. 'Sorry, boss. I'll go.'

Fauna threw a powder compact at him and it glanced off his shoulder. 'You're not going anywhere, Tomasso Galli. I hate you. I wish I'd never met you. I wish it had never happened, but that doesn't mean that I'll get rid of it. You can walk away from this, but I can't. You're going to pay for what you've done to me. I'll kill you.'

'Trust me, you stupid girl. I'm already paying for it.'

Quinn's voice was calm. 'You're entitled to your feelings, Fauna, but so is he. He's worried about your future, and I understand his concerns. But, Tomasso, this is her decision.'

He turned to Quinn. 'She's not thinking straight. This circus is our future.'

'And what about our child? Doesn't it deserve a chance?'

The argument spiralled, and Quinn tried to diffuse the tension. 'Guys, this isn't helping anyone. Tomasso, you laid down like a man. I expect you to behave like one now. You both need to take a step back and think about what's best for everybody.'

Quinn's words broke Tomasso's resolve and his anger gave way to defeat. Fauna wiped her tears. And Quinn hoped their eyes wouldn't be red when they stepped into the ring—if they ever got that far.

As a fragile truce settled, Fauna stood up, her face a mask of anger. 'You don't understand, either of you. I'll make you sorry you crossed me. "Sweet Fauna. Good Fauna. Always thinking of other people." You don't know what I'm capable of.' She stormed out of the tent, the flap fluttering in her wake.

'Where the heck did that come from?' Quinn said.

'I've no idea. I thought she was calming down.'

They exchanged a helpless look, but before they could react, a crash came from outside, followed by a scream of pain.

Fauna was sprawled at the bottom of the steps to the raised platform, her body twisted at an unnatural angle.

'No.' Tomasso's voice was a guttural cry. His eyes were extended with shock as he knelt by Fauna's side. 'Oh, God. Not the baby. I'd never forgive myself.'

'Call for an ambulance. It's all right. She'll be okay. Let's keep calm.'

Time passed in a blur and each second counted them down to the performance. Quinn's mind was already working on replacements.

There were flashing lights, hurried voices, and the urgent scramble to stabilize Fauna's condition. He saw Nash and his boyfriend running across the field to help them.

As they loaded her onto a stretcher, Tomasso's face was a mask of guilt. Quinn put a reassuring hand on his shoulder. 'She'll be okay.'

'Can I go with her?' Tomasso asked the ambulance driver.

'You stay away from me, Tomasso Galli. This is your fault,' Fauna was crying.

The lights of the ambulance competed with the twinkling bulbs around the field as it pulled away, leaving them bewildered. The argument that was so important to Fauna, Tomasso, and all of them seemed trivial in comparison to the fragility of life and the twisting guiles of fate.

'Get her sister, and I'll start the car,' Quinn said.

'The show?' Tomasso asked.

'Sod the show. Mac can stand in for me tonight.'

When they got there, the hospital room was awash with sterile light, the beeping of machines a dissonant backdrop to the heaviness of their emotions. Quinn stood by the window. His eyes were fixed on the street below. He'd offered to wait in the corridor, but Fauna wouldn't hear of it. Quinn didn't know if he was there to act as a referee between them.

'You're like a father to her. She wants you here,' Tomasso said. He sat in a chair by Fauna's bedside, his fingers laced with hers as they watched the monitor beating a tattoo with their unborn child's heartbeat.

Quinn shouldn't be there. It was private, but he couldn't move from the window, not yet. When he'd heard the song of the little one's life on the monitor, a tear leaked from his eye and he felt like a fool. The tension that had driven a wedge between them was replaced by a palpable sense of unity—the kind that only comes from a parent seeing their baby for the first time, and Quinn was honoured to be part of it.

He remembered his own unborn child. He'd seen him once, on a machine much like this one. It was before the accident that took his wife and child from him. They were so happy that day. The next time he saw his son was when he said goodbye to him.

They delivered him the night of the accident, but he never breathed. Quinn called him Michael. His wife wasn't there to give her opinion and it was his heartbreaking choice to make alone. She'd died before Michael was pulled out of her stomach. And all these years later, some people still thought he was responsible for wilfully taking their lives.

He should go. He wiped his face and got as far as the door.

'Boss,' Tomasso said.

He had his hand on the door handle. He'd nearly escaped the emotion.

'Somebody here wants to meet his godfather—that's if you don't mind.'

He hugged them, and he cried like a fool. And the three of them laughed together, staring in awe at the light and shadow on the screen—buttocks, and hand, and head.

'Look he's already doing somersaults.' Quinn said. 'I'd be honoured to guide this young man. Maybe he'll be a great ringmaster,' he laughed as Tomasso gave him the rise he was after.

'He will not. He'll be a great acrobat.'

Quinn grinned. 'The best there ever was.'

'Have you two finished?' Fauna looked happier than Quinn had ever seen her, a real beauty.

'How are you feeling now?' Quinn asked.

'Better. They say we'll be fine.'

'I was so scared,' Tomasso said.

Fauna brushed a strand of hair away from his forehead. 'I was scared too,' she said. 'We do dangerous things for a living—but this little man fighting to live is real bravery.'

'My son,' Tomasso said.

'Our son,' Fauna said. 'He's called Gabriel.'

'I like that,' Tomasso agreed, and Quinn nodded his approval.

'It's such a shame that Flora was still mad with me and wouldn't come.' Fauna burst into tears again.

'Tomasso smiled and kissed her hand. She wasn't mad, darling. She spoke to the ambulance man before he drove you away and he told her you'd be fine. She had a show to do.'

'See. If she cared about us, she'd have come.'

'You're wrong. She gave me a message, and said to tell you that she loves you with all her heart—and that tonight she's dancing for both of you.'

'The circus is in your blood,' Quinn said.

He watched. The fractures in their relationship were healing, and their love was stronger than their doubts.

After the machine was turned off and the radiographer left the room, Fauna's smile left her. Her mood pivoted again, the perfect arabesque turn of temperament.

'What is it? Are you in pain? Should I get somebody?'

Fauna's expression shifted. 'Tomasso, you told me to kill our baby,' she murmured. Her words were slurred and the heavy sedation they'd given her to keep her and the baby calm was in full effect.

Her words gained momentum, growing more frantic. 'You wanted me to get rid of him because you did it, didn't you? You knew about the murders.' The change in mood had come out of nowhere.

'What are you talking about? I would never hurt anybody.'

'He's the murderer, Mr Quinn. It's Tomasso.' Fauna's voice escalated to a state of hysteria. 'Keep him away from me. He's going to kill me.'

Delusion had taken hold of Fauna, and she was terrified.

'That's not true. I would never hurt anyone, especially not you.'

Fauna's tears flowed, and her breath was ragged as she struggled to make sense of her thoughts. 'I don't know what to believe.'

Quinn was a steady anchor grounding their turmoil. 'Fauna, love. Tomasso was with you every time. He couldn't have been involved in the murders.'

'But he wasn't. I remember it clearly. The night Alessio disappeared, so did Tomasso. I saw it in his eyes, Mr Quinn. He's been lying to me.'

Tomasso's gaze pleaded with Quinn for understanding. 'We had an argument. I'd had to do the show and you were glaring at me, Fauna. In between dances, you were throwing up backstage in a bucket. I was scared and I felt so helpless. When all the commotion about Alessio erupted, I ran and hid in the castle walls to think about my future.'

'And what about when Madam Selena and Finley Ross were murdered?' Fauna asked.

'You were sleeping.'

A fragile silence fell over the room, the accusation and denial hung between them like a gossamer curtain that could heal or harm. And then as quickly as her mood had switched, it changed again.

'He's healthy,' she whispered. Her voice was filled with awe.

Tomasso looked confused. He was young and couldn't deal with life's experiences yet—or a pregnant woman's hormones. He had a lot to learn.

'It's the drugs. She doesn't know what she's saying,' Quinn whispered. 'We should let her sleep.'

But was it just Fauna's medication making her come out with wild accusations? He remembered one of his bally girls had developed a psychosis when she was pregnant, and there was a chemical imbalance in her brain. If that had happened to Fauna, what might she be capable of?

Tomasso's eyes softened at the mention of his child. He brushed Fauna's cheek. 'Our little boy,' he murmured, his voice filled with something fierce.

The love between them was as undeniable as the life growing in Fauna's womb. But the suspicion was a doubt that hadn't been dispelled for Quinn.

He stepped back, giving them the space they needed to heal. But he couldn't ignore the truth—it turned out that Tomasso couldn't provide a solid alibi during any of the three murders.

When Fauna had been interviewed by the police, she'd said they were together on all three occasions. Quinn noticed that she'd rested her hand on her stomach the whole time—who was she protecting?

He left the hospital. He couldn't keep this burden to himself and had to talk to Nash. The man Fauna loved might be connected to the events plaguing the circus. Tomasso hadn't been with them long, just under six months and he came with no history. No questions asked. Quinn wouldn't allow his thoughts to stray further than Tomasso tonight. He didn't want to think about the twins.

He'd known those girls all their lives.

His decision settled on his shoulders. Talking to the police wasn't the carney way, but Nash was a good man.

They needed a good one on their side.

Chapter Twenty-Seven

The autopsy report had taken almost twenty-four hours to come back. After talking through some of the relevant details with Quinn, it lay on Nash's desk as a reminder of the darkness ruling the circus. He read the findings again with his third coffee but there was nothing he didn't already suspect. Ross Finley's death was a bizarre puzzle, but the cause of death was clear. The pieces were coming together.

Nash's fingers drummed on the edge of his desk as he absorbed the information. The toxicology results painted a grim picture—psilocybe poisoning followed by strangulation. A kindergarten full of corpse children didn't kill Ross Finley. It was somebody very much alive.

Nash gave Quinn the basic facts. 'Psilocybe is a popular fungus known for its psychoactive properties. Most people know it better as magic mushrooms. It induces hallucinations and altered states of consciousness,' he explained. 'Ross ingested an astounding number of magic mushrooms. The sheer quantity was staggering, a disturbing glimpse into the mind of a murderer with no conscience.'

They talked some more until Quinn said he had things to do and left Nash to his thoughts.

Finley was drugged before he was murdered. Psilocybe feeds on paranoia. While Quinn and the crew were shutting down the grounds, the killer was in Finley's trailer forcing him to take them and filling his head with stories about the dead children and curses. The magic mushrooms took the horror stories, wormed them into his brain, and did the rest of the work. Later, while Quinn sat with him, the maniac set the carousel off to feed into Ross' paranoia and draw him to the ride. Then all the killer had to do was knock Quinn out, and strangle Ross. He carried him to the carousel to stage his tableaux. It was bold. The killer was strong—stronger than most men. And he could have been seen at any point. How did he get the dead man on a horse with all of those people standing around gawping at the ride?

Selena had seen the dead children but she was drugged, and so was Finley. Our killer is establishing an MO, Nash thought. The investigative team had been out talking to locals, the fields around camp were full of psilocybe. It was a well-known haunt for the local party people to take a trip to Happytown. Did the killer stumble on the crops accidentally, or did he know they were there?

Nash's spine tingled. The autopsy concluded that Finley Ross had been strangled and had his eyes removed. They were found in his jacket pocket. Had he seen too much? The graphic and unsettling details of the violence made Nash hurt for the state of the world, and he missed Kelvin when he wasn't around.

The connection between Ross' death and the curse was undeniable, but the motive was elusive.

A knock on his caravan door stemmed his thoughts, and he looked up to see Quinn with two breakfast rolls courtesy of Jolene.

'Have you got any further with finding the source of the magic mushrooms? They're not easy to come by,' he said.

Quinn could be trying to throw him off the scent. On the other hand, he could reasonably have no idea how easy they were to obtain at this time of year. Especially around the castle fields. 'On the contrary, Mr Quinn. It's common knowledge among the local youth and party scene that they grow prolifically here.'

'I stand corrected. However, the fact remains that someone gave him those mushrooms. And then killed him and carried him to the carousel. I don't know whether to be delighted or terrified that it wasn't ghosts.'

'Be scared, Quinn. People can hurt you more than stupid stories.' Nash leaned forward, his fingers tapping the autopsy report. 'I'm going to find out who had the motive and the means to carry out these killings. People are still lying and some of the alibi's are at best shaky.'

'I've been meaning to talk to you about that. I've looked into Tomasso Galli. His lack of an alibi during the murders is suspicious. And a recent argument with Fauna brought out a lot of accusations.'

Nash's brow furrowed as his mind raced to process the information. He opened a file and checked her statement as he bit into delicious sausage, bacon and egg. 'Fauna said they were together on all three occasions, they provided the alibis for each other—and the other sister was with them.'

'Not true, apparently.'

'What about the twins? They say they were together, but like many other statements, because they were sleeping, it can't be corroborated. PACE don't jump to conclusions. We need solid evidence over suspicions.'

'I know. But you can't ignore the signs, either.'

'Signs and omens and talismans. I'm getting fed up with all this hocus pocus. We'll keep digging and follow the evidence. The rubbish about curses stops now.' He banged his hand on the desk and his coffee mug jumped like a puppet. 'Put the word around camp. No more. Is that clear?'

Quinn smirked. 'I'll tell them. But you can't stop them talking.'

There was a knock on the door and Kelvin came in. 'I'm sorry. I didn't realise you were in a meeting.'

'That's okay. I was just leaving,' Quinn said.

They waited for the door to shut and Kelvin sat on the edge of Nash's tiny desk. His head touched the ceiling and he had to curl his spine and rest his forearms on his knees. 'Are you ready for lunch? I've had a fabulous morning in Critter Cave.'

'Crikey, is it that time already?' Nash didn't let on that he'd just demolished a huge roll. He put Fauna's file down and smiled. Kel had been in the sun. His black skin glowed and he made Nash want to jump his bones every time he saw him. 'Is that right? How the other half lives.'

'You wouldn't believe the fun I've had. It's been a hoot.'

Nash had a headful of work and murders but he felt his smile widening as he saw Kelvin's happiness. He reminded himself that one of them was on holiday.

'I stroked a lion. Can you imagine that?'

'I can. Imagine it. I wouldn't want to do it. I've heard that thing roar.'

'And Billy's taken a shine to me.'

'Billy?'

'The orangutang.'

'Right. I'm glad you've been making friends and influencing people.'

'All right, snarky. You need a shoulder rub.' He moved behind Nash as he talked. 'But I haven't come here to tell you about my Doctor Doolittle impersonation.'

'No? Afternoon delight in a tiny cramped caravan that smells of mothballs?'

'Dream on, big boy. No. While I was belly rubbing a lion and dancing with a bear I melded into the background, though with good looks like mine I can't see how.'

Nash laughed. 'I'm a busy man. Is there a point to this?'

'There is.'

'What did you find out?'

'The trainers were talking about Magnus. They mentioned something about a disagreement with Finley Ross.'

Ross was part of the ground crew. He seemed like an unlikely figure to be falling out with the strong man.

'Did you catch any specifics?'

'Not much, just that there was tension between them. Something related to Magnus' act.'

Nash's mind reeled. The puzzle pieces shifted again as new information was brought onto the board.

Nash and Kelvin had lunch together and then Nash said he had to get back to work. Kel was spending the afternoon painting scenery with Noor and Octavia. He said he'd see if he could find out anything else. If anybody could get people talking without realising it, it was Kelvin.

'Okay, but I'm very worried about you.' Nash had a serious look on his face.

'Don't worry about me. You've got enough on your plate. I'm fine. I can look after myself.'

'It's not that.'

'What, then?'

'You're enjoying yourself far too much. I'm scared I'm going to lose you to the circus.'

'You just want to see me in a leotard.'

'Get out of here.'

Nash had a full afternoon lined up, and he had a favour to ask of the clowns. After that, there was a more serious task to finalise. Tomasso was at the hospital picking up Fauna. She'd been kept in overnight but was free to come home with a full bill of health. It was with a heavy heart that Nash arranged for Tomasso to be apprehended and taken to the station for questioning. He'd lied in his interviews and had no alibi. Nash was being leaned on from above to bring him in.

Detective Nash and the PACE team gathered outside Tomasso's caravan. The couple weren't back yet, and Nash was using the time to make a thorough search. He had a lot of people to keep safe, and when they got there, his priority was getting the pregnant girl out of the way in case things were violent.

Nash stood with one hand holding a search warrant. His gaze was fixed on the caravan.

'What are you doing? Lyara asked.

'Looking.'

'At what?'

'Everything. Before going into a potential crime scene, you should visualise everything there is to see.'

Quinn looked sick, and Nash knew he had a soft spot for the kids involved. Nash said he had to wait outside so as not to contaminate possible evidence. The owner was still high on the list of suspects and Nash wanted him out of the way so there could be no tampering.

'All right. Let's start the search.' Nash stopped himself from calling them his team. These people weren't his team, they were temporary colleagues. His guys were a thousand miles away at home in England.

As a new arrival, Tomasso was allocated a trailer from the caravan graveyard. The interior was lit by the glow of a lantern casting flickering shadows on the walls. Nash's gaze swept over the space, taking in the cluttered shelves and personal belongings that spoke to him about Tomasso's life.

Lyara crouched, her gloved hands sifting through the items on a shelf. Nash scanned the room and saw everything that looked right—and the things that didn't.

He searched a sideboard and pulled everything onto the floor. After emptying all three drawers, he took them out and put them to one side. At the bottom of the space behind the drawers, he found a coil of rope. He covered his gloved hand in an evidence bag and took it out without contaminating it.

'What's that?' Lyara asked taking an interest and reaching for the camera.

'It's a rope, but not any rope. I'd lay money on it being the one used in the strangulation of Ross Finley. Get some pictures.'

'Already on it.'

This could be a breakthrough or a plant. He unrolled a rug in the corner expecting blood stains and laughed at himself when it was clean.

As they searched outside, Lyara found a baggie tucked behind Tomasso's caravan underneath his chemical toilet. She picked it up with forensic tweezers. Nash was glad she'd been the one to examine the unpleasant toilet. It crossed his mind that he should have taken the job himself and felt ungallant. But it was a fleeting thought. He recognized the residue at the bottom of the baggie—magic mushrooms.

Lyara laid it on the Formica tabletop and snapped some photos from several angles.

Quinn had seen Lyara pick up the bag and tried to step into the caravan. 'Get out. And don't touch anything.' Nash, was holding up the baggie. After having it photographed he'd put it inside an enclosing evidence bag.

Quinn's eyes widened when he saw it. 'What is it?' he asked. There was only a small residue of vegetable matter at the bottom. The delicate mushrooms with their fawn caps had lost their form. Nash had seen them before. Quinn might well be familiar with them, too. It could be a ruse to appear ignorant.

'Is that the magic mushrooms?' Quinn said. 'Are they the same kind that Ross Finley took?'

Nash ushered Quinn away to keep him clear of the investigation. 'Rest assured, we'll be having them tested for verification.'

Quinn's face was grim. 'It can't be a coincidence.'

'You understand that we need to bring Tomasso in for questioning?'

'Of course. Do what you have to.'

They waited for Tomasso to return from the hospital with Fauna. Nash had asked Flora to be there and get her sister out of the way.

As the taxi pulled up outside the trailer, Tomasso helped Fauna out of the car. He waved at them, and Nash saw Quinn wince as he waved back. Flora embraced her sister and gushed as she hugged her, tactically moving her away from Tomasso one step at a time. 'Hey, sis, how are you? I can't wait to see the picture of my nephew. I'm so sorry about yesterday. I was horrible.'

'It's forgotten. Come on, let's get inside, I'm dying for a cup of tea.'

'Before we go inside, can I borrow you for one second? I want to show you something.' She nudged her another couple of feet away from Tomasso.

'Can't it wait? She needs to get in and lie down. The doctor said complete bed rest. She shouldn't even be standing up,' Tomasso said.

'I'll bring her straight back.'

'Go,' Nash shouted.

Three officers came from behind the row of caravans to Tomasso and tackled him to the ground. The twins were escorted into Octavia's trailer which was closest. Nash saw the woman wrap Fauna in her plump, hairy arms and lead her to a seat. 'Cup of tea for the shock, my love. That'll sort you out.'

Nash's gaze locked with Tomasso who was handcuffed on the grass. This was a difficult moment, but Nash knew it had to be done. Lyara read him his rights.

'Tomasso Galli. You are under arrest on suspicion of the murders of Alessio Silvestri, Selena Debois and Ross Finley.'

Tomasso's disbelief mingled with a show of shock. 'What? Are you crazy? I didn't do anything.'

She cut him off, her voice unwavering. 'You have the right to remain silent. Anything you say can and will be used against you in a court of law.'

Nash's gaze shifted to the periphery. Flora was a few feet away, staring at Tomasso in disbelief. Beside her, Fauna was devastated, her tears flowing as she clung to her sister for support. 'What are they doing, Flo? What are they doing to Tomasso?'

Nash saw the pain Fauna was going through. She didn't need to see someone she loved being arrested.

Flora wrapped her arms around Fauna and he couldn't hear what they said, but he understood the depth of their connection.

Nash saw the turmoil in Tomasso's eyes. The anger, and perhaps guilt. He had done his duty, but he couldn't shake the unease.

As Tomasso was led to the police van, the worry settled on Nash's shoulders as he turned and walked away.

Chapter Twenty-Eight

Nash adjusted his nose. Knowing the family was rehearsing, he looked through the window of the Silvestri's trailer. The carneys were milling around doing the usual morning routines and Nash had rounded up the troupe's children to join them in the glorious sunshine. They sat on the grass excited for the break from their tasks and rehearsals.

It was worrying. If Nash could get this close to the family's trailer without being seen from inside, so could anybody else—and yet he'd been left alone. Nash would never understand the culture or dynamics. He didn't linger but wanted to check on Luca huddled on his bed inside.

The child wore depression like a straitjacket, and Nash was reminded again that this kid was twelve. He looked so weak. As well as reverting to childlike ways, he seemed smaller. With any other kid his age, Nash could have bribed him to snap out of it with a KFC, and the kid would have upped the ante by getting some Minecoins thrown in. The weeks since his brother was kidnapped had gone by in silence, and every attempt to break through his locked-in state fell short.

Hypnotism had failed, leaving Nash frustrated and helpless. Time was running out. He felt it. The killer had escalated his timeframe with Ross Finley's murder—he was bold. Invisible. He wasn't afraid to kill in plain sight and was a risk-taker.

It was time to instigate the next attempt to get through to the boy. He called the guys over. And Nash tapped on the window. He didn't want to scare him, so he moved with purpose and a wave—Luca was already frightened into silence.

His pale face appeared at the window as he knelt up. His shock was apparent as he looked at the unexpected visitors. But Nash was glad he looked like a kid on Christmas morning, and not one who'd seen the ghosts in the carousel. He'd never seen a little boy that looked so fragile. His eyes had sunk in their sockets—and he could have played with those dead children without standing out. Nash remembered Aurora saying she was making him smoothie milkshakes to try and get fluid and nourishment into him.

The four other clowns—Jellybean, Nifty, Shadow, and Jinx—had gathered on the grass outside, forming a semi-circle. They wore their usual mismatched outfits, each clown exuding a unique charm and presence.

With a flourish, Patches pulled a colourful megaphone from behind his back and held it to his mouth. 'Ladies and gentlemen, boys and girls, and our special guest, Master Luca Silvestri. Today, for one day only, this special day, we present to you an extravaganza that's bound to tickle your funny bone.'

Nash watched as Luca's expression shifted from wide-eyed surprise to a cautious interest. The clowns began their new routine, a choreographed skit that revolved around the idea of not talking. It was a delicate theme, given Luca's condition, but they wove it into a light-hearted performance that even had Nash chuckling—and he'd spent hours rehearsing it. Conrad Snow said Luca wanted to be a clown to bring joy into the lives of others. Despite being twelve, Nash hoped he wasn't too old to be enthralled by the show.

Jellybean mimed talking to a friend, with gestures and funny faces. Nifty tried to communicate using body language, resulting in a comical dance that had everyone in stitches. Shadow donned a pair of oversized glasses and pretended to read a newspaper, his expressions increasingly perplexed.

And then there was Jinx, the mute clown. With a huge plastic mobile phone in his hand. He launched into a series of hilarious gestures, telling a story about looking for his voice without uttering a word. His physical comedy was a hit, eliciting a laugh from Luca. Nash was delighted at his response.

As the routine reached its climax, Patches stepped forward with his megaphone. 'And so, what can we learn from all this laughter? Not talking is a lonely path, my friend. Our voices bring us together. They tell our stories, and they create friendships that can't be replaced.' Patches high-fived a couple of the children sitting on the grass.

The other clowns nodded, their painted faces reflecting earnestness beneath the slapstick. Nash watched as Luca's lips curved into a smile. He saw a glimmer of warmth in his eyes.

The performance ended with a bow from the clowns, and Luca's trailer window slid open. A smattering of applause followed, with Patches joining in. He grinned and winked at Luca, his painted face expressing genuine fondness.

'Remember, Luca,' he called out. 'Your voice is your superpower. Don't let it go to waste.'

'Use it or lose it,' Jellybean shouted, and Jinx, who'd been mute from birth, looked under a hedge for his missing voice.

As the other clowns waved and left, Patches stayed at the window. He felt lighter. It was a tiny moment, but it was still a step forward—the clowns had done what Nash couldn't achieve on his own. They'd cracked a smile from the boy who had been locked down for weeks, and Nash felt a renewed sense of hope.

Nash, disguised as Patches the clown, made a show of falling over his big feet. Luca's giggles were a precious sound and Nash felt that there was a way back for him. After suffering deep trauma, some people hid inside selective mutism for years—and some never spoke again. He wasn't going to let that happen.

'Hey there, champ.' Nash greeted him in a playful tone, his voice muffled by the ruff on the colourful clown suit he was wearing. As Patches, he was a riot of mismatched patterns—stripes, polka dots, and stars clashed and mingled in a parade of hues. A wide, floppy hat perched on his head, with a red pom-pom at the tip that wobbled when he spoke, and his shoes were enormous, making comical squelching sounds as he walked.

Nash gestured to the space inside the trailer. 'Mind if we come in, Luca?' Nash gestured Lyara over.

Luca's eyes sparkled as he nodded. Nash ducked through the doorway, his exaggerated movements causing his oversized shoes to squeak on the floor. He made a performance of it, then settled on the edge of Luca's bed, his posture intentionally comical. Lyara was there for safeguarding purposes and sat on the sofa in the living area waiting for them to come out. There was no room for three of them in the sleeping pod.

'Luca, my friend,' Nash said in a mock-serious tone, 'I've heard you've got a superpower, but you've been keeping it quiet. Is that true?'

Luca's laughter bubbled out of him, the sound was like music to Nash. He grinned behind the clown makeup, heartened by the response. Putting him at ease, he chatted playfully with Luca and mimed a conversation as Patches the Clown. He used exaggerated gestures, made silly faces, and pretended to get tied up in the curtains. It elicited more giggles from the kid, who shook his head pretending he was too cool for clowning around. Nash took the boy into the living area to give him more room, and so as not to crowd him in the intimate setting of his tiny bed space.

'Now, Luca,' Nash said, making sure that his tone didn't shift, 'I heard your superpower is holding you back from talking. But you know, superheroes use their powers for good, right? What if you used yours to tell us what's on your mind? It's a brave thing. And it's a good thing to do. Try it. Once you start, you won't want to stop talking again.' Patches mimed his ears hurting from the anticipated noise.

Luca looked at Nash, his laughter stopped and his face morphed into a contemplative expression. Nash kept his mannerisms level when Luca nodded, a small but significant gesture. Progress. It was progress.

Nash continued the charade, asking simple questions that could be answered with yes or no nods. Luca participated without stress. It was slow, but it was communication.

When Nash thought he'd pushed the boundaries of their breakthrough as far as he could, he was ready to back off. Enough for one day. But Luca's gaze shifted to Nash's face, locking eyes. There was a moment of connection, an unspoken understanding that transcended words. Nash knew what the child was asking.

'It's okay. You can trust me, Luca.'

The boy pointed out of the window.

At that moment, dressed as Patches, Nash couldn't have been more grateful to look like a fool. His face itched under the heavy greasepaint and the green wig made his scalp feel as if it was alive. He didn't know how the guys stood it. But he'd have stayed in the ridiculous costume for the rest of his career if it meant saving one frightened boy. The path forward was unclear, but the mystery gripping the circus was killing people. He'd made a strong connection with the child who held the key to their investigation. Nash was excited that Luca was ready to talk about the ordeal he'd been through. The nodding to benign questions and pointing were progress—but he had to tread carefully. He forced his expression to hold its smile and didn't leap on it as he wanted to. One wrong move and he could scuttle back into his protective shell.

Nash mimed falling off the sofa in shock and winced, knowing that his back was going to punish him for it.

'You did it, Luca. You took the first step towards finding your voice. That's incredibly brave. I wonder if it's been hiding under the sofa all this time?' He hauled himself to his knees, the groan of complaint genuine, and looked. 'Nope. Not there.'

Luca giggled.

He was about to ask Luca more when the sharp report of a gunshot shattered the air. Nash's instincts kicked in, and he rushed outside, his gaze scanning the scene. Snow's warning loomed in his head. They were coming for the boy.

He threw off the clown shoes that slipped over his own and wiped his hand across his painted face. There was so much make-up, and he smeared the big red and white painted lips across his cheek. He gave up on the discomfort, there were more important things to deal with. His heart was pounding as he saw Billy, the gentle orangutan, darting away in a panicked frenzy. The ape was screaming, one set of knuckles grazing the earth as he loped away at incredible speed.

Nash sprinted to Mac McKenzie, the boss hostler. 'Mac, what happened?'

Mac took in the clown outfit. 'Patches?'

'No, it's me.'

'Nice costume. I never believed them when they said the police were a bunch of clowns—but if the cap fits.'

Nash gave a wry grin, the urgency of the situation pushing aside his embarrassment. 'What's going on, Mac?'

'It's a nightmare. Somebody let Billy out and all hell's let loose. They fired a shot to frighten him, and he ran off terrified. Look how far he's got, we'll never catch him.'

Nash stared at Billy. He was a distant figure racing through the circus grounds. He cursed under his breath. 'Protestors?'

'Not this time.'

'Lyara, get back to Luca. Keep him safe,' Nash said.

'No,' Mac said. 'We need every spare pair of hands on this.'

'I need her at the caravan.'

'He'll be fine. If that ape goes rogue, you'll have more to worry about than a frightened kid.'

Lyara looked at Nash and he nodded. 'Okay, but stay close.'

'Billy's tame, and ordinarily, I wouldn't be too worried about rounding him up. He'll do anything for an ice lolly. But Creya

Brieanna, his handler, is away this week and without her, he could be unpredictable.

'What do you need?' Nash asked. He battled the clown costume as he rummaged in his own clothes for his phone.

'What are you doing?' Mac asked.

'Backup.'

'We don't need a load of coppers frightening him and making things worse. This is a circus issue and we'll deal with it.'

'I couldn't give a damn that your monkeys escaped. My job is to protect the public.'

Mac called the main castle office to tell them to lock down the grounds to contain Billy. It was a blessing that the circus wasn't open to the public yet. But the castle was. It was an empty gesture, the orang was more than capable of scaling the walls. Nash listened in to Mac's side of the call and picked up that the castle manager was incensed to hear there was a wild animal on the loose, especially as the grounds had public visitors. They'd been there three weeks longer than their original leaving date and their welcome was as thin as the hole in a fisherman's sock.

When Mac got off the phone, he spoke to Quinn who was rallying the carneys. 'I'll take some of the crew. We'll spread out and track him down. Creya Brieanna's away, so it's up to us to keep him safe.' Mac handed Nash a walkie-talkie. 'If you see him, don't approach. He'll panic. We've trained them not to go with strangers. Get me on this if you find him, and his relief trainer will walk him back. Billy will listen to him.'

The gunshot and the released orangutan were more reminders that danger was everywhere. They were facing challenges beyond Nash's initial investigation.

Clown costume or not, Nash was ready to face whatever this was. The public was in danger, and he felt a responsibility as one of the investigating officers to keep them safe.

Another shot rang out and chaos erupted as Bobo the chimp darted away from Quinn, his distressed cries echoing through the circus grounds. The two species, orangutans and chimpanzees, had never mixed well, and Bobo's fear was palpable. His frantic movements drew the attention of the circus members, and the atmosphere shifted from controlled urgency to bedlam.

Quinn shouted, 'Spread out and find Billy. Watch out for Bobo.' The urgency in his tone was mirrored in the reactions of the crew members. They were aware of how dangerous all the animals could be. The story was told to every child growing up in the circus about the trainer thirty years before, who had her face ripped off by an adolescent chimpanzee. Circus people were taught animal respect early in their lives.

The crew split into groups, going in different directions, calling for Billy and keeping an eye out for the frightened chimp.

In the confusion, Nash lost sight of Billy and Bobo for a second. But he saw Quinn coaxing the chimp from the branches of a tree.

'Bobo, come to Daddy. There's a good boy.'

Bobo shook his head and screamed at him, showing his teeth in fear.

'Do you want a bun, sweetheart?' The chimp shook his head, signed no and screamed again. Bobo had been taught to communicate with Makaton and simple signing. He knew how to make his displeasure felt. He argued again and gave Quinn the middle finger.

'That's too bad because I'm going to go in the trailer where it's safe. And I'm going to eat two cream cakes where it's safe. And then I'm going to drink a cup of sweet tea with sugar, and I know that's your favourite. And I'm going to drink it in our trailer where it's safe. Too bad that I'm going to be sad and lonely without Bobo.'

Nash halted for a second to check that at least one of the escaped animals was contained. Quinn made a show of walking with his head down and ignoring the chimp. It was too much for Bobo, and he ran down the tree trunk screaming at Quinn. The interaction between man and beast was inspirational and Nash was humbled. Quinn locked Bobo in his caravan and lost precious time getting him a cream bun and a cup of tea. Nash heard the chimp's distressed cries as Quinn closed and locked the door. 'Sorry buddy. I won't be long. Pick something for us to watch on TV, and by the time you're done, I'll be back.'

The circus grounds were a whirlwind of activity. People shouted directions and tried to create order amid the chaos. The clowns, who had just come from entertaining Luca, were part of the search party. Their costumes added a comical touch to the scene, and the practical advantage of pinpointing the search parties.

Jellybean ran past Nash and shouted, 'How's Luca?'

The words hit him like a jolt of electricity. Shock smacked him like a cannonball to the chest. He scanned the area around him to see if Lyara was near Luca's van. He saw her with a group of visitors, herding them to the exit. The boy was unattended. His parents were practising their flying routine with their performance music loud enough to hear it on the high trapeze in the Big Top, and the boy was alone. Nash realised they couldn't have heard the gunshot and was torn between sprinting back to the trailer and going to the tent first to get his family. Urgency made the decision for him.

He charged to Luca's trailer. He'd forgotten about him in the uproar. Fear and guilt gnawed at him. He'd failed in his duty to protect Luca. If anything had happened, he'd never forgive himself.

The escaped ape and the gunshots got him out of the way so the killer could—What?

He knew that when he got to Silvestri's trailer, it was going to be empty and Luca would be dead. Despite Nash's promises, he'd let the boy down.

Chapter Twenty-Nine

He burst into the trailer, and relief floored him when he saw Luca sitting on the bed. The boy looked frightened again and lost. After the giggles of earlier, Nash could have kicked himself. Luca had been abandoned.

'I'm sorry, son. Are you okay? Are your folks still in rehearsal?'

Luca's gaze flicked to the window as the sounds of chaos from outside filtered in. Nash noticed that he'd closed it while he'd been gone. Billy was missing, Bobo was distressed, and the place was going crazy out there.

'Lyara, can you bring his parents, please?'

The boy was a mess. Nash looked around but there was nothing out of place. He felt reassured that it was just the commotion that had frightened him. Nash's voice softened as he crouched in front of him. 'I'm sorry I left you alone. I should have stayed with you.'

Luca was a mass of internal emotion but Nash saw the accusation first, then uncertainty, and terror. Luca pointed at the window, his fingers knitting into anxiety.

There was a knock on the door and Luca jumped. Jimmy's head appeared around it. 'Inspector, somebody's seen the shooter running away. The boss said you'd want to know.'

'Thanks, Jimmy. Tell him I'll be right there.' Jimmy waved at Luca as he left.

'Luca, we need to get you somewhere safe until your folks get here,' Nash said. He was taking no argument, not that the child had one to give. 'Let's go, kid.'

As Nash's hand made contact, Luca flinched, his eyes welling with tears. Being left alone wasn't the only thing that had terrified him while Nash was out monkey hunting. Something had happened in those five minutes.

Luca was rooted to the spot and refused to move. He had to feel in control and there was no way Nash was going to force him. He knelt and coaxed Luca to tell him what had happened. 'Luca, you can talk to me. I'm here to listen. Remember your superhero power? Your voice can overcome anything.'

Luca was fixed on Nash.

'What happened while I was gone?'

His breathing was ragged. He opened his mouth to speak, but it was barren.

Nash imagined the struggle inside him. The boy was battling fear against the need to communicate. He wished he could take the pain away.

As much as Nash hoped for the return of their earlier breakthrough, Luca wasn't ready. He remembered Snow's reading about seeing a boy with a box and his mouth sewn shut. Luca's fear had closed him off again, locking him behind a wall of silence.

Nash refused to give up. He'd seen Luca's resilience. 'I know something scared you. It made you feel that you can't talk to me. Did you see something while I was gone?'

Luca shook his head. No.

'Did somebody come in?'

His eyes shimmered with tears, and he nodded, searching for something. Perhaps it was hope. Nash held his gaze, willing him the courage to open up.

'Your voice is your superpower, Luca. Talk to me and you can conquer anything.'

As Nash talked, Luca's frustration grew. It was apparent that he was still too terrified to talk. Nash felt helpless.

A knock on the door made them jump and interrupted their conversation. Nash sighed, it was like a bloody train station in this trailer.

Bence Jaeger came in and a wave of relief washed over Nash. He was a familiar and reassuring presence that Luca trusted.

'Hey there, tough guy,' Jaeger said with a smile, as he stepped into the trailer. 'Mind if I join the party?' He threw a chocolate bar on the table in front of Luca.

He didn't say anything or reach to take it.

'Don't want chocolate? It's official. We need to ask Detective Nash to investigate if you're a double agent from the broccoli brigade.'

Luca lowered his eyes. The fear was riding him, and he was shaking. Nash was grateful for the help as Jaeger crouched beside him. His presence was calm and reassuring.

'It's me. Bence. You remember me, right? Because the way you're ignoring me, little buddy, is making me think you took a knock to that head of yours and it made you forget me. Are we still friends?'

Jaeger produced a butterfly from behind Luca's ear that settled on the boy's knee. Jaeger covered it with his hand. 'We need to keep him safe, don't we, Luca?'

Luca nodded, his eyes hidden under his fringe. And when Jaeger raised his hand the butterfly took flight and fluttered around their heads until it found the open door and escaped. 'Give me a bro-hug, little man.'

Luca found Jaeger's chest and buried his face into his jumper, trembling with fear. His skinny arms wrapped around Jaeger's neck and he clung on as though his life depended on it.

Nash sat on the sofa as Jaeger tried to put Luca at ease, his affection for the boy was evident from his voice. He patted him on the knee and Luca flinched. 'It's okay, Luca. I heard the orangutan's been hurt.' Jaeger turned to Nash. 'The circus is asking for police involvement. There are a few guys milling around up there but they don't seem to be doing much. They sent me to come and get you, so here I am at your service.'

At the mention of Billy, concern replaced Luca's fear. Nash exchanged a glance with Jaeger, acknowledging the change. Billy's welfare had stirred something in Luca, even if he was too frightened to communicate verbally.

Nash sat back to give Jaeger and Luca more space, his thoughts shifting to the new twist regarding Billy. 'I need to check this out. Are you okay here for a few minutes, Bence? I don't want to leave him alone.'

'Sure. No problem. We're fine, aren't we, kid?'

'Is that okay, Luca?' Nash asked. 'Are you good with your uncle Bence while I nip out to see Mr Quinn?' Although he'd never heard it said before, he purposefully used the avuncular noun to instil the idea of family. 'I won't be long. Bence will look after you.'

As Jaeger and Luca huddled together, Jaeger pointed the remote control at the TV. He understood kids and knew how to distract them from their fears. He was used to dealing with the adult psyche, Nash knew that, but his work didn't involve understanding children, that part of him was intrinsic. Nash stood up.

He was relieved as Jaeger took over with Luca. Kelvin was sightseeing, but Nash felt guilty that they hadn't had much time together and it was mid-afternoon already. Jaeger took the pressure off by waving him away and comforting the terrified boy. Nash hesitated for a second, torn between his duty to stay with Luca and the urgency of the situation outside.

The kid was rigid with fear and Nash being there was one person too many in the confined space. He'd got through to him best in a one-to-one situation and Jaeger was doing a great job of doing the same. The events had etched a mark on Luca's soul. His small body trembled, huddling against Jaeger as he pulled him close.

As Nash looked on, Luca was crying. He seemed to be in discomfort. His silent sobs were an expression of what he'd been through. It was too much for him, and Nash saw a dark stain spread across the crotch of Luca's pants. It was a reminder of how deeply the boy's trauma affected him. His basic sense of safety was shattered.

Jaeger's voice pulled Nash from his thoughts. 'I've got this, detective. Get Aurora,' he said. His tone was gentle, evidently wanting to spare the boy's embarrassment.

Nash was doing more harm than good. He needed to go before he upset Luca any further. He said a quick goodbye and was glad to get out of there. It was oppressive, but Jaeger was already working on distracting the boy with his parlour tricks.

He'd taken a few steps away from the trailer when a sudden crash from behind made him whirl around. His instincts kicked in as he rushed inside.

Luca was on the floor, his body convulsing in another seizure.

Nash knelt on the other side of him. Jaeger was putting him in the recovery position his voice filled with concern as he reassured the boy. 'Luca, it's okay. I'm here. Breathe, buddy, just breathe.'

'Can he hear you?'

'Sure he can. He's going to be okay any minute now. Aren't you, Luca?'

The boy jerked violently. Nash rang for an ambulance and they worked together to ensure Luca's safety. The seconds felt like an eternity as they waited for the seizure to subside. They supported him through the ordeal.

As Luca's body relaxed, Nash exchanged a worried glance with Jaeger.

Jaeger's demeanour was calming. He was a professional with a good understanding of first aid. He talked all the time, low and soothing, a steady stream of comfort as he sat on the floor with Luca. Nash watched as Jaeger's hands moved over Luca's chest, checking his breathing and making him comfortable. He talked to him, and his tone was kind.

'I'm right here with you. You're doing great. Just keep breathing. You're stronger than you know.'

'The ambulance shouldn't be much longer,' Nash said to break the silence.

Bence's response was a nod. Time stretched out as they waited for the medics. 'Luca's come out of his fit, but he's tired,' Jaeger said. 'His brain worked hard during the convulsions and his body needs time to rest. 'That's all,' he said. 'He'll be okay.' And Nash realised he was reassuring him with the same skill he used on Luca to calm him.

'Where the hell are his parents? I sent Lyara for them ten minutes ago.' Nash said. It had only been a few minutes but it seemed like hours. He thought he'd always been pretty good in a crisis but he was scared for Luca. Jaeger's words gave the boy comfort, his voice was a ladder for him to climb back into the boat. When they heard the sirens, Nash felt better. At last. Jaeger said he'd find Luca's folks.

Nash gave the paramedics room to take over when they arrived. As they tended to him, Nash nodded his thanks to Jaeger. He'd risen to the occasion. There were moments of humanity and kindness in every day and not all of them were big things like this.

Nash stepped outside and calmed Luca's terrified parents as they ran across the field to him. 'We were rehearsing, we had no idea,' Aurora said. Isabella was crying, and Aurora pushed past him to get to her son. Nash put a gentle hand on Mauritzio's shoulder to hold him back. 'I'll take you in the car,' Nash said.

They watched the paramedics wheel Luca into the ambulance. Aurora was still dressed in her training leotard and her hair was damp against her scalp as she climbed into the ambulance and sat beside her son. Nash watched them drive away.

Luca would be safer elsewhere.

Chapter Thirty

Quinn looked at the faces around the table and then the notes in front of him. The discussion about the safety and well-being of the animals had been going on for half an hour.

'News of Billy's escape has leaked to the press and they've made a meal of it,' Mac said.

'The frightened ape only wanted to be taken home to the security of his enclosure,' Quinn agreed.

'When his stand-in trainer found him, he walked meekly back on the promise of food.'

The night before, the protesters were back with their chanting and abuse. The police had been called out for the second time that day, and although nobody was hurt, it wasn't good for the circus.

Mac's argument against secondary padlocks made sense—quick access during emergencies was crucial. But Quinn's concern for the animals' security was equally valid.

'We have to balance safety with efficiency,' Mac insisted, his voice carrying the weight of experience as the boss hostler. 'If we lock everything down too tight, we risk losing precious minutes in a crisis. It's a no-win situation.'

Quinn's irritation showed in the way he leaned back in his chair, and Bobo parted his hair, grooming him for fleas to calm him. The Critter Cave was home to a variety of animals with unique needs and potential dangers. The bosses' differing viewpoints were a reflection of the complexity of decisions that came with running the circus.

An uneasy solution was reached. Ground staff would rotate in shifts, guarding the Critter Cave. It was a compromise that balanced safety and efficiency. It ensured the animals were secure and had somebody on hand for swift action if it was needed. A sofa was brought into the animal enclosure with a fridge that ran from the generator. For their comfort on shift, they were given a variety of snacks and a kettle. The meeting adjourned and everybody went back to work, leaving Mac and Quinn alone.

The responsibility of managing the circus in the wake of the murders and everything else was getting to Quinn. He exchanged a nod with Mac. Despite their differences, their friendship and respect were intact. Their goal was to protect the circus and its human and animal members. Mac was the one person Quinn could always rely on when things were tough.

Another pressing matter had come to the forefront and still played on Quinn's mind. The suspicion surrounding Tomasso Galli as the murderer was a hot topic in camp, and the troupe had him judged, tried and put away for life before he'd had the chance to request a pillow in his cell. The evidence was compelling. The rope in his trailer was used to strangle Ross Finley. His DNA was found embedded in the fibres. The mushrooms were the same genus as the ones that poisoned him.

Quinn hadn't known Tomasso for long and had seen him suffering the stigma of the offcomer before any of this happened.

New folk coming in either settled or they didn't. He'd seen Tomasso joking around camp more, though there was still some tension with his acrobat colleagues. Meyer, Kotch and Wolf were a tight act of serious Germans a couple of years older, and more experienced, than Tomasso. They hadn't taken to him well. The evidence seemed damning, but Quinn struggled to reconcile the image of the wiry acrobat in the role of cold-blooded killer.

'The detective doesn't think Galli would be strong enough to carry Finley over the field,' Quinn said and laughed.

'He's letting the kid's physique fool him. We've seen him flinging Meyer around like a little girl. The kid's wiry, but he's got more strength than most bodybuilders. He's stronger than he looks.'

'Strong enough to carry Finley, and clever enough to make Alessio disappear?'

Mac chuckled and handed Bobo a tangerine. 'You've got a point. That one's got that fancy PACE team scratching their heads and it's keeping them awake at night.'

'Like they're the ones with monsters invading their dreams,' Quinn said.

'Even so, if he can carry Finley, he's capable of handling Selena.' Mac's next question hung in the air and a silence extended between them. 'But how did he make Alessio disappear?'

'Beats me. Ask the detective, he's the one with all the answers, and he's had long enough to think about it.'

Octavia knocked on the door and came in. She'd heard the tail end of their conversation. 'Well, it wasn't ghosts and curses, that's for sure. Whatever happened to that boy it was done by human intervention,' she said.

'Great observation, but I still don't see how. What can I do for you?' Quinn said.

'I've just come to ask if you ordered the lingerie tape for the girls. If not they'll be dropping out all over the place tonight.'

'Sure. The order came in this morning, check the boxes over there.'

Octavia delved into the three cardboard boxes and the men watched her without speaking. Her voice was muffled as she groped to the bottom of a large box. Quinn and Mac were privy to a rare glimpse of her furry lower legs.

'Sod's law. It had to be in the last one, didn't it? Couldn't have been in the first. That would be too easy. I'm not buying it,' she said.

She'd launched from one subject into the next without a segway. 'Not buying what? The tit-tape?' Quinn asked.

She emerged, pulling the top half of her body from the crate. 'If he killed anybody, I'll shave my hair and stuff a teddy with it. He's a good kid.'

Quinn had been fifty-fifty. But one thing he did know was that Octavia had the shrewdest mind of anybody he'd ever met. If she said Tomasso was innocent his balance sheet shifted from fifty-one to forty-nine in favour of innocence.

'It was him all right. Shifty eyes. I've never trusted a man who can't look you straight in the eye,' Mac said.

Fifty-fifty.

'You say he did it—but what you don't know is that Tomasso was spending time learning to dance because he was about to propose to Fauna. I was giving him lessons.'

'And you never thought to mention it to the police?'

'I was sworn to secrecy, why would I break that trust? And anyway, I can't give him a firm alibi, but it was all happening around that time so he could have been with me. But then Fauna got pregnant, and it went to pieces. He's a sweet boy.'

Sixty-forty to innocence.

'I'm telling you a boy who wants to abort his own bairn is as guilty as sin.'

'Have it your own way, Mac Mackenzie, but there's those that might call you shifty when you're out of their hearing.' She smiled at them and left with the tape.

That night the atmosphere under the big top was electric as the audience settled. They were at the height of the tourist season, and there was a big crowd. Nothing can fill a seat like a murder or three. Anticipation hung over the troupe like a tangible thread sewing them together. Rivalries were put aside and backstage egos were doused. Quinn was sitting behind the curtain on Chandra. Posture on. Smile on. They were ready.

The spotlight illuminated the centre ring. The five clowns—Jellybean, Nifty, Shadow, Jinx and the real Patches—followed the elephant and prepared to kick off the show with their signature antics in the opening walk-on. Quinn's eyes swept over their colourful costumes and exaggerated makeup looking for any slip in standards.

He led the troupe into the ring and the audience was enthralled. It went well, and when the last performer strutted out, the clowns ran back in to perform their opening act, while above their heads the rigger released the trapeze swings ready for the flyers. Ignatius ate fire and the audience applauded on cue.

As the clowns goofed around, Quinn watched. Murder was no excuse for tardiness and every footstep was choreographed.

Their synchronised movements and playful interactions were a testament to years of friendship and working as a unit. Quinn loved the joy the clowns brought to the audience.

As the routine progressed, his smile faded. In a comedic moment, Patches was supposed to trip over a hidden wire, causing a series of props to collapse in a heap of colourful chaos. But as he stumbled and fell, the props remained intact, defying the laws of physics—and comedic timing.

It was as if the act had been suspended, and the clowns went into frantic ad-libbing. Something was off and he exchanged a look with Mac.

The clowns continued with their act, improvising through the unexpected prop-fail. The audience's laughter didn't waver. The guys' professionalism left them unaware of the behind-the-scenes problem.

As the clowns wrapped up their routine and took their bow. The glitch in the choreographed performance was a mystery.

'Some bastard glued the jig,' John Sutton said, coming out of character as Jellybean.

The runners grabbed the props and pulled them out of the ring as the Silvestris, minus Aurora, took their opening bow. She was at the hospital with her son, and the meagre father-daughter team had to simplify their performance to carry the act alone.

Mac's fingers brushed over the wooden framework of the clown's prop, searching for signs of tampering. Everything looked normal, but Jelly was right, the collapsible joints had been glued into position.

Quinn felt a sense of dread churning his stomach into cottage cheese. A few bits of wood were harmless, but his eye flicked to the swings thirty and forty feet above his head on two raised platforms. The Silvestris were already in flight. Even the most routine things were tinged with unknowing.

Whether it was a harmless prank or an accident, the show wasn't the time to be playing with people's lives.

The performance continued, and on cue, the audience's attention shifted to the main ring where a team of eight magnificent horses and riders in full plumage cantered in. The sight of them with their sleek coats gleaming in the spotlight, drew gasps from the crowd. Quinn never tired of hearing it.

The horses moved in syncopation, their hooves pounding in rhythm as they circled the ring. The audience was captivated. Applause rang with admiration as the riders executed daring stunts and formations on the horses' backs. The display of skill showcased the bond between humans and animals. The children's faces were excited and that's what kept the blood flowing through Quinn's veins. After thirty years, he still had a thrill from seeing an upturned face in love with the horses.

The girls were balanced. The smiles were practised, and it was all working as it should.

The awe was shattered when the third mare, Candy, stumbled. She righted herself but something was wrong. The horse slewed and threw her hind-left, knocking her rider off balance. Jade fell into a seated position over Candy's neck and the rest of the horses and riders were jolted out of sequence. The horse stumbled again, but before Quinn could get into the ring and motion them out, Candy collapsed. Her rider was caught in a precarious position on her back and her leg was crushed underneath the horse. Gasps of shock echoed through the audience as the circus team rushed to the fallen horse's side.

Every person in the audience felt the ground shudder as the huge horse hit the sawdust. For a few seconds, they reacted with screams and pandemonium as Quinn cleared the rest of the horses out of the ring. The crew had to move Candy to pull the injured girl out and carry her to safety.

'Bloody hell, it's only gone and died,' somebody shouted from the front row.

And then, when the ring was empty apart from Quinn and the fallen horse, there was silence.

Chapter Thirty-One

Quinn waved in the clowns. Like tuned pistons on a motor, and as if this happened every night, the crew ran in with shielding curtains to cordon off the area where the stricken horse lay.

Alexander Bavic stood at the back of most performances in case he was needed to treat any minor mishaps, and he ran in with his bag at his side. It wasn't his job to be a showman, he was there to save Candy's life. And if the audience saw his concern, that was too bad, and he'd deal with the flack later. He saw the way the horse had fallen and it looked as though she'd dropped dead mid-canter in the ring. He went to his knees in the sawdust to examine the fallen horse. Quinn looked on as his trained eyes scanned Candy's body for injury and cause. He assured the troupe that she was alive and took a blood sample from her.

Nash came in and said he'd heard the commotion from his trailer as carneys called the news to each other across the field. He was there in minutes. Quinn waved Mac over and told him to grab his top hat and cane and take over the show. The hostler went out in jeans, a checked shirt and a fine top hat with Quinn's iconic ringmaster's jacket hastily thrown over the top.

'What happened, Alex?' Quinn asked.

'She's fine and she'll sleep it off. I suspect she's been doped with Ketamine. Someone may have tampered with her feed or injected it directly.'

'Who would do that to an innocent animal?' One of the girls was squealing backstage loud enough for the front rows of the audience to hear. Quinn hissed for everybody to get out of the tent.

'Where did they get the drug?' Nash asked.

'Dark web? Local dealer? Who knows?'

'Can she be moved?' Quinn asked.

'Mr Quinn, you could put her in a tutu and fit her with a diamond tiara and she wouldn't wake up until the final act of Swan Lake.'

'Never mind smart answers. Is she okay? Can we get her somewhere more private?'

'Sorry. Yes. Left to come around naturally, she'd be out for a while. However, when you've got her out of here, I'm going to give her a stimulant to bring her back.'

One of the ground crew appeared with a blanket and six of the strongest men rolled the supine horse onto it. They dragged her out of the performance area.

Quinn's jaw tightened, and the implications of sabotage sent a surge of anger through him. Three people were dead, and he was reacting with a violent rage over an animal being doped.

The clowns came offstage. They'd done a couple of standby routines as Mac brought order to the program. Still fuming from the earlier sabotage, they were in uproar and exchanged heated words with anybody who'd listen. Their frustration was evident in the animated gestures and raised voices.

'This is getting out of hand,' Patches said. 'If that poor horse dies, the circus won't recover from the bad blood.' His eyes were red with anger. 'First our routine, now Candy? Someone's messing with us. It's Ravenswood and his damned curse.'

'It could be the protesters. We won't stand for it. We're a team, and we won't let anyone hurt any more of our people and animals. This is outsiders' work, this is.' Jellybean said. 'No carney would ever hurt an animal—not in this circus. Not even Ravenswood.'

Nifty made a sign of the Cross and glanced at the horse as the men dragged her across the field to a clean stall. 'Jesus and Mary, I love you. Save souls.' He chanted it as a mantra, then grinned. His affirmation to his saviour was complete, and all would be well now. 'Right guys into the clown car, let's hunt some demons.'

The troupe rallied. The acts of sabotage had pushed them to their limits, but they were united in their resolve to protect the integrity of the circus.

In the ring, the fallen horse had cast a shadow over the rest of the performance. The night was marred by the incident, and the acts limped through the rest of the show. Mac put a stop to any high wire or dangerous acts being used. In a change to the programme, the clowns, dogs, and jugglers completed the show.

Alexander worked to ensure Candy's well-being and brought her around. She stood up immediately and Quinn watched her wobble on unsteady legs. Alexander ordered her to be supported to stop her from falling and breaking a leg as the effects of the drug wore off. When she was able, they walked her in the exercise paddock, making endless circuits of the space to raise her blood flow and send the after-effects of the drugs through her system. The troupe cheered when Alexander stated that she was going to be fine and there was no lasting damage. 'She just had an unscheduled nap, that's all. It looked more dramatic than it was.' Although the horse was sedated, Nash said he couldn't shake the feeling that the harm was intended for the rider, not the horse.

They grappled with the news of Tomasso Galli's arrest and split into two camps—those that thought him guilty, and those that didn't. Suspicions were cast wider, enveloping even those who had never crossed their minds. A whisper circulated and grew. It painted Magnus in an unfavourable light. The reasons for the suspicion were vague and nuanced. They were fuelled by flimsy circumstantial evidence that aligned with the times of the murders.

Magnus' towering presence and immense strength set him apart. He was a figure of admiration among the circus crowd. But it was these qualities that cast accusation over him. Normally gentle, his physical power and occasional temper raised questions.

It wasn't only his strength that stoked suspicion. It was the timing of his movements. He'd been seen near the crime scenes on more than one occasion. His imposing figure was recognisable even in silhouette. Some of them were outspoken as the alcohol after a stressful day soaked into them and made them brave. They saw him as a threat, and Quinn had to prevent the troupe from evicting him from the camp.

The spark of suspicion ignited when two innocuous incidents came to light. The first was when Magnus visited Luca in his trailer while his parents were rehearsing. It turned out that Mauritzio had asked him to look in on the boy. But the other piece of evidence was more concerning. Flora had gone to Magnus' trailer seeking help with moving a cabinet. Nobody locked their doors, and she tapped and walked in as was the custom. Magnus wasn't there, and Creya Brieanna, was away on holiday. As Flora turned in the cramped space, she saw a distinctive shawl belonging to Madam Selena in the corner at the head of his bed.

It was one that Madam Selena had worn during her readings. It didn't belong in Magnus' trailer. Their love affair had been over for years, and he was seeing somebody else. Why did he have Selena's scarf? Everybody knew he was still in love with her, and this was seen as proof. Fauna hadn't held back on spreading gossip about what she'd seen.

At dinner that night, the discovery fuelled whispers and speculation. Three times a week the trestle tables were laid with communal food provided from circus funds for those who wanted to eat together. During the afternoon on those days, a rota of crew would give up their downtime to help Jolene cook. Quinn maintained that eating together fostered kinship and community. When belts had to be tightened, the communal dinners were always brought up as something that could go, but Quinn wouldn't hear of it. It was the only proper meal some of them would get, and he was aware of that.

Some of the troupe connected the dots. Magnus' strength, his presence near the crime scenes, and now this unexpected link to Madam Selena's belongings—it was enough to foster an uprising of accusations.

They were coping with the aftermath of the murders. The arrest of Tomasso Galli was one thing, but he had his supporters, and the shadow of suspicion still loomed over everybody. Saar was smug about not making anybody's suspect list until Daft Damien pointed out that Saar and Noor could have done it together.

'And how would that work, Brains?' Saar asked.

'I don't know, do I? Just saying, that's all.'

'Maybe you did it, Damien, what with that temper of yours. Oh, hang on. The killer's clever so that's a stupid idea,' Noor said.

The insult was lost on him and he smiled around the troupe happy to be included in the suspect list. If there was a list, Damien wanted to be on it.

'It's not impossible, though,' one of the ground crew said. 'Saar and Noor could have done it with the help of a third accomplice?'

'Really, Joe? Straws and clutching my friend,' Octavia laughed.

While Magnus' guilt was unfounded, his presence in the Silvestri's trailer and the circumstantial evidence planted seeds in the minds of friends who'd always seen him as a pillar of honesty. Creya Brieanna was back from her leave and wasted no time falling out with Flora over the dinner table. Brother was turning on brother, friend on friend. Tensions ran high as murmurs of suspicion transformed into heated exchanges.

Quinn broke another piece of bread from a homemade loaf and dunked it in his lamb stew. He took in the raised voices and clenched fists. Performers who had once shared camaraderie were divided by fear. It was a heartbreaking sight, a fracture in the unity that defined the family. He tried to calm everybody, but their sap was rising.

He'd invited Nash, Kelvin and Lyara to eat at the communal gatherings for the length of their stay in Prague. But Lyara preferred to get home as soon as her shift was finished. Nash said it was enlightening and confessed to Quinn that many snippets of things were said around the table that he wouldn't normally be privy to. Nash's professionalism meant that he kept Kelvin as distant from the case as possible, but the Carneys loved him. In particular, the girls had taken a shine to him. Kelvin told Quinn that his normal life as a solicitor was very staid and he loved being at the showground.

During the escalating arguments, Nash's presence exuded authority and calm. Quinn was grateful for the backup, even though it was nothing he couldn't handle on his own. His determination to restore order was evident in his expression. Nash and Kelvin, the voices of reason, were ready to offer support if things got out of hand.

Nash didn't interrupt until the remarks were too personal and not based on fact. 'Let's all take a step back and think about what we're saying. We're on edge, and accusations won't get us anywhere,' he said. Quinn noticed the detective included himself to lessen the impact of disapproval.

'We think you should interview Magnus again, inspector,' Berdini said.

Magnus stood, almost toppling the long bench that seated twelve people. He held his emotions with a controlled rage, and Quinn saw his lid coming unstuck. His bulk emphasised the intensity of his anger. 'I don't know where this is coming from. I didn't do anything.'

Quinn watched a storm of emotions threatening to erupt from various people at any moment. His voice was firm but measured. 'We need to remember that wild accusations won't solve anything. We're better than this.'

'For God's sake. Whoever did it, just own up so that we can get back to some kind of normality.' Ignatius touched the puckered scarring on his cheekbone from his recent burn. A habit, Quinn noticed, that he'd fallen into. 'Yeah, Ignatius, just own up so we can move on,' Jimmy said.

Nash's calm mirrored Quinn's sentiments. 'You're in this together and need to support each other. Don't let suspicion tear you apart. My door is always open and you can come and talk to me at any time.'

'Like anybody's going to do that. We don't talk to coppers,' Damien said.

'Or eat with them,' Jackson, one of the ground crew said. Quinn noticed that there was still resentment over having a detective staying onsite coming from some of the troupe.

'And I thought we were friends, Jackson. Who am I going to come to when I need a cup of sugar now?' Kelvin said, and everybody laughed.

The tension wavered, and the collective anger subdued—for now.

Magnus' jaw was tight. He could blow, or he could calm down. He nodded, an acceptance of the truth. 'Get them off my back or I'll sue the lot of you. Slander. That's what they call it.'

The tension ebbed, the anger dissipated, and the performers exchanged kinder words for the rest of the meal. They were resilient.

Chapter Thirty-Two

When Nash and Lyara got to the hospital, the family were sitting around Luca's bed, comforting him. Nash watched for a minute before he tapped on the glass and gestured for them to come into the corridor. Aurora kissed her son on the forehead and they left the room. A nurse stayed with Luca.

'What's happened to my son?' Mauritzio said without any preamble.

'Is he talking? Has he said anything?' Lyara asked.

'Of course not. And he certainly hasn't given us any answers about what's been happening.'

'If it's alright with you, we'd like to try asking him some questions,' Nash said.

'I don't think so. Last time you talked to him, he had a fit and ended up in a hospital bed.' Mauritzio looked as though he was ready to thump Nash, and Aurora put a hand on his arm. Isabella was crying and clung to her mother's side.

'I can't tell you how sorry I am about that, Mr Silvestri, but I must insist on speaking to your son. Whatever you believe, he isn't safe, and we need to find out what he knows.'

'I'll keep my son safe, inspector. Me. I won't have him upset. Can't you see he's ill?' Mauritzio said.

Nash was going to go into the room but Mauritzio blocked his way.

'Don't you want to know what happened to Alessio? Your son is the only one who knows.'

It was as though Nash had punched him in the face, and he was ashamed of using a bullying tactic against him. But if he kept Mauritzio's children alive, it would be worth it. Mauritzio slumped into one of the orange plastic chairs and put his head in his hands.

'You can speak to him, but not without us being there,' Aurora said.

'Please, Mrs Silvestri. I know you have the right to be there while we question a minor. However, there may be things he's unwilling to say in front of you. I beg you, for the sake of your children, please give us just five minutes with him. I promise I'll be gentle.'

'No, I'm sorry, it's out of the question.'

'You can wait out here and I'll call you the second we're done. I wouldn't ask if it wasn't important.'

'You've got two minutes,' Aurora said.

'Thank you.'

'If you hurt him in any way, I'll break every bone in your body, policeman.'

'I won't. I promise. You could get coffee and something to eat, you must be exhausted.' He handed her a carrier bag. 'Some clothes that I had Octavia pack for you all. There's some toiletries in there too.' Aurora broke down, the last of her strength stripped by his thoughtfulness, and the tears came. Nash touched her arm. No words were needed.

The hospital room was quiet when Nash and Lyara went in. It was late afternoon and the sun bathed the room in warm orange light. The boy at the heart of their investigation lay on the bed, staring at the window beside him, but with an empty expression as though he wasn't seeing through it. The events of the past weeks had damaged him, and Nash was put in mind of TV shows he'd seen of children possessed and decimated by supposed demons. He hesitated about getting too close to the bed in case the kid sat up, twisted his head three hundred and sixty degrees and spewed pea soup at him. Luca had the same wild but vacant look as those kids, and Nash wondered what horrors haunted him.

He looked at Nash as he stood by his bed and said hello. And Luca was back in the room from whichever hell he'd been visiting. There was a glimmer of strength in his eyes, a resilience that excited Nash. Something was different, and he wondered if the boy was ready to fight.

'Hey, Luca. How are you feeling?'

A smile tugged at the corners of Luca's lips. It was another sign of progress, a connection that had been hard-fought. Nash and Lyara had spent time with him, trying to build trust in the face of his trauma.

'Hi,' Luca said, and Nash almost fell over in shock. 'I'm okay,' Luca mumbled. His voice was a whisper and it carried a new weight, representative of a twelve-year-old. It was the first time Nash had seen grit in the kid. He'd always seemed so much younger.

'Can we sit down?'

He nodded, and while there was caution and wariness on his face, the unbridled terror of earlier was gone. He looked scared but wasn't at the point of collapse.

Nash settled in the chair next to him, his posture relaxed and open, and Lyara took the one against the wall further away. 'I'm glad to hear that. You gave us quite a scare. How's the hospital food? Is it as bad as everyone says?'

Luca's lips twitched into a grin. 'It's not great, but not the worst. It's okay if you like red jelly.'

They laughed, and the light chatter continued, a dance of words that sought to offer a respite from the fear that had surrounded Luca. Nash was pleased that he was talking in full sentences and volunteering information. It was a complete transformation. He was thrown for a loop and had to let his brain play catch up and work out how to move forward with him. Luca's voice was hoarse, but otherwise, as strong as he'd expect from a twelve-year-old. Nash avoided probing questions. The boy's guard was a protective barrier that couldn't be dismantled with force. If he tried to break it, rather than letting Luca invite him in, he could revert back to the way he'd been in a heartbeat. Initial signs were good, and if all they did was talk about sloppy cottage pie and jelly, Nash would have to curb his impatience.

His hand rested on the edge of the bed, his fingers tapping a quiet rhythm that conveyed his presence and support. It was a small gesture, one he'd learned on a counselling course. The idea was that the monotony of the beat acted like a metronome to soothe an anxious mind.

Luca reacted, but not in the way Nash expected. His steady breathing quickened, and Nash saw the heart rate increase as the graph on the monitor drew spikes and the heart icon blinked with increasing speed.

Luca shifted up the bed as if he was about to take flight, but as Nash watched, he got a grip of himself and covered Nash's hand with his. Nash thought about the butterfly trapped beneath Jaeger's hand.

'Don't tap,' Luca said.

'Okay, Luca. It's all right. Relax. You're safe,' Nash said.

'I'm not safe.'

Nash had never wanted to probe a response so much in his life but closed his mouth and waited. The way he acted over the next few minutes was crucial. Luca moved his hand from his and closed his eyes. A hush fell over the room, and the conversation hung dormant between them like a fragile thread. Nash thought back over his time with the circus and a hideous pattern formed.

Luca opened his eyes and fixed them on Nash's hand. His expression was animated. With a sudden movement, he caught it, his fingers clutching him as if it was a barometer to measure trust.

Nash felt a revelation coming from the sudden movement and the raw emotion he saw on Luca's face. If the kid started screaming obscenities in a strange language, he wouldn't have been surprised. He needed a holiday, and Prague wasn't it.

In a voice laced with certainty, Luca spoke two words that resonated in the heightened atmosphere.

'It's him.'

The words cut through the layers of protection Luca had built to guard himself. Nash waited.

'Do you know who's responsible for everything, Luca?' Lyara asked. She stood and came towards the bed. Nash held his hand up to keep her back and she froze where she was.

'It's okay, she can come.' Luca motioned Lyara forward and she pulled her chair up to the other side of the bed. She reached into her bag and took out a digital Dictaphone. She handed it to Nash.

Luca's grip on Nash's hand tightened. His eyes filled with fear and determination.

Nash's mind was a whirlwind of colliding possibilities. He thought he knew, but he had to hear it, and couldn't put anything into the boy's mind. It was a fragile moment that could shatter with the wrong move.

He leaned in closer to Luca, his voice gentle as he kept the urgency from it. 'I need you to say it, Luca. Who was it? This is nothing to be scared of.' He held up the recording device to show him. 'Is it okay if we record what you say?'

Luca nodded.

'Can you tell us? Who you are talking about?'

Luca's gaze was locked on Nash's, his grip on his hand strong. His breathing quickened, and the monitors responded. Nash saw the internal struggle playing out.

Luca whispered.

'It's Bence.'

Chapter Thirty-Three

The name hung in the air, a revelation that sent a ripple of disbelief through the room. But Nash already knew and was furious that he hadn't seen it sooner.

He got on the phone to PACE. 'We've got him. It's Bence Jaeger. Confirmation from the boy. I'm with Luca Silvestri now, getting his recorded statement. Get eyes-on at the circus. Find out where he is and don't let him out of your sight. Do not engage until backup arrives.'

Nash knew who the killer was the second he thought about the butterfly trapped underneath Jaeger's hand. Events ran through his head like a cine film. The panic every time Luca was near him was profound. Bence Jaeger, the hypnotist who had been with the circus for years, was the prime suspect. He had to allow for the boy to be mistaken, but he knew he wasn't. Nash remembered the veiled threats. No wonder the boy was terrified. 'I am powerful. I am the one you should listen to. You don't have to talk.' And the worst one of all, the way Jaeger kept saying, 'I can end this.' He'd threatened to kill the kid right under Nash's nose, and he'd missed it.

'Bence Jaeger? Luca, it's a very serious allegation. You have to be sure.'

'I was there.' Tears came to his eyes and rolled down his cheeks. Lyara got up and gave him the box of tissues from the nightstand.

'He killed Alessio.'

Nash processed the enormity of Luca's accusation. Bence Jaeger had gained their trust. It was Nash who brought him in to hypnotise the boy. He'd promised Luca's parents to keep their son safe, and then he'd brought a monster into their home. He felt sick.

'Why didn't you tell us before? We'd have taken him away.' Nash said.

'I couldn't.'

'But you're speaking now.'

'I broke it.'

'I don't understand. What did you break?'

'The spell. He said some stuff to put me in a trance, and then he took my voice out and locked it in a box.'

'I don't understand what you're saying, Luca. What do you mean? Are you saying he'd hypnotised you before?'

'Yes. He brought a box with him the morning after Alessio disappeared. Everyone was out searching—and I knew where Alessio was. It was my fault. I said I was going to tell the police and he said that's what he was afraid of. He had this red metal box, the kind you keep money in with a lock.' Nash had seen it on a shelf in Jaeger's trailer.

Luca was still crying and he choked on mucus at the back of his throat. Lyara stroked his arm and made soothing noises.

'Take your time. You're doing well.'

'I was scared. He said some words and touched my forehead. And then he pulled my voice out of me and locked it in the box. I kept trying to talk, but there were no words. I couldn't speak. And every time I tried, it got worse. He said he'd kill my family if I told anybody. "Keep your hands by your sides and don't let them talk for you," he said. And if I told anybody, he said he was coming for Isabella first.'

He stopped talking and Lyara gave him a glass of water. 'Drink some of this, sweetheart. You're doing great.'

Nash was grateful that she'd spoken because he couldn't. It was worse than he'd imagined. The enormity of what Jaeger had done to the child was horrific. The threats against his family were standard behaviour. He wouldn't expect anything else. But that's all he'd expected. Jaeger had literally stolen the kid's voice and tortured him with hypnosis and bullying.

'Luca, science says you can't be hypnotised against your will. That's one of the reasons Jaeger wasn't high on our suspect list.'

'Do you want to try that one on me again? Or better yet, why don't you let him root around in your mind, and then tell me what he can and can't do? He made me little,' Luca said.

Nash patted Luca's knee and the boy flinched.

'You're doing so well now,' Nash said.

'One of the doctors helped me to break the spell. He said the mind is so powerful that it can induce terrible conditions on people—but with strength of will you can stop it,' Luca said. 'It took a long time, but the doctor helped me to talk.'

'Bence messed with you because you were vulnerable.'

'Gee, thanks. I'm hitting puberty, that's not the image I want to portray to the girls,' Luca said, and Nash laughed. Luca had stopped crying and looked older. Nash was blown away by the maturity of his vocabulary.

'I used the same concept and figured if he could hypnotise me, if I tried hard enough, I could break through it.'

'Who'd have thought there was such an intelligent lad fighting inside that terrified little boy,' Lyara said.

Luca laughed and it was genuine mirth at the start. Nash let it play out until the laughter became bitter. 'That wasn't me.'

'Son, you're doing a great job of baffling this old policeman.'

'It was Jaeger. "You're seven years old," he said. "You're a small, weedy, pathetic seven-year-old who can't even speak because you let somebody steal your voice. What does it feel like to be seven again?" he said, and I couldn't even tell him to piss off.' The rage had come up in a second. He caught himself. 'Sorry. Please don't tell my dad I swore.'

'I think we can let that one slide, don't you, Lyara?'

'Most definitely. I want to kill the bastard myself.' She said it deadpan in her thick Swedish accent. It broke the tension and Luca's rage. Nash and Luca laughed at her.

'What?' Lyara said.

Luca went on with his story. 'Every time he came near me, he used hypnosis and threats to make sure I didn't talk.' He held his hand up and wiggled his thumb. It was pale and wrinkled and showed signs of skin damage. 'I was so ashamed, but I started sucking my thumb when nobody was watching. Now I have to stop doing that, too. Can you imagine what the other kids would say?' Nash laughed with him, but it wasn't funny.

The last pieces of the puzzle were falling into place. Nash drew comparisons between Jaeger's actions, Luca's trauma, and the sinister undercurrent of the haunted carousel. Jaeger had used his longstanding position to manipulate and control people. But he still didn't know why. There was so much he didn't know, and a limit to how far he could push Luca.

Lyara's expression mirrored Nash's horror as each new piece of information was told. 'Bence Jaeger? Why? What would drive him to do it?'

'He said he was going to make us world-famous and real celebrities.'

'The circus?' Nash asked.

'No. Alessio and me. It was a trick, the greatest illusion ever performed.'

'The night he was killed?'

'No. The night he disappeared.'

'What happened?'

Luca's voice quivered as he told them about the night of Alessio's disappearance. It crept out of him in a torrent of emotions. The fear, manipulation, and the haunting memory of witnessing the unthinkable. It was a story that painted a chilling picture of Jaeger's real nature.

'We practised with Bence in secret. I was going to be fantastic, and he told me I had an important part and had to get the swinging just right. But I swear I didn't know. Honest.'

The monitor's beeping increased. 'It's okay, Luca. You're not in trouble. We know it wasn't your fault. But I still don't get how he did it.'

'Alessio was never there.'

'On the trapeze?'

'Yes. I was alone on the platform. He was hiding in Bence's trailer through the whole show.'

'He couldn't disappear. But two hundred people saw him vanish in front of them.'

'The lights were flashing and set in the right places. But it was a hologram. A recording of Alessio doing his act.'

'You didn't know he was going to vanish?'

Luca hung his head in shame. 'No, I did. But it was just a trick. The best illusion ever performed, he said. But that was all. Alessio was supposed to appear backstage and run on. He was finishing the show. I didn't know any different until everybody else did.' He buried his head in his hands and sobbed.

'Go on, Luca.'

'Everybody thought he was dead, but he was alive. I knew what Bence was doing, but I couldn't warn anybody. If I did as he said, he'd break the spell and leave us all alone. But then Alessio came back.'

'Can you tell us what happened?' Nash was sweating and felt the perspiration on his forehead. Why did they keep hospitals so damned hot? He wiped his brow with his sleeve.

'I woke up when Bence came in. And he put his finger to his lips—as if I could speak anyway. I sat up in bed. Bence slit Alessio's throat in front of me. I tried to scream. The trailer's tiny. My parents were just a partition away, but I sat on my bed and did nothing. Nothing. Blood squirted out of Alessio's neck. His hands came up to his throat. It hit me in the face. Some of it went in my mouth. I screamed the place down, but there was no sound.'

Nash had seen the blood spatter and photos of the state of Luca Silvestri covered in Alessio's blood. He'd sat with his knees to his chest for another five hours beside his brother's corpse.

Luca's words faded. Bence Jaeger had committed heinous acts in the guise of friendship.

'Thank you for talking to us, Luca. We're going to make sure this ends, and that Bence pays for what he's done.'

'I can end this,' Luca said and gave a bitter laugh.

Nash wanted to cut his tongue out. He sounded like Jaeger, even his placating tone was the same. He coughed. 'Sorry. Poor choice of words.'

'You don't say.' Luca grinned at him, letting him off the hook.

'Your mother's probably ready for storming the room, so we'd better let them in. You've been incredibly brave. I promise you, nobody but your parents are getting in this room.' He said the words but he didn't know if he could uphold them. Jaeger had power over people. He remembered when the mentalist made him feel ill just by suggesting it.

Lyara went into the corridor to speak to Luca's family. Nash warned her not to say too much. The last thing they needed was Mauritzio on the warpath before the police could detain Jaeger.

'I want to help. I don't want anyone else getting hurt,' Luca said.

'We're going to bring Bence to justice and make sure he can't hurt anyone else.'

Bence Jaeger had charisma and the ability to befriend people. He'd offered assistance during the crisis and fooled everybody. Luca's parents demanded answers, but Nash kept his cards close to his chest. He left Luca with his family but didn't feel the boy was safe there or anywhere else.

Lyara's voice broke through his thoughts as they walked down the corridor. 'Are you okay? This has hit you hard.'

'I fed him to the lions.'

'You weren't to know. He had us all fooled.'

'I genuinely liked Bence, I trusted him, probably more than any of the others. And now we have to face the fact that he's a deeply disturbed man, capable of anything.'

Lyara touched his shoulder. 'It's tough. But now we know the truth, we can stop him.'

'Can we? In my career, I've never been so scared of being able to stop somebody that I knew was guilty. We have no idea what this guy's learned to do to people's minds. What he put that kid through was barbaric.'

'We need to make sure he doesn't get away with it.'

Nash's driving on the way to the circus was erratic. He gathered information from Quinn and some of the other carneys as they waited for the arrest warrant to come through. He liaised with the PACE team to move into position. Then he ordered armed guards to go to the hospital and protect Luca. Before leaving, he spoke to the hospital administrator and, working through his limited English, explained that Jaeger was a very dangerous man, and must not be let in or underestimated.

Nash coordinated with the team to ensure that Bence Jaeger's arrest was swift and thorough.

As he spoke to the PACE members, his voice was laced with urgency. He'd resisted the temptation to go straight to Jeager's trailer and drag him out by the testicles. This had to be done right. 'We need to move quickly. He mustn't escape. He can't have any inkling that we're onto him until we have the grounds cleared and backup in position.'

The team members acknowledged his instructions, and Nash felt charged. He had a duty to bring Jaeger to justice for the circus community, but also for Luca—a child that he'd let down.

The pieces were in place, and the evidence against Bence was damning. They had him.

Lyara's voice broke through his thoughts. 'Nash, are you sure you're up for this? Why not let the team handle it? You're too close, and it's okay to take a step back.'

'I have to do it. I owe it to Luca.' It was more than that. He had to be there when they took that bastard down. He had to see it for himself.

Chapter Thirty-Four

Nash was in Quinn's office. He told him what was happening and that the grounds were being cleared of public visitors.

When he came out, an officer screamed at him. 'He's on the castle walls with a hostage.'

'Shit. I thought he was in his trailer?' Nash said.

'He got to my guard. Hypnotised him. He's still puking in a bush.'

More backup arrived with the negotiator in a convoy of police vehicles with flashing lights. The intrusion of blaring sirens grabbed the attention of everyone in the circus community. All visitors to the grounds had been shown out, but only a few of the troupe had already left. They'd been told to act normally and leave in small groups so as not to rouse Jaeger's suspicion.

The last of the performers and crew members emerged from their trailers and show tents.

Quinn and Kelvin ran to the officers. Mac was screaming into his walkie-talkie. Armed police in riot gear fanned out to surround the castle walls.

'What went wrong?' Lyara asked.

Quinn exchanged a glance with her. 'He smelled a rat.'

'What's the latest?' Nash asked and turned to Kelvin. 'I want you out of here. Go.'

'I'm not going anywhere until I know you're safe. I'm staying. I can help get some of the vulnerable people to safety.' Nash didn't have time to argue with him.

'Talk to me,' he said to Officer Brunovich as he put his earpiece in. He ran up the steep hill to the castle.

Quinn looked terrified. 'He's got Fauna.'

'Oh, Jesus.' Nash knew he had a hostage, but they didn't know who it was. 'The pregnant one?'

Brunovich said in his mic, 'The other sister's hysterical, but we've got her.'

'Good.'

They got to Vysehrad Castle and he assessed the situation. Jaeger was standing on top of the castle wall. It was thirty feet tall at its highest point. There were taller buildings to fall from and survive, but Fauna was pregnant. This time they had two lives to save. Three if they brought Jaeger in alive.

Nash looked at the growing crowd. He raised his voice to address everyone. 'Listen up, everyone. We have reason to believe that Bence Jaeger is involved in the recent events—the murders, the unrest and everything else.'

Gasps and murmurs rippled through the crowd as the weight of Nash's words sank in. Performers exchanged worried glances, and the atmosphere was charged with tension and disbelief.

As the performers and crew exchanged uneasy looks, Nash's gaze swept across their faces. 'Stand back and keep out of the way. Let us do our job.' He spoke to one of the officers. 'Move them.' He wanted the area to be cleared, but there was no time. He had more to worry about than the people standing in a semi-circle in front of the castle.

'Stay alert.' Nash's voice was a whisper as he spoke to the team, holding his earpiece, the tension was evident in his tone. He stood behind the negotiator who'd positioned himself on the ground below Jaeger and the terrified hostage. Nash could hear her pleading for her life and her baby.

'Mr Jaeger, my name's Boris Ridzen, and I'm not going to insult your intelligence by trying to talk you down.'

'Go on, it'll be fun. Give it your best shot, Megaphone Man.'

'I'm simply going to ask what you want for this to end. What can we do for you?' The negotiator said.

Nash's focus was honed on Jaeger's every move. They were dealing with a master of mind control. They had to be one step ahead at every turn.

Jaeger pushed Fauna forward so the toes of her shoes were hanging off the edge of the wall. The girl screamed and clutched behind her, grabbing Jaeger's jacket. 'Please. Let me go.' He could have hypnotised her into compliance—but Nash knew this bastard. He wanted to feed off her terror.

'You want me to let you go?'

He jerked her and she screamed. 'No. Don't drop me.' She stared at the distance and sobbed. 'I'm pregnant.'

'Sucks to be you, honey.'

'Don't do something you'll regret, Mr Jaeger. She's just told you she's having a baby. You don't want to harm a mother and child do you?' Boris said.

Jaeger's lips curved into a smile, and there was a glint of confidence in his eyes. He could plant doubt and confusion. But they were prepared.

Jaeger ignored the negotiator. 'You've come a long way, Inspector Nash. But do you have what it takes to catch me?' His words were a challenge.

'I'm taking you down. You're surrounded.'

The negotiator glared at Nash for interfering and motioned for him to stand down. 'You still haven't told me what you want. Let's talk, Bence. You can call me Boris. What do you want?'

'You look like ants. Stupid, ineffectual, crawling ants. Why would you assume I want anything from you? Ask Nash what I want. Let's see if he can come up with something. Isn't that right, Scooby Doo?'

'What?' Boris asked.

Jaeger ignored him but waved his hand without letting go of Fauna.

It was a fleeting distraction that caught Nash off guard. The world shifted around him, and his senses were disoriented. In a panic, he looked at Lyara.

'You okay, boss?' He was going to answer but stopped when Lyara morphed into DI Molly Brown. 'Nash?'

Nash's training kicked in, his mind battling against the mental intrusion. He focused on breathing and grounded himself in reality. Bence's mentalist tricks might work on others, but Nash was determined not to succumb.

'Nice try.' Nash's voice was steady with a hint of triumph. Jaeger was making this personal.

Jaeger's smile faltered. Surprise crossed his features. Nash's mental defences held strong.

'Everyone stay back. We need to diffuse this situation carefully,' Nash said.

The onlookers complied. Their murmurs of concern were a backdrop to the tense stand-off. With his senses back in reality, Nash's focus was locked onto Jaeger, and his mind raced ahead to find a way to resolve the crisis without anyone getting hurt.

'Jaeger, this won't end well for you,' Nash called out, his voice projecting authority. 'Let the girl go. We can find a way to talk this through.'

Jaeger's laugh was bitter. His grip on Fauna tightened. 'Talk? You're always talking with nothing to say. Do you think I'll just surrender and be taken down? You underestimate me.'

'That's the one thing I'll never do, Bence. I know what you're capable of. You have a better mind than me.' He flattered the mentalist's ego, playing for time.

Nash's instincts guided him. His eyes scanned the area for any possible advantage. And he saw a brief distraction as one of the officers moved into position, to flank Jaeger from behind. If he could keep him calm long enough for the shooter to get onto the wall, they might stand a chance of ending this without any casualties.

But Jaeger was quick. He manipulated Fauna so that she was shielding his exposed side. People in the crowd cried out, and Nash heard Flora shouting obscenities from the ground. He couldn't risk a shot that might harm the pregnant girl.

'Let her go. You're only making things worse for yourself.'

Jaeger's expression twisted into a malevolent smile. 'I know what I'm doing. I always have a plan.'

'And what is it? Because I'm buggered if I can see a way out of this.'

'I'm going to take out the miserable lot of you—Every *kibaszott* one.'

Mac was coming with the giant inflatable. Eight of the ground crew were dragging it across the field to put it in position under the wall. It was an enormous bouncy pad that acted as a net to catch the performers when they were in rehearsals.

'You fools. Do you think I didn't anticipate that? Bravo for effort, men. I'd give you a round of applause but as you can see my hands are full with the Madonna and Child.'

'Let her go, Bence. We can talk. Let's cut a deal,' Boris said.

'You have as much power as your air-filled bed, Nash. The castle walls surround the grounds. I can move her a lot faster than you can move that bouncy castle. Splat. Missed. Oh, dear. Good effort.'

'You're a heinous bastard.'

'Your insults have no impact. My intellect is greater than yours. Why would your words bother me?'

Quinn had been held back with the rest of the carneys and he tried to break through the line of riot police holding them away. Nash signalled to let him through.

On the castle wall, the wind whipped Jaeger's hair as he held Fauna, his grip tight and his eyes wild. Quinn stepped forward and looked terrified.

'Don't show any weakness,' Nash whispered. 'He feeds from it.'

'Get back, Isiah,' Jaeger said.

The ringmaster didn't listen. He straightened his shoulders and drew himself up to his show-ready posture. 'Bence. Get down and let that poor girl go. What are you doing?' His voice resonated with a strong command. 'I've seen you face demons and rise above them. Remember where you came from, and who you were before you joined us. Shame on you.'

Jaeger's grip on Flora eased as he looked at Quinn. He was the one who'd given him a chance when no one else would.

Nash saw his hold relax. 'Jump, Fauna,' he shouted. The girl hesitated and closed her eyes to leap.

Her chance was lost. Jaeger gathered his wits and increased his grip around her waist until she cried out in pain. 'My baby,' she screamed. Fauna trembled and it was a stark reminder of her vulnerability in the turmoil.

'Bence, let me help you, my friend.' Quinn's voice was intimate.

'You can't help me, Quinn. No one can.'

'Your mother's death was a tragedy. We know that, but you have to let it go, Bence.'

A flicker of pain crossed Jaeger's face, but he hid it beneath the anger. Nash watched and prompted Quinn as his words stirred memories that had been buried under layers of survival for a long time. He wondered what had released them and triggered the awful string of events.

'I know how much her death hurt you. I was there for you. I still am, Bence. You were lost, and struggling to hold onto your sanity—you were then and you are now. Don't you see? You aren't well, but you can trust me.'

'Shut up. Get my dead mother and bring her back to life. Do that and I'll let Fauna go.'

'He's spiralling. Be ready,' Nash said into his earpiece.

'You don't have to do this, Bence,' Boris said.

Quinn carried on talking. 'I saw something in you back then. After two years in the state hospital, you displayed such strength. You were resilient and brave.'

'You're playing the player, Quinn. I know what you're doing.'

'Do you know why I took you in?'

'Please, great oracle. Enlighten me. I've got nothing else to do before I kill this waste of humanity. And then I'm coming for you, if for no other reason than to shut you up.'

Somebody said in Nash's ear, 'I've got the shot.'

'Hold position. On my mark.'

'I saw a survivor, Bence. You were defined by tragedy but were determined to rebuild. I know you left that candle burning in your trailer, but your mother's death was a tragic accident. You've got to stop punishing yourself. It wasn't your fault or anybody else's.'

'I lit that candle. I got drunk. I left her there to die. And now everybody else can die because she didn't deserve to. I'm doing this for her.'

'Why do we deserve to die? We made you better. What's gone wrong, my friend? You did great, Bence. You built a life that mattered. You worked harder than any man I've ever seen. Even in the hospital, while others drowned in their psychosis and conditions, you worked to build a career in mentalism and magic. You found family and friends who care about you. Stop this.'

Jaeger was doing something to Fauna. Her eyes closed as she listened. Fauna's breathing aligned with the rhythm of Jaeger's words as he muttered in her ear. Her sobbing stopped. She was quiet and compliant. Things were escalating and Boris nudged Quinn to continue.

'Your mother wouldn't want this. She was a good woman. A kind soul and she loved you so much.'

Nash saw Jaeger's shoulders shaking. He was laughing.

'What would your mother say if she saw you now? Your Jonna.' Quinn's voice carried the essence of memories.

'She wouldn't want you to be eaten alive by anger and despair,' Nash said.

Jaeger's grip on Fauna wavered. His gaze locked on Quinn's. His hands moved to cover his face.

And Fauna fell.

Screams rose from the crowd and Flora buried her face in Octavia's bosom as her sister fell from the castle walls. Jaeger didn't even seem to notice that she'd gone. She fell face up on the inflatable as the men hauled it under her. The fact that Jaeger had subdued her with hypnosis possibly saved her baby's life as she fell without tensing or trying to protect herself. Two officers escorted her to a waiting ambulance as Flora extracted herself from Octavia's embrace and ran to her.

The riot police moved in, their weapons trained on Jaeger. 'Don't shoot,' Nash ordered. 'Bence, give it up. It's over. Let me help you.'

As Nash engaged Jaeger in empty conversation, he signalled to his team to maintain their positions and be ready to act. The tension in the air was suffocating.

Bence Jaeger was defeated and crumpled like a little boy. As the situation reached a boiling point, a distraction took his focus. A gust of wind blew, causing his long hair to whip around his face. In that moment of disorientation, he tottered on the lip of the castle wall.

It had gone on long enough. The commander seized the opportunity and gave the order to the man with the best vantage point to fire. Quinn screamed, 'No.' Nash opened his mouth to plead with the commander. But it was too late. The sniper fired a well-aimed shot, striking Jaeger's upper arm.

The shock of the impact made him scream in pain and he stumbled.

He fell onto the inflatable and writhed on it clutching his arm and screaming in agony as he bled.

The police team moved in fast. Jaeger was subdued and was handcuffed.

As the chaos of the stand-off subsided, Nash couldn't shake the danger of the situation. It had been averted, but the knowledge that Jaeger had been willing to use Fauna and her child as a shield haunted him. It was a reminder of the lengths the killer was prepared to go.

***

As they led Jaeger away, a doctor was called to look at his arm. The marksman was excellent. It was a flesh wound that bled greater than its worth. A couple of stitches, a bandage, and Jaeger would be fine. There could have been a very different outcome.

Quinn and Nash shared a nod of understanding. 'He's not well,' Quinn said.

'I know.'

'Look after him.'

'We will.' But Nash had no authority here—and no empathy for the killer. He was paying lip service to Quinn's request out of respect for the owner of the circus who cared about his people. For Nash, Jaeger could rot in hell where he belonged.

The atmosphere in the circus had shifted. A feeling of disbelief, and whispered words circulated through the troupe. Jolene rallied some of the carneys and went to the cooking tent. It was Thursday, one of the nights that dinner wasn't provided and the guys sorted themselves out, but she didn't bother asking Quinn's permission. She told him this was a time to eat together and re-band. As he walked among the people, he saw the weight had been lifted from them. The rumours of haunting and ghosts that plagued them were illusions. They were a smokescreen created by fear. There was a collective sense of astonishment, as they came to terms with the revelation that the carousel, shrouded in myth and mystery, was just a ride. Ambrose clung to his guns. 'My carousel might not be the cause of Jaeger's killing spree, but you mark my words, it's still haunted. Give me a break,' he spluttered. 'I needed a job.' He was called a wily old rogue, but with affection—he was one of their own now.

Already, feeble jokes were told and backs were slapped. Nobody had forgotten their dead, and Quinn knew more than one toast would be raised to them that night. 'But now,' Octavia said, 'is a time for the living.'

Shadow the clown—still in full costume—chuckled. His painted smile, exaggerated by his grin, spread even wider than usual. Quinn smiled back, the camaraderie and shared relief was infectious. Now wasn't the time to share his concerns.

Patches had been the heart of the clown routine that brought laughter to Luca, and Quinn nodded when Nash said he'd never forget his stint in costume.

He saw performers hugging and celebratory high-fives. The oppression of the murders and even the supernatural had been lifted, replaced by the triumph of truth and the strength of their community. Mauritzio and Isabella had come home from the hospital but were still weighted by their grief. They went to their trailer to let the troupe have fun without guilt.

Quinn smiled at everybody and tried to join in the fun, but Nash had told him what Jaeger whispered as he was dragged away. 'You fell for my little-boy-lost act up there? Fool.' He was laughing as they forced him into a riot van.

When the troupe gathered at the table, Quinn banged his cup on the surface. 'Five minutes until it's served.' He winked. 'Who's for a ride on the carousel?'

Chapter Thirty-Five

Nash and Kelvin took their seats in a dimly lit restaurant near the bustling chaos of the police station. The trauma of the day's events was etched on their faces.

'I couldn't be more proud of you, Silas.' Kelvin's voice held a rare sincerity, with none of his usual banter.

Nash smiled. 'I've had my share of wild situations, but that was something else. If you ever put yourself in danger like that again, I'm placing you on house arrest for the next thirty years.'

In the heart of Prague, they were in the renowned The Dog's Bollocks restaurant. The aroma of high-end cuisine wafted through the air, mingling with the soft melodies of live music.

'Terrible name—great choice,' Nash said.

'I aim to please,' Kelvin grinned. 'I found it yesterday when you were being a hero and I was killing time sightseeing. I couldn't wait to bring you here.'

They were at a table suffused with candlelight, sitting by the window. Nash's tired eyes brightened as the waiter put a menu in front of him. He studied the list of tantalizing descriptions that distracted him from the demands of his role. The team didn't need him tonight and he'd left them to get Jaeger attended to by the medics and booked in ready for interviewing in the morning. It was a welcome night off to be with Kelvin, and a chance to just be. He was away from the chaos that defined his working life.

Nash ordered the risotto that was described as a symphony of flavours. Kelvin went for a rare steak. Kel always went for steak no matter the town or country. Nash leaned back, gazing at the lively streets of Prague and remarked that the sometimes simple food of the city was some of the best he'd ever eaten. He commented on the quality of the, often simple, cuisine and Kelvin agreed.

'The other day I came out of the subway tunnel by the bus stop and I was ravenous. I found a tiny restaurant that looked as though it needed a good clean but I was too hungry to think about food poisoning. They served the best—and I mean the very freaking best—stew and potato dumplings you've ever tasted. It was amazing.'

Nash smiled but didn't answer. He was too full of love, his enthusiasm for life, and the simple things in it. The city's energy wrapped around him like an embrace, and the weight of responsibilities lifted. The clink of glasses and the laughter of other patrons created a backdrop for a romantic ambience. And he was happy.

'Here's to our holiday,' he said.

'Babe, if this is your idea of a holiday, I'm getting another man.'

As the evening progressed, Nash savoured every bite, letting the flavours dance on his palate. The harmony of tastes was supplemented by the beat of contentment. Even in a murder investigation, there were remote pockets of peace to be found.

The night draped over the city, and Nash joined Kelvin at the hotel. The circus was the last place he wanted to be that night.

Weariness clung to him like a shadow but lightened as he saw the wonderful double bed again, and the coffee machine. He stripped out of his clothes and they shared a shower. The events of the day faded away for a few hours as he slipped under the covers.

Lying in Kelvin's arms, Nash's thoughts drifted, blending with the gentle lull of the night. Kelvin brought tranquillity to their lives and he couldn't bear the thought of them ever being apart.

He felt as though he'd been asleep for minutes when the silence was shattered by the ring of his phone. It cut through the stillness of the early morning where even the traffic hadn't woken yet.

He reached for his mobile and knew it was bad before he answered.

'Nash.'

He recognised the voice of the station commander. 'We've got a situation. Jaeger's escaped.'

Nash's senses were sharp as the words hit him like electricity. 'When?'

'We're still piecing the details together. But he slipped away through the night. We've got officers combing the area, but we need you here fast.'

'I'll be there.' The fog of sleep evaporated. He hung up and dressed. Kelvin was sitting up when Nash disconnected the call. 'Trouble?' His voice was heavy with sleep and his accent, which was rarely apparent, made Nash melt.

'Jaeger's escaped. They need me at the station.'

'I'll come with you.'

'No. Stay here. I need to do this without worrying about you as well.'

'Okay. More sightseeing for me, then. Come back safe, Si.'

Nash kissed him goodbye and went into the cold. As he left the hotel, dawn painted the sky with orange and pink. He took a second to be awed by the beauty. The city that had been quiet fifteen minutes ago, pulsed with early morning activity.

Station Commander Savilek met him at the door and filled Nash in as they walked. The police station had a shift change at six. But because of the delicate nature of their new guest, the day shift was asked to come in early for an extended changeover. However, when they arrived, the officers found the front door wide open.

Nash felt the chill of dread as Savilek continued his story. 'Nobody was manning the front desk. The place was like the *Marie Celest,* and the scared officers went into their rounds without even taking their greatcoats off. They knew it was Jaeger and pulled their weapons,' the commander said.

He told him that Jaeger's cell, which should have held his sleeping presence, was empty. They searched the rest of the building and found the night-duty guards in a storage cupboard. They were bound together at the wrists, but were seemingly asleep, their heads bowed in a deceptive stillness. The day staff would have checked they were still alive. But the snoring confirmed it.

Nash listened and interrupted with questions twice, but for the most part, he let the commander tell him the story. Nash noticed that he wore odd socks—it seemed he'd dressed in a rush as well.

The day shift boys shook the guards but struggled to rouse them. When they came to, they were confused and lacked coherence. The truth was inescapable—despite being warned to be wary of him, they'd been hypnotized by Jaeger. Their senses were manipulated by the man they were supposed to keep locked up.

Their most dangerous prisoner had escaped by simply asking the guard to open his cell. After sending them to sleep and locking them up, the CCTV showed Jaeger opening three other cells and letting the petty criminals out. It added extra chaos.

As the officers scrambled to bring in manpower, their radios crackled to life with urgent messages, spreading the news of Jaeger's escape through the force.

His trail grew cold. He'd slipped into the morning mist, leaving fear in his wake.

In the aftermath of the discovery, the staff faced the fact that the hunt was on. A dangerous fugitive was out there.

In the confines of the police station's briefing room, Nash sat with his fellow detectives. The situation meant that every available officer was called to patrol the streets. The airport and train stations had already been alerted and roadblocks were in operation thirty minutes after the escape was discovered. An early press conference was arranged and Commander Savilek sat in borrowed socks behind the press conference table, with cameras flashing in his face. He warned the public that a dangerous criminal had escaped custody and must not be approached under any circumstances. A stop-press was held on the *Bleck Daily News* until a photo of Bence Jaeger could be released to them. And social media was red hot. The morning's revelation of Jaeger's escape sent shockwaves through the department. And soon the city would be in a state of panic. The room buzzed with hushed conversations and the hum of technology.

Commander Savilek stood at the front of the press room. 'We can't underestimate the threat Jaeger poses,' he said. 'This man is dangerous, cunning and resourceful. Our priority is to apprehend him before anybody else gets hurt.'

Nash absorbed the details. Luca's vulnerability was at the forefront of his mind. Unfinished business? He tried to think like Jaeger. He knew him well enough to predict his potential targets, and the boy in hospital topped the list. Nash's fingers tapped a report of worry on the table as his mind raced ahead of his body.

The briefing outlined the deployment of extra security to the hospital, ensuring Luca's safety. Nash's conviction in his assumption was strong. Jaeger wouldn't pass up an opportunity to strike.

A voice pulled him back to the present. 'Nash, you're with me. We're leading the task force from base,' the commander said.

'Yes, sir.' It was a long time since he'd had orders barked at him. He wasn't the lead on this case and it was a humbling experience. He wanted to be at the hospital guarding Luca himself but was shouted down. He had to follow orders like any other subordinate.

After the briefing, he followed Savilek out of the room. The circus was a place of strong bonds, and it was likely Jaeger would exploit that. He could be going there.

Lyara headed up the field task force. They moved fast, and their brief was to locate and neutralize the threat Jaeger posed.

Hours passed. The sun climbed high in the sky as the force scoured the area and reported back to base. Nash's anxiety intensified with every dead end.

A call came in at eleven. Quinn had been taken into protective custody at the circus and he was safe—for now. Nash's shoulders sagged with relief, and a burden lifted from his chest. Everybody else was accounted for. The grounds were locked down and Vysehrad castle was under heavy guard.

With everybody safe, Nash's focus shifted to the pursuit of Jaeger. The next move had to be strategic. He closed his eyes and thought like the murderer. Their encounters ran through his brain, driving him to come up with a plan to outwit a person with the mind of a genius.

Nash tuned into Jaeger's obsession with his mother.

He sent word to Quinn to find out where she was buried. He could be going there or to his old home in Hungary. Quinn didn't know, and they lost time with the research team scouring births, deaths and marriage notices. With every researcher hitting the computers, they located her resting place in a tiny village in the south of Hungary. More time was spent liaising with the Hungarian police to have the graveyard and his former home monitored.

Nash was immersed in a multitude of tasks, focussing on police procedures and investigation. Papers shuffled, screens flickered with data, and voices hummed with updates as the team worked together to formulate their next moves.

He was absorbed by a map spread across the table. Marker-drawn lines connected the relevant locations. It was a mosaic of evidence and possibility. Think like Jaeger. He analysed the patterns, ticking through scenarios, and tried to predict the killer's next move.

His phone vibrated, taking his attention away from the task. He'd given the killer his personal number to contact him fast if he needed Nash in regard to Luca. Instinct told him it was Jaeger.

It was

He steadied himself, making time to tap record as he answered the call. His voice was calm despite the urgency. He didn't open with a greeting.

'Where are you, Jaeger?'

'That's not very friendly, is it?' Jaeger's voice dripped with mockery, his words coated in the layers of taunting.

'What do you want?'

'You keep asking me that. You're obsessed, old man. Let's start with a chat and we can work up from there. We'll take a moment to savour the dance between us.'

'Let's meet. Just you and me.'

'A tryst? I've wondered what it's like to be queer. What would your other half say?'

'Cut the crap. Now.'

'You're so manly, but not really in a position to call the shots. You're chasing shadows. You'll never catch me. But my friend—We are friends, aren't we? You said so. I'm going to leave a trail for you to follow. A scatter of bodies that I'll leave in my wake. Breadcrumbs for you, Hansel.'

Nash's grip on the phone tightened, and his jaw clenched. Jaeger's sadistic mind games were as terrifying as they were calculated. Nash took hope from the fact that he said he'd leave the trail, and not that it was already waiting for him. It didn't sound as though he'd killed anybody yet. His mother's tragic death was his trigger point, and Nash had to exploit it.

'I suppose Jonna's accident was heartbreaking for you. But no one else cared about it. It was a bore, really. But you kept banging on until people were sick of hearing about your grief. I wonder how many of them will care about you now?' Nash aimed the venomous barb and fired.

'More to the point, how many bodies will it take before you find me?' Jaeger asked.

'Tit for tat? I expected more from you. You're not that bright when it comes to it, are you? You can do a few party tricks, but that's it.'

'I'll kill you,' Jaeger said.

'Me? I'm on your hit list? Come on. I'm waiting for you. Do it in the next hour and you'll still be in time for lunch.' He wouldn't let Jaeger's mind games derail him. 'I'm going to catch you, Bence. We're going to get justice for the victims.'

Jaeger's laughter echoed through the line. 'We'll see, won't we? The game is afoot, Nash. But can you keep up?'

The line went dead, leaving Nash with a maelstrom of emotion. He stopped the recording and recentred himself, clasping his hands together to stem the tremor.

The map, the evidence, the team. They were his weapons. But this was personal. He spoke to the commander. 'I'm sending you the recording.'

Savilek nodded and gave him a thumbs up.

The team used the incoming number to triangulate the location between the three closest towers. Minutes later, the report came in that the payphone was left dangling on its cord, and they were combing nearby streets looking for him.

Nash's phone rang again a few minutes later. 'Nice try, Mr Detective. But you'll have to do better than that. The sad thing is you'll try the same tactic again. Testing, one, two. Testing.' He laughed.

'God, you're stupid. I thought you were coming for me. Chicken shit? Balls gone? Who's the dumb-arsed Neanderthal now?' Nash's voice was hard.

'Let's have some more fun first. Keeping you on your toes.'

Nash clenched his fist, his patience wearing thin. The last call had come unexpectedly, he was ready for him this time. 'Cut to the chase. What's your game?'

A deep laugh echoed down the line. 'I thought we'd up the stakes. I was going to hypnotise you over the phone and make you jump off the police station roof, but I've had a better idea. You've been trying to outwit me. That you'd even think you could is an insult. Who the hell do you think you are, Nash? You can't step up alongside me. You aren't man enough.'

'Leave the kid alone. We've got more people on the ground than you could ever get through.'

'The kid? He's yesterday's news. I always liked him and I'm prepared to grant him his life—but there has to be a pay-off. Nothing comes for free. What about your precious Kelvin? Where is he?'

Kelvin had joked that if Nash was abandoning him for work, he was going sightseeing. He was exploring the city's wonders. Nash felt the cold seep into his spine. The fear for Kelvin's safety overrode his attempts to rile Jaeger.

'What have you done?' Nash's voice quivered with rage.

'Nothing. Yet.' Jaeger's voice took on a sinister edge. 'But the possibilities are endless. It'd be a shame if something happened to him. A shame, but entertaining, too, don't you think?'

Nash's mind raced. His thoughts were consumed by a frantic worry that eclipsed everything else. 'If you lay a finger on him, I'll kill you.'

'Temper. I'm not heartless. I'll give you a chance to save him.' Jaeger's words were a twisted promise, laden with menace.

'How?'

'Find him before I do. Do you want a clue?'

'Yes.' Nash was motioning for a second phone to call Kelvin while he kept Jaeger on the line.

'Say please.'

'Please. Yes, please.'

'He's not in Paris. You have one hour.' The call ended.

Nash's hands trembled as he stared at the phone. He rang Kelvin. His phone was off. He never turned his phone off. Jaeger had it. He had Kel. He had to act fast. He turned to his colleagues, relaying the situation and mobilising a team to search for Kel.

'He said he's not in Paris, but knowing his warped mind, it might not even be a valid clue.' The research team shook their heads.

The police station was alive, with officers coordinating their efforts to locate Kelvin in the ancient city.

Nash had to protect the person he loved. The chase for Jaeger had taken a more personal turn, and Nash would move planets with his bare hands to ensure Kelvin's safety. He couldn't sit there any longer, he had to look for him. But he had no idea where to start.

He saw a man sitting in the waiting room. 'Excuse me. I'm doing a puzzle about Prague. Does "He's not in Paris," mean anything to you?'

The man smiled. 'Certainly. We have our own Eifel Tower in Prague. We call it the Petrin Tower.'

'Thank you. You may have just saved a man's life.'

The station hotline buzzed with a call and Nash was called back in. It brought a rush of relief so intense it was overwhelming. He answered. 'Tell me you've found him.'

'Good news, Nash. Mr Jones is fine. We found him visiting the tower.'

Nash felt tears well in his eyes and wiped them away before anybody noticed. 'Thank you so much. Could you pass on a message? Please tell him that I love him.'

'Of course. He's standing beside me. He heard you, and he's smiling. I'd pass the phone over but I have more news.'

'Good, I hope.'

'It doesn't get much better. We've got him. He's at the airport.'

'Jaeger?'

'No, the pope,' he heard Kelvin say in the background. Nash thought he might never hear his voice again, and it was the sweetest thing he'd ever heard.

'I'm five minutes away. I'll be there.'

The officer was still talking. 'Jaeger was trying to slip out of the country.'

'Be careful,' Nash said. 'I can't stress that enough. Please, be careful. And thank God.'

'We're keeping eyes on Kelvin. Just until he's back safe with you. We're bringing him in. The voice soothed the remnants of Nash's anxiety.

'Thank you for everything.'

The officer on the line understood. 'It's our job, Nash. We're here to protect and serve.'

As the call ended, Nash gathered his thoughts. He was already sprinting to get the car.

He got to the airport, ignoring all the signs that said *No Parking*, and left his car with the door wide open at the entrance.

He ran.

Chapter Thirty-Six

Nash burst into the chaotic scene at the airport. He flashed his badge and the commanding officer handed him an earpiece. 'You took your time,' he said.

Jaeger was ahead of him but far enough away to be blocked by the crowd. The magnitude of people and cacophony of panicked screams assaulted Nash's senses. Blaring sirens and urgent orders from the police melded into a dissonant sonata of madness.

It was horrific. There were two dead bodies on the floor, and a third officer was being worked on by paramedics. Nash gathered his determination with every step as he fought against the surging tide of people. His focus never changed.

Jaeger was near the terminal entrance with a malicious grin on his lips and Nash saw a predator revelling in the chaos he'd orchestrated. He held an armed guard in front of him, though his vacant expression betrayed the eerie truth—he was a puppet under Jaeger's control.

The guard's eyes led to a soul that had stopped being his own. The grip on his issued weapon was steady, an extension of Jaeger's will and not of his doing.

The SWAT team took their positions, and their precision broke through the bedlam. Nash saw the hostage's fingers twitching with controlled urgency.

One of the SWAT snipers spoke into the earpieces of every man on the team.

'I've got the shot.' He was on one knee beside a suitcase trolly.

He had Jaeger lined up in his sights, the NIR target light steady on his forehead.

This was the moment.

Jaeger's cold voice shattered the stillness. 'Shoot them,' he commanded, his tone dripping with icy confidence. 'I command it.'

Nash's eyes widened as the guard under his control squeezed the trigger. The gunshot echoed through the terminal.

But it wasn't the only one.

There were two deadly shots fired in the chaos. The hypnotised guard fired first as the puppet master pre-empted the fire strike. There was no expression on the man's face. His eyes were empty as Jaeger held him by the shoulder and aimed him like a joystick.

The marksman returned fire a split second after the hostage. His body jerked as the bullet struck solid matter, sending the shot aimed at Jaeger high. A crimson Rorschach spattered across the floor as his bullet lodged into the wall. The other one buried into the hollow of the marksman's throat. A perfect kill shot on a man almost engulfed in riot gear. A snowflake of plaster fell, leaving a brown splodge and a hole above a holiday poster that proclaimed *Paradise Found*.

The snuffed-out life of the sniper made Nash wonder if he had a family. He was a young man. The cruel triumph in Jaeger's eyes was grotesque as their take-down had been turned against them.

The sound of gunfire was deafening. The battle cries of police were in stark contrast to the terrified screams of civilians caught in the crossfire. Nash's muscles tensed as he looked for cover. The world around him blurred. His focus narrowed to a singular point. This had to end.

His eyes never left Jaeger. An eternity of decisions condensed into a single moment. With a surge of adrenaline, Nash charged forward, drowning out the chaos. The time for negotiation had passed—there was only action left.

A voice barked across the wasteland between them. 'Stand down, Nash,' Commander Savilek shouted.

Nash ignored him.

'Stand down. That's an order,' he repeated

'Listen to me. Listen only to my voice.' Jaeger's monotone sliced through the air like a haunting melody. It carried an unnatural power, a siren's call that ordered control over multiple minds. Nash realised what he was doing and covered his ears. Dread clawed at his chest as he heard the madman's hypnotic words and saw the first people succumb to the hypnosis.

The initial wave of Jaeger's mass takeover cascaded outward, a psychic ripple that bent the will of the SWAT team in its path. The human mind is a labyrinth of complexities. Resistant to intruders, a few officers avoided the invasive call to Jaeger's power. They broke free of the hypnotic grasp. Fear painted their faces as he tried to take their minds, but defiance won the battle for those few. They ran for cover, propelled by a primal instinct for survival.

But for most of the SWAT team, the fact that they were in full riot gear was of no consequence. Their expressions contorted with agony as they doubled over, throwing up as if their souls were purged from their mouths. They yielded, vomiting across the terminal floor until the puddles joined to make abstract art before the officers collapsed to the ground unconscious. Their weapons slipped from unresponsive fingers.

Jaeger raised his arms to the sides, a faux messiah in the form of a man.

He was still talking, louder this time. A potent surge of his power unleashed the second wave of attack. It was aimed at the civilians.

Nash's stomach churned as he watched in horror while ordinary people turned into marionettes on the end of Jaeger's strings. Men, women, and children moved with docility. Their eyes were glazed, and their minds were shackled to the invisible force.

He called out as a family of four walked forward with eerie synchronicity. They didn't hear him. Their expressions were devoid of emotion. Fear was replaced by a blank acceptance.

The group grew, with others joining the bizarre procession, forming a human barricade that stood as an army in front of Jaeger. The sight defied the essence of humanity. It was a perversion of free will that he'd never have believed if he hadn't seen it. Rage boiled inside him.

Jaeger revelled in his perverse triumph and Nash glanced at the few people strong enough to resist to see if they were safe. Jaeger had no use for them and would kill them without conscience. Some of their faces were streaked with tears and etched with terror, but they were free and running. It was a prophecy of hope and a reminder that the human spirit can be unbreakable.

Nash took deliberate steps forward, displaying no fear. He held his hands out to show he was unarmed. The air was electric with tension, a charged standoff that held the balance of lives in its grip.

Nash advanced, and the stern voice of the commander cut through the madness. 'I will not tell you again, Inspector Nash. Stand down.'

Jaeger was a predator relishing the plight of his prey. His voice was honeyed poison. He spoke quietly with the sound of damnation. 'This is a delightful turn of events. Our valiant hero has entered the stage. But you didn't ride in on the elephant, and there's no sparkly show costume, inspector.'

Nash's jaw clenched. He refused to be cowed by the malevolence radiating from the killer.

Jaeger repeated the commander's threat and his voice dripped with sadistic amusement. 'Yes, stand down, Super-Agent Nash, or I'll end this fool's life right here.' He shook the man's shoulder. There was no reaction.

With a nod, Nash paused, his body tense but compliant. He stood in the open, playing to Jaeger's ego. 'I'm impressed, Bence. Your greatest performance yet. And it will be showing now, live on every news channel across the world. Is that what you want? Fame? You've got it. Take your bow. You deserve it.'

'Don't mind if I do.' He inclined forward a few inches, careful not to lose his hold on the hostage. Nash opened his hand to halt any intended attempt to shoot Jaeger from behind. 'But that's what you've always been good at, the grand performance. A mirage of smoke and mirrors hiding your pathetic nature.'

'You're an astute observer. But do you think your words matter to me?'

'Of course they do. You singled me out because I'm important to you. It's not power that defines a man. It's how he wields it. But you're a coward. Your strength lies in hiding behind innocent lives, especially the children.'

Nash's tone was biting with disdain. 'That's the legacy you're leaving behind, Jaeger. The man who preyed on children. I'm thinking about your media name now, I can put it out there you know, before they invent one. Bence Jaeger, the man who hid behind children. The Yellow-Belly Mesmeriser. It suits you. What do you think?'

'Don't mock me. I'll kill him.'

'If you're going to, you will. Take down as many as you can in the time it takes these men to put a bullet in your head.'

'Detective Chief Inspector Nash, you're playing with people's lives,' Savilek said, running in a crouch from the entrance.

Officers were regaining consciousness, but they were unable to do anything in their misery. They were still vomiting violently. The terminal floor was like a skating rink in the iceodrome of hell, and the foul stink filled Nash's throat every time he opened his mouth. He couldn't help it, he retched and Jaeger laughed as a torrent of thick vomit sprayed through his lips. It pooled on the floor in front of him, some hitting his tie and his trousers. He wiped his mouth with his sleeve and didn't miss a beat.

'You're going to die today, Jaeger. Are you ready?' Nash said.

A flicker of uncertainty crossed Jaeger's eyes.

'You think you're Moses. But you're pathetic. Nobody worships you. Look at you. Hiding again. Soft, motherless boy, sheltering behind his puppets. Go on. Part the Red Sea and face me. I dare you.'

Nash took a step closer to a row of chairs where the corpse of a fallen officer lay. He saw a weapon in his holster. Adrenaline lit every synapse of his nervous system.

Jaeger recovered from his flicker of self-doubt. His laughter rang out. A hoarse crow-caw of madness filled the air. He was standing in his omnipotent stance with his arms wide again. 'You think I can't?' He was still laughing as he made a spreading motion by bringing his palms together and then opening them. The crowd of people parted in front of him. They moved in a trance in two perfect halves of equal distribution. The sight appalled Nash.

He took advantage of the mocking laughter as Jaeger's head flung back. Nash dropped to his knees next to the dead officer. His fingers closed around the metal of the gun's grip. With a fluid motion, he pulled the weapon free from the holster and measured the weight—and the moment.

With it in his firing hand, Nash dropped to the floor in a well-practiced manoeuvre. He went down on his side, hard. His body took the full impact of the concourse. And he rolled to tuck himself behind the chairs. The polished tiles were cool against his abused body. And then he rose to one knee with the unerring aim of a man used to the shooting range.

The gunshot rang out, a thunderclap that shattered the fragile equilibrium—and Jaeger's kneecap. His triumphant laughter turned into a pained scream as the bullet struck his leg. He stumbled, his control over the hostage faltering as he reacted to the agony tearing through him.

Nash's movements were as slick as oil. His focus was solid as he advanced on Jaeger across the floor. The madman staggered, grabbing to reclaim his hostage.

Nash's finger squeezed the trigger again. Another shot found its mark in his other leg. Jaeger crumpled to the ground. His eyes were wide with disbelief.

The balance of power had shifted. With Jaeger focused on his pain, his mind released the people he had under his control. They woke, and looked confused, wrinkling their noses at the sight around them, and the smell. The spell was broken and vomiting tapered away to gurgled retching. When they were purged, the afflicted officers righted themselves.

Jaeger lay on the ground. Nash watched him slip into unconsciousness. The storm of action subsided.

The place had the feeling of the aftermath of a bomb attack during WWII. They were shell-shocked. Children sobbed, but most of the adults were in clinical devastation and too traumatised to make a sound. Nash was aware of a bird that had flown into the terminal and was flying between the rafters. It was free.

He pushed himself up from the floor and was out of breath but triumphant. His body ached, every movement testimony to the battle that had run its course. His hip and shoulder throbbed. He felt the tenderness of bruises forming. His airport souvenirs of the struggle.

Gritting his teeth against the pain, Nash managed to stand up on shaky legs, two officers ran forward to help him. His vision swam and the world spun around him.

A hand reached out, strong and steady, and Nash's gaze lifted to meet the eyes of Commander Savilek. The man holding Nash up released him.

'Need a hand?' the officer asked, and Nash heard respect. He hoped that's what it was and not the voice the Commander used for arresting subordinates.

Nash managed a smile, his gratitude was evident. With a nod, he accepted the support and leaned on the case lead. It was a simple gesture, a silent camaraderie shared between two men who had faced evil together.

His bruised hip and shoulder were badges of honour earned in the pursuit of justice.

Two men held Jaeger down, and Nash warned them to be careful as it could be a trick. Savilek had his hand out with a pair of handcuffs dangling from his fingers. 'When a man takes down his prey, he should be the one to bring it in.'

'My pleasure,' Nash said. He had trouble bending down and that's when he felt his broken rib, defined from all of his other aches. But he took huge pleasure in slapping the cuffs on Bence Jeager.

Nash returned to his colleagues at the base with news of Jaeger's capture. A cheer went up, but it wasn't like the celebration he'd have with the guys when he got home.

After a stint in hospital, Jaeger was transferred to an armoured van in handcuffs. After his surgery the same day, Commander Savilek told the consultant in charge that his prisoner was too dangerous to be admitted as a patient, and he signed the discharge papers.

Nash had no doubt that Jaeger could get out of handcuffs in less than thirty seconds. He was gagged against speaking, and the driver and his mate wore noise-cancelling headphones. It was dangerous driving in them, but nowhere near as bad as giving Jaeger the opportunity to get inside their heads. It was a temporary measure but the best they could do until they had him secured.

The real problem was how to imprison a man who could escape any box you locked him in.

As the day turned into late afternoon Kelvin burst through the door and Nash ran into his arms. They kissed in the public foyer. A Pragian waiting to be interviewed fired off a volley of homophobic filth, and Nash didn't need to speak Czech to get the gist. He dragged Kelvin into the back office where they could have a few minutes of privacy. Jaeger's threats against Kel turned out to be a smokescreen, but for a while, Nash thought Jaeger had him and it was too much. He burst into tears. As Kelvin held him, he thought back to the year before when he was terrified of anybody finding out he was gay. He heard DI Molly Brown's voice in his head. 'Boss, get over yourself. Nobody cares.' It was a lesson he'd finally learned.

With Jaeger apprehended—again—the stakes were higher than ever, and the measures put in place reflected the gravity of the situation.

He was transported to a top-security prison, a fortress designed to contain the most dangerous psychopaths in society. The prison's reputation for impenetrability was well-earned, and Jaeger would stay there while he awaited trial. The officers assigned to guard him were handpicked for their expertise.

It wasn't just the guards who were integral to Jaeger's containment. The keys to his cell, an innocuous pair of metal objects, took on huge significance. They were kept in a locked vault, an additional layer of security to prevent any possibility of escape through manipulation, hypnotism or brute force.

Three specially chosen officers were tasked with a unique responsibility that had never been put into force before. They would guard the vault working on a three-shift rotation. It was meticulous and unyielding, a perpetual cycle of vigilance with no room for complacency. But that wasn't enough. There was a chance that Jaeger could still get to them from his sound-proofed padded cell.

Recognising the danger posed by his ability to manipulate minds, a top medical hypnotist was brought in. With precision, the hypnotist worked with the officers, implanting a failsafe prompt into their subconscious minds. This prompt would act as a defence mechanism, preventing anybody from infiltrating their thoughts and compromising the security of the keys. In simple terms, the court-appointed hypnotist ensured that no other hypnotist could get in. She inserted a special password to lock their minds.

The coordination of these measures was a masterpiece of collaboration. Jaeger was confined to a cell designed to thwart the most ingenious escape attempts.

The guards, the keys, the failsafe prompts—every layer of security came together in a resolve to safeguard the world from a terrible human being.

It was over.

Chapter Thirty-Seven

The interrogation room was a stark environment. Its bare walls and harsh lighting cast an atmosphere of solemnity. Nash sat at one side of the table. His gaze fixed on the man across from him. Bence Jaeger, who'd been so charismatic and in control, was less assured. Lyara, Nash's partner in this investigation, sat beside him, her presence was a quiet reassurance in the volatility of the room.

Nash wanted to kill him.

All of them had been given the same failsafe under hypnosis as the officers guarding the prisoner. The duty solicitor was a composed and professional figure. He sat next to Jaeger, his legal expertise evident from his demeanour.

In the days since his arrest, Jaeger's wounds were healing and one of his legs was encased in a cast from ankle to thigh. The other was stitched and bandaged. This bastard was in no position to run. Getting him sitting had been difficult enough.

Nash tried to read the emotions Jaeger was hiding. The murderer was wound as tight as his bandage, but there was a depth of complexity in his eyes.

Nash opened the interrogation. His voice was firm as he began with the standard introductions for the tape. They could be translated into relevant languages later. 'Mr Jaeger, you're here in connection with a series of murders that have taken place within Quinn Brothers Flying Circus. We have evidence and witness testimonies that point to your involvement in these crimes.'

'I am innocent,' he sneered.

Nash continued, his tone measured. 'We believe you manipulated and exploited those around you. That you used your skills in hypnotism to control and silence those who might have spoken against you. You've preyed upon their vulnerability and fear.'

The room was stifling and Nash loosened his tie, undoing the top button of his shirt that he always kept closed. His eyes locked onto Jaeger's to pierce the layers of deception.

Nash was glad Lyara was with him. She'd proven to be a steady and capable detective proficient at leading her team. They deserved this moment together. Her support lent strength to Nash's resolve to put the bastard away. The duty solicitor's role was to present his case. He observed the interview with a watchful eye, his pen documenting every point of conflict. He was ready to intervene if needed.

'Mr Jaeger, the evidence against you is substantial. We've linked you to the murders of Alessio Silvestri, Selena Debois, also known as Madam Selena, and Ross Finley. Witnesses have come forward, and physical evidence, gathered since June 3rd, places you at all three scenes.'

Jaeger's eyes were cold, his expression a mask of defiance. The weight of the accusations hung in the air, a challenge that demanded a response. Nash's patience had worn thin by the lies Jaeger told.

Lyara's voice was calm but assertive. 'We've spoken to members of the circus, Mr Jaeger. They've revealed the extent of your abuse. Your tactics won't work anymore.'

Franklin, the duty solicitor, leaned forward to remind Jaeger of the legal process. 'Mr Jaeger, with seven people dead, it's in your best interest to cooperate. The evidence against you is overwhelming. Providing your side of the story can only benefit your case at this juncture.'

Jaeger produced the damned smile that made Nash want to punch him. His expression was arrogant. 'No comment.'

'We have a hundred witnesses to what you did at the airport. The rope used to strangle Ross Finley was found in your trailer. The same genus of hallucinogenic used to poison Madam Selena and others was found in your possession. Witnesses have seen you at the time of the murders. And semen belonging to you was found in the vaginal cavity of Selena Debois. Need I go on?'

'Ah yes. The lovely Selena.'

'You confessed to me that you were in a secret relationship with her. Witnesses saw you together, and her belongings were found in your trailer.'

'Secrets are what keep life interesting, detective. I told you that before. Selena and I had a connection that few could understand. She was drawn to my abilities. She liked my special skills.'

'In fact, isn't it true that you admitted to me that you'd been in a long-standing relationship with her?'

'Damn, you're tedious. "But I love her so much, Inspector. You can't tell anyone, though, because it's a secret." You fell for any line I fed you.'

'Are you saying you weren't involved in an intimate relationship with Ms Dubois?' Nash asked.

'That depends entirely on your definition of the term intimate relationship.'

'I can see you're dying to tell us.'

'Did I shag her several times a week for seven years? Hell yes, I did. And mighty fine she was too, after a little suggestion of how to whore like a whore.'

'But?' Nash was playing along and feeding Jaeger, but he adopted an expression of being bored by the performance. It couldn't have been further from the truth. After weeks of confusion and intrigue, he wanted to know every detail of the man's dealings, the better to put him away. The art of a police interview is for the interviewer to say as little as possible, while the suspect spills his guts. Nash was happy to let the monster ramble.

'The question you should be asking is: was Selena a willing participant?'

Nash kept his disgust in check. 'And was she?'

'Most definitely. You have no aptitude for this, Mr Nash. Wrong question again. You let me guide you. Who is leading this interview? Don't answer that. No need. The question this time is, was she consenting?'

'And the answer?'

'Not in the least.' His demeanour changed from smug to outraged. He slammed his handcuffed wrists on the table making them jump and overturning a plastic cup of water that they ignored. 'That bitch. That evil slut-whore insisted on giving me a reading when I arrived at the circus. She did it for everyone, apparently, wanting to prove she was supernatural. She was the biggest freak of the sodding lot of them. Queen bee. She turned her stupid cards over. "I can't say it," she said. She pretended to make me drag it out of her. But she made a big mistake that night.' He stopped, panting, and spittle flew from the corners of his mouth in his rage.

'What happened, Bence?' Lyara said.

'I'll tell you what happened. That bottom feeder, who wasn't fit to wash my mother's feet, said my beautiful mama was a lady of the night. She was stunning, a star. Every man alive wanted to have her on his arm. My mother was an angel.'

'That must have hurt you very much, Bence.' Lyara was good, and Nash was happy to let her take the lead while he fantasised about grabbing Jaeger by the hair and ramming his face into the table until it was pulp.

'I showed her. I made her pay.'

'What did you do?' Lyara asked.

'Three times a week, I made her my whore. I implanted a suggestion that she would meet me at a hotel of my choice whenever I played *Swan Lake* over the phone to her. I even made the silly cow pay for the hotels. That's why she never had any money. I showed her what a whore was really like. I implanted behaviours and suggested how she should act, what she should wear, and what she must do to me.'

Nash was floored. He thought making her pay meant murdering her, but it was worse than mere death.

'And she didn't know anything about it?' Lyara sounded as though she was about to vomit.

'Are you okay?' Nash said, touching her arm. She nodded.

Jaeger laughed. 'She knew what was happening, all right. She knew, but she was powerless to stop it. We got thrown out of a lot of motels until she learned not to scream. They weren't the type of establishments that would call the police if you get my drift. Sometimes I didn't have sex with her. Sometimes I just listened to her cry.'

Lyara couldn't continue.

'Why didn't she report you?' Nash asked.

'Because I'm a genius, and she was an amoeba. That's the clever bit. Before we left, I made her forget everything that happened. Until the next time, and then I removed the memory block and she remembered every sordid second of every sordid detail—and knew it was going to happen again. She had no idea what I was doing to her during her normal life. But she always knew she hated me.'

'Why did you kill her?'

'I was bored of her. And after Alessio, it was so much fun. I got the taste for it.'

'What about Alessio? Were you shagging him, too?'

He pointed at Nash. 'I'm not the dirty queer.'

'Why did you kill him?' Nash was the hunter, not the prey.

'Because he was golden. He got greater applause than me and he was an arsehole about it. Sweet boy, smug boy.'

'And let's have the hat trick. What about your motive for killing Ross Finley?'

'The rumour about the stupid ride was too much fun. Do you blame me for having fun with that one?'

'Were there any others?'

'Alas, no. I tried with that big-headed fire eater, and again with the horse girl. She had tickets on herself. I was going to start on the freaks next. No, nobody else. But there will be. You'll have to update your home security, and look around corners, Mr Nash.'

'What I don't understand is what made you start. Quinn said you were doing so well and seemed happy.'

'What does he know? He's a fool. Another one that had better watch himself. They always took her side. That whore, Selena. How would you feel if they kept threatening to get rid of you, and ordering you to be nice to somebody you hated?'

'I should imagine I'd deal with it in an adult and responsible way.' Nash's voice didn't waver as he indicated the tape deck. 'We have your taped confession and evidence that connects you to these crimes. It's time to face the consequences.'

Lyara's voice was strong when she spoke again. 'Your victims deserve justice, Mr Jaeger. We won't stop until we put you away for the rest of your life.'

The solicitor spoke for the first time since Jaeger began his confession and Nash wondered what the point of him was. 'Please refrain from making antagonistic remarks. My client has been cooperative and as such, I insist that he's treated cordially.'

'For the tape,' Lyara said. 'Screw you.' She glared at the solicitor first and then his client. Nash put his hand on her arm to calm her and noticed the solicitor's smile before he smothered it. Nash realised that Franklin had given Jaeger enough rope to hang himself, and was performing at the minimum legal requirement to represent him.

The solicitor spoke again. 'Consider your options very carefully, Mr Jaeger. Cooperation can mitigate the severity of the charges against you. Though not by much, I shouldn't think.'

'Let's talk some more about the murder of Selena Debois, Mr Jaeger. We didn't really cover that. Details you see, pesky things, but they do like them covered. Ms Debois was found drugged, strangled, and inside the tiger cage. Care to explain your involvement?' Nash said.

Jaeger smirked, his posture relaxed. 'Selena. I loathed her, but she was quite the enchantress, wasn't she? Even when she wasn't under my control, she was a woman of allure.'

Nash's tone sharpened. 'Cut the theatrics, Jaeger.'

'But we were kindred spirits.'

Nash leaned in, his voice menacing. 'A kindred spirit who ended up dead? You left her inside the cage like a twisted exhibit.'

'Fate takes unexpected turns, detective. Selena's demise was tragic, so they say. I certainly had nothing to do with a tragedy.'

Nash's gaze bore into Jaeger's, his determination unyielding. 'Are you retracting your earlier confession? Witnesses place you near the tiger cage that night. We have evidence that links you to the crime scene. Not to mention your full confession on tape.'

'You're skilled at constructing a narrative. But evidence can be misleading, can't it? People see what they want to see.'

'The evidence ties you to the murder weapon. It all adds up.'

'Selena's death was tragic, but my involvement was not. I enjoyed every sweet moment.'

'Your games and lies won't protect you.'

Jaeger's arrogance was a thin veneer. Any backtracking was a play for confusion to plead diminished responsibility at a later date. Nash had seen it many times before. There was no doubt that Jaeger was insane, and would probably be sentenced as a sick man—but there was no mind less diminished than his.

'How did you make Alessio Silvestri disappear in the middle of a trapeze act? Witnesses saw him on that trapeze one moment, and the next he was gone. How did you do it?' Nash didn't let on that he already knew.

'The art of illusion is a craft I've perfected over the years. People only see what's in front of them, but the reality is more malleable than you think.'

'Not a hologram then. My bad.'

Jaeger's face darkened. Nash would swear later that it changed colour with rage because Nash knew the secret of his greatest trick. His voice rose in anger. 'Alessio was an expendable pawn in a much bigger game.'

'One that ended with a young man's life taken away and a family destroyed. You're a monster.'

'Despicable Me. Perhaps. But I'm effective. Alessio's demise served a purpose, and he was a means to an end. And don't forget the little brother who saw it all. Such a tragic sight. It will stay with him forever. Memories are made of this.'

'How did you get Ross on the carousel with everybody milling around?'

'Milling? Did you see anybody milling or all the imbecilic carneys I hypnotised to watch in a trance? That's how I got Ross' body on the carousel in full view?'

'For what? Sick satisfaction?'

Jaeger was cool, his words dripping with arrogance. 'Art, my darling detective. It was a statement of my genius. Satisfaction, power, control. These all drive me. And you're a pawn in my game. Welcome to the board, worthy white knight with your black rook.'

Nash boiled over, seething with anger. 'I'm warning you. Leave my personal life out of this. You won't win, Jaeger. Remember, I can end this.'

Jaeger's laughter echoed in the room, a chilling sound. 'Bravo. Excellent wordplay and well-remembered. See? Worthy. The game is far from over.'

'I've had enough of you. And I have a marvellous fillet mignon waiting for me. While you'll be taken back to a cell in handcuffs. Your move.'

'You can't take my intellect. I'll be quite comfortable wherever you decide to try and confine me.'

With a nod, Nash signalled to the room. 'Finish up and take him down. He bores me.'

'I'll kill you.'

'No, you won't. But you will paint my nightmares in dark colours for a long time.' Nash turned to the recorder. 'For the tape, detective Silas Nash has had his life threatened by a dangerous man intent on revenge. The suspect, Bence Jaeger, has admitted, without coercion, to three murders and additional crimes, including mental manipulation, kidnapping and the abuse of a minor.' He smiled at the people in the room. 'Interview ended at 11:33. Turn it off.'

The officers moved, their grip firm as they led Jaeger out of the interrogation room. Despite his bravado, his demeanour wavered and Nash saw a crack in his façade of arrogance.

He watched as Jaeger was led away, his thoughts focused on the long road of the trial ahead. Nash sighed at the thought of the judicial system. The jury would find him guilty. He'd appeal on the grounds of insanity. He'd scream diminished responsibility and he'd get locked up in a high-security hospital rather than a prison. He'd probably kill somebody at some point, and that would be it. Life in solitary.

Nash could live with that.

It was time to go home—and he realised that he couldn't wait. Among much public outcry, he'd seen that not all circuses were bad places steeped in the exploitation of animals and vulnerable people. He'd look on his time as an honorary carney with fondness. In the recent words of a great man called Isiah Quinn, 'The show will live forever.'

***

An hour later, despite Nash wanting to get straight on the road, Kelvin insisted that they say goodbye to some of the friends they'd made. Nash hated goodbyes, and apart from at the trial, he'd probably never see any of these people again, but Kel made all the usual empty promises about keeping in touch.

The Good Lady Diana was already loaded, and with all the Czech memorabilia Kelvin had bought to keep himself amused, she groaned under the added weight.

Jolene insisted on packing them enough sandwiches and cakes to last all the way to New Zealand, never mind England, and Nash had to drag Kelvin away before he accepted a job as a costume designer alongside Noor.

It was sunset as they were leaving. With nobody around the camp, the sound of laughter and ribbing came to them from the trestle tables of another communal camp meal.

He'd miss the circus, but nowhere near as much as Kel would. Nash put the van into first gear and drew away.

'Wait,' Kelvin shouted, getting his phone out. 'One last picture for the road.' He positioned the screen in front of them and Nash leaned in for the selfie.

At that moment, the van lit up with a thousand lights. They looked out of the back window, startled, to see the empty carousel turning. The lights seemed brighter than they'd been before.

The calliope music was out of tune again.

This book is dedicated to, and written in respect of:
Joseph Merrick
Chang and Eng Bunker
Charles Sherwood Stratton
William Henry Johnson
Annie Jones
Stephan Bibrowski
Simon Metz
Abdul Kareem
Isaac W. Sprague
Ella Harper

Printed in Great Britain
by Amazon